QUICKSILVER is...

"A wickedly witty, mercurial tale, filled with [Quick's] own sexy brand of humor-laced sensuality."
—*Library Journal*

"Dark, chilling...engrossing."
—*Midwest Book Review*

"A perfect reading experience."
—*Fresh Fiction*

New York Times bestselling author Amanda Quick "serves up another fascinating, engaging addition to her Arcane Society saga with this second installment in the Looking Glass Trilogy."*

Virginia Dean wakes after midnight beside a dead body, with a bloody knife in her hand and no memory of the evening's events. Dark energy, emanating from the mirrors lining the room, overpowers her senses. With no apparent way in or out, she is rescued by a man she's met only once before, but won't soon forget . . .

Owen Sweetwater inherited his family's talent for hunting the psychical monsters who prey on London's women and children, and his investigation into the deaths of two glass-readers has led him here. The high-society types of the exclusive Arcane Society would consider Virginia an illusionist, a charlatan, even a criminal. But Owen knows better. Virginia's powers are real—and so is the power she exerts over him simply with her presence. And if her abilities can be relied upon in the midst of great danger, they just might be the key to his investigation.

"[A] chilling addition to this exceptional paranormal series!"
—*Fresh Fiction*

"A wickedly witty, mercurial tale, filled with her own sexy brand of humor-laced sensuality, an abundance of intriguing characters . . . and a lively adventure successfully resolved but lightly peppered with tantalizing hints of what's to come."
—*Library Journal*

"The story line grips the reader . . . and never slows down until the final denouement. There are some quirky secondary characters who add whimsy to the otherwise dark, chilling but engrossing story line."
—*Midwest Book Review*

continued . . .

"Quick deftly distills intrigue, romance, and a dash of the paranormal into a beguiling story." —*Chicago Tribune*

"Another dazzling combination of superbly realized characters, an intrigue-studded plot, and spellbindingly sexy romance." —*Booklist*

"Compelling . . . The story grabs you from the first page and refuses to let loose until you read the final words . . . It's just another example of why you can't go wrong with a Jayne Ann Krentz–written book—no matter what name she uses." —*The (Columbia, SC) State*

The River Knows

"Well-plotted, adventurous, and suspenseful, *The River Knows* takes the reader downstream with lots of surprising twists and undercurrents." —*The Seattle Times*

"An alluring combination of foggy nights and steamy afternoons." —*Publishers Weekly*

"The incomparable Quick has once again penned a superbly tantalizing romantic suspense, replete with smart and snappy dialogue, witty humor, and fast-paced action." —*Booklist*

"Quick . . . does it again with a naughty-and-nice romp." —*Kirkus Reviews*

Second Sight

"With her witty dialogue, multidimensional characters complete with eccentricities and psychic abilities, clever plotting, and generous humor, the perennially popular Quick has penned another surefire winner."

—*Booklist* (starred review)

continued . . .

"Clever dialogue, well-handled paranormal elements, and an intriguing plot merge with Quick's lively wit in this thoroughly entertaining romance."

—*Library Journal* (starred review)

"There is no one who understands what we long for in a man as well as Amanda Quick."

—*BookPage*

Lie by Moonlight

"Quick's trademark wit and humor run gracefully throughout this suspenseful and satisfying novel."

—*Booklist*

"This rousing, steamy story is a captivating read."

—*Library Journal*

Wait Until Midnight

"Terrific historical romantic suspense . . . Regardless of the time period, Ms. Quick provides a fabulous tale that seems always to land on the keeper shelf."

—*The Best Reviews*

"[A] wonderful story of mystery and romance."

—*A Romance Review*

QUICKSILVER

AMANDA QUICK

JOVE BOOKS

New York

THE BERKLEY PUBLISHING GROUP
Published by the Penguin Group
Penguin Group (USA) Inc.
375 Hudson Street, New York, New York 10014, USA

Penguin Group (Canada), 90 Eglinton Avenue East, Suite 700, Toronto, Ontario M4P 2Y3, Canada
(a division of Pearson Penguin Canada Inc.) • Penguin Books Ltd., 80 Strand, London WC2R 0RL,
England • Penguin Group Ireland, 25 St. Stephen's Green, Dublin 2, Ireland (a division of Penguin
Books Ltd.) • Penguin Group (Australia), 250 Camberwell Road, Camberwell, Victoria 3124, Australia
(a division of Pearson Australia Group Pty. Ltd.) • Penguin Books India Pvt. Ltd., 11 Community
Centre, Panchsheel Park, New Delhi—110 017, India • Penguin Group (NZ), 67 Apollo Drive,
Rosedale, Auckland 0632, New Zealand (a division of Pearson New Zealand Ltd.) • Penguin Books
(South Africa) (Pty.) Ltd., 24 Sturdee Avenue, Rosebank, Johannesburg 2196, South Africa

Penguin Books Ltd., Registered Offices: 80 Strand, London WC2R 0RL, England

This is a work of fiction. Names, characters, places, and incidents either are the product of the author's
imagination or are used fictitiously, and any resemblance to actual persons, living or dead, business
establishments, events, or locales is entirely coincidental. The publisher does not have control over
and does not have any responsibility for author or third-party websites or their content.

QUICKSILVER

A Jove Book / published by arrangement with the author

PUBLISHING HISTORY
G. P. Putnam's Sons hardcover edition / April 2011
Jove mass-market edition / April 2012

Copyright © 2011 by Jayne Ann Krentz.
Excerpt from *Canyons of Night* by Jayne Castle copyright © 2011 by Jayne Ann Krentz.
Cover design by Richard Hasselberger.
Cover illustration © 2011 by Craig White.
Stepback design by Jane Hammer.
Stepback photograph of Entrance to Kings College © Neleman Initiative, LLC / Getty Images;
photograph of Houses of Parliament © r.nagy.

ISBN: 978-0-515-15056-8

JOVE®
Jove Books are published by The Berkley Publishing Group,
a division of Penguin Group (USA) Inc.,
375 Hudson Street, New York, New York 10014.
JOVE® is a registered trademark of Penguin Group (USA) Inc.
The "J" design is a trademark of Penguin Group (USA) Inc.

PRINTED IN THE UNITED STATES OF AMERICA

10 9 8 7 6 5 4 3 2 1

ALWAYS LEARNING   **PEARSON**

For Frank.
You are my hero.

QUICKSILVER

ONE

The visions of blood and death blazed violently in the mirrors. The terrible scenes, lit by gaslight, reflected endlessly into a dark infinity.

Virginia lay very still for a moment, her heart pounding while she tried to make sense of the nightmare in which she had awakened. Myriad reflections of a woman lying on a tumbled, bloodstained bed surrounded her. The woman was dressed in only a thin linen chemise and white stockings. Her hair cascaded around her shoulders in tangled waves. She looked as though she had recently engaged in a passionate encounter. But her dazed eyes were wide with shock and horror, not fading desire.

It took Virginia a few seconds to realize that the woman in the mirrors was herself. She was not alone in the bed. There was a man beside her. The front of his unfastened shirt was soaked in blood. His head was turned away, but she could see enough of his handsome face to recognize him. Lord Hollister.

She sat up slowly, unconsciously letting go of some unseen object that she had been gripping in one hand. Part of her insisted that she was living through a dreadful dream, but her other senses warned her that she was

awake. It took everything she had to touch the side of
the dead man's throat. There was no pulse. She had not
expected to find one. The chill of death enveloped
Hollister.

A fresh surge of panic flared through her. Tiny icicles
lanced the nape of her neck and the palms of her hands.
She scrambled frantically out of the bed. When she
looked down she noticed that a portion of her chemise
was stained crimson. She raised her eyes and saw the
knife for the first time. It was half hidden by the rumpled sheets. The blade was covered in blood. The hilt
lay very close to where her hand had been a moment
earlier.

At the edge of her vision she saw disturbing shadows
shift deep within the mirrors. Hurriedly she shuttered
her psychical senses. She could not deal with a reading
just now. Her intuition was flaring wildly. She had to
get out of the mirrored room.

She turned quickly, searching for the new bronze-
and-black gown that she had worn to the Hollister mansion that evening. She saw the dress and her petticoats.
The garments were crumpled carelessly in the corner,
as if they had been hastily discarded in the throes of
passion. The toes of her high-button walking boots were
just visible beneath the folds of the cloak. For some
incomprehensible reason, the thought that Hollister had
partially undressed her before she had sunk a knife in
his chest was more unnerving than awakening next to
the body.

*Dear heaven, how could one kill a man but have no mem-
ory of the violence?* she wondered.

Dark energy seethed again in the mirrors. Fear and

the need to escape were making it hard for her to control her senses. Once again she managed to suppress her talent. The shadows receded deeper into the looking glasses. She knew she could not banish them entirely. It was no doubt still night outside. Glasslight energy trapped in mirrors was always strongest after dark. There were scenes lurking in the looking glasses that surrounded her that she needed to confront, but she could not read the afterimages now. She had to get out of the room.

She looked around and realized that there was no obvious door. The walls of the small chamber appeared to be entirely covered in mirrors. But that was not possible, she thought. The air in the room was fresh. The gas lamp burned steadily. There had to be some concealed means of ventilation, and somewhere there was a door. And where there was a door, there would be a draft over the threshold.

Forcing herself to focus on one thing at a time, she crossed the chamber and picked up her gown. It took an enormous amount of effort to fasten the petticoats and pull the dress up around herself because she was shivering so violently.

She was struggling with the bodice, trying to get the front hooked, when she heard the soft sigh of concealed hinges. Another wave of panic rattled her nerves. She looked up quickly. In the mirrored wall in front of her she watched a glass panel open behind her.

A man moved into the room, riding an invisible wave of dark power. She recognized him at once even though they had met on only one occasion. But then, she would know him anywhere. A woman did not forget a man whose dark, shadowed eyes held the promise of heaven or hell. For an instant she could not move. She froze, the front of the gown clutched to her breasts.

"Mr. Sweetwater," she whispered.

He gave her a swift, head-to-toe assessment. His hard, implacable face was sculpted in light and shadow by the glary light of the lamp. His eyes narrowed faintly. In another man, the expression might have indicated concern. But this was Owen Sweetwater. She was certain that he did not possess anything resembling normal human emotions.

There were only two possible explanations for his presence in the death chamber tonight. He was there to kill her or to save her. With Sweetwater there would be no middle ground.

"Are you injured, Miss Dean?" he asked, as if merely inquiring after her health.

The cool formality in his tone triggered a flash of clarifying indignation.

"I'm unhurt, Mr. Sweetwater." She glanced at the bed. "But the same cannot be said for Lord Hollister."

He crossed to the bed and studied Hollister's body for a moment. Virginia sensed energy whisper through the room and knew that Owen had heightened his talent. She did not know the nature of the psychical ability he commanded, but she sensed that it was dangerous.

Owen turned around. "Excellent work, Miss Dean, although somewhat untidy."

"*What?*"

"It is clear that Hollister will no longer be a problem, but we must get you safely away from here before you are arrested for murder."

"No," she managed.

Owen's brows rose. "You do not wish to leave this chamber?"

She swallowed hard. "I meant I did not kill him."

At least I don't think I did. She realized she had no memory of anything after she had read the looking glass in the bedroom of the Hollister mansion. She had no choice but to claim that she was innocent. If she were arrested for the murder of Lord Hollister, she would surely hang.

Owen gave her another swift appraisal. "Yes, I can see that you did not plant that kitchen knife in his chest."

She was startled. "How can you know that I am innocent?"

"We can discuss the details somewhere else at a more convenient time," Owen said. He came toward her, moving with the purposeful stride of a beast of prey closing in for the kill. "Here, let me do that."

She did not comprehend what he intended until he was directly in front of her, fastening the small hooks that closed the front of her gown. He worked with swift, economical movements, his hands steady and sure. If the fine hair on the nape of her neck was not already standing on end, Owen's touch would have electrified it. The energy around him charged the atmosphere and her senses. She was torn between an overpowering urge to run for her life and the equally strong desire to throw herself into his arms.

That settled it, she thought. The events of the night had unhinged her mind. She could no longer trust any of her obviously shattered senses. She sought refuge in the self-mastery that she had spent most of her life perfecting. Mercifully it came to her aid.

"Mr. Sweetwater," she said coldly. She stepped back quickly.

His hands fell away. He gave the front of her gown a critical once-over. "That will do for now. It's after midnight, and the fog is quite thick. No one will notice you once we are outside."

"Midnight?" She reached down to the small chatelaine watch pinned to the waist of her gown. When she saw that he was right about the time, she shuddered. "I arrived at eight, as instructed. Dear heaven, I have lost four hours."

"I apologize for the delay in my own arrival. I did not get word that you were missing until an hour ago."

"What are you talking about?"

"Later. Put your shoes on. We have an unpleasant walk ahead of us before we are free of this place."

She did not argue. She lifted her skirts and petticoats and shoved one stocking-clad foot into a boot. She did not bother with the laces.

Owen contemplated the body on the bed while he waited. "You're sure you are unhurt?"

She blinked, trying to comprehend the lethal edge on his words.

"He did not rape me, if that is what you are wondering," she said crisply. "You will have noticed that he is still fully clothed."

"Yes, of course," Owen said. He turned back to her, his odd eyes even colder than usual. "Sorry. It is just that for the past few hours I have been consumed with the sensation that something was wrong. When I came through the door a moment ago, I discovered that I was right."

"You were too late to save his lordship, do you mean, sir?"

"No, Miss Dean, too late to save you. Fortunately, you were able to save yourself."

She got her other foot into the second boot. "I certainly do not mourn Hollister. I believe he was a monster. But I cannot take the credit for his current condition."

"Yes, I can see that now," Owen said with a chilling calmness.

"Do not pretend to humor me, sir." She leaned down to scoop up her heavy cloak. "I want to make it quite clear that I did not murder his lordship."

"Frankly, it does not matter to me. Hollister's death is a benefit to the world."

"I could not agree with you more, however—" The sound of sighing hinges stopped her.

"The door," she said. "It's closing."

"So it is."

They both rushed for the door. Owen reached it first, but the mirrored panel swung back into place just before he could get his booted foot into the opening. Virginia heard an ominous click.

"It's locked," she said.

"It's all of a piece," Owen said. "This entire affair has been a source of great annoyance to me from the start."

"My condolences," she murmured.

Ignoring the sarcasm, he went back to the bed and picked up the bloody knife. He crossed the room again and smashed the heavy hilt of the weapon against the door panel. There was a sharp, splintering crack. A large fissure appeared in the mirror. He struck again. This time several jagged shards fell to the floor, revealing a portion of a wooden door.

She studied the new lock that had been installed in the ancient door. "I don't suppose you're any good at picking locks, Mr. Sweetwater?"

"How do you think I got in here tonight?"

He took a thin length of metal out of the pocket of his coat, crouched and went to work. He got the door open in seconds.

"You amaze me, sir," Virginia said. "Since when do gentlemen learn the fine art of lock-picking?"

"The skill comes in quite handy in the course of my investigations."

"You mean in the course of your unfortunate campaign to destroy the careers of hardworking people such as myself who are guilty of nothing more than trying to make a living."

"I believe you refer to my efforts to expose those who earn their livings by deceiving the gullible. Yes, Miss Dean, that is precisely the sort of research that has intrigued me of late."

"Those of us who are practitioners of the paranormal can only hope that you will find a new hobby soon, before you destroy our business entirely," she said.

"Come now, Miss Dean. Are you not at least somewhat relieved to see me tonight? If I hadn't arrived when I did, you would still be trapped in this room with the body."

"Your point is well taken," she admitted.

"You can thank me later."

"I'll try to remember to do that."

He tossed the knife aside, wrapped his gloved hand around her wrist and drew her toward the door. She did not trust Owen Sweetwater. She could not afford to trust him. In the past few weeks it had become clear that he was engaged in a personal quest to expose practitioners of the paranormal as charlatans.

He was not the first so-called investigator to attempt to label all practitioners as frauds. But she had privately begun to wonder if, in his zeal, Sweetwater had decided to take matters a step further. Two glass-readers—women with talents similar to her own—had died under mysterious circumstances in the past two months. The authorities had declared the deaths accidental, but she had her doubts.

Perhaps Owen Sweetwater had taken it upon himself to do more than try to destroy careers. Perhaps, in addition to acting as judge and jury, he had assumed the role of executioner. There was something in his eyes, in the energy around him, that told her his nature was that of the hunter and that his chosen prey would be human.

Sweetwater was certainly no friend or ally, but all indications were that he did not intend to kill her, at least not here and now. Going with him seemed a wiser choice than attempting to find a route to safety on her own. She did not even know where she was.

They went through the doorway. Owen paused long enough to light a lantern that he had evidently left on the other side of the entrance. The flaring light illuminated an ancient corridor fashioned of stone.

"Where are we?" she whispered.

"In a basement below the grounds of the Hollister

mansion," Owen said. "The house was built on the ruins of a medieval abbey. There is a warren of tunnels and cells down here. The place is a maze."

"How did you find me?"

"You probably don't want to know the answer to that question."

"I insist on knowing how you found me, sir."

"I have had two people watching your house from an empty house across the street for the past few nights."

For a moment she was too stunned to speak.

"How dare you," she finally managed.

"I told you that you would not like the answer. When you set off tonight for a reading, my watchers thought nothing of it. You go out several nights a week to practice your art. But when you did not return in a reasonable length of time, the watchers sent word to me. I went to your town house and asked your housekeeper for the address of your client."

"Mrs. Crofton told you that I came here to do a reading?"

"She was concerned that you had not returned. When I arrived on the grounds of the Hollister estate I knew at once that something was very wrong."

"Your talent told you as much?" she asked, deeply wary.

"I'm afraid so."

"How?"

"Let's just say that you are not the first woman to disappear into these tunnels. The difference between you and the rest of Hollister's victims is that you are alive."

"Dear heaven." She took a moment to grasp the meaning of what he had said. "You detect violent death?"

"In a manner of speaking."

"Explain yourself, sir."

"Trust me, you are better off not knowing."

"It's a bit late to concern yourself with my delicate sensibilities," she snapped. "I just woke up in a bed with a high-ranking gentleman who was recently stabbed to death."

"Your nerves are obviously quite sturdy. Nevertheless, this is not the time or place to discuss the nature of my talent."

"And why is that?" she asked.

"We have more pressing priorities at the moment. I would remind you that if you did not stab Hollister to death, then it follows that someone else did. That individual may still be in the vicinity."

She swallowed hard. "Right, then. I'll save the questions for later."

"A wise decision," Owen said.

He stopped so suddenly that Virginia stumbled against him. He did not seem to be aware of the impact. He raised the lantern and held it so that the yellow glare lit the passageway to the right.

"Do you feel some energy?" he asked in low tones.

A strange flicker of icy awareness brushed Virginia's senses.

"Yes," she said.

The sensation grew stronger. It was accompanied by a rhythmic clank-and-thud.

A miniature carriage rolled toward them out of the

darkness. When it came into the light Virginia saw that it was drawn by two clockwork horses. The toy vehicle stood about a foot tall. The equipage was a work of art, not a child's plaything. Every detail was exquisitely rendered. The cab was finished in gleaming black enamel and elaborately gilded. Small windows glinted in the lantern light. The horses were realistically sculpted, complete with flowing black manes and tails. Their harness fittings were trimmed with gold.

"Why would someone leave such an expensive toy down here?" Virginia asked.

Owen took her arm again and drew her back a step. "That thing is no toy."

She could not take her eyes off the carriage. It fascinated her.

"What, then?" she asked.

"Damned if I know."

Another wave of chilling energy feathered her senses.

"I can sense the power in the device," she said. "It's glasslight, the same kind of energy that I read in mirrors. But only humans can generate psychical energy. How is that carriage doing it?"

"We are not going to investigate." Owen hauled her around a corner, out of the direct path of the clockwork carriage. "We must keep the wall between us and that device, whatever it is. Stone blocks psychical currents."

A faint, frightened voice came out of the dark passageway behind the carriage.

"Is there someone out there? Please help me."

Owen stilled. "Damn," he said, very softly. "One complication after another."

Virginia turned back toward the intersection of the hallways.

"Who's there?" she called in a low voice.

"My name is Becky, ma'am. Help me, I beg you. I can't get out. It's very dark here. There are bars on the door."

"Another one of Hollister's victims," Owen said.

Virginia glanced at him. "We must do something."

"We can't get to her unless we can get past that clock-work mechanism."

"It is producing my kind of energy," she said. "I might be able to control it."

"Are you certain?"

"I must try. Let me take a look."

Owen's fingers closed like a manacle around her wrist. "Whatever you do, don't let go of my hand. Understand?"

"Yes, yes, of course," she said, impatient now. "I need some light."

He held the lantern out and aloft so that it partially illuminated the intersecting corridor.

The clank-and-thud noise had ceased. Virginia risked a peek around the corner.

In the flaring light the windows of the miniature vehicle glinted ominously. As though sensing prey, the automaton lurched forward again.

"Interesting," Owen said, listening. "It seems to be activated by movement. Since it is a psychical device of some sort, it is probably reacting to our auras."

"Yes, I think so." She pulled back out of range of the

carriage and flattened herself against the stone wall.
"The energy is infused into the windows. I cannot be
absolutely positive until I try, but I believe I may be able
to neutralize the currents, at least temporarily."

In the adjoining corridor the clank-and-thud noise
ceased again.

"It definitely reacts to motion," Owen said. "If you
can neutralize it long enough for me to get to it, I may
be able to smash it or disable it. If it is a true clockwork
mechanism, there will be a key."

"Are you still there, ma'am?" Becky called from the
darkness. "Please don't leave me here."

"Coming, Becky," Virginia said. She worked to keep
her tone calm and reassuring. "We'll just be a moment."

"Thank you, ma'am. Please hurry. I'm so scared."

"Everything is under control, Becky," Virginia said.

Owen tightened his grip on her wrist. "Give it a try.
If it feels as though you are being overcome, I will pull
you back out of range."

"That sounds like a reasonable plan."

She gathered her nerves, heightened her talent and
stepped cautiously around the corner. Owen angled the
light so that it fell on the motionless carriage.

There was a brief, tense silence before the dark windows of the miniature vehicle started to glitter as
though illuminated from inside the cab. Virginia sensed
energy pulsing once more in the atmosphere. The
mechanical horses started forward. The wheels of the
carriage began to turn. The device was much closer to
her now, only a few feet away.

Without warning, currents of senses-freezing energy

lashed at her. Although she thought she was prepared, she nevertheless flinched at the impact.

Owen tightened his grip. She knew he was preparing to pull her around the corner and out of reach of the carriage weapon.

"It's all right," she managed. "I can handle this."

Ignoring the freezing wave of energy, she found a focus the same way she did when she looked deep into a mirror. She established a counterpoint pattern, dampening the oscillating waves of power coming from the device. The effect was swift, almost immediate. The currents smoothed out rapidly. The carriage continued to roll forward, driven by the clockwork mechanism.

"It's done," Virginia said. She did not dare look away from the carriage. "Do what you must. I'm not sure how long I'll be able to maintain control."

One could draw on one's psychical reserves for only so long when employing them to the maximum degree, as she was doing now.

Owen did not waste time asking questions. He released her and moved swiftly around the corner into the passageway, where she stood facing the device. He used one booted foot to tip the entire miniature equipage onto its side. The legs of the horses continued to thrash rhythmically but uselessly in the air.

Virginia became aware of a muffled *ticktock, ticktock.* "Sounds like a clock."

Owen crouched beside the weapon. "There must be a way to open this thing."

He stripped off a glove and ran his fingertips lightly over the elegant curiosity.

"I thought you were going to smash it," Virginia said.

"I'd rather preserve it intact, if possible. I want to study it. To my knowledge, no one has ever succeeded in infusing energy into an inanimate substance like glass in such a way that the currents could be activated by mechanical means. This device is really quite extraordinary."

"Perhaps you could conduct your examination another time?" she suggested icily. "I cannot maintain control indefinitely."

"Are you still out there, ma'am?" Becky called plaintively.

"We're here, Becky," Virginia responded. "Mr. Sweetwater, if you don't mind?"

"Got it," Owen said.

His fingers moved on the roof of the carriage. The top swung open on small hinges. He reached into the cab. A few seconds later the ticking ceased. The currents of energy that Virginia had been holding in neutral winked out of existence. Cautiously, she relaxed her senses. There was no more energy coming from the toy's windows.

"A standard clockwork mechanism." Owen got to his feet. "One stops the carriage just as one would a clock. Come, let's find that girl."

Virginia was already in motion. She went past a row of ancient dark cells, the lantern held high.

"Becky?" she called. "Where are you?"

"Damn it," Owen muttered. He moved quickly to catch up with her. "Have a care, Virginia. There may be other traps."

She was vaguely aware that he had used her first name as though they were longtime friends rather than near strangers, but she paid no attention. She stopped in front of a heavy wood-and-iron door. A small opening in the door was blocked by bars. A terrified young woman of no more than fourteen or fifteen years looked out, fingers gripping the iron rods. Her eyes were hollow with fear and tears.

"Are you badly hurt?" Virginia asked.

"No, ma'am. But it's a good thing you came along when you did. There's no telling what would have happened to me."

Owen took out his lock pick. "I'll have you out of there in a moment."

"What occurred here?" Virginia asked gently.

Becky hesitated. "I don't remember too much, ma'am. I was at my usual corner outside the tavern. A fine carriage stopped. A handsome gentleman inside leaned out and said he thought that I was very pretty. Said he'd pay me twice my usual fee. I got into the carriage, and that is the last thing that I recall until I woke up in this dreadful place. I called and called for the longest time, but no one ever answered. I gave up. Then I heard you and your gentleman friend."

Owen got the door open and stood back. "Come along, Becky. We've wasted enough time here."

Becky hurried out of the cell. "Thank you, sir."

Owen did not respond. He was looking at the stone floor. Virginia felt dark energy shift in the atmosphere and knew that he had raised his talent, whatever it was.

"Interesting," he said.

"What is it?" she asked.

"I believe this may have been where Hollister encountered the person who planted that knife in his chest."

He kept his voice very low, but Virginia knew that Becky was not paying any attention. The girl was wholly focused on getting out of the stone tunnel.

"You can *see* that sort of thing?" Virginia asked.

"I can see where the killer stood when she did the deed," Owen said.

"A *woman* killed him?"

"Yes. What is more, she was mad as a hatter."

"Dear heaven. Lady Hollister."

TWO

It occurred to Owen that he had no right to be offended by Virginia's deeply wary attitude. After all, he was a Sweetwater. As a rule, women were either fascinated or repelled by the men of his family. There was rarely any middle ground. But regardless of which group they fell into, women intuitively considered Sweetwater men dangerous. According to his Aunt Marian, an aura-talent, something about the auras of the Sweetwater males made sensible people—male and female, talented and untalented alike—uneasy.

Nevertheless, romantic fool that he was, Virginia's edgy suspicion had blindsided him. He was chagrined to realize that he actually felt rather crushed. It was his own fault for employing poor tactics, he thought. In hindsight, establishing himself as a psychical investigator who specialized in exposing fraudulent practitioners had been a mistake. But he had not been able to think of any other way to gain entrée into the tightly knit community of practitioners affiliated with the Leybrook Institute.

There would be time enough to ponder his blunder later, he told himself. He now had two females to escort to safety.

He picked up the clockwork carriage and tucked it under one arm. The small horses dangled in their harnesses.

"Miss Dean, if you would take the lantern," he said.

"I have it," she said, hoisting the lantern.

He looked at both women. "Stay close." He started forward. "We will leave this place the same way I entered, through the old drying shed. There is a carriage waiting nearby."

He heard a small muffled sound behind him. The lantern light flared wildly on the stone walls.

"Are you all right, Miss Dean?" he asked.

"Yes, of course," she said coolly. "I stumbled on one of the floor stones. They are very uneven, and the lighting is quite poor down here."

In spite of his ill-tempered mood, he smiled a little to himself. Virginia Dean was living up to his expectations. It would take more than a bloody corpse and an encounter with a deadly clockwork curiosity to shatter her nerves.

Not that he had anticipated weak nerves from her. He had known from the beginning that she was a formidable lady infused with determination and a strong spirit. She was also a woman of considerable talent. He had never doubted that, unlike the talents of so many of her colleagues at the Institute, her gifts were genuine. There was an exhilarating energy in the atmosphere around her—at least he found it exhilarating.

In his experience, the vast majority of her competitors and colleagues were outright frauds. The best that could be said of most of them was that they were entertainers who, like magicians and illusionists, had perfected showy tricks based on sleight of hand. At worst, they were villains who deliberately deceived and exploited the gullible.

But Virginia Dean was different. He had been transfixed by her from the first moment he saw her. That had been a week ago, when he had stood at the back of a small group of Arcane researchers gathered in Lady Pomeroy's elegant drawing room and watched Virginia perform a mirror reading. When she looked into the glass above the fireplace, he had been acutely aware of the energy that had crackled in the atmosphere.

Their eyes had met fleetingly in the mirror before she looked away. He had sensed in that brief connection that she was as aware of him as he was of her. At least, that was what he had wanted to believe.

She had worn a dark, conservatively tailored gown with a high neck; long, tight sleeves; and a small, discreetly draped bustle similar to the one she had on tonight. Her hair had been pinned beneath a crisp little confection of a hat. If she had chosen the sober attire in an effort to offset the feylike quality bestowed by her red-gold hair and haunted, blue-green eyes, she had failed spectacularly. She was not beautiful in the traditional sense; she was something far more intriguing to a man of his nature: a woman of mystery and power. Everything that was male in him was enthralled.

He had been certain that she was aware of his intense interest that day, and he'd known something else as well. She had been quietly seething. Lady Pomeroy, the woman who had commissioned the reading, had not informed her ahead of time that there would be an audience of paranormal investigators. He could see that

Virginia had not appreciated having the surprise sprung on her.

He did not know what Virginia had seen in the mirror that evening, but when she was finished she had turned away to speak very quietly to Lady Pomeroy. The others in the crowd had clamored loudly, demanding to ask questions and conduct experiments on her talent.

She had faced them with an air of icy disdain that would have suited a very displeased Queen Victoria.

"I do not read mirrors for the purpose of entertaining others or satisfying their curiosity. When I accepted this commission, I believed it to be a serious request. I did not realize that I was to be tested and examined. I'm afraid I don't have time for that sort of nonsense."

At that point she had given them her back and walked out the door without another word. The shock that had momentarily electrified the small group that was left behind in the drawing room had amused Owen to no end. Lady Pomeroy and the researchers from the Arcane Society all moved in eminently respectable—and in some cases exclusive—circles. They were not accustomed to enduring the cold scorn of a lowly psychical practitioner, a woman who actually went into the world to earn her living with her talents.

When they had recovered, they awaited the verdict from a flushed and very annoyed Lady Pomeroy.

"What did she tell you, madam?" Hedgeworth asked.

"Miss Dean informed me that my husband was not murdered, nor was his death a suicide, as some suspected," Lady Pomeroy said brusquely. "According to her, Carlton was alone here in the drawing room when he died of natural causes, as I have always believed. There was no indication of violence."

"Well, that was a perfectly safe thing for her to say, wasn't it?" one of the other observers pointed out. "There is no proving otherwise after all these months."

"She no doubt researched the matter of your husband's death before she came here today, Lady Pomeroy," Hobson said. "The particulars were in the papers, after all. The press called it a stroke."

"Quite right," one of the others said. "The Dean woman could well be a fraud. The charlatans in that field are very clever. And since none of us is a glasslight-talent, we cannot be certain that we, ourselves, were not deceived."

But Owen had known with every fiber of his being that Virginia Dean possessed a true talent. The shadows in her eyes told him that she had witnessed death many times over. He knew those shadows well. He saw similar ghosts in his own eyes every time he looked into a mirror.

He turned down another hallway, Virginia and Becky at his heels.

"I admire your fortitude, Miss Dean," he said. "And that of Miss Becky, as well. You have both been through a great deal tonight. Many people, male or female, would have been thoroughly rattled by now."

"Never fear, Mr. Sweetwater," Virginia said. "Becky and I will indulge ourselves in a bracing case of shattered nerves at a more convenient time, won't we, Becky?"

"Yes, ma'am," Becky said. "Right now I just want to get out of this place."

"My sentiments precisely," Virginia said. "Becky, are you certain you can't recall anything after getting into the man's carriage earlier today?"

"No, ma'am." Becky hesitated. "Just that the gentleman seemed so handsome and so charming. And the flowers. I remember those as well."

"What flowers?"

"I'm not sure, but I think I smelled something sickeningly sweet, like dying roses."

"Chloroform," Virginia said grimly. "You were drugged, Becky. That is why you don't remember what happened to you."

Owen opened the door at the top of the stairs and ushered them into the old drying shed.

"Please do not mistake me, sir, ma'am," Becky said. "I am truly grateful to both of you. But I don't understand how the two of you managed to find me tonight. How did you know where I was?"

"Mr. Sweetwater is an investigator," Virginia said. "A sort of private inquiry agent. Finding people is what he does. Isn't that right, sir?"

"In a manner of speaking," Owen said.

"Oh, I see." Becky's expression cleared. "I've never met a private inquiry agent. It sounds a very interesting profession."

"It has its moments," Owen said.

He opened the door, heightened his senses and looked out into the night-shrouded gardens. Nothing moved in the fogbound darkness. The walled grounds that surrounded the mansion were as eerily silent as they had been earlier, when he had arrived. The mansion also appeared deserted. No light glowed in any of the windows.

He led the women out of the shed.

Behind him, Becky spoke quietly to Virginia.

"Are you Mr. Sweetwater's assistant, ma'am?" she asked.

"No," Virginia said firmly. "I do not work for Mr. Sweetwater."

"Ah, then you are his mistress," Becky said, speaking with the wisdom of the streets. "I thought so. It must be very exciting to be the mistress of a private inquiry agent."

Owen winced and braced himself for the thunderstorm he knew was about to light up the garden. But to his amazement, Virginia did not lose her temper. She kept her voice polite, almost gentle. One would never know that she had just been grievously insulted.

"No, Becky," she said. "I do not have any sort of personal or intimate relationship with Mr. Sweetwater."

"I don't understand," Becky said. "If you don't work for him and if you're not his mistress, why are you out here with him in the middle of the night?"

"I was at loose ends this evening," Virginia said. "I thought it might be amusing to go out on an adventure with a private inquiry agent."

"I expect it was thrilling," Becky said.

"Yes, indeed," Virginia said.

Owen glanced back over his shoulder. "Thrilling, was it, Miss Dean?"

"Perhaps that is not the perfect word," Virginia said.

He got them through the garden gate and down the

alley to the waiting carriage. The figure on the box stirred and looked down.

"I see you found not one but two ladies, Uncle Owen," Matt said. "A good night's work."

"There was a bit of luck involved, but everyone is safe." Owen opened the door of the cab. "We are going to drop our guests off at their respective addresses."

"Aye, sir," Matt said.

Virginia drew Owen aside while Becky got into the vehicle.

"We will take Becky to the charity house in Elm Street," she said quietly. "She will be well taken care of there tonight. The woman who operates the house will give Becky a clean bed, a good meal, and offer her a way off the streets."

"I know the place," Owen said. He smiled. "Are you aware that it has recently come under the auspices of the Arcane Society?"

"Arcane is operating a refuge for young prostitutes?" Disbelief rang in Virginia's voice. "I don't believe it. When did the Society develop an interest in charity?"

"I'm told it is the modern era, Miss Dean. The world is changing, and so is the Arcane Society."

"*Hah.* I sincerely doubt that lot of arrogant, hidebound old alchemists is capable of change."

She turned and went up the steps and into the cab. He climbed in behind the women, put the clockwork weapon on the floor of the vehicle, sat down and closed the door. The carriage rattled forward down the lane.

Becky frowned at the clockwork device. "Is that a toy?"

"No," Owen said. "It is an automaton, a clockwork

curiosity. Someone evidently left it behind. Thought I'd salvage it."

"Oh," Becky said. "It is very pretty."

"Yes," he said.

She lost interest immediately and sank back into the corner of the seat with a small sigh. "Do you think the handsome man in the carriage will try to find me? He will no doubt be very angry when he discovers that I am gone. He knows the corner where I conduct my business."

"I promise you that you will never see him again," Virginia said. She touched the girl's hand. "You are safe."

THREE

They delivered Becky into the warmth and welcome of the Elm Street charity house's matron, Mrs. Mallory. Becky seemed bewildered, but the prospect of a hot meal and a safe bed persuaded her to tolerate the situation, at least for the night.

"Whether or not she accepts the offer of going off to the charity-house school for girls, where she can learn a respectable trade, like typewriting or telegraphy, will be up to her," Virginia said when she got back into the carriage. "But Mrs. Mallory is very skilled at encouraging the girls to enter the school."

Owen sat down on the opposite seat.

"You are a strong believer in education for the girls of the streets?" he said.

The carriage rolled forward.

"It is the only hope for a woman alone in the world," Virginia said.

"You speak from experience?"

"I was orphaned at the age of thirteen. If my father had not left me a small inheritance that ensured that my boarding school fees were paid until I was seventeen, I would very likely have wound up on the streets like young Becky."

"No," Owen said. "Not you. With your talent and intelligence you would have found another way to survive."

She looked out into the darkness. "Who knows? It does seem rather ironic that I am pursuing a career that requires me to work at night."

"Will there be anyone who will have been concerned about you tonight?" he asked. "Aside from your housekeeper, I mean."

"No. Actually, I'm surprised Mrs. Crofton was worried. She is new and still learning my unusual routine. I am often out late in the evenings, although rarely this late."

From the way Virginia spoke he knew that she was not accustomed to the notion of anyone worrying about her or fretting because she was late returning home.

"Why do you work at night?" he asked.

"The energy in the mirrors is usually stronger and more easily read at night. I can work in a heavily draped room if necessary, but I prefer to do my analysis in the evenings. I see things more clearly then."

"I hadn't realized that." Intrigued, he considered the matter briefly. "My talent is sharper and more focused at night as well. I wonder if it has something to do with the absence of the energy produced by sunlight. Perhaps those sorts of currents interfere with certain paranormal wavelengths."

She looked at him. "I am aware that you and your associates within Arcane hold a low opinion of those of us who make our livings with our talents. I know that you consider the vast majority of us to be charlatans. I also realize that the fact that I have frequent evening appointments does nothing to improve my reputation in your eyes or those of the Society's. I would like to make it clear that I do not give a fig what you or the arrogant members of Arcane think of me and my colleagues at the Leybrook Institute."

"You have already made your opinion of me and the Society quite clear, Miss Dean. Perhaps I should mention that I am not a member of Arcane."

"Why were you in that group of so-called researchers who wanted to test my talent at the Pomeroy reading?"

"It's a long story. You are exhausted. You need rest and time to recover from your ordeal tonight. I promise to tell you everything in the morning."

She ignored that. "You risked your own neck to come looking for me tonight. Why?"

"I told you, I have been keeping an eye on you. I think you may be in danger, although I admit I had not anticipated the situation in which I found you tonight. I have been searching in another direction."

"You said you were not a member of Arcane."

"Arcane is a client."

"A *client*?" She appeared stunned. "You work for the Society?"

"I am currently conducting an investigation for Arcane's new psychical investigation agency, Jones & Jones. Perhaps you have heard of it?"

Her jaw tightened. "I have heard rumors of the new agency, yes."

"You do not approve?"

"In my world, there is a strong suspicion that J & J is in the business of putting those of us who use our tal-

ents to make a living out of business. Arcane believes
that psychical practitioners, in particular those at the
Leybrook Institute, give legitimate study and research
of the paranormal a bad reputation."

"Because there are so many charlatans in your midst,
and those frauds deceive and mislead the public.
I understand. But I think it is safe to say that J & J currently has more work than it can handle dealing with
truly dangerous psychical criminals. Trust me when
I tell you that Caleb and Lucinda Jones, the directors of
J & J, are not concerning themselves over much with
mediums, séance-givers and other fraudulent practitioners these days."

"That remains to be seen."

"I comprehend that you do not trust Arcane, but I
need your help. I am hunting a killer, Virginia, one who
is operating in your world."

"What are you talking about?" she asked.

"Two glass-readers have died recently. J & J has asked
me to investigate."

"Why would J & J care about the deaths of two practitioners? The police certainly weren't interested. They
don't even believe that Mrs. Ratford and Mrs. Hackett
were murdered. Neither does anyone else. The authorities concluded both women died of natural causes."

"But you suspect that is not the case, don't you?"

She hesitated. "Yes."

"So does J & J. So do I. As I said, it is a long story, and
the hour grows late. I give you my word that I will
explain everything in the morning."

"You will not fob me off without some further
explanation, sir. You said you are investigating the

glass-reader deaths on behalf of Arcane. What talent do you possess that enables you to conduct such an investigation?"

"Let's just say that you were close to the truth when you told Becky that I am a sort of private inquiry agent. I am, in fact, a hunter."

"Who or what do you hunt, Mr. Sweetwater?"

"Monsters of the human variety, Miss Dean. Like you, I do my best work at night."

His own house was dark and silent when he got home, but that was the way it always was at night. He lived alone. His housekeeper arrived early in the morning and left in the late afternoon. The arrangement provided him with the solitude that he found himself seeking more and more after dark. There was no one about to notice when he went out to walk the night, no one who might casually mention the new habit to another member of his closely knit family.

At least the glass-reader case was temporarily distracting him from the late-night strolls and the abyss that beckoned ever more strongly.

Owen carried the clockwork carriage into the cluttered library and set it down on a table. The dark windows of the miniature vehicle glittered malevolently in the light of the gas lamp. Before he went to bed tonight, he would lock the device securely in the safe in the basement. He was certain that he had disabled the weapon, but he did not intend to take any chances. The thing was something entirely new in his experience. He would proceed with great caution.

He crossed the room to the brandy table and poured himself a healthy dose of the spirits. Glass in hand, he sat down in front of the cold hearth and contemplated the beautifully crafted curiosity. The inquiry he was conducting had taken an ominous twist. Hollister's death was the least of it. There were still far more questions than answers, but one thing was clear. Virginia Dean was the key to the entire affair.

FOUR

The following morning Owen took the carriage out of the safe, hauled it upstairs to the library and put it on a table. He collected a variety of small tools and set to work dismantling the curiosity. He was in the process of carefully removing one of the windows in the cab when a knock sounded on the door.

"Not now, Mrs. Brent." He did not look up from the delicate task of disassembling the carriage. "I told you, I do not want to be disturbed this morning."

"Yes, sir, I know, sir." The housekeeper's voice was muffled by the door. "It's Mrs. Sweetwater, sir."

"Which Mrs. Sweetwater? There are half a dozen of them in London at any given moment."

The door opened. Mrs. Brent fixed him with a stern look. "Mrs. Aurelia Sweetwater, sir. She just arrived, and she insists on speaking with you."

Of course it would be Aurelia, he thought. She was the oldest of his great-aunts and enjoyed the status of being the family matriarch. He had known this visitation was coming, he reminded himself. But he had been dreading it.

"Damn it to hell," he said. But he said it very softly. "Very well, Mrs. Brent, show her in here, if you would."

"Yes, sir." Mrs. Brent started to retreat into the hall.

"But I warn you that it will be worth your position in this household if you bring in a tea tray," Owen vowed. "I do not want to give my aunt any excuse to hang about here."

Mrs. Brent's mouth twitched in amusement, but she kept her professional composure. "Yes, sir."

"I heard that," Aurelia Sweetwater announced. She swept into the library, elegantly regal in a dark purple gown. Her gray hair was caught up in a towering chignon and crowned with a feather-trimmed hat that matched the dress. Her street-sweeper petticoats rustled ominously on the carpet. "As it happens, I do not have time for tea today, but that is beside the point."

"Good morning, Aunt Aurelia," Owen said. He left the table and crossed the carpet to give her an affectionate kiss on the cheek. "You are looking in excellent spirits today. A bit early, is it not? What brings you here at this hour?"

"You know perfectly well why I was forced to call on you at this ungodly hour of the morning. It is the only time I can hope to find you at home. You have been avoiding me, Owen."

"Not at all. I have been busy of late. New client, you know."

"I am aware that the family has taken on Arcane as a client. I'm not certain that is a wise move, but we shall see."

"Arcane is changing," Owen said. "Under the new Master, it has assumed new responsibilities. It seems the Joneses feel an obligation to protect the public from the monsters."

Aurelia raised her brows. A thoughtful expression crossed her face. "If that is true, then we will likely be seeing a great deal of business from J & J in the years ahead."

Owen angled himself on the corner of his desk. "Precisely. There is never a shortage of monsters to hunt."

Aurelia smiled. So did Owen. It was a moment of silent, familial communication and mutual understanding that only another Sweetwater would comprehend. The men of the Sweetwater family were compelled to hunt the monsters. It was the nature of their talent. But they had long ago concluded that it made excellent financial sense to have a client pay for the work whenever possible.

Aurelia stopped smiling. "As it happens, I came here today to discuss Arcane with you."

"What about it?"

"It seems the Society is now offering a matrimonial consulting service that specializes in introducing people of talent to each other."

It took him a split second to realize where the conversation was going. When the full horror of it struck home, he came off the corner of the desk very suddenly.

"Do not even think about registering me with the Society's matchmaking agency, Aunt Aurelia," he said.

"Oh, I cannot do the registering for you." She waved that aside, unfazed by his dark mood. "You would have to take care of the details yourself."

"I am not about to employ a matchmaker."

"My understanding is that Lady Milden, who operates the agency, has a true gift for matching people endowed with strong psychical natures. She has a number of resources to draw on, including Arcane's extensive genealogical records."

"Forget it." He went to the window and stood looking out at the rain-dampened garden. "I am not interested in that approach."

"Why not?"

"Sweetwaters find their own women."

"Except when they don't," Aurelia said. She spoke quietly, but the words were heavy with meaning. "We both know what happens when a Sweetwater man goes too long without a true mate."

He did not respond. There was no need.

"You have begun the nightwalking, haven't you?" Aurelia said quietly.

A cold chill iced the nape of his neck. The Sweetwaters were very good at keeping secrets from outsiders, but it was damned difficult to keep a secret within the family.

"I have always hunted at night," he said, trying to claw his way out of the trap. "Everyone in the family knows that. It's the nature of my version of the family talent. I see the evidence of the monsters more clearly after dark."

"What everyone in the family *knows*," Aurelia said, "is that you are spending more and more time on the streets late at night. It is one thing to troll for monsters occasionally. In this family, that passes for sport, rather like fishing. But it is quite another to go out alone night after night, searching for your prey. That way lies madness for a Sweetwater man."

"I am not hunting at night for the sport of it. I have a particular client, J & J, and I have a specific target, a psychical maniac who is murdering glasslight-talents."

"I realize that you have recently acquired a client, but that is only a short-term diversion. It will not change what is happening to you. Owen, your parents and the rest of the family are starting to worry. If you do not find the right woman soon, you will become a nightwalker."

"What makes you think Lady Milden can find me a match?"

"I am told she is very skilled at what she does. What do you have to lose?"

"Time," he said. "Time that I can spend searching for my own true mate."

"You said yourself this is the modern era. You should take advantage of modern, more efficient ways of doing things."

"I'll consider it," he said, lying through his teeth.

"I will take that as a promise."

He swung around. "Damn it, Aunt Aurelia."

"I will ignore the bad language this one time, because I am aware that you are under considerable stress." She went toward the door. "You have wasted too much time already. You must not wait any longer, Owen. Your family does not want to lose you to the night."

FIVE

I do not usually report to clients until the job is finished," Owen Sweetwater said.

Caleb angled his chin in acknowledgment of the great favor that Sweetwater appeared to think he was granting to Jones & Jones. In the few months that he and Lucinda had been doing business at the agency, they had discovered that the only people more troublesome than the clients were the powerful and unpredictable talents the firm was obliged to hire in order to conduct the investigations.

"We appreciate that you are making an exception for us," Caleb said.

His cousin Gabe, the Master of the Society, studied Sweetwater with a considering expression.

"You came highly recommended, Mr. Sweetwater, but please understand that this sort of business is new to us," Gabe said.

The three of them were standing in an abandoned warehouse near the docks. Sweetwater had chosen the location for the meeting, just as he had selected the location the first time, when Caleb had contacted him about the possibility of employment. It had become clear immediately that when one engaged the services of the

Sweetwater clan, one accepted the arrangements stipulated by the particular Sweetwater with whom one was dealing.

At the first meeting Caleb had been convinced that Owen Sweetwater was a hunter-talent of some sort but not the traditional variety. The psychical abilities of the average hunter tended to be of a more physical nature. Such talents were usually endowed with preternatural reflexes, speed, hearing and night vision. They hunted by detecting the psychical spoor of their prey.

Owen Sweetwater moved with a predatory ease and control that put one in mind of a hunter, but Caleb had grown up in a family that boasted a number of hunters sprinkled throughout the bloodline. He knew true hunters, and he was quite certain that whatever Sweetwater was, he was not a traditional hunter-talent.

"What we want to know," Caleb said carefully, "is whether you have found any evidence that supports my belief that the two glass-readers were killed by paranormal means. If not, then this case is not J & J's problem. I will give what information we have to an acquaintance at Scotland Yard. The police can take responsibility for finding the killer."

"The way they took responsibility for the murders of an untold number of prostitutes in the past several years?"

Gabe frowned. "What the hell is that supposed to mean?"

"Tomorrow or the following day, you will read of the tragic death of Lord Hollister in the morning papers," Owen said. "The official cause of his demise will likely be a heart attack or stroke. In reality, he died of a knife in the chest."

Caleb raised his brows. "Your work?"

"I cannot take the credit. I suspect the wife. I found the body when I explored the basement beneath the mansion."

"What the devil were you doing in Hollister's basement?" Gabe asked.

"That is where my investigation led me," Owen said a little too smoothly. "What the press will not be aware of is that Hollister preyed on young prostitutes for years. He lured them into his carriage and took them to the basement beneath his mansion, where he raped and murdered them. There is no telling how many he killed. While I was on the premises, I found another girl who was still alive. I took her to the charity house in Elm Street."

"I have seen nothing in the papers about missing streetwalkers," Caleb said.

"That is because the press rarely notices when girls go missing," Owen said. "Prostitutes are forever vanishing from the streets. Sometimes they turn up in the river, sometimes they simply disappear. But unless the death is a particularly bloody one, the public has no interest. Hollister was careful to dispose of the bodies so that they did not draw attention."

Gabe thought about that. "You say Hollister was a talent?"

"Yes, I'm sure of it, possibly a glass-reader."

"That is why your investigation led you to his basement," Caleb said, mentally assembling the pieces of the puzzle. "Was he the one who murdered the glass-readers?"

"No, but there is some connection between Hollister and the murders of the glass-readers," Owen said. "My investigation is ongoing."

"That does not tell us a great deal," Gabe said without inflection.

"I can give you one or two other interesting facts. I came across a rather dangerous psychical weapon disguised as a clockwork curiosity in the Hollister mansion. There may be other such devices out there."

Caleb groaned. "I had hoped that the crystal guns that gave us so much trouble in the course of a recent case were the end of our problems with paranormal weaponry."

"Evidently not," Owen said. "I can also tell you that the link between Hollister's death and the deaths of the glass-readers runs through the Leybrook Institute."

Irritation flashed through Caleb. "That damned Institute is rife with charlatans and frauds."

"When you consider the matter closely," Gabe said, "it is the ideal place for a true psychical killer to conceal himself."

"A genuine talent hidden among the fakes." Caleb sighed. "Very clever."

"It's called hiding in plain sight," Owen said. "The monsters are very good at that."

It seemed to Caleb that there was a new chill in the atmosphere. It was not coming from the river or the fog that shrouded the warehouse. It emanated from Owen Sweetwater's aura. *We are doing business with a very dangerous man*, he thought.

"It seems you were right, Caleb," Gabe said. "But then, you generally are when it comes to this sort of thing."

Caleb did not respond. There was nothing to say. He was almost always right when it came to seeing patterns. He was especially skilled at noting the dark evidence that indicated crimes that had been committed by villains endowed with psychical talent. But no one was right one hundred percent of the time. Deep inside, he lived with the knowledge that someday he would miscalculate and innocents might die. It was the theme of his darkest dreams.

He frowned at Owen. "How do you intend to proceed?"

Owen shrugged, as if the question had an obvious answer.

"I will identify the killer and remove him," he said. "I will then, of course, send you a bill for services rendered."

Gabe leaned back against a large, empty wooden cask and folded his arms. "A simple plan."

"I have always found that they work best," Owen said. "Now, then, I am rather busy at the moment. If there is nothing else, I trust you will excuse me."

He turned and walked away through the deep shadows at the back of the warehouse. In a moment he was gone.

Gabe watched the darkness where Sweetwater had vanished. "I do not think that he told us everything he knows."

"You can place a wager on that assumption," Caleb agreed.

"He's one of us, though, isn't he?"

"A hunter?" Caleb said. "Yes, I'm sure of it. But he is not like any hunter-talent I have ever met."

"How do you think he hunts?"

"From what little I have learned about him, I suspect that he has the ability to discern what it is that compels the killer. Once he knows that, he can make some predictions."

"Such as the possible identity of the killer's next victim?"

"Yes."

"What if he's wrong?"

"Then I was wrong to employ him," Caleb said. "If another innocent glass-reader dies, I will bear a good portion of the blame."

"No," Gabe said. "You took the only step you could take to try to stop the person who is murdering the glass-readers. And as the Master of the Society, I authorized the hiring of Sweetwater for this venture. It was, I believe, a very logical move. We are sending a man who hunts monsters out to hunt his natural prey."

Caleb exhaled slowly. "What gives us the right to do such a thing?"

"Damned if I know," Gabe said. "But if J & J doesn't go after the psychical villains, who will? It is not as if the police are equipped to track down killers who are endowed with paranormal talents."

"No."

"I would remind you this is not an act of pure altruism on our parts," Gabe said. "Our survival and the survival of those like us may well be at stake. Arcane has a great interest in protecting the public from the monsters."

"I am aware of that."

At the moment, the press and the public were fascinated by the paranormal. But if it became common knowledge that there were those who could use their psychical abilities to commit murder, the popular interest would transmute instantly into panic.

Gabe strode toward the door. "As long as I am Master, I will do everything in my power to ensure that we do not return to the days when those with even a scrap of paranormal talent were branded as witches and sorcerers. If that means occasionally hiring a psychical assassin, so be it."

Caleb fell into step beside him. "You have certainly become a good deal more obsessed with protecting the members of the Society and future generations of talents since Venetia delivered your firstborn last month."

Gabe opened the door and moved out into the fog-shrouded night. "It is astonishing how becoming a father focuses one's priorities."

SIX

Owen went up the steps of the modest town house in Garnet Lane, keenly aware of the sense of anticipation that had been whispering through him all morning. The prospect of seeing Virginia again energized him in ways that probably should have been deeply disturbing or at least mildly concerning. It was invariably a mistake to allow himself to give free rein to any strong emotion when he was on the hunt. The Sweetwaters were a notoriously passionate lot. A side effect of their talents, some said. But indulging in strong passions while hunting violated all of the family rules.

Virginia Dean was proving to be the exception to every rule he had lived by for all of his life.

The door at the top of the steps opened before he could knock more than twice. Mrs. Crofton, the housekeeper, stood before him. She was a tall woman in her late thirties, garbed in a gray housedress trimmed with a white, crisply starched apron. A neatly pleated white cap covered most of her tightly pinned blond hair. There was a mix of curiosity and veiled assessment in her blue eyes. He knew from their initial encounter that she was not accustomed to finding a man on her employer's front steps. The knowledge that Virginia did not, apparently, receive a lot of gentlemen callers pleased him more than he wanted to admit.

"You're back, then, Mr. Sweetwater," Mrs. Crofton said.

Her voice was laced with the cool, professional accents of a woman who at one time or another had served in a far more exclusive household. He wondered how she had come to work for an employer who was obliged to go out into the world to earn a living. House-keepers and others in service were as concerned with their social status as everyone else. The social standing of one's employer mattered.

"I believe I am expected." He gave her his card.

"Yes, sir. Miss Dean said you would be calling today, sir. She will see you." Mrs. Crofton stepped back and held out a hand for his hat and gloves. "I'll show you into her study."

When she closed the door, a heavy gloom descended on the front hall. It took him a moment to realize that there was no mirror on the wall over the console as was commonplace in many homes, to add the illusion of light and space.

He followed Mrs. Crofton down a narrow corridor and into a snug, book-lined study. The window at the far end overlooked a small, attractive garden. There was a mirror in this room, he noted. It looked new.

Virginia was seated behind a compact rolltop desk. She looked up, pen in hand. For a heartbeat, he just looked at her, fascinated by the way the morning light burnished her red-and-gold hair.

"Mr. Sweetwater to see you, ma'am," Mrs. Crofton announced.

"Thank you, Mrs. Crofton," Virginia said. She put aside the pen. "Please sit down, Mr. Sweetwater."

Mrs. Crofton hesitated in the doorway. "Will you be wanting tea, ma'am?"

Virginia looked suddenly uncertain. Having faced the same weighty question earlier that day, Owen smiled to himself. Offering tea was a silent way of inviting a guest to linger longer than might otherwise be necessary. Virginia's decision would provide him with a clue to how she viewed their association.

"Yes, please," Virginia said with an air of sudden decision. "Thank you, Mrs. Crofton."

He had his answer, Owen thought. Virginia was still wary of him, but she had accepted the fact that she could no longer avoid him. Serving tea did not mean that she would cooperate fully, but it was a silent acknowledgment that they were bound together, if only temporarily, by the events of the night.

Mrs. Crofton closed the door. Owen sat down in a chair facing the desk and the window.

"I must admit I'm curious to know how you explained your late return home last night to your housekeeper," he said.

"I simply said that I had been detained at the client's house longer than expected." Virginia indicated the copy of the *Flying Intelligencer* on top of the desk. "There is nothing on Hollister's death in the morning papers, so Mrs. Crofton has no reason to ask any questions."

"Do not be too sure of that. In my experience, housekeepers always know more than anyone realizes. The reason there is no gossip yet is because, as of midnight last night, no one except us and the killer was aware that Hollister was dead. For all we know the body is still down there in that chamber, waiting to be discovered. When it does appear in the papers, the death will no doubt be attributed to natural causes."

"Yes, of course. The family will make certain of it. They will not want the scandal of a murder investigation, especially if the killer was the wife, as we suspect."

"No."

Virginia clasped her hands on the blotter. "Given that no high-ranking family wants to become involved with the police, I cannot understand why someone tried to arrange matters so that I would be found at the scene of the murder with a knife in my hand."

"I'm almost certain that was not part of the original plan. I think it is far more likely that something went very wrong with a carefully set scheme last night."

"Do you think it was a coincidence that Lady Hollister commissioned a reading last night?"

"When it comes to murder, there are no coincidences. But in this situation there are other possibilities."

"Such as?"

"Perhaps you were the intended victim all along."

Virginia stilled. "Me?"

"If you had been found at the scene, you would have been arrested and very likely hung for murder."

"Good grief."

"Do you have any enemies or rivals, Miss Dean?"

She drew a breath. "No outright enemies that I know of, but there is always a great deal of competition among practitioners. So yes, I have some rivals, but I cannot think of any who would go so far as to implicate me in the murder of a high-ranking gentleman just to get me out of the way."

"It is only one possible explanation for events. I'm sure there are others."

"What a cheerful thought. You must have spent some time thinking about the case last night, sir. Is that the best you could come up with?"

"I will admit that my thinking last night was not terribly productive. There are too many unknowns at this stage."

She raised her brows. "Did you get any sleep at all?"

"Very little."

"Neither did I." Virginia sighed. "I spent most of the night trying to make some sense of events. I am absolutely baffled."

"There is a great mystery here. The one thing I am certain of is that although we succeeded in destroying someone's carefully laid trap, you are still in danger."

"But why?"

"Because you are a very powerful glasslight-talent, Miss Dean. Your psychical ability is the key to this affair. Tell me what you remember of last night."

"I have gone over each moment again and again." She rose and went to stand at the window. She gripped the edge of the green velvet drapery and looked out into the garden. "Mr. Welch, the gentleman who manages the consultation appointments at the Institute, booked a reading for me at the request of Lady Hollister. I arrived at the Hollister mansion at the specified time, eight o'clock in the evening."

"Did Lady Hollister send a carriage for you?"

Virginia's mouth curved into a faint, wry smile. "No,

of course not. People like Lady Hollister only extend
that courtesy to those they perceive to be their social
equals. As far as my clients are concerned, I rank a rung
or two lower on the social ladder than a governess or a
paid companion, because unlike women in those two
respectable careers, I go out into the world to make my
living."

"But judging by the fact that you have your own
house, employ a housekeeper and dress rather fashionably, I would hazard a guess that you make considerably
more money than women in either of those two
professions."

She laughed a little and turned her head to look at
him. "Your guess would be correct, Mr. Sweetwater. The
house is rented, Mrs. Crofton kindly agreed to take
wages that she assures me are considerably lower than
those she received from her last employer, and my
dressmaker does not even pretend to be French, as the
most exclusive ones do. But yes, I do manage nicely.
What is more, my business has flourished now that I
am affiliated with the Leybrook Institute. Mr. Leybrook
is very skilled at attracting high-quality clients."

"Such as Lady Hollister?" he asked without
inflection.

Virginia winced. "In retrospect, it would appear that
she was not the best of clients."

"Go on with your recollection of events."

Virginia returned to the view from the study window. "Let me think. I recall being shown into the library.
The room seemed cold and dark, although there was a
fire on the hearth and the lamps were lit. Something
about the energy in that house, I suppose. Very depress-

ing. Lady Hollister was waiting for me together with her companion. Tea was served. I asked Lady Hollister to tell me why she had requested the reading."

"Did she explain?"

"It was obvious almost immediately that Lady Hollister was not entirely sane. Her conversation was disjointed, and she became easily agitated. Her companion had to calm her at several points. But Lady Hollister was very clear about why she had summoned me."

"What mirror did she want you to read?"

"The looking glass in her dead daughter's bedroom." A slight but unmistakable shudder shivered through Virginia. "I dread those sorts of readings. The children . . ."

"I understand."

She glanced at him again. "Do you?"

"I have seen the taint of the monsters who prey on children. If you dread those readings, why do you do them?"

"I feel somehow compelled." Virginia returned her attention to the window. "Sometimes, not always, I am able to provide a sense of finality to the bereaved parents. It is as if the reading closes a gate into the past and frees them to move forward into the future. And on rare occasions, I have been able to perceive clues that have led the police to the killer."

"You take satisfaction from those readings? The ones that lead to justice for the victim?"

"Yes," she said. "They comfort me in some way I cannot explain. But last night I was unable to give Lady Hollister what she wanted and needed. Instead, I suspect that I drove her deeper into madness."

"What happened?"

"Lady Hollister told me that her daughter had died at the age of eleven. Officially it was declared an accident. The girl's body was found at the foot of the staircase. When I was shown into the bedroom, it was clear that nothing had been changed in the room since the poor child's death."

"Where was the mirror?"

"On a small dressing table," Virginia said. "It faced the bed. I knew that I did not want to look into it, but I felt I owed the truth to Lady Hollister."

"What did you see?"

Virginia closed her eyes. "The girl was assaulted by someone she knew well. Someone who terrified her. She cried. That is probably why he strangled her. He wanted to silence her and used too much force. Afterward I suspect that he tossed her body down the stairs in an effort to feign an accident. But I know where she died."

"In the bed."

Virginia crushed the green velvet drapery in her tightly clenched fist. "Yes."

"Hollister. She was raped and murdered by her own father."

"I think so, yes."

The familiar ice-and-fire energy of the hunt splashed through Owen's veins. He suppressed it with an act of will. That particular monster was dead, he reminded himself. He needed to concentrate on the new prey.

"Did you tell Lady Hollister the truth?" he asked.

"I did not name Hollister as the killer. After all, I had no proof to offer. A woman in my position must be very careful with her words in a situation like that. The thing

is, I do not see the afterimages of the murderers, only
those of the dead. The visions tell me a great deal, but
they do not provide all of the answers. It was possible
that another close family member was the killer, an
uncle or a grandfather, perhaps."

"But you did tell Lady Hollister that the person who
had murdered her daughter was someone the girl knew
and feared."

"Yes."

"How did she respond?"

Virginia's brows came together in a troubled frown.
"I'm not entirely certain. That is where my memory of
the night starts to blur. I think she may have left the
room without speaking, but I cannot be positive. After
that, everything is a blank until I woke up in that mirrored chamber."

"You were drugged."

"That is the only explanation," Virginia agreed. "But
by whom? Lady Hollister? Why would she do that?"

"You told her a truth she did not want to hear. You
said yourself she was clearly unbalanced."

"We know Hollister used chloroform on Becky so it
may have been on the premises, but I'm sure I would
have recalled the smell or at least a struggle."

"I'm told one does not always remember the odor,
but I think in this case, it's more likely that the drug was
in the tea."

"In which case Lady Hollister intended to drug me
even before she knew what I would see in the looking
glass," Virginia said. "But again, why?"

"We do not yet have the answers, but we will get
them."

Virginia turned away from the window. "'*We,*' Mr. Sweetwater?"

"I cannot conduct this hunt—" He stopped and cleared his throat. "I mean this investigation, without your assistance."

She went back to her desk and sat down. "You seem very eager to help me, Mr. Sweetwater. I suspect that is because you believe that I am the key to solving the case for your client."

"You are a very suspicious woman, Miss Dean. Is it not barely possible that my client wishes to protect you and other potential victims of the glass-reader killer?"

"It is highly unlikely that Arcane has any interest in protecting practitioners like myself."

"Well, as it happens, I am the one requesting your assistance, not J & J. You will be dealing with me, not Arcane."

"Is there a difference?"

"Oh, yes," he said very softly. "A vast difference. I am no more a member of Arcane than you are. As I told you, J & J is a client."

"No offense, sir, but I trust you will understand that I know less about you than I know about Arcane or J & J."

He smiled. "By the time this affair is concluded, we will know each other very well, Miss Dean. Meanwhile, I give you my word that I am not going to ruin your career, nor will I allow J & J to do so."

"*Hmm.*"

"You do not believe me?"

"I'm not sure what to believe," she said. "There is the

matter of your reputation. Only last week you exposed another medium in the press."

"I admit that I did expose a couple of mediums in order to establish my credentials as a legitimate researcher," he said. "I can see that it was not the wisest course of action, because now you do not trust me. If it matters, I can tell you that I chose the two mediums because practitioners who claim to speak to the dead annoy me far more than those who pretend to levitate or read minds."

"Why is that?"

"The levitators and mind readers are harmless entertainers, for the most part. They are guilty only of parlor tricks. But the mediums practice a cruel deception."

She drummed the fingers of one hand on the desk. "As it happens, I agree with you. Nevertheless, that does not give you the right to interfere in the business affairs of others who are merely trying to make an honest living. Well, mostly honest."

"Believe me, exposing practitioners is not my goal in this affair. I posed as a researcher who investigates psychical phenomena in order to provide myself with a cover that I could use to enter your world."

"I see."

"Your colleagues affiliated with the Leybrook Institute may not trust me, but by now they are convinced that I am a researcher."

"It is almost impossible to prove the existence of psychical talent. There are no instruments that can measure or record that kind of energy. I doubt if I convinced any of your associates who were present at the Pomeroy reading."

"They were not my associates. And I am aware that you feel you were tricked into doing that reading for Lady Pomeroy and those Arcane investigators."

She narrowed her eyes. "Did you arrange for that test?"

"No, Miss Dean. Believe it or not, what I intended that night was a proper introduction. I asked Lady Pomeroy to request a reading so that I could meet you. I knew that she had always had some questions about her husband's death. I swear to you that I did not know that she intended to invite several researchers from the Society to watch you at work."

She studied him for a long time with her haunting eyes.

"I believe you," she said at last.

It was as if a mountain had been lifted off his shoulders.

"Thank you," he said.

"I almost walked out that evening without doing the reading," Virginia said. "I have a strict rule when it comes to dealing with those who want to conduct research on me. I always refuse to cooperate in any sort of test. But on a whim, I decided to go through with that reading."

"Because of Lady Pomeroy?"

"I could tell that she truly did have questions about Lord Pomeroy's death. But that was not the reason I stayed to read the mirror."

"You did the reading because of me, didn't you?"

"I think so, yes."

"Why?"

"I sensed that you were a man of considerable talent," Virginia said. "I thought, perhaps, that if you witnessed me at work you might comprehend that my talent was real, also. I suppose it was a challenge of some kind."

"So you broke your own rule that day. Because of me."

She smiled coolly. "In my experience, breaking the rules that I have established for myself is almost always a mistake."

"I have had the same experience."

"Have you ever broken your own rules, Mr. Sweetwater?"

"It seems I am shattering a number of them in this case."

An odd silence descended. The housekeeper's footsteps sounded in the hall. Mrs. Crofton opened the door and brought in the tea tray. She looked at Virginia.

"Shall I pour, madam?"

"Yes, thank you, Mrs. Crofton," Virginia said.

Mrs. Crofton poured two cups of tea and handed them out. She left the room, unobtrusively closing the door. It seemed to Owen that the study was suddenly even smaller and more intimate. He opened his senses a little, allowing himself to savor the sensation of being so close to Virginia.

"Will you assist me, Miss Dean?" he asked after a while.

"Someone has murdered two glass-readers in the past two months," she said. "Yesterday I was lured to the scene of a rather spectacular murder that involved a mirrored room. And then there is that clockwork curiosity that we encountered in the tunnels beneath the Hollister mansion. All in all, there is simply no way to explain any of those events by invoking coincidence. Yes, Mr. Sweetwater, I will assist you in your investigation."

"I am very pleased to hear that."

"Before we begin, I trust you will understand when I tell you that I have some concerns for my reputation in this affair."

Out of nowhere, cold outrage flashed through him. "I assure you, Miss Dean, the men of my family may be hunters, but we consider ourselves gentlemen. I have no intention of harming your good name."

She blinked in surprise, and then smiled. "Thank you for that assurance, but it is unnecessary. It is not my personal reputation that matters to me. At my advanced age and given the nature of my career, I need no longer worry about that sort of thing."

"What the devil are you talking about? You are hardly elderly."

"I am twenty-six, sir. That puts me well and truly on the shelf, as I'm sure you are aware. I will not be looking to contract a respectable marriage. It is my professional reputation among my colleagues that concerns me."

He frowned. "I don't see the problem."

"Really, sir, you are being quite dense. Let me spell it out for you."

People had called him a great many things, but dense

was not among the words that were typically used to describe him.

"Please do," he said.

"It is imperative that none of my associates conclude that I am assisting you to expose other practitioners. That is the sort of rumor that would ruin me."

"Of course." He really had been quite dense, he thought. "I had not considered that aspect of the matter."

"It must be very clear to one and all that I am allowing you to study and observe my work only because I am convinced I can prove to you that I really do possess some talent."

"Yes, Miss Dean. That was my plan."

"If there is any gossip to the effect that I am betraying my colleagues, I will soon lose all of my friends and the connections I require to conduct business in my world."

"You have made your point, Miss Dean. I will do everything in my power to make certain that your colleagues believe that I am devoting all of my attentions to you and you alone."

"Excellent." She sat back in her chair. "In that case, let us discuss your plans. I can advise you whether or not they are viable. I expect you will have to make some modifications. After all, we will be operating in my world, not yours, sir. I am the expert."

He wondered just when he had lost control of the discussion. If he was not extremely careful, Virginia Dean would take charge of the entire investigation, and that would put her in even more danger than she was in already.

An oddly disturbing shock of awareness whispered through him. He had embarked upon the investigation because his talent had compelled him to accept the case from J & J. There was a monster preying on the paranormal practitioners of London, and he had been called to the hunt. It was what the Sweetwaters did. It was in the blood.

But somewhere along the line the driving force behind his decision to find the killer had altered. Now he hunted to protect Virginia. The only way to do that, it seemed, was to put her at risk by involving her in the investigation. *Be careful what you wish for, Sweetwater.*

"I have one more question," Virginia said.

"Only one?"

"What do you intend to do if we are able to identify the killer?"

He set his cup and saucer aside, propped his elbows on the arms of the chair and put his fingertips together. "Caleb Jones informs me that J & J has developed a policy that applies to situations such as this."

"What is J & J's policy?"

"If there is sufficient evidence that is not of a paranormal nature, evidence that will hold up in a court of law, said evidence will be turned over to Scotland Yard. The authorities will then take charge, and the criminal will be arrested and tried in the normal, routine manner."

"I see. What are the odds that that policy will be effective in this case?"

"Very poor."

She watched him intently. "But one way or another,

SEVEN

The following morning, Virginia called on her closest friend, Charlotte Tate, and told her the whole story.

"Thank heavens you are safe and were able to save that poor street girl." Charlotte poured tea into two cups. Behind the lenses of her spectacles, her unusual amber eyes were shadowed with concern. "But I still can't believe that you came so close to being arrested for murder."

"I expect that I will have nightmares about waking up next to Hollister's body for some time," Virginia said.

Charlotte set the pot down. "I don't want to even think about what might have happened if Mr. Sweetwater had not come along when he did. You would likely never have escaped from that mirrored chamber, let alone figured out how to rescue the girl from that underground cell."

"It's true, I do lack lock-picking skills," Virginia said. "Perhaps I will ask Mr. Sweetwater to teach them to me. He was very adept, I must say."

They were sitting at the small table in the back room of Charlotte's bookshop. Charlotte had inherited the shop from her mother, who had, in turn, received it from her mother. The women of Charlotte's family had a true talent for locating ancient and rare books and manuscripts linked to the paranormal.

The bookshop did not stock the latest sensation novels or penny dreadfuls. The weighty, leather-bound tomes on the shelves ranged from archaic treatises on ancient Egyptian, Indian and Greek theories of the paranormal to journals devoted to the investigations of modern researchers. In between there were medieval works on metaphysics and Newton's speculations on alchemy.

Three of the shelves in the shop contained an extensive collection of the *Journal of Paranormal and Psychical Research,* the Arcane Society's official publication. There were, however, no copies of the Leybrook Institute's own very popular *Leybrook Journal of Paranormal Investigations.* Unfortunately, the Institute's publication was replete with papers that bore titles such as "An Investigation of the Usefulness of Certain Musical Instruments in the Summoning of Spirits" and "A Study of Levitation and Astral Travel." In other words, Virginia thought, Leybrook published a great deal of fiction. But as Gilmore Leybrook had explained, the Institute's *Journal* sold far more copies than Arcane's decidedly more esoteric publication.

"Lock-picking is no doubt a useful ability for a man in Mr. Sweetwater's profession," Charlotte said. She frowned. "I certainly didn't turn up any information about psychical talent in the bloodline when I looked into Mr. Sweetwater's background for you a couple of weeks ago."

"Something tells me the Sweetwater family keeps a lot of secrets."

Shortly after Owen Sweetwater had embarked upon his investigations of Leybrook Institute mediums, Virginia's intuition had been aroused. She had asked Charlotte to see what she could find out about the dangerous newcomer in their midst. When it came to research, no one was more talented than Charlotte. It was an aspect of her ability.

"I'll dig deeper and see what I can learn," Charlotte said. "All I could discover for certain is that the family is an old, established one with a reputation for being reclusive. Evidently the Sweetwaters rarely go into society, although with their money and connections they could probably do so if they wished."

"The Sweetwaters appear to have a few things in common with the Joneses," Virginia said. "That no doubt explains why they are doing business together."

"A very odd business it is, if you ask me. I can't stop thinking about what would have happened if you had been found in that room with Hollister's body."

"Ah, but there was no murder." Virginia glanced at the copy of the *Flying Intelligencer* on the table. "According to the morning papers, Lord Hollister expired from natural causes."

"Right, a heart attack. Obviously someone had to come up with a different version of events when it was discovered that you had departed from the scene. Imagine overlooking a knife wound in a man's chest."

"It's amazing what can be covered up by a wealthy, exclusive family."

"Well, I doubt that anyone is in deep mourning, least of all his poor wife. Do you really think that she was the one who killed him?"

"That is what Mr. Sweetwater believes. He perceived traces of energy that were left by the killer. He said whoever put the knife in Hollister's chest was definitely unbalanced. He also feels certain that the killer was a woman."

"*Hmm.*" Charlotte pursed her lips and looked thoughtful. "He can tell that much from the residue of energy at the scene?"

"So he says."

"And you believe him?"

"Why not?" Virginia smiled wryly. "After all, he believes in my talent."

A bright, sparkly look appeared in Charlotte's eyes.

"I see," she said. "Well, now, that's certainly interesting."

There was no need to discuss the matter further. Charlotte understood the situation perfectly. Virginia's talent had always created problems for her when it came to romantic relationships. Over the years there had been men who had found her attractive. Strong talents often drew the attention of the opposite sex. The energy of a powerful sensitive could be felt even by those who did not possess any measurable talent themselves.

But although men were sometimes intrigued, even fascinated, by her psychical nature, sooner or later the very quality that had initially drawn them to her began to make them uneasy and eventually repelled them. Virginia did not entirely blame them. The prospect of marrying a woman who claimed to see the dead and the dying in mirrors struck most gentlemen as daunting, to say the least.

When she turned twenty-six several months ago, she had shared a bottle of wine with Charlotte and officially abandoned the last of her romantic dreams. She would never marry. Charlotte had arrived at a similar conclusion regarding her own fate. Faced with lonely spinsterhood and inspired by the wine, they had resolved to chart an alternative course for themselves.

The initial plans had involved flinging themselves recklessly into a series of romantic liaisons with handsome men. Simple and brilliant though the scheme seemed to be in the glow of the wine, in reality things had not worked out very well. It transpired that there was a severe shortage of handsome men who were sufficiently interesting to warrant the risks involved.

They were now engaged in researching another safer and far more sensible option. The new plans appeared promising.

"I'm not telling anyone except you about the true nature of my association with Mr. Sweetwater," Virginia said. "As far as everyone else at the Institute is concerned, I have agreed to allow Mr. Sweetwater to study and observe me as I work."

Charlotte frowned. "Are you certain you can trust Owen Sweetwater? He may be using you for his own ends."

"Oh, he makes no bones about doing just that," Virginia agreed. "He has been quite open about the fact that he needs my assistance in his investigation. My intuition tells me that he can be trusted insofar as my personal safety is concerned. After the events of last night, I feel certain that he means me no harm. But I am well aware that the only reason he has taken an interest in me is because he thinks I'm the key to the case he is trying to solve."

"Yes, well, as long as you are going into this with your eyes wide open. Promise me that you will be very careful."

"Believe me when I tell you that being careful is my highest priority," Virginia said. "But let's move on to a more interesting topic. How goes your research into medical therapies for female hysteria?"

"I am still making inquiries, but the name of one doctor in particular keeps popping up," Charlotte said. "Dr. Spinner. His patients rave about his skill in treating hysteria. They say he uses the very latest electrical medical device to achieve astonishing results."

"How does it work?"

"I have heard that the instrument vibrates. Evidently a number of women have booked standing, weekly appointments with Dr. Spinner. They say they wouldn't miss a treatment for the world."

"It is always good to hear positive testimonials about a doctor before one books an appointment," Virginia said. "But I must admit I am not keen on the notion of a medical procedure that involves an electrical device. It sounds rather dangerous."

"According to what I have heard, Spinner's treatment is very safe. I have been assured that the vibrating device he uses to induce the therapeutic paroxysm is of the most modern design and extremely efficient."

"The treatment he prescribes is for female hysteria," Virginia reminded her. "Neither of us actually suffers from that condition."

"How difficult can it be to fake an attack of female hysteria, for goodness' sake?"

"Good point," Virginia agreed. "In any event, after what I went through last night, I'm certain my nerves are very fragile indeed."

"Of course they are," Charlotte said enthusiastically. "So are mine. I doubt very much that Dr. Spinner is overly exacting when it comes to establishing a diagnosis, in any event. After all, the one thing everyone knows about patients who suffer from female hysteria is that they represent a great source of repeat business for a doctor."

"The disease doesn't kill the patient, but the patient must be treated on a regular basis in order to achieve a therapeutic effect."

"In short, the hysteria patient is the ideal patient," Charlotte said. "Furthermore, those in the medical profession are convinced that spinsterhood itself is enough to produce hysteria in women. Something to do with the problem of female congestion. We both qualify as spinsters now. Very hard on the nerves, they say."

"I expect an unfortunate marriage would be equally hard on the nerves." Virginia shuddered. "Only consider poor Lady Hollister's situation. She must have suspected that she was wedded to a monster, but there was nothing she could do about it. In the end it obviously drove her mad. I would much prefer the problem of female congestion."

"Let's be honest here," Charlotte said. "Neither of us would have put up with a creature as vile as Hollister any longer than it took to determine his true nature.

Had he married either one of us, he would have expired on his honeymoon."

"Well, there is that," Virginia agreed. "But you and I both possess a considerable degree of talent, and with strong talent comes strong intuition. I doubt very much that either one of us would have married such a beast in the first place. We would have sensed the monster in him."

"We both know that one of the reasons we are facing spinsterhood in the first place is because of our talents." Charlotte wrinkled her nose. "Strong intuition is all well and good, but it certainly gets in the way of romantic relationships. Just think, Ginny, we will both be twenty-seven years old, and neither one of us has found a man we could love with any degree of passion. Which is why we really must give serious consideration to Dr. Spinner's therapy."

"I agree, but I'm afraid I won't be free to try Spinner's treatment until after I've finished assisting Mr. Sweetwater with his investigation." Virginia put down her empty cup and rose from the table. "Let us hope that my nerves survive intact long enough for me to seek medical therapy for my hysteria and congestion when this business is completed."

EIGHT

Virginia left the bookshop a short time later. It was late afternoon, but the fog had brought on an early twilight. The buildings on either side of the narrow street loomed in the eerie gray dusk. The vaporous mist was so thick that she did not notice the carriage in front of her town house until she was close to the front steps.

Owen vaulted down from the cab and came toward her. He wore a long, dark coat and a low-crowned hat pulled down over his eyes. At the sight of him, a thrill of excitement flared deep inside her. It had been this way when he had walked into her study yesterday. She responded to his presence in a way that was new and intoxicating to her senses. It was also somewhat disorienting. She had never experienced this reaction around any other man.

She paused at the bottom of her front steps, aware of a pleasant sensation that she had not experienced for a very long time. It took her a heartbeat or two to recognize the feeling. In spite of recent events, she felt happy, a little exhilarated.

She smiled. "Mr. Sweetwater. I wasn't expecting you."

"I have been waiting for you," he said coldly. "Your housekeeper told me that you had gone to visit a friend."

The sparkling excitement inside her was instantly transformed into irritation. The one great, extremely positive aspect of spinsterhood, she thought, was that a woman was not obliged to answer to any man.

"I am returning from paying a call on a very good friend," she said crisply. "Not that it is any of your affair, sir."

"Under the circumstance, I had hoped that you would have the good sense to exercise some caution when it comes to your daily schedule. I told you that I have people watching your house at night, but I did not think it necessary during the day."

She raised her chin. "What did you expect, sir? That I would lock myself in the house and sit by the fire until you concluded your investigation? I'm afraid that will not be possible. I have a living to make."

"I comprehend that fact. But I do not like the idea of you going out, unescorted, while there is a killer running around who preys on women with your talent."

"I am not an idiot, Mr. Sweetwater. This afternoon I walked along crowded streets and spent some time in the company of my friend in a shop. I was never alone at any time. I did not stroll down dark alleys or take shortcuts through empty parks. I even managed to refrain from accepting rides in carriages with strangers. Not that any strangers offered me a ride."

He contemplated her with faintly narrowed eyes. "You are correct, of course. I have no right to tell you how to go about your daily life."

"Is that an apology?"

"No, an observation. There is no point in my apolo-
gizing, because I will very likely lecture you again on
the same subject in the near future. You can probably
place a wager on it."

"Why?"

"Because I'm trying to keep you safe and catch a
killer, damn it. And because between the two of us, I am
the one who has had some experience in dealing with
the monsters."

"I do realize that your intentions are honorable, sir,"
she said, gentling her voice a little. "The problem we
have is that you are obviously accustomed to issuing
orders, and I am not at all accustomed to taking them."

"I can see that."

"I'm certain we shall muddle through. Now, then,
why did you come here to see me today? Have you some
news?"

For a moment she thought he was going to ignite the
embers of their disagreement into a full-blown quarrel.
But evidently concluding that he did not have logic on
his side, he abandoned the field. She suspected the
retreat was only temporary.

"Later tonight I would like you to accompany me on
a visit to the house of one of the glass-readers who was
murdered, Mrs. Ratford," he said. "I noticed at least two
mirrors on the premises when I went inside. Perhaps
you will be able to perceive something helpful in one
of them."

Anticipation ghosted through her. "Yes, of course."
She went up the steps to the front door. "There is no
reason to stand around out here. Won't you come in?
I'm sure Mrs. Crofton will want to serve tea. I fear that

if I do not invite a few more guests into the house, she will grow bored and quit."

Mrs. Crofton opened the door. She gave Virginia a disapproving look.

"Mr. Sweetwater has been waiting for you, ma'am."

"Yes, I know, Mrs. Crofton," Virginia said. She removed her bonnet and stepped into the hall. "It is his own fault. He did not send word that he intended to call this afternoon."

"I invited him to wait in the parlor and offered tea, but he declined," Mrs. Crofton said. "He and his carriage have been standing in the street for nearly forty-five minutes."

"I understand, Mrs. Crofton." Virginia put some steel into her words. "You may serve tea to him now. We will be in my study."

"Yes, ma'am." Mrs. Crofton took Owen's hat and gloves with a solicitous air. "I have some tarts fresh out of the oven that will go nicely with the tea."

Owen smiled at her. "That sounds wonderful, Mrs. Crofton. I haven't eaten in hours."

Mrs. Crofton beamed and sailed away in the direction of the kitchen.

Owen followed Virginia down the hall. This was only his second time on the premises, but she was acutely aware that he seemed very much at ease in her house now, as if he were in the home of a longtime friend. *Or the home of his lover.* Where in blazes had that thought come from? She had obviously spent far too much time discussing treatments for female hysteria with Charlotte today.

"Your housekeeper is an interesting woman," Owen said. He sounded amused.

"I'm afraid Mrs. Crofton does not really approve of me," Virginia confided as she led the way into the study. "She has recently come down in the world, you see. Her previous employer was a wealthy woman who moved in exclusive circles. Sadly, the lady was somewhat absentminded. She died owing her staff several quarters' worth of back wages."

"Let me hazard a guess. The heirs saw no reason to pay the back wages."

"No. Poor Mrs. Crofton found herself without funds and without a post. She was obliged to accept the first position that came along. I'm afraid the post was in the household of a woman who not only conducts business but often does so at night."

"You."

"Indeed." Virginia sat down behind her desk.

Owen lowered himself into one of the reading chairs with a fluid, masculine grace that struck Virginia as decidedly sensual. She realized that he had brought an aura of energy into the room that stirred her senses.

"Have you considered letting Mrs. Crofton go and perhaps replacing her with an employee who might not be so concerned with her own social status?" he asked.

She took a grip on her overheated imagination and forced herself to pay attention to the conversation.

"That would be quite impossible," she explained. "Those in service are every bit as concerned with their social standing as those who move in society. Besides,

Mrs. Crofton is an excellent housekeeper. I am very fortunate to have her."

Laughter glittered in Owen's eyes. "I have the impression she is well aware of that."

Virginia sighed. "Yes, and there is no doubt but that she can do better than this household. In fact, between you and me, I am quite certain that I will not have her much longer."

"Why do you say that?"

"She received a letter earlier this week. I could not help but notice the return address. The letter was from the Billings Agency. That is the agency that sent her to me. I have a feeling that Mrs. Billings now has a better post to offer Mrs. Crofton. But enough of my domestic problems. Did you learn anything when you examined the clockwork carriage?"

"A few things," he said, "but I'm not sure any will prove helpful. The quality of the materials used to construct the device and the fine detailing are reminiscent of some of the elaborate clockwork curiosities crafted during the Renaissance. That leads me to believe that the person who created the carriage considers himself to be a true artist."

"But the carriage is a weapon, not a work of art."

"The distinction between the artist and the armorer has not always been obvious. During the Renaissance, fine weapons were produced that were also masterpieces of craftsmanship. There is a long tradition of swords and armor and daggers that are encrusted with jewels and detailed with gold."

"Have you started searching for the clock maker?"

"I've asked my cousin Nicholas Sweetwater to pursue that angle of the investigation."

"There are no doubt a great many clock makers in London."

"Yes," he said. "But Nick has a talent for that sort of hunting."

Owen went home an hour later, satiated by the excellent tea and tarts that Mrs. Crofton had served, and energized by the time spent with Virginia. He could grow accustomed to calling regularly on Number Seven Garnet Lane, he reflected.

NINE

Owen returned to Garnet Lane that evening in an anonymous hired carriage. Virginia was waiting for him. She wore a hooded cloak against the chill of the night. He sensed the mix of excitement and foreboding that animated her. When he took her gloved hand to assist her into the carriage he could have sworn that electricity sparked between them. The hair stirred on the nape of his neck.

They spoke little on the drive to the quiet street where Mrs. Ratford had rented a small house, but Owen was intensely conscious of Virginia's nearness the entire time. He would have given a great deal to know if she felt the same sense of awareness.

When they reached their destination he sent the carriage on its way. There would be other cabs about later, when they left the scene of the murder.

There was an empty, shuttered feeling about the house where Mrs. Ratford had died. The curtains were drawn closed across the windows.

"You're certain there is no one home?" Virginia asked.

"I checked again earlier today. The house is still vacant. The rumors concerning the former occupant's death have probably made it difficult to attract new tenants. Prospective renters are no doubt reluctant to move into a house in which the previous resident may have been dispatched by spirits from the Other Side."

Virginia looked at him. A gas lamp burned close by in the mist, but he could not see her face clearly. Her features were shadowed by the hood of her cloak.

"There are always rumors about those of us who read mirrors," she said. "Many people are convinced that we see ghosts and spirits. They do not understand that what we perceive are simply afterimages caught in the glass. Mirrors are nothing more than paranormal cameras that capture some of the energy given off at the time of death or near death."

"I understand."

They went down the alley behind Number Fourteen. Owen opened the gate that guarded the tiny garden. They went up the back steps. Owen inserted the lock pick into the kitchen door. The lock gave way immediately.

"May I ask where one buys that sort of tool?" Virginia asked.

He smiled a little at the bright curiosity in her voice.

"This particular pick was crafted by one of my uncles. He has a knack for that sort of thing."

"Yours is an interesting family, sir."

"That is certainly one way to describe my relatives." He opened the door and listened for a moment with all of his senses. "Still vacant."

Virginia moved past him to enter the house. He heard the soft, sultry swish of the ruffles at the hem of her gown as they brushed across the toe of his boot. Her scent briefly clouded his mind. He was aroused not just by the anticipation of the hunt but by the woman who shared it with him tonight.

He followed her into the narrow hall, closed the door and turned up the lantern he had brought along. The light did little to alleviate the heavy gloom.

"Death always affects a house, doesn't it?" Virginia looked around. "One can sense it in the atmosphere."

"Yes. Which is why so many people find it easy to believe in ghosts."

"What, exactly, are we looking for?" she asked.

"Something, anything, that will give us a clue to how Mrs. Ratford was killed. I went through this house, and Mrs. Hackett's as well, shortly after I accepted the case. I am certain that both deaths were caused by paranormal means, but I do not think the killer was present at the time of the actual murders. He has come and gone on several occasions since the murders, however."

"You can detect those sorts of details so plainly?"

"It is the nature of my talent, Virginia," he said, willing her to understand and accept the compulsion that drove him.

Virginia said nothing. She halted in the doorway of the small parlor. "There is a mirror over the fireplace. I may be able to discern something in the glass."

Owen stood behind her and waited. The light of the lantern flashed on the mirror, casting ominous shadows around the room.

Virginia walked forward and stopped in front of the fireplace. Her eyes met his in the darkly silvered glass. He felt the atmosphere heat and knew that she had raised her talent.

She turned her full attention on the mirror, gazing into it as though into another dimension. She concentrated intently, not speaking for a time.

A moment later she lowered her talent and turned to face him with eyes that were still filled with mysteries.

"The mirror has been hanging above the fireplace for a very long time," she said. "There are certainly shadows in it but nothing distinct. Certainly nothing of violent death."

"That makes sense. The body was found upstairs in a bedroom. There is a mirror on the dressing table."

They went back out into the hall and up the narrow staircase.

"I noticed that the mirror over your own mantel is new," he said.

"I purchased it when I rented the house. There was an old one in that room and another in the front hall. I removed both of them."

"You do not like old mirrors?"

"Looking glasses absorb energy over the years. The old ones hold a lot of shadows. I find them disturbing."

"Yet Mrs. Ratford kept the old one in this house."

"Perhaps she could not afford to replace it. It is also possible that it did not bother her greatly. She had some talent, but she was not a very strong glass-reader. Only powerful glasslight-talents find old mirrors disturbing."

At the top of the stairs they paused. The light of the lantern revealed three doors. Two stood open. The one at the far end of the hall was closed.

"That is the room where she died," Owen said.

They both heard the muffled scraping, clanking noise at the same time. It came from the nearest open doorway.

"What in the name of heaven?" Virginia whispered.

Owen angled the lantern for a closer look. An elegantly made mechanical dragon appeared from the darkened room. The clockwork device was the size of a small dog. Its segmented tail, set with crystals, snaked from side to side. Long, gilded claws rasped on the floor. The glass eyes radiated a cold, compelling paranormal fire.

"Another one of those damned weapons," Owen said. "Where the hell did that come from? It wasn't here the last time I visited this house."

He seized Virginia's arm and started to haul her back toward the staircase.

She moved willingly and with some speed, but it was too late.

A dark fog descended. The nightmare exploded around him, inundating the hall with hellish visions from a madman's fevered dreams. The dead and the dying descended on him, mouths open in silent screams.

TEN

All the terrible shadows that Virginia had seen in mirrors since she had first come into her talent at the age of thirteen prowled the eerie mist that filled the hall. The dying stared at her with horrified, dread-filled eyes, as if they somehow sensed that she bore witness to their deaths. They did not plead for her to save them. They knew there was no hope. They asked for something else from her, something she could almost never provide: justice.

The ghastly visions whirled around her. She was suddenly dizzy. Her stomach roiled. For an instant she thought she would be ill, and then she realized she could not orient herself in the strange fog. There was no way to distinguish up from down. If she put one foot wrong she might tumble down the staircase that she could no longer see.

A voice came out of the mist, edged with the grim determination of a man who is hanging on to sanity by sheer force of will.

"Hallucinations," Owen rasped. "Get down. This energy is so thick we won't be able to find the stairs."

He used the grip on her arm to pull her down onto

her knees and then into a sitting position beside him. They locked hands and scrambled backward, feeling their way, until they came up against a hard surface. *The wall*, Virginia thought. At least she now had a sense of direction.

"It's glasslight energy," she said. "The same energy that was infused in the clockwork carriage. But there's so *much* of it. It's as if I'm trapped in a nightmare. I can't lower my talent."

"Neither can I," Owen said. "Too much stimulation. The radiation is so intense, it's electrifying our senses."

"This thing is a far more powerful weapon than the carriage."

"I think the carriage was designed to induce unconsciousness. This device was made to kill."

"Or drive one to one's death," Virginia said.

"Can you control it? If not, we're going to have to feel our way to the staircase."

"I am doing my best."

She strained to concentrate her senses in an effort to perceive some image in the mist that she knew was real. The horrific visions blurred and faded slightly. The clockwork dragon came back into view. It wavered in and out of focus as it slithered, scraped and clanked toward her.

"Much better," Owen said. "A little closer and I will be able to kick it over."

The device halted several feet away. The nightmarish scenes flickered on and off like visions in some ghostly magic lantern show.

"Not close enough," Owen said. "But given the erratic

way in which it is generating energy now, I may be able to reach it."

She felt him shift beside her and knew that he was about to push himself away from the wall.

"Wait," she said quickly. "I've managed to neutralize some of the energy, but if you get too close, it will get a better fix on you. Right now it appears to be confused."

"You speak of the damn thing as though it were alive. It's just a machine, a bloody damn clock."

"I'm aware of that, thank you very much," she snapped.

"Right," Owen said, his tone suddenly very neutral. "Sorry."

This was hardly the best moment for a quarrel, she thought. She concentrated on holding the currents steady.

"I believe the problem from the machine's point of view is that we are touching each other," she said. She tightened her hand around Owen's gloved fingers and pressed her shoulder more firmly against his. "Our auras are overlapping. I think we appear to be a single entity to the dragon."

"A single entity with two auras. It can't get a strong fix."

"Yes, I think so. But I cannot hold it still much longer. Let's remove our gloves. Perhaps we can increase the confusion with skin-to-skin contact."

"Worth a try."

Arms linked, they each stripped off a glove. Seconds later Owen's powerful bare hand closed firmly around

Virginia's fingers. A shock of awareness shivered through her. The surging currents of masculine energy thrilled her. It seemed to her that she was drawing power from him, as if the currents of her aura were now carried along on the rush of Owen's energy field. *Like a swimmer taking advantage of a powerful ocean wave*, she thought. She should have been terrified, but the unfamiliar sensation was exhilarating. *Because it is connected to Owen.*

On the heels of that thought came another: *What is happening here between us?*

But there was no time to try to understand the sense of intimate connection that she was experiencing. The dragon's energy was becoming increasingly violent.

She drew on the link with Owen to heighten her talent and intensify her focus. Underneath the waves of raw power that she was wielding, she sensed a danger, one she had never before encountered. Like the swimmer riding the crest of the wave, she had to remain in control of the dazzling white-hot storm she had created. She did not know for certain what would happen if she failed, but her intuition warned her that if she lost her focus for even a second, she and Owen would both drown in the raging sea of energy.

For a heartbeat or two it seemed that the effort was not working. But in the next breath the room steadied around them. The visions did not evaporate entirely, but they faded to ghostly images. The eyes of the clockwork dragon continued to spark and flash with ominous light, but the death masks in the magic lantern show that filled the hall grew pale and erratic.

"Let's approach it together," Owen said. "With luck, it will remain confused."

Hands tightly clasped, they pushed themselves to their feet against the wall. Virginia kept up a high level of dampening energy. They waited a moment. When the paranormal storm did not flare up again, they moved toward the dragon.

When he got within range, Owen lashed out with one booted foot. The dragon toppled onto its side, glass eyes rattling in their sockets in an attempt to obtain another focus on its target. Virginia breathed a sigh of relief as the last of the dreadful hallucinations evaporated.

"I am no longer seeing visions," she said.

"Neither am I," Owen said. "Let's get this damn thing deactivated."

Keeping his grip on Virginia's hand, he stripped off his other glove and crouched beside the device. He moved his fingers over the enameled body of the dragon and pressed a spot on the side. The back of the device opened on small hinges, revealing a complicated clock-work mechanism. Owen reached into the beast and did something to the metal innards. The dragon's gilded claws froze in midair. Its eyes went dark as the energy inside faded.

In the eerie stillness that settled in the hall, Virginia was suddenly conscious of the rapid beat of her own pulse and an edgy sensation. She was acutely aware that Owen still gripped her hand. Little frissons contin-ued to crackle through her, jangling her senses, arousing them in unfamiliar ways.

Owen released her fingers. The strange sensations dimmed a little, but they did not vanish altogether. She was certain that if Owen touched her again the thrilling feelings would flare up at once. She took a step back, putting some distance between herself and Owen, who seemed oblivious to the stirring energy in the atmosphere.

"I've got the key," Owen said. He slipped it into the pocket of his coat. "I'm certain the device won't operate now until it is rewound."

"Like a clock?"

"Exactly like a clock." Owen inspected the insides of the dragon. "And an elegantly made one, at that. Our clock maker spares no expense when it comes to materials."

"Why on earth would anyone leave such an expensive device in an empty house?"

"It is hardly likely to be stolen," Owen pointed out. "The average housebreaker would not survive an encounter with this toy."

"True. Which implies that someone left it behind to guard the premises."

Owen gave that a few seconds of close thought. "But it was not on guard when I came here the first time. That means that on one of his return visits the killer realized that someone else had been inside. He set the dragon to make certain that any future intruder would not survive."

"He is protecting something that is very important to him."

"I found nothing of value here on my first visit."

Owen got to his feet and looked at the closed door at the end of the hall. "I overlooked something. We must find out what there is in this house that warrants such an exotic guardian."

ELEVEN

O wen collected the lantern and walked to the end of the hall, very aware of Virginia beside him. His senses were still on fire from whatever had just happened between them a few minutes ago. Had she felt that compelling intimacy, too?

"If there is something of value in the last bedroom, there may be another clockwork curiosity guarding it," Virginia warned.

He glanced at her, but it was impossible to tell if she had experienced the same surge of psychical connection. In the glare of the lantern her intelligent face appeared concerned but resolute. A casual observer would never guess that she had just faced a withering hail of nightmares. She was concentrating on the project at hand. He should be doing the same, he reminded himself.

"This time we are prepared," he said.

He put his back against the wall and opened the door with great care, listening for the telltale clink and thud of another clockwork device. But no sound came from the room.

He pushed the door wider, moved into the opening

and held the lantern aloft. The light fell on the bed, an old chest of drawers and the dressing table.

"Everything is just as it was the last time I was here," he said.

"You're right, there is nothing in this room that is obviously of great value." Virginia crossed her arms, hugging herself, and surveyed the small space. "But the energy is certainly disturbing, is it not?"

"This is the room where Mrs. Ratford was murdered," Owen said. "I am certain of it. And I am equally certain that the killer has been here a number of times since committing the crime. So, yes, there is a lot of bad energy in this room."

He walked into the small space and heightened his senses. The hot, dark currents of violence fluoresced in the shadows, painting the room in the deepest shades of ultralight. Although he was braced for the impact, there was nothing he could do to suppress his response. The hunter in him was always aroused by such energy.

Virginia watched him. "What do you see?"

"What I perceived the last time I was here. She was murdered, but no gun or knife was used to commit the crime. It was murder by paranormal means, but it was not a swift kill. Whoever did this wanted Mrs. Ratford to suffer for a time."

"But you are sure that psychical energy was involved?"

"There can be no doubt." He concentrated on the residue of iridescent energy in the room. "Strong psychical currents were employed to commit murder in this room, but the killer was not present at the time. I can usually identify the precise location where he or she stood at the moment the murder took place. There is always a great deal of energy generated when one kills."

"As the adage says, murder always leaves a stain."

"Yes. We have made some progress this evening. We have found a means by which the killer could have committed the crime without being physically present in the room."

"He used a clockwork curiosity," Virginia said. "Perhaps the dragon."

"It is a possibility." Mentally he went through the logic and nodded once, satisfied. "He would have had to enter the room to set up the device, of course. Then he would have left and returned later when he was certain the clockwork weapon had performed the kill and had time to wind down. He retrieved the dragon but brought it back when he realized an intruder had been inside the house."

"You said he has been here several times since the murder."

"Yes." Owen opened a drawer and glanced inside to make certain he had not overlooked anything on his first visit.

"Why would he do that?"

"To savor the energy of the kill," he said absently.

There was a short, awful silence behind him. He closed the drawer and looked at Virginia.

"The killer comes here to savor the energy of death?" Virginia asked uneasily.

"In my experience it is not uncommon."

"I see." Virginia turned back to the mirror. "There were rumors after Mrs. Ratford died. She made her living claiming to communicate with spirits through mirrors. There are some who are convinced she really did manage to summon a malevolent entity from the Other Side. They believe it killed her."

"We know one thing for certain: If Mrs. Ratford claimed to communicate with the dead, she was, by definition, a fraud."

"No, not in her own mind."

"I thought we agreed that there is no such thing as communicating with the dead," he said flatly. "All those who claim to be mediums are, by definition, frauds of the lowest order, because they prey on the gullible and those who are made vulnerable by grief or a weak mind."

"I was acquainted with Mrs. Ratford because she was a member of the Institute." Virginia contemplated the mirror on the dressing table. "We were not close, but we had what you would call a professional connection. We occasionally had tea together in the Institute's tearoom. We talked. I am convinced that she actually did have some degree of genuine glasslight talent."

"Then why the devil would she claim to speak with spirits? Why not use her talent in an honest fashion, as you do?"

"Probably because she did not understand what she saw in the mirrors, let alone know how to interpret the visions and images. I told you, her talent was only middling at best. She did not comprehend that what she was viewing was the psychical residue that is absorbed by a looking glass. She was convinced that she really did see ghosts. One cannot blame her."

"It's true that most people with psychical abilities

lack a scientific understanding of their talents," he said. "I will concede that some with certain forms of clairvoyance might mistakenly believe that they are, in fact, sensing ghosts or spirits."

"That is very broad-minded of you, sir."

"Gabriel Jones is right. One of Arcane's primary missions in the years ahead should be to educate the public on the physics of the paranormal."

Virginia raised her brows. "You refer to the new Master of the Society?"

"Right. Jones is convinced that until there is a scientific understanding of psychical energy, those who possess talent will continue to be treated at best as entertainers. At worst, we will be regarded with fear and suspicion."

"I wish Mr. Jones luck with his plans to inform and enlighten the public."

Her dry tone caught his attention. "You don't think it can be done?"

"I suspect it will be very long indeed before attitudes change. Meanwhile, those of us with a little talent must rely on our wits."

"You have more than a little talent, Virginia Dean. And we are wasting time. If you would be so good as to examine the looking glass?"

"Yes, of course." She turned her attention to the dressing-table mirror. Once again he felt currents of energy pulse in the atmosphere. He heightened his own talent so that he could watch Virginia with all of his senses.

She concentrated intently for a long moment.

"There are some images here," she said at last. Her

brows came together in a baffled frown. "I can see the afterimage of the victim. It is burned deeply into the mirror. But there is something else in there as well."

"What?"

"There is raw energy trapped in the mirror. It is very odd. Like frozen fire."

"Take your time. Describe the victim."

"She is sitting at the table, gazing into the mirror. She is dying, and she knows it. She clutches her chest and looks to the right. She is both terrified and bewildered by whatever she sees."

Owen glanced to the right of the dressing table. "The bed. The killer hid the device underneath it. The dragon, or whatever curiosity was used to commit the murder, emerged when it sensed the victim enter the room and sit down at her dressing table."

"She never had a chance. She died just at the instant she began to comprehend the means of her death."

"Is there any indication that she knew her killer?"

"No. I think all she can see is the device that is murdering her."

"It is, nevertheless, quite possible that she did know the killer. She simply was not aware that he was the one who placed the clockwork device under the bed."

"I think you're right." A visible shudder went through Virginia. In the mirror her eyes were wide and haunted.

Owen crossed the room and stopped behind her. Instinctively he put his hand on her shoulder. He could feel the heat generated by the use of her talent through the fabric of her cloak and gown. He knew that particular fever in the blood. He had experienced it often.

"That's enough," he said gently. "We have discovered

what we came here to find, the cause of death. It is time to go home."

They found a hired carriage two streets over. Both horse and driver were asleep. The coachman roused himself when Owen opened the door of the carriage and ushered Virginia up inside.

"Garnet Lane," Owen said.

"Aye, sir." The driver collected the reins.

Owen had wrapped the dragon in a quilt. He set the shrouded automaton on the floor of the carriage and sat down across from Virginia. His senses were still flaring. That was only to be expected, he thought. A close brush with danger or violence always resulted in an edgy tension that lingered, sometimes for hours or even days. But the events in the Ratford house had left him physically as well as psychically aroused. He knew that part of what he was feeling now was directly linked to Virginia's presence. Something had happened when they had held hands to battle the clockwork dragon, something as intimate as it was inexplicable.

He was certain the experience had strengthened the growing bond between them. He longed to ask Virginia if she was aware of the connection, but he was worried that the intimate question would alarm her. She was already wary enough about their association.

He did not know how much longer he could wait for her to acknowledge the link between them. For now the bond was of a psychical nature, but the need to seal it with the hot energy of physical passion was stirring his blood.

He looked at her. In the low glow cast by the carriage

lamps he could have sworn that he saw some heat in her eyes. *She feels it, too,* he thought. But perhaps the energy he perceived in her was simply the remnants of the fever that had resulted from the use of her talent tonight. It always took one a while to cool down after such an intense burn.

"Are you all right?" he asked, unable to think of anything else to say.

"Yes," she said. She pulled her cloak more snugly around herself. "But I must admit that my senses are still rattled. I have never before encountered anything like that storm of hallucinations."

"Neither have I. If it is any consolation, my nerves are also badly frayed."

She smiled. "It would take more than a clockwork dragon to shatter your nerves, sir."

"Or yours. You are the one who slew the dragon tonight."

"I could not have done it without you." She looked down at the blanket-wrapped dragon. "It is very powerful. Unlike a human, it would not tire until it winds down. It is a machine, capable of radiating that high level of energy for a considerable length of time. No person of talent, regardless of the degree of that talent, could control such a device for long before exhausting the senses."

"It is astonishing that someone actually possesses the ability to construct such a weapon. I talked to my cousin Nick today. Thus far he has not had any luck finding the clock maker, but he has picked up a few intriguing rumors from some rather eccentric collectors."

The carriage halted in front of Virginia's town house. He opened the door, vaulted down to the pavement and turned to lower the carriage steps. Virginia gave him her hand and descended to the pavement. She had put her gloves back on, he noticed.

"I believe I need a strong dose of medicinal spirits tonight," she said.

He smiled. "I certainly plan to take the same therapeutic medicine when I get home."

She contemplated the dark windows of the town house for a moment, and then she turned back to face him. In the shadows cast by the gas lamp and the hood of her cloak it was impossible to make out the expression on her face. But he could sense the heat in her eyes.

"Would you care to share a glass of my tonic with me, sir?" she asked. "I have some excellent brandy."

His blood was suddenly several degrees warmer. He felt as if he had just received an invitation to enter paradise.

TWELVE

Virginia held her breath. She could not believe what she had just done. The invitation had been an uncharacteristically impulsive act inspired by the edgy sensation that was generating a fever deep inside her. It was surely a mistake, one she was certain she would regret. If Owen hesitated for even a heartbeat she would change her mind.

He did not give her time enough to catch her breath.

"I would like that very much," he said.

The even, casually polite tone of his voice told her absolutely nothing. But his eyes heated a little in the darkness. She knew that he was in the grip of the aftermath of a heavy burn, just as she was. No one but another powerful talent could understand the sensation.

She pulled her cloak around her and started up the front steps. "It is not as if either of us will be getting much sleep tonight, is it?"

"No," he agreed.

He paused long enough to pay the coachman. Then he followed her up the steps.

She dug her key out of the small chatelaine purse she wore. "And like it or not, we appear to be colleagues, at least for a while. We might as well share a drink and discuss the case."

"It sounds like a very useful way to proceed," he said.

She fumbled with her key and managed to drop it.

Owen snagged it in midair with no apparent effort.

"Allow me," he said.

He inserted the key into the lock and opened the door. She moved into the dimly lit hall. Mrs. Crofton had taken herself off to bed two floors above, but she had left a wall sconce burning.

She'll know I'm home, Virginia thought. *She'll know that I am not alone.* Housekeepers always knew everything that went on in their domain.

Owen set the dragon on the floor, stripped off his leather gloves and reached out to help Virginia with the cloak. When his warm fingers brushed the sensitive nape of her neck, another flicker of awareness went through her. The feverish sensation got more intense, but she did not feel the least bit ill.

He hung her cloak on a brass wall hook and then he set his hat on the console table alongside his leather gloves.

It is as if we were two lovers coming home late after an evening at the theater, she thought.

Her imagination was running wild, and her nerves were still tingling with the icy-hot sensation. She desperately needed a shot of brandy.

She led the way down the hall and into the darkened study. Inside the small, cozy room she turned up a lamp and went to the little table that held the brandy decanter.

Owen crossed to the hearth, struck a light and lit the fire with the easy familiarity of a man making himself at home. When he was finished he rose, peeled off his coat and tossed it over the back of a chair. He was not wearing a waistcoat, Virginia noticed. He unknotted his tie and left it hanging loosely around his neck. Next he opened the collar of his shirt. With deft movements of his fingers he removed the cuff links that secured the sleeves of his shirt, and tucked them into a pocket.

Virginia caught her breath. Oh, yes, he was definitely making himself at home.

She splashed brandy into two glasses. The decanter clinked lightly against the rim of one glass. She realized her hands were trembling. She set the decanter aside and gave Owen one of the glasses.

"To both of us getting some sleep tonight," she said, raising her glass.

"To us."

Not quite the same toast, she thought, but she did not think it would be a good idea to correct him.

His eyes never left hers as he downed some of the brandy.

She took a more cautious sip and lowered the glass.

"May I ask what you saw tonight when that storm of hallucinations struck?" she said.

"I saw the victims of the murders that I have investigated over the years," he said. "The ones I failed."

She exhaled slowly. "You mean those poor souls for whom you could not find justice?"

"And those I arrived too late to save. They are the ones who haunt me." He went to stand in front of the fire. "What did you see, Virginia?"

She crossed the carpet to join him at the hearth.

"My visions were not unlike your own. Like you, I saw the ones I failed, those who died by violence. The ones for whom there was no justice because the killer was never caught."

He nodded once, understanding.

For a long moment they stood side by side, gazing into the fire.

"Do you ever wonder why we have been cursed with talents such as ours?" she asked after a time.

"There is no such thing as a curse," he said. "That is superstitious nonsense."

She almost smiled. "I was speaking metaphorically, Mr. Sweetwater."

"Of course. My apologies." He drank some more brandy. "I tend to be quite literal when it comes to matters involving para-physics."

"I understand."

"I will tell you the truth, Virginia. The reason I responded so sharply just now is because there have been many times when I have asked myself the very same question."

He had used her first name again. But she now thought of him as Owen, she reminded herself. It was astonishing how sharing danger had a way of injecting a degree of intimacy into the atmosphere between two people who were otherwise barely acquainted.

"I am a modern thinker, sir," she said. "Like you, I certainly do not believe in the supernatural. But have you ever come up with an answer to the question?"

He gripped the edge of the mantel and contemplated the fire. "I can give you an answer that conforms to the laws of para-physics, at least what I know of those laws.

There is, as I'm sure you know, a great deal left to be discovered in the field."

"I am aware of that. Well? What is the scientific answer to the question?"

"A person who commits murder or an act of violence generates a heavy surge of psychical energy. Even the coldest of killers leaves a hot trail."

"Yes," she said. She shivered at the memory of some of the images she had seen in the mirrors.

"The same is true of the victim if he or she has time to react to the assault," Owen continued. "Strong energy does not simply evaporate. It continues to oscillate in the atmosphere of a space and is absorbed into the surfaces of furniture, walls and floors."

"And looking glasses."

He inclined his head. "Yes, although I cannot perceive what you do when you look into a mirror. The physics of looking glasses are quite unique."

"I comprehend that both of us are sensitive to the residue of the energy that is laid down by violence. But why do we both feel the need to find answers for those who are left behind?"

"I cannot answer that."

She swirled the brandy in her glass. "Do you think that all of those who possess talents like ours experience the compulsion to seek justice and answers?"

"No, far from it." He downed the last of the brandy and set the glass on the mantel. He did not take his attention off the flames. "There are people endowed with talents similar to our own who savor the atmosphere of murder in the manner of connoisseurs who appreciate fine art and great wine."

She nearly dropped the brandy glass.

"What?" she said, and gasped.

Owen's jaw hardened. He looked at her. A cold fire replaced the other kind of heat that had lit his eyes only a moment ago.

"There are those who seek out the scenes of murder and horrific violence in order to indulge their senses in the sensations that were generated in the moment of death," he said.

It seemed to Virginia that the room chilled. "That is difficult to believe."

But she had sensed the unwholesome excitement of the killers when she had looked deeply into the mirrors, she thought. She had witnessed that terrible thrill through the eyes of the victims. Owen was right, there were those who savored the act of murder.

"Some with talents similar to ours revel in violent energy to such a degree that they become addicted to it," Owen said. "In order to satisfy their craving they do not merely seek out murder scenes, they create them."

"They kill."

"Again and again. With their talents." He looked at her. "Those are the ultimate predators."

Comprehension flashed through her. "Those are the killers you hunt."

"Yes."

"It is the desire for justice that drives you."

The faint curve of his mouth held no trace of humor. "I cannot claim any such noble excuse, Virginia. I do not understand the need within me. I only know that I cannot escape it." He paused. "It is an addiction of another kind."

She knew then that he was not seeking absolution. He was telling her a truth about himself, waiting to see if she could accept it.

"I think," she said, choosing her words with great care, "that we can turn to Mr. Darwin and the theory of evolution for guidance here."

Owen looked first startled and then he frowned, his eyes narrowing. "What in blazes does evolution have to do with this?"

"Well, it occurs to me that nature has a way of keeping things in balance, and so does society. We have criminals among us, so it follows that there are those who are drawn to stop them. Such people perhaps become policemen or detectives, or they choose to study the criminal mind."

"I am not a policeman," Owen said in a voice of stone.

"If human predators with strong psychical powers have evolved, which is clearly the case, then it is also logical that there are those like you who have evolved to hunt them," she concluded.

Owen said nothing. He just watched her with his hunter's eyes.

She cleared her throat. "It is the way of the natural world."

"That is an interesting theory."

"I certainly thought so."

"Why are you bothering to search for a scientific explanation for the existence of a man like me?"

She finished her brandy and set the glass on the mantel, alongside the one he had placed there.

"I suppose it is because I would like to find a similar rational explanation for my own talent and the compulsion I experience whenever I am summoned to the scene of a violent death," she said quietly.

"We are not two of a kind, Virginia. I can kill with my talent, and I have done so."

She stared at him. "Truly?"

"Yes. Do you think that makes me one of the monsters?"

She took a breath, very certain now. "No. You are a dangerous man, Owen Sweetwater, but you are not one of the monsters."

"You are sure of that?"

She met his eyes in the mirror. "You would not have risked your own life to rescue Becky as well as me the other night at the Hollister mansion if you were a monster."

Owen drew her into his arms. She caught a fleeting glimpse of their reflections in the mirror and was quite certain that she saw lightning flash deep within the looking glass.

"*Virginia,*" Owen whispered.

Her name sounded as though it had been dragged from the very core of his being. His kiss held the same raw power. It ignited the fires of passion that flared between them. Whatever came tomorrow, she would never forget, never regret, this night.

With a soft, muffled cry she wrapped her arms around his neck, abandoning herself to the storm that swirled in the room. He kissed her long and hard, drinking deep.

When she was breathless and shivering with need, he started to undress her. He undid the hooks that fastened the bodice of her gown with fingers that trembled with the force of his own desire. Knowing that he wanted her as badly as she wanted him filled her with a rush of soaring, feminine confidence. She began to unfasten the buttons of his shirt.

He got the bodice of the gown open, revealing her thin chemise. He tugged the dress away from her breasts and pushed the heavy folds of fabric down over her hips. The gown crumpled to the floor and pooled around her ankles. He untied her petticoats. The yards of white linen splashed on top of the dress. She stood before him, knee-deep in the heap of discarded clothing, clad only in her chemise, drawers, stockings and low-heeled walking boots.

She reminded herself that this was not the first time he had seen her partially undressed. She had been in a similar state two nights ago when he had discovered her in the mirrored room beneath the Hollister mansion. But tonight everything was different.

Owen looked at her as though she were a creature of magic come to life.

"You are so beautiful," he said. He sounded awed, even worshipful.

She was no great beauty, she thought, but in that moment she felt like a goddess.

"So are you," she blurted, without thinking.

His laugh was a low, husky growl. "I don't think so."

"Yes, you are." She got the last of the buttons on his shirt undone and flattened her palms on his bare chest, fingers tangling in the crisp hair she found there. His skin was warm to the touch. The feel of the firm contours of his sleekly muscled body intensified the stirring deep inside her. "You are magnificent."

"You are the magnificent being here in this room."

She smiled. "Are we going to argue about our mutual magnificence?"

He laughed again, sounding somehow younger, almost lighthearted, like a man who, for a time, at least, had shed a great burden and the responsibilities that accompanied it.

"Not tonight," he said. "This is no time to argue."

He crouched in front of her and undid the buttons of her walking boots. She gripped his shoulders while he eased the boots, one by one, off her feet. He slid his hands up under the chemise and drew the drawers down to her ankles.

"Owen," she whispered.

He got to his feet and kissed her again, silencing her. He moved his thumb across her nipple, caressing her through the delicate fabric of the chemise.

She was so sensitive that even the light touch sent tiny shock waves through her. She sucked in a sharp breath, not certain if what she felt was pain or pleasure. His hand stilled instantly.

"Did I hurt you?" he asked against her mouth.

"No." She pulled back a little and then leaned close again to drop a featherlight kiss on the side of his hard jaw. "It is just that I have never felt anything quite like this sensation."

"Neither have I."

The earnest declaration amused her. "There is no need to pretend that you are inexperienced in such matters, Owen. You are a man of the world."

"This is different." The statement was flat, categorical, not open to debate. "You are different. You are the one."

In spite of the currents of passion that had inflamed her senses, the familiar flicker of intuition tingled through her. *This man is dangerous.*

"The one?" she repeated, baffled. "I do not understand what you mean."

"Never mind." He picked her up in his arms, lifting her free of the pool of skirts and petticoats. "This is not the time for explanations."

The room spun around her. He carried her to the large leather reading chair. Just before he sank down into the depths of the chair with her in his arms, she caught another glimpse of their reflections in the mirror. Energy flashed and sparked like hot sunlight in the depths of the looking glass.

And then she found herself draped across Owen's strong thighs, her stocking-clad legs dangling over the padded arm of the big chair. In the firelight Owen's face was taut with passion and something akin to hunger. He kissed her again, a slow, intoxicating kiss.

While he held her in thrall with the kiss, he explored her body with his free hand, touching her as though she were the rarest and most valuable work of art ever created. She gave herself up to the sensual storm that was breaking over her, engulfing her.

She was aware of his palm gliding down her leg, but she was occupied with the kiss and did not pay close attention until she felt his hand slip beneath the hem of her chemise. A moment later she realized that his fingers were on the inside of her thigh.

"So soft," he growled against her mouth.

She knew then what he intended, but she was torn between shock and wonder. He cupped her gently. She tensed, her fingers twisting in the expensive white linen of his shirt.

He tore his mouth away from her lips and kissed her throat. "I want to feel you melt for me."

This is the night, she thought. She was on the edge of exploring the great mystery she had yearned to discover with the right man. At last the secrets of passion were being revealed to her. She would not turn back now.

He probed deeper with his fingers. Everything inside her seemed to be liquefying. She clutched the front of Owen's shirt, crushing the fabric, hardly able to catch her breath. A great restlessness and a sense of urgency consumed her. The tension caused her whole body to tighten.

"Owen." She twisted in his arms, needing more. *"Owen."*

"I'm here," he said. It was a vow.

He lifted her again. This time he settled her astride, her knees gripping him on either side of his thighs. She did not understand what he intended until she looked down and discovered that somehow he had managed to open his trousers. The size of his engorged shaft shocked her senses all over again.

She had seen nude statues of the male figure. She and Charlotte had pored over the lascivious drawings of couples engaged in intercourse in the books that Charlotte kept tucked away in a locked closet. But nothing had prepared her for this.

Fascinated, she reached down and touched him lightly.

Owen groaned and half closed his eyes. "Ahh, my sweet, have a care."

"Did I hurt you?" she asked, horrified.

"No." His mouth curved at the edges. "But I am very sensitive to your touch, Virginia Dean. You have a great deal of power over me."

"I find that hard to believe."

He stopped smiling. The heat in his aura and his eyes seemed to intensify.

"It's the truth," he said. "I have known that from the start. I need you, Virginia."

"Why?" she asked, utterly bewildered.

"Later," he promised.

"You keep saying that."

"Because it's complicated and I cannot talk coherently at the moment," he rasped.

"Owen?"

"Please, if you have any generous feelings toward me at all, not now."

"All right," she said. "But later."

"Later," he said again.

He groaned and kissed one breast and then the other through the chemise. The gossamer fabric was no barrier to his hot, hungry mouth. He moved his hands up the insides of her thighs. When he reached her heated core he found the wellspring of the growing urgency that consumed her.

"Yes," she gasped. Her fingers clenched around his shoulders. She closed her eyes against the rush of exquisite tension.

He stroked her, finding places of intense sensation that she had never known existed. Everything inside her shivered and tightened until she could not abide it any longer.

A surging energy flashed through her. Suddenly she was sailing on a glorious tide. The release stole her breath. She clung to Owen, her rock in the storm.

She was only vaguely aware of him pushing into her, forcing his way gently but relentlessly into her passage. She paid no attention, too enchanted with the cascading waves of energy.

He thrust suddenly, deeply. Even though she knew enough to be prepared for some initial discomfort, the sharp, lancing pain caught her off guard. The electrifying sensation was not just physical. It crackled across all of her senses.

She flinched, gasped and bit the nearest thing at hand, Owen's earlobe, quite fiercely. The small act of retaliation was as much of a surprise to her as it was to Owen.

He sucked in a harsh breath and held himself very still within her.

For a couple of heartbeats neither of them moved.

"I think we both just drew blood," Owen said. He sounded as though he was speaking through gritted teeth.

She took a breath and was shocked by the coppery taste on the tip of her tongue. Good grief, she really had bitten the man. It wasn't his fault that she was new to this business.

"My apologies." Mortified, she dropped her face back down onto his broad shoulder. "One reads about this sort of experience and one thinks one is prepared, but I wasn't expecting quite such a jolt."

"Neither was I. Tomorrow I must remember to purchase a gold ring to insert into the ear that you just pierced."

She raised her head again, alarmed. She stared at the small drop of blood welling on his earlobe. As she watched, the tiny crimson rivulet dripped onto the collar of his pristine white linen shirt.

"Oh, dear," she said. "This is awkward."

"Not as awkward as the position we are in at the moment."

She could feel the steel-hard tension in his muscles. She sensed that he was holding himself in check for her sake.

She cleared her throat.

"Well," she said, "is that all there is to the business? I must say, after waiting so long to escape spinsterhood, I did expect something a bit more interesting."

"Interesting," he repeated, a bit too neutrally.

"In sensation novels there is always a transcendent metaphysical passion that accompanies the physical act. I expect when that occurs, it compensates for the uncomfortable side of the experience."

"You didn't experience anything of a transcendent nature just now?"

"Actually, I was engaged in an extremely transcendent experience, but you just ruined it."

"It is my turn to apologize. I did not expect you to be a virgin."

She glared at him. "Why not?"

"You are a woman of strong passions," he said. He kissed her cheek. "I assumed that by now—"

"You mean at my age—"

"I assumed that by now," he repeated deliberately, "you would have found some way to explore those passions."

"Well, I was considering an appointment with Dr. Spinner."

He caught her face between his hands. "Could we discuss this some other time?"

"Certainly," she said politely. She winced, trying to adjust to the feel of him inside her. "Do, please, get on with it. We've come this far. We may as well carry on to the conclusion."

"That's the spirit."

"Are you laughing at me?" she asked, suddenly suspicious.

"No, Virginia, believe me, I am not laughing. It would hurt far too much. I doubt that I would survive."

He began to move slowly inside her, using his grip on her hips to guide her into the rhythm. She was raw from his initial entry, but she was increasingly certain that she could at least endure the remainder of the process.

To her astonishment, the pain began to transform into a stimulating sense of urgency again. She was still exquisitely sensitive, but the sensation was now a compelling force. Her fingers locked around Owen's shoulders.

One of his hands left her rear and shifted to the place between her legs where their bodies were joined. She felt his fingers on the bud that was the center point of sensation.

A short time later he struck an invisible chord, launching her back out on the fabulous waves of sparkling energy. Small, powerful currents flashed through her, sweeping her along on the dazzling tide. She wanted to scream with the pleasure of it all; she wanted to laugh, to sing, to cry.

But she could do none of those things, because with another low, savage groan, Owen crushed her mouth beneath his own, swallowing any sound she might have made. He thrust heavily into her one last time, and then he went rigid. She felt the shuddering power of his climax slam through him in near-violent waves.

For a timeless moment they sailed the storm together. Then with one last heavy, groaning sigh of release, Owen relaxed deep into the chair.

When Virginia opened her eyes she saw that he was watching her with the lazy satisfaction of the hunter after a successful hunt.

"I knew you were the one," he said.

THIRTEEN

The scientist entered the laboratory the way he always did, through the kitchen door. He stood quietly for a moment, savoring the faint currents of energy that still shivered in the atmosphere. They were starting to fade. That was only to be expected. The experiment was concluded.

He took out the specially designed gold pocket watch that the clock maker had given him and walked down the narrow hall to the stairs.

The atmosphere thickened quite pleasantly as he made his way to the floor above. There were still hints of dread interlaced with the exciting nuances of incipient panic. He admired the aura of escalating fear that he had succeeded in capturing. But it was the dark power of the energy preserved at the moment when the subject understood that death was imminent that was the signature of his great talent.

The subject in this particular experiment had not been a strong talent. There were very few truly powerful glass-readers. But like Ratford, Hackett had served well enough for his purposes.

A muffled clink and thud stopped him at the top of the stairs. In spite of the fact that he was prepared, a cold chill wafted across his senses, rattling his nerves. The clockwork devices that he used to conduct the experiments were ideally suited to the great work. They were, in fact, the key to the perfection of his engine. But they were extraordinarily dangerous, not to mention expensive. He did not like having to leave them on guard, but after discovering that burglars had contaminated the scenes of both experiments, he'd been forced to take precautions. That was a problem with letting a house stand empty. They were magnets for housebreakers and thieves.

He struck a light and then flipped open the pocket watch. The interior of the watchcase was fitted with a special mirror. He held the watch so that the mirror inside was focused on the dark doorway.

The flaring light fell on a praying mantis the size of a house cat. The eyes of the clockwork insect glittered with malevolent energy. The increasing chill in the atmosphere warned him that the device had obtained a focus on him. The energy level started to escalate. His insides chilled. For an instant, panic assailed him. What if the mirror in the pocket watch no longer worked?

He shuddered with relief when the mantis clanked to a halt. The icy currents ceased emanating from the faceted glass eyes.

The scientist breathed a shaky sigh and continued down the hall.

The Hackett and Ratford experiments had both been unqualified successes, thanks to what he had learned during his preliminary research in the basement of the Hollister mansion. In the course of that work he had discovered how to calibrate the clockwork devices.

After Hackett and Ratford, he had been satisfied that the devices worked on glasslight-talents precisely as he had theorized. He had been ready for the final experiment, the one that, if successful, would energize his magnificent engine. But everything had gone wrong the other night.

That was always the way with scientific progress, he reminded himself. One had to expect setbacks.

He opened the door of the bedroom. Inside, all was just as he had fashioned it on the night of the experiment. The body of the subject and her personal possessions had been removed immediately after the death, of course. They were not important. What mattered was that he had achieved his goal of igniting some energy deep inside the dressing-table mirror. The currents were quite weak, because Hackett had been weak, but that was not important. What mattered was that he had proven the validity of the theory.

He opened his senses. The mirror on the dressing table still contained a little fire, but the energy was fading rapidly. There was no reason to return again to this house. He had learned all he could from this experiment.

He left the bedroom and went back along the hall, pausing long enough to collect the praying mantis. The device was still frozen as a result of the effects of the mirror, but he knew that status would not last long. The only certain method of ensuring that the curiosity would not activate was to remove the key from the back of the machine. He set about the task cautiously, holding his breath until he had the key safely out. When the mantis was secured he put the key in the pocket of his coat and dropped the curiosity into the canvas bag that he had brought with him for that purpose.

He carried the mantis downstairs. Outside on the street, he walked to the corner and whistled for a hansom. It was only a short distance to the scene of the second experiment, but he did not feel comfortable walking alone at such a late hour. The newspapers were full of stories of hapless citizens who had been set upon by violent criminals at night.

Ten minutes later he got out of the hansom at the corner, paid the driver and walked quickly to Ratford's address. Excitement and anticipation built rapidly within him. The second experiment was still fairly fresh. In addition, Ratford had been somewhat stronger than Hackett. He was very curious to see if the fires in the glass would last longer.

He opened the door and moved into the kitchen, pausing to absorb the atmosphere.

The first faint, discordant currents drifted across his senses. The atmosphere in the house had been disturbed again. Anger flashed through him. Another ruffian had entered the premises. Really, the rise in crime was appalling. The dragon would have taken care of the problem, but there would likely be a body in the upstairs hall. Disposing of the corpse would be a nuisance.

Annoyed at the thought that yet another intruder had entered the carefully staged experiment, the scientist took out his pocket watch and went up the stairs. At the top he paused, struck a light and listened tensely for the mechanical clink and thump of the clockwork dragon he had left on guard.

He was greeted with a disturbing silence. He looked around, fearful that he might accidentally stumble over the lethal device. But there was no sign of the automaton.

It occurred to him that the weapon might have failed. When all was said and done it was only a clockwork mechanism, and clocks sometimes stopped for no good reason. Holding the pocket watch at the ready, he went slowly along the hallway, searching the darkened rooms. At the far end he was forced to come to the inescapable conclusion: Not only was there no corpse, the dragon was gone.

Panic shot through him. He threw open the door of the laboratory. Everything inside appeared to be untouched, but when he heightened his senses he could detect the faint currents of energy that told him the experiment had been disturbed again, this time by someone who had been capable of overcoming the dragon. Only an extremely powerful glasslight-talent could have managed that feat. Even he could not control the toys without the aid of the pocket watch.

Rage boiled inside him. The vast majority of glass-readers were weak, insipid creatures like Ratford and Hackett who did not begin to comprehend their own abilities. Many actually believed that the images they saw in the mirrors were genuine spirits. But he knew of one who might have been able to survive the dragon long enough to disable it.

He had saved Virginia Dean for last because he had sensed that she was the one he needed, the glass-reader who might be strong enough to ignite the fire in the mirrors of his Great Engine. She had now proven that she was even more powerful than he had realized. Excitement shivered through him.

Two questions immediately sprang to mind: Why had Virginia Dean come here tonight? And had she come alone?

FOURTEEN

Owen opened his eyes when Virginia started to extricate herself from the chair and his arms. He watched her get to her feet, aware of a deep sense of satisfaction that went beyond the physical. She had no notion of how deliciously disheveled and erotic she looked dressed only in her rumpled chemise and stockings. Tendrils of her sunset-bright hair had come free of the pins and tumbled around her shoulders.

She looked down at her stained chemise with dismay.

"Oh, dear," she said. "It was new."

"I will replace it."

"There is no need for that," she said, quite sharply. "I'm sure it will all wash out."

Flushed, she hurried across the room, stepped into the pile of clothing and hastily drew first her petticoats and then her gown up around herself.

As if she were putting on a suit of armor, he thought.

He crumpled the handkerchief he had used to clean both of them a short time earlier and put it into a pocket. Reluctantly he pushed himself up out of the chair, closed the front of his trousers and fastened his shirt.

"Virginia," he said. He stopped. Not certain what to say next.

"Yes?" She concentrated hard on the last hooks of her gown.

He went toward her. "Are you certain that you are all right?"

She raised her chin. "Of course I'm all right. Why wouldn't I be?"

"This was your first experience of this sort of thing."

"Well, yes," she said. "But that is hardly my fault. Really, society makes it very difficult for a single woman to take a lover."

"Difficult but not impossible. Many single women find a way around the problem. Why did you wait so long?"

She sighed. "One has to reach the point where one realizes one has nothing left to lose and that there is no reason to save oneself for marriage because it is unlikely that the man of one's dreams will ever appear."

"I see." That certainly crushed any romantic notions he might have entertained concerning the nature of their relationship. She had given herself to him tonight because she had concluded that nothing better was likely to happen along.

"Actually, I did reach that conclusion a few months ago on my twenty-sixth birthday," Virginia continued. "But unfortunately, the situation did not become any less complicated."

"Why was that?"

"There remained the problem of employing the right man for the position, as it were."

"You intended to *hire* someone?" He had never envi-

sioned himself as a man who was easily shocked, but
Virginia had just succeeded in stunning him.

She reddened. "Perhaps that was not the best way to
put it. One wants this sort of thing to be accompanied
by strong passions, of course."

"One would certainly hope so."

"Really, it is not at all like hiring a gardener."

"I'm relieved to hear that. I think."

Her brows snapped together. "It is not as if there is
a wide selection of suitable gentlemen just lolling about,
waiting to be picked up like ripe tomatoes in a market.
There are so many requirements to be met. And as it
turns out, the older a woman gets, the more requirements she accumulates."

"I see."

"By the time one reaches my age, the list is very long
and one knows that it will be impossible to find the
right man. So one must be prepared to compromise."

He caught her chin on the heel of his hand. "What
were your requirements, Virginia?"

"I had cut my list back to include only strong passions," she said.

"But I failed to meet even that minimal require-
ment?"

She blinked. Her eyes widened. "Not at all. Whatever
gave you that notion, sir?"

"As I recall, somewhere in the middle of the exercise
you mentioned that you had been hoping for a transcendent metaphysical experience."

"But it was transcendent," she said earnestly.
"Exceedingly so." She waved the issue aside. "Well, per-

haps not in the middle, but certainly at the beginning and most assuredly at the end, it was quite transcendent."

He smiled and brushed his mouth across hers. "I cannot tell you how pleased I am to hear that. Because it was transcendent for me, as well."

She smiled, radiant and relieved. "Oh, good. I was concerned about that aspect of the matter, what with my limited experience and all. But I am a quick learner, I assure you. I expect it will all get more efficient with practice."

"Efficiency is not a priority for me." He whispered another kiss across her mouth and then released her. Turning away, he scooped up his coat and shrugged into it. "I must be off. It is late. You need rest, and so do I."

"Do you want me to examine the scene of the other glass-reader murder?"

"In due time." He went to the door and opened it. "After what we learned tonight, my intuition tells me that it is more important to take another look at the mirrored chamber where Hollister died."

"How do you intend for us to do that?"

"We will go in the same way we got out the other night."

In the front hall he collected his hat and gloves. She opened the door. He went out onto the steps and stopped, aware that he did not want to leave.

"Good night, Owen," she said softly.

"Good night, my sweet. Lock the door."

"I will."

He went down one step and paused. "You're sure it was transcendent?"

"Absolutely. And very stimulating. I vow, I don't feel the least bit exhausted anymore. Do you know I was seriously considering taking one of Dr. Spinner's treatments for female hysteria in order to experience the hysterical paroxysm that his patients rave about? But I very much doubt that his therapy can compare with the sort of transcendence we experienced tonight."

"Who the devil is Dr. Spinner? And what is this therapy for female hysteria? I have never heard of it."

"I'm not precisely certain of the details, but evidently it involves an electromechanical machine called a vibrator. It's a very modern medical instrument."

"Good Lord. How long has he been offering this treatment?"

"Quite a while, from what I understand. It is a very common treatment, of course."

"It is?"

"Oh, yes, it has been for years. There are any number of doctors who offer a similar therapy for hysteria, but not all of them use such a modern device to induce the therapeutic paroxysm. Many still do it manually, which, I understand, can take a great deal of time. Dr. Spinner's machine is said to be extremely efficient."

"Damnation. You say these treatments are widely available to the women of London?"

"Yes, of course. I understand they are quite popular in America, as well. Good night, Owen."

"Hang on." He started back up the steps. "I want to ask you a few more questions about this Dr. Spinner."

"Some other time. I'm really not in the mood to discuss the latest medical practices. Good night, Owen. Be careful on the way home. London streets can be dangerous at night."

She closed the door gently but firmly in his face.

FIFTEEN

Clive Sweetwater was seated in his favorite chair, feet propped on a leather ottoman, when Owen walked into the library the following morning.

"Good morning, Uncle," Owen said.

"Huh." Clive did not look up from his copy of the *Flying Intelligencer*. The day's edition of *The Times* was lying on the table next to the chair, but Clive always read the scandal sheet first. He claimed it was far more interesting. "Hollister's death finally made the papers. Heart attack, of course."

"Of course."

"How goes the Arcane investigation?"

"All I have at the moment are a great many questions." Owen picked up the silver pot on the table and poured himself a cup of coffee. "I stopped in to see Nick. I called at his lodgings a few minutes ago. His housekeeper informed me that he was on his way here, to make use of your library."

"He arrived shortly before you showed up. Headed straight for the kitchen, as is his habit. Matt and Tony returned home just before dawn, after keeping watch on the Dean house for you. They slept for only a couple of hours, and now they're in the kitchen as well. Don't know where they get the energy."

"Youth."

"The three of them are eating me out of house and home."

"Blame your housekeeper." Owen swallowed some coffee. "Mrs. Morgan's cooking is remarkably good."

Clive lowered the paper with a sharp, rustling motion and peered at Owen with his hunter's eyes.

"Your aunt Aurelia has announced that she's going to register you with Arcane's new matchmaking agency," he said.

"That won't be necessary." Owen kept his tone very even.

"When you think about it," Nick said from the doorway, "it makes great sense to employ a matrimonial agency that specializes in matching people of talent. It sounds like a very efficient way to proceed with the business."

"Do not," Owen warned, "use the word 'efficient' in my presence today, unless it is to describe your progress in locating that damned clock maker."

"What's the matter with you? Did you get enough sleep last night?"

Owen looked at him, not speaking.

"Right," Nick said. He sauntered into the room and headed for the coffeepot. "Got a solid lead from a collector who specializes in paranormal artifacts. Said he'd heard rumors of a clock maker who created exquisite mechanisms that could induce unconsciousness and create hallucinations. There were hints that for a suitable amount of money, the clock maker will take a commission for a curiosity that can kill."

Owen halted his cup halfway to his mouth. "Which clock maker?"

"He didn't have a name, but he said that the clock maker is said to use an alchemical symbol as a signature."

"That fits. There was a small alchemical sign on both devices."

"I'm doing some research on those marks. I'm hoping to turn up more information today." Nick peered at him with keen interest. "What is your problem with the word 'efficient' today?"

Owen looked at his cousin. Nick was a couple of years younger. He was tall and lanky, with the sharp, ascetic features that were common to the men of the Sweetwater family. But unlike most of the males in the clan who possessed a certain intuitive good taste in clothes, Nick had a perpetual air of scruffiness about him. It had been too long since he'd bothered to get his curly brown hair cut. His gray coat and trousers, although expensively tailored, were already rumpled, even though it was only eight-thirty in the morning.

Nick struggled manfully with the latest fashion in neckties, but he invariably produced lumpy mounds of fabric instead of elegant knots. He had always had a difficult time, sartorially speaking, but there was no denying that the situation had worsened after he moved into his own lodgings, because his mother was no longer able to keep an eye on him.

The unkempt appearance concealed a razor-sharp psychical gift for unraveling the secrets of dead languages, codes and other such mysteries. Nick was never happier than when he was deciphering an ancient manuscript, especially one that contained paranormal secrets. It was the nature of his version of the Sweetwater family talent.

Ethel Sweetwater appeared in the doorway, saving Owen from having to come up with an answer to Nick's question about the word "efficient."

Ethel was a fine-looking woman, fashionably dressed in a dark red-and-black gown. Like all of the women in the Sweetwater family, she was formidable, a force of nature. The Sweetwater men did not marry weak women. They required women who could handle the talent of the men of the line, women who could keep dark secrets.

"What is this about efficiency?" Ethel asked.

"Good morning, Aunt," Owen said. "You are looking spectacular today."

"Do not evade the question," she said crisply.

Like many of the women who married into the Sweetwater family, Ethel was highly intuitive.

"Have you ever heard of a Dr. Spinner?" Owen asked.

"Yes, of course," Ethel said. "He has an excellent reputation. Noted for his very modern treatment of female hysteria, I believe."

"I am told his therapy is highly efficient," Owen said.

"I wouldn't know," Ethel said. "I have never experienced an attack of hysteria in my entire life."

"But you are aware of his therapy?"

"Certainly. Dr. Spinner is a very fashionable doctor at the moment. He uses a new electrical instrument to achieve excellent results. Why do you ask?"

Owen cleared his throat. "The subject came up in conversation recently."

Ethel raised her brows. "It must have been a very interesting conversation."

"Yes," Owen said. "It was." He made a valiant effort to change the subject. "Were you able to learn anything from your research into the Hollister family tree?"

"Very little that will be useful, I'm afraid. The line ended with Hollister. There are no surviving close relatives, no uncles, brothers or cousins. It was not a prolific family. I did, however, turn up traces of madness here and there in the family tree. At least one cousin and a grandfather were confined to asylums. I suspect there were others who were mentally unstable, but in earlier times families generally kept their mad relations in the attic."

"But there is evidence of strong talent in the line?"

"Yes," Ethel said. "However, from what I could tell, the truly powerful talents in the family were the ones most likely to show indications of instability and insanity."

SIXTEEN

The door of the shop opened just as Millicent Bridewell started to wind up the gleaming silver-and-bronze lobster. The latest creation from her workshop was exquisite, complete in every detail, right down to the snapping claws. She had not yet infused energy into the eyes. That was the last step of the process, an added touch that she provided for only her very special customers. There was, of course, an additional charge.

She removed the key and put it into her pocket. The customer who called himself Mr. Newton entered the shop, bringing with him an air of unsettling energy.

"I wish to commission some more curiosities, Mrs. Bridewell," he announced in a low, raspy voice. "They must be powerful."

Everything about Mr. Newton, from his fine clothes to his watch fob, screamed money. By rights he should have appeared distinguished, Mrs. Bridewell thought. He ought to have commanded respect. Instead he seemed oddly bland and innocuous, more like a butler than a gentleman. He was rather short, with thinning hair that was a dingy shade of blond. His features were neither handsome nor ugly. In every aspect he was

monumentally forgettable, the sort one passed on the
street without a second glance.

But Newton had now purchased several of her special curiosities, and she was becoming very uneasy. In
general, her customers tended to be desperate wives or
impatient heirs. They preferred to rent a clockwork
device with the intention of using it only a single time.
When the difficult husband or the lingering wealthy
relation was out of the way, clients were more than eager
to return the toys. The power infused in the devices
made most of her customers nervous. Beautiful as they
were, the curiosities were not the sort of objects that
one put on display in the library, where well-meaning
maids, visitors or children might attempt to wind
them up.

But Newton was different from her customary clients. He bought the toys outright, and he had not
returned any of them, although she had assured him
she would refund some of his money if he did so. She
did not care to know how Newton was using her lovely
creations. She never questioned her customers. What
they did with the devices was their business.

What concerned her about Newton was that he was
using the toys far too often. If he got careless the police
might stumble onto her profitable little sideline. The
police, however, did not worry her nearly as much as
Arcane's new psychical investigation agency did. Rumor
had it that the firm of Jones & Jones had assumed the
responsibility of looking into crimes of a paranormal
nature. Not that the agency had any right to interfere
in the private business affairs of those who happened
to possess a little talent, she thought. Nevertheless, she

did not want any trouble from that quarter. The Joneses were a dangerous lot.

"I don't have any more curiosities prepared, Mr. Newton," she said. She bustled around behind the counter, instinctively putting some distance and some glass between herself and the client. "I thought I made it clear that my special curiosities are made to order. It takes time to infuse the energy into the glass."

"Yes, yes, I know. I want you to start work immediately. I am in something of a hurry."

She cleared her throat discreetly. "May I ask if there was a problem with any of the other curiosities that you purchased? Did they fail to work?"

"No, no, they functioned as you said they would. But I need more power. I have concluded that if I employ several of them at once I will be able to achieve the effect I require."

She hesitated. The sad truth was that the pursuit of her art took money, a great deal of it. There was never enough. The fine materials and components required to create the curiosities were expensive. Many of her clients had trouble coming up with the rental fee, but Newton never questioned her prices. Clients who did not try to bargain were scarce and, therefore, valuable.

"I suppose I could have some more curiosities ready for you in three days," she said finally.

"Excellent. Remember, they must be as powerful as you can make them."

"I will see what I can do," she said briskly. "But I must have the full amount in advance."

He was not pleased with that, but he did not argue. "Very well."

She waved a hand to indicate the several curiosities on display. "You may choose the ones you want me to enhance."

"Let's start with the Queen," Mr. Newton said. "She'll be quite appropriate for what I have in mind."

SEVENTEEN

Virginia followed Owen through the iron gate and into the night-shrouded gardens that surrounded the Hollister mansion. She contemplated the darkened house from beneath the hood of her long gray cloak. The windows appeared to be fashioned of obsidian. They glinted, black and opaque, in the moonlight. No gaslight or candles lit the interior of the house. There was no sign of a glowing hearth.

"You were right," she said. "It does appear to be vacant."

There was a muted clang of iron on iron as Owen closed the gate.

"I made a few inquiries. I learned that Lady Hollister dismissed the staff very early on the morning after we found Hollister's body," he said. "A discreet undertaker took away the body. No one has seen Lady Hollister since that day."

"Where did she go?"

"No one seems to know. Hollister had a country house in the north. She may have gone there by train."

"One can hardly blame her for wanting to escape this dreadful place."

They made their way into the old drying shed. Nothing inside had been disturbed, as far as Virginia could tell. She waited while Owen turned up the lantern. When the yellow light flared they started down the stone steps into the ancient abbey ruins beneath the mansion. She sensed Owen heightening his talent.

"Do you perceive anything?" she asked.

"Nothing to indicate fresh violence," he said. "But the old energy is still here. He brought the girls in through this passageway and removed the bodies the same way. That kind of thing soaks into the very walls."

"Just as it does into mirrors."

"I suspect that there is a second entrance inside the house."

"Why do you say that?"

"Convenience, if nothing else."

They went past a familiar intersection.

"That is the corridor where we found the carriage," Virginia said. "The one that leads to the cell where Becky was held prisoner."

"Yes. We are not far from the mirrored chamber."

They rounded another corner. The lantern light splashed down a short stone passage. There was a door midway along the hall. It was closed.

Owen stopped. "That is the door to the mirrored room."

She halted beside him. They were standing so close together in the narrow confines of the stone passage that the hem of her cloak brushed against his leg.

"This corridor looks just like all the others," she said. "How did you find me the other night?"

"The place reeks of violent energy. That room is the

focal point." Owen studied the closed door. "The other night when I came down here I feared that I would be too late."

She knew from the flat, cold way he spoke that if he had found her body in the mirrored chamber, her name would have been added to his personal list of those he had failed.

"But you weren't too late," she said gently.

He did not respond to that. He went toward the door, flattened his back against the ancient wall next to it and motioned for her to do the same.

"In the event we encounter another clockwork guard," he explained. "The stone is our best protection."

He reached out with one gloved hand and opened the door. It was not locked. The heavy iron-and-wood door swung inward slowly. The interior of the room was drenched in darkness. Virginia listened closely. She knew that Owen was doing the same. There was no clank and thump of mechanical claws.

Owen pushed the door wider and moved into the opening. He held the lantern aloft.

"Empty," he said. "No clockwork devices. But someone has recently redecorated."

Virginia looked past him. The bed still stood in the center of the chamber, but it was neatly made up with pristine, crisply ironed linens and a pretty quilt patterned with pink roses. There was no sign of the bloodstained sheets.

"I can understand that the person who removed the body would have taken the bloody sheets," she said. "The killer did not want to leave any evidence of the crime. But why take the time to remake the bed?"

"If whoever stabbed Hollister had no practical means of getting the bed out of this room," Owen said, "he or she might have remade it in an attempt to conceal the bloodstained mattress in the event that someone else discovered this chamber."

Virginia studied the bed. "No, I don't think that was the motivation. That bed was made up with great care and the highest-quality linens. The quilt is beautiful and expensive."

"Hollister was a wealthy man," Owen reminded her. "All the linens in the household are no doubt costly."

"No, not all," she said. "The servants would have had separate, much less expensive bedding. Whoever changed the sheets on this bed used the finest available, the ones that would have been reserved for the master and mistress of the household. In fact, that quilt looks feminine. I suspect it was intended for Lady Hollister's bed."

"An interesting observation," Owen said. He looked intrigued. "It fits with my suspicion that Hollister was murdered by his wife."

"But she is at least half mad," Virginia said.

"Only a madwoman would kill her monstrous husband and then use her own fine linens to make up the deathbed."

Virginia shuddered. "Yes."

Owen walked into the center of the room. Virginia followed, her talent still lowered in an effort to suppress her intuitive reaction to the terrible energy in the chamber. All of her senses were shrieking at her to run. She knew that Owen was aware of the same ghastly currents.

She looked around uneasily. The flaring light of the lantern reflected endlessly off the mirrors, creating walls of cold flames that extended into an infinite darkness.

"It's as if we were standing in some anteroom of hell," she said.

"Yes." Owen turned his attention away from the bed long enough to survey the walls of mirrors. "Which raises the obvious question: Why did Hollister create a room like this? If he was a glasslight-talent, surely he would have found the effects of the reflections disorienting and disturbing."

She met his eyes in the mirrors. "I'm sorry to tell you this, but I'm afraid that there are some talents with an affinity for mirrors who would find this room thrilling to the senses. I suspect Hollister was one of them."

He raised his brows. "Something to do with the stimulating effects of the mirrors, do you mean?"

"Yes." She walked slowly around the room, heightening her senses very cautiously. "Mirrors reflect energy from across the spectrum. Those of us who work glasslight are especially sensitive to that reflected energy. Indeed, one of the difficulties in reading the afterimages in looking glasses is dealing with the reflections. When mirrors are arranged as they are in this chamber, to create an infinity of reflections, the effects can be quite . . . dramatic."

"When it comes to the laws of para-physics, glass is always unpredictable."

"Trust me, there is no need to remind me of that fact. I have been dealing with glasslight since I turned thirteen."

"Yes, of course. My apologies for the lecture. What do you mean when you say that the effects are dramatic?"

She looked at the endlessly repeating scene in the mirrors. "Some glasslight-talents might find that their powers were enhanced by the reflected energy in this chamber."

The dangerous heat in Owen's eyes burned hotter. "Permanently enhanced?"

"No," she said. "The effects would last only while one was inside the mirrored space. But the sensation could be quite exhilarating, I suppose, at least for some talents. The effects would act like a powerful drug on the senses. And if one were inclined toward some dark obsession, as Hollister obviously was . . ." She let the sentence fade.

Owen looked thoughtful. "In other words, this chamber would have acted like an intoxicating elixir on Hollister's senses while he committed murder."

"Yes. Once the afterimages were burned into the mirrors, he could come down here to experience them again and again before they began to fade. You told me that some killers return to the scenes of their crimes to savor the energy that is left in the vicinity of the murders. I think the effects of the mirrors in this room would be similar for a murderer who was also a glasslight-talent."

"And when the images did start to dim?"

She swallowed hard. "He was no doubt driven to kill again. Like any drug, he would crave more and more of the stimulation he got from the mirrors."

"Each time he killed, he would have burned yet more layers of afterimages into the looking glasses."

"Yes."

She did not say anything else. There was no need. When she met Owen's eyes again in one of the mirrors, she knew that he understood.

"Raising your talent in this chamber will be like walking into hell," he said.

She sighed. "It is never easy looking into mirrors that have witnessed death. I have seen some terrible things in looking glasses. But this chamber is different."

"Because more than one woman died here?"

"In part, yes." She thought about the first wildly disorienting sensations that had struck her elevated senses like shocks of lightning when she had awakened in the bed next to Hollister's body. "But there is something else involved here, something I do not understand. Perhaps when I start to read the glasslight it will become clear."

Owen came up to stand behind her. He put one powerful hand on her shoulder. "You need not do this, Virginia. I can learn a great deal here on my own."

"Of course I must read these mirrors. We need all the information we can get from this place. But before I begin, tell me what you see in this chamber."

Energy flared when Owen elevated his talent. He looked around slowly, taking in the bed and the table with a measuring expression.

"I didn't have time to take a good look the other night," he said. "But now I see that murder was done in this room, not once but on several occasions." He walked to the bed. "The victims all died here."

"What of the killer?" she asked.

"His energy is all over this chamber, but the darkest currents are concentrated near the bed." Owen frowned. "The majority of the murders were done the old-fashioned way. Hollister strangled his victims. But the three most recent murders were committed by paranormal means."

"He started using the curiosities to kill his victims."

"Yes, I think so." Owen prowled the small space. "There is other strong energy in here besides Hollister's. It is difficult to distinguish from his, but I can see traces of it clearly, now that I am looking closely. It is the same energy I detected in Mrs. Ratford's house."

"A second killer?"

"Yes. But why does the energy blur with Hollister's?" Owen crouched on the floor, removed one glove and touched the stone. A visible frisson of awareness went through him, and his eyes got a little hotter. "Ah, yes. I understand now."

"What is it?" Virginia asked.

Owen rose to his feet. The energy in the atmosphere around him raised the hairs on the nape of Virginia's neck.

"My aunt assured me Hollister had no close relatives, but I am certain that the second man in this chamber is related by blood to him," Owen said.

"Hollister left no surviving children."

"None that we know of. It does not necessarily follow that he did not leave any offspring."

"Illegitimate offspring," Virginia said quietly. "Yes, that is always a possibility, isn't it?"

Owen glanced at her, curiosity in his eyes. "What are you thinking?"

She forced herself to concentrate. "I am thinking about Lady Hollister."

"What of her?"

"She is a very small woman. In a fever of insane rage she might have been able to kill her husband, but how did she manage to lift him onto the bed? For that matter, how did she get me out of the dead daughter's bedroom and into this chamber?"

"Obviously she had help."

Virginia thought about it. "The companion, perhaps. Or one of the servants." She composed herself and prepared to raise her talent. "Now it is my turn to see if I can add anything more to the evidence that you have discovered."

She summoned her inner control and raised her senses cautiously.

Shadows began to shift in the mirrors. Her pulse beat faster.

"What do you see?" Owen asked.

She took a firm grip on her nerves and rode the waves of energy higher, opening her talent more fully. The dreadful afterimages appeared like dim, moving photographs deep within the glass.

"I see the victims," she whispered. "So many of them. They are all about Becky's age. Some of the afterimages are quite faded. Hollister started murdering in here years ago."

Owen watched her in the looking glass.

"Virginia," he said. "Are you all right?"

She could not answer him. The ghastly afterimages

shifted and seethed in the mirrors. The visions transformed the room into a chamber of horrors. The ghostly
figures screamed silently and reached out to her as if to
pull her into their dark universe behind the looking
glasses.

Owen's voice came to her out of the storm.

"Virginia, if you can't handle this, tell me."

Rage spiked through her. She would not allow the
monster who had created this chamber to win. She
pulled mightily on her control.

And found it.

The afterimages in the mirrors sank back into the
glass. She could still see them, but they were no longer
inundating her senses.

"I'm all right," she managed. "It was just the initial
shock. I thought I was prepared, but I did not realize
how many afterimages had been captured in these mirrors. Hollister was truly one of the monsters."

"I regret that he did not come to the attention of my
family early on in his career," Owen said. He sounded
grim. "That is the problem with monsters. They find it
easy to conceal themselves, especially in a large city like
London. In the future perhaps Jones & Jones will be able
to assist us in the hunt."

"Perhaps."

"You do not have a lot of faith in J & J, do you?"

"No."

"I would remind you that it was Caleb Jones who
sensed that there was a strong possibility that Ratford
and Hackett had been murdered by paranormal means.
Furthermore, he commissioned me to hunt for the killer

even though neither of the victims were members of the Arcane Society."

She made a face. "Very well, I will concede that this new J & J appears to be taking an interest in investigating psychical murders outside the Society. But there is no getting around the fact that those in Arcane do not approve of people like me and likely never will. That is not important now, though. There is something else in these mirrors."

"Besides the afterimages, do you mean?"

"Yes. There are faint flames burning deep in these looking glasses, just as there were in the mirror on Mrs. Ratford's dressing table."

"Are you certain?"

"Yes. The fire in these mirrors is weak, but it is perceptible. I think that when the curiosities are used to commit murder they somehow lock energy, not just afterimages, into the glass."

"You said the fire trapped in Mrs. Ratford's mirror was stronger. Why would that be? More people died in this chamber."

"Yes, but those who died here were not glasslighttalents. Mrs. Ratford was. I think that may make all the difference."

"Son of a bitch," Owen said softly. "That's why he is now focusing on victims who are glass-readers."

"Yes, I think so. They provide more of the kind of energy he wants to trap in the mirrors."

"But why does he seek to lock the fire in the glass?" Owen asked.

"I don't know."

"Is there any way to release the flames?"

"The energy seems to be in stasis. I'm not sure if I can ignite it. But even if it is possible, I don't think it would be a good idea. What I see is pure, raw energy. There isn't a lot of it, to be sure. Nevertheless, there is no telling what would happen if I tried to pull it out of the mirrors."

"Enough." He urged her toward the door. "We have our answers. I think we have spent enough time in this miniature hell."

EIGHTEEN

The hunter in him sensed that he was closing in on his prey. He ought to be feeling the icy-cold rush of energy that always hit toward the end of the hunt, Owen thought. But for some reason he was consumed with an edgy, restless sensation that told him he had left at least one door unopened.

"Owen?" Virginia said. "Is there something wrong?"

He realized he was hurrying her so swiftly along the stone passage that she was obliged to hold her skirts up almost to her knees and trot briskly to keep up with him.

"Sorry," he muttered. He forced himself to slow to a rapid walk. "I am eager to get you out of here."

"I appreciate that. I assure you I have no desire to linger. But I have the impression that you are not satisfied with what we learned in that chamber. At least we have some clue to the identity of the man who murdered Mrs. Ratford and Mrs. Hackett. We know that he is a blood relative of Hollister's."

"That information is useful," he agreed. "I will ask my aunt to pursue her genealogical research."

"You are concerned about the fire that is trapped in the mirrors, aren't you?"

"Yes. Hollister was an out-and-out killer. He raped his victims, and then he murdered them. That was all he cared about. But there is something different about the second man. He does not assault his victims physically before he kills them."

"I see what you mean." Virginia sounded thoughtful.

"It is almost as if he has been conducting experiments."

"To what purpose?"

"To trap fire in mirrors, or so it appears. There is much more to this affair than meets the eye, Virginia."

"Lady Hollister might be able to tell us something useful, but she really is quite insane, Owen."

He turned another corner and saw an ancient wood-and-iron door set into the wall of the tunnel. He stopped abruptly. So did Virginia.

"Lady Hollister," he said softly.

"Surely you are not going to pursue her? Speaking personally, I am grateful that she murdered her husband."

"She certainly did the world a favor." He contemplated the door. "But I am curious about how she came and went from the scene of the murder."

Virginia looked at the door. "Do you think that leads to the mansion?"

"Yes. The lock on it is new."

He took the pick out of his pocket and set to work. "The house is empty. We may as well search the premises while we are here."

"That could take hours, even days. It is a very big house, Owen. What do you hope to find?"

"I don't know. I never do until I see it."

When he got the door open they found themselves in an empty basement room. A well-worn trail of footprints cut through the decades of dust and grime that covered the stone floor.

"Someone came this way often over the years," Virginia said.

He angled the lantern and crouched to view the footprints. "It is impossible to make out individual tracks because there are so many of them, but most appear to have been left by a man."

"Hollister."

"No doubt. I see the prints of a woman's shoes, as well. More than one woman, to be precise. Whoever they were, they came through here recently."

"Lady Hollister and the servant who helped her carry me down here, perhaps."

"No doubt." He straightened and aimed the lantern at the flight of steps at the far end of the room. "Let us see where that leads."

They climbed the steps. The door at the top opened onto a darkened library. When they emerged into the room Owen saw that the opening they had come through was concealed as a section of bookshelves.

"A house of secrets," Virginia said. "But obviously Lady Hollister knew at least some of those secrets."

Owen set the lantern on the desk and began opening and closing drawers. "Others may have known them as well. Lady Hollister's companion, for example. Or some of the servants."

"I do not recall seeing any servants other than the housekeeper when I arrived. There must have been a couple of daily maids and a gardener, at the very least. One simply cannot run a household this size without staff. But I can't believe that they would have remained silent if they had suspected what was going on down in that chamber."

"By all accounts this was a rather eccentric household." He closed one drawer and opened another. "If most of the staff came in daily and did not live on the premises, it's possible that they never knew about their employer's unpleasant hobby down in the basement."

Virginia came toward him. Her shoes made no sound on the expensive carpet. "Are you searching for anything in particular?"

"It would be rather useful to find a record of the purchase of one or more of those damned clockwork devices." He closed the last drawer. "But there is nothing of that sort here. Just some blank paper and a few odds and ends."

Virginia began plucking books at random off the shelves. After half a dozen volumes, she opened one and paused.

"This is interesting," she said.

He rounded the desk. "What have you got there?"

"There are a number of photographs concealed in this book. They all appear to be of young women and girls about Becky's age." Virginia looked up quickly. "Dear heaven. I fear that this is a record of Hollister's victims."

He took the book from her and examined the photographs. Each showed a young woman dressed like a prostitute. Each girl in the pictures was lying on the bed in the mirrored room, clearly dead.

Wearily Owen closed the book. More victims he had failed to save, he thought. More images to haunt his nights. "He indulged his obsession for years, and no one ever knew."

Virginia touched his hand. The knowing look in her eyes told him that she understood what was going through his mind.

"There is no changing the past," she said. "There will always be monsters. You cannot hunt them all. You will do what you can, but you must accept that you will not be able to save every victim."

"Knowing that truth and accepting it are two very different things."

"One accepts such truths by concentrating on the present and the future, not the past."

He smiled. "Where did you learn such wisdom?"

"My mother told me that when I was thirteen and just coming into my talent. She said I must never forget that although I would see a great deal of evil in the mirrors, once in a while I would be able to find justice for some of the victims and provide a sense of peace to some of those left behind. She said those rare moments must be enough to sustain me or I would be driven mad by the afterimages I would view in the years ahead."

"Your mother sounds like a very wise woman." He tucked the book under one arm. "I will give these pictures to Caleb Jones. He can turn them over to his friend at Scotland Yard. Perhaps the police will be able to notify the families of some of Hollister's victims and assure them that the killer is dead."

"That is a good plan," she said.

He went toward the door that opened onto the hall.

"Let's go upstairs. People are inclined to keep their most closely held secrets in their bedrooms."

They went down a long hallway and started up the broad stairs to the floor above.

"I remember coming up this staircase," Virginia said. She looked around uneasily. "The bedroom that Lady Hollister wanted me to examine was on this floor at the end of the hall."

"That was the room in which you were overcome by the drug?"

"Yes. I remember nothing after that until I woke up in that mirrored chamber."

The faint creak of a rope twisting on wood brought him to an abrupt halt. He looked up.

"Virginia," he said quietly.

She froze. "What is it?"

"If I am not mistaken, it is Lady Hollister."

The flaring light of the lantern revealed the body of a woman hanging from a rope secured to the banister two floors above.

"Dear heaven," Virginia whispered. "I'm sure that's her."

Owen went swiftly up the next flight of stairs. Virginia followed on his heels. They both looked over the banister. The light fell on the face of the dead woman.

"It is, indeed, Lady Hollister," Virginia whispered. "Was she murdered, too?"

Owen opened his senses and looked at the fluorescing light that clung to the rope and the wooden banister. Madness and despair radiated like a terrible poison.

"No. It is the same psychical energy that I saw downstairs in the tunnels where Hollister was killed. After she avenged her murdered daughter, Lady Hollister went about her wifely duties. She saw to it that her husband's body was quietly removed. She made up the bed and dismissed the servants. And then she hanged herself."

"And she managed it all without creating a scandal in the family."

NINETEEN

Virginia was in her study, a cup of tea in one hand, a note from a grateful client in the other, when she heard the carriage in the street. She ignored the rattle of wheels and the stamp of shod hooves until she realized that the vehicle had stopped in front of Number Seven. Her pulse kicked up a beat and then immediately settled back into its normal rhythm. *Not Owen*, she thought. If he came by cab today it would be in a fast, sleek hansom, not a large, private equipage.

She listened to Mrs. Crofton's quick footsteps in the hall and knew that the housekeeper had also recognized the unmistakable clatter of an expensive vehicle.

The front door opened. There followed a low, indistinguishable murmur of voices. Not a client, Virginia knew. She met those at the Institute. It was one of Gilmore Leybrook's policies, and she thought that it was a very sound one.

In her early years as a glass-reader she had been obliged to interview clients in her personal lodgings. Some of those who sought out the assistance of a glass-light-talent were more than a bit odd, to say the least.

A few of the truly distraught had appeared on her doorstep at midnight, demanding second or even third readings, convinced that she had been wrong the first time. There had been some threats from time to time. All in all, life was vastly more peaceful when clients did not know the address of the reader.

But if the new arrival was not a client and not Owen, Virginia could not imagine who would be calling on her in such a fine carriage.

The door of the study opened abruptly. For all her professional polish and aplomb, Mrs. Crofton's eyes sparkled with excitement. She raised her chin and assumed a commanding tone of voice that was certain to carry out into the front hall.

"Lady Mansfield to see you, ma'am. Shall I tell her that you are at home?"

"Good grief, *no*."

Virginia set down the teacup with more force than she had intended. There was a sharp, jolting crack of china on china. Tea sprayed across her hand and the note she had been reading. Mrs. Crofton frowned.

"Did you burn yourself, ma'am?"

"No, no, the tea has gone cold." Virginia seized a napkin and dabbed at her hand. "There must be some mistake."

"With the tea, ma'am? I'll bring in a fresh pot."

"I'm not talking about the tea, I meant the identity of my visitor. Are you certain it is Lady Mansfield?"

"Her card, ma'am." Mrs. Crofton produced the calling card with a triumphant flourish. "I put her in the parlor."

"Well, get her out of there." Virginia crumpled the

napkin. "Please tell Lady Mansfield that I am not at home."

Mrs. Crofton got a steely look in her eyes. She moved into the study, closed the door and lowered her voice. "Too late to send her away. I already told her that you would be with her shortly."

"Now, see here, Mrs. Crofton, I am well aware that you feel you came down in the world when you accepted the post in this household. Nevertheless, I regret to inform you that I am your employer and I give the orders under this roof."

"Have you lost your senses, ma'am? Lady Mansfield is quality of the most exclusive sort. She moves in very elevated circles. Why, I cannot believe that she has called upon you in person."

"Neither can I," Virginia muttered.

"It is extraordinary. Most ladies of her station would have sent around a note summoning you to their homes to give them a psychical consultation." Mrs. Crofton waved her hands in exasperation. "You would likely have been shown in through the tradesmen's entrance."

"You know very well that I never accept commissions if I am expected to use the tradesmen's door. And for your information, Mrs. Crofton, Lady Mansfield did not bother to send me a note summoning me to an interview because she knew very well that I would have refused."

Mrs. Crofton was aghast. "Why would you do a thing like that?"

"I really don't think I need to explain."

"I must remind you, ma'am, this is precisely the sort of client we've been attempting to attract."

"*We?*" Virginia repeated, gravely polite.

Mrs. Crofton refused to be intimidated. "I have been giving your career a great deal of thought."

"I beg your pardon? *You* have been thinking about *my* career?"

"If you want to advance yourself in your profession, you must acquire a better class of client. This is a golden opportunity. I will not allow you to pass it by. Our futures depend on it."

"I am flattered that you have aligned your fortunes with mine, Mrs. Crofton. Does that mean that you have abandoned any hope of moving back up in the world by finding another employer?"

"It's not as if I've got a great deal of choice at the moment, now, do I? Neither do you, I'm afraid. You know as well as I do that if you intend to better yourself, you need a housekeeper like me who knows the ways of the quality."

"Do you know, Mrs. Crofton, until I met you I had not actually planned to better myself? I thought that I was doing rather nicely as it was."

"Nonsense," Mrs. Crofton said. "You mentioned at breakfast just last week that you wanted to earn money so that you could make some investments to secure a comfortable retirement."

"Yes, but that is another matter entirely."

"I've got to think of my own retirement as well. As you just pointed out, we are stuck with each other. So I strongly suggest that you go into the parlor and accept Lady Mansfield's commission for a looking-glass reading."

Reluctantly Virginia pushed herself to her feet. "It is obvious that you are not going to follow my instructions to show her the door, so I will perform the task myself."

"Don't you dare be rude to her," Mrs. Crofton warned. "Once word gets around that you have performed a reading for Lady Mansfield, other fashionable ladies in her circles will want to commission readings. This is how one builds a quality clientele."

Virginia crossed the small room toward the door. "I appreciate the advice, Mrs. Crofton. Now, if you'll be so good as to get out of my way."

Mrs. Crofton did not move. "One more thing."

Virginia paused. "Yes?"

Mrs. Crofton lowered her voice a bit more. "Whatever you do, don't appear too eager or grateful for the commission. Just be reserved and polite. Professional. Tell her that you'll have to check your calendar before you commit to an appointment. Make her think she's fortunate to be able to obtain your services."

"I really don't know how I managed to conduct my business without your advice before you came to work in this household, Mrs. Crofton. Now will you kindly get out of the way?"

"Right, then." Mrs. Crofton stepped smartly aside and wrapped her hand around the doorknob. "I can hardly believe our good fortune. I wonder how your name came to Lady Mansfield's attention. Perhaps it is your recent association with Mr. Sweetwater. And here I've been worried about that."

"I have no idea why Lady Mansfield chose to call on me today, but I can tell you exactly how my name came to her attention. Indeed, she has been aware of me for thirteen years."

Mrs. Crofton opened the door. "How's that?"

"My mother was her husband's mistress until both

Lord Mansfield and Mama were killed in a train accident. They were returning from a tryst at Mansfield's hunting lodge in Scotland."

Mrs. Crofton blanched. "What on earth?"

"Lord Mansfield was my father," Virginia explained in a tight voice. "I do apologize, Mrs. Crofton. I realize you had no way of knowing that you had assumed a post in the household of the illegitimate daughter of a high-ranking gentleman, but there it is. I don't think you need bother with a tea tray."

Virginia went out the door and down the hall. She paused on the threshold of the parlor and collected herself.

Lady Mansfield stood at the window. She looked out into the street as though there were something of great import there.

"Lady Mansfield," Virginia said.

Helen, Lady Mansfield, turned to face her. "Thank you for seeing me, Miss Dean. I apologize for the intrusion. But I am quite desperate, and I have nowhere else to turn."

"Lady Mansfield, I really don't think we have anything to discuss."

"Please, I wish only to ask you a simple question. If you will be so kind as to answer it, I assure you I will not linger under your roof a moment longer than necessary."

The thing that had always struck Virginia as inexplicable was the fact that Helen was a remarkably beautiful woman. Blond-haired and blue-eyed, she was endowed with a classic profile and a fine figure, enhanced by the latest fashions. She was one of those women who drew the eye. At the age of eighteen, when she had married her much older husband, she must have been breathtaking, Virginia thought. She had also been a great heiress, a fact that always enhanced a bride's charm.

With such a wife gracing his home and his arm when he went out into society, what had possessed Lord Mansfield to continue his long-standing, illicit relationship with a lowly glass-reader? Virginia wondered. It was not as if her mother had been a dashing actress or a much younger or more beautiful woman. Yet the relationship that Mansfield had begun with her mother years before his marriage to Helen had endured.

On those rare occasions when she allowed herself to sink into a dark mood and brood for a time on just how very much alone she was in the world, she summoned up the shards of memories of her childhood. When she did so, she took some comfort from knowing that Mansfield had loved her and her mother. One's parents were always great mysteries, she reflected.

She started to speak the little speech she had rehearsed on the short trip down the hall. *There has been a mistake, Lady Mansfield. I am not receiving visitors this morning. I'm sure you will understand.* But one look at the pleading expression in Helen's blue eyes caused the words to evaporate from her mind. She had seen that same look in the eyes of too many clients who came to her, seeking answers.

"What was it you wanted to know, madam?" she heard herself say instead.

"I am well aware that this is difficult for you, Miss

Dean," Helen said. "Surely you realize that I find it equally uncomfortable. I would not have come here today if there had been any other course of action open to me."

I'm going to regret this, Virginia thought. But there was nothing else to be done. Helen was clearly in considerable anguish. Nothing short of desperation would have brought her here today.

"Please sit down," Virginia said. She motioned to one of the two dainty chairs that bracketed the unlit fireplace.

"Thank you."

Helen sank gracefully onto the chair, arranging the elegant folds of her expensive blue day gown with small, practiced movements of her gloved fingers.

Virginia took the matching chair and twitched the skirts of her plain copper-brown housedress into position.

"I realize that you have no reason to help me," Helen said. "But I am hoping you will feel some degree of compassion for me in my hour of need."

"Perhaps if you would get to the point, madam?"

"Yes, of course. My daughter, Elizabeth, has disappeared."

In spite of everything, Virginia felt herself grow cold. "You believe she is dead?"

Helen's eyes widened in shock. "God forbid." She pulled herself together. "I meant that she has vanished from her home. She ran away sometime this morning. She told no one where she was going. No one saw her leave. I will come straight to the point, Miss Dean. Is she hiding here with you?"

Virginia was so taken aback by the question that for a moment she could not think clearly.

"Good heavens, no," she finally blurted.

"Please do not lie to me. I must know the truth. I have been absolutely frantic since I discovered that she was missing."

"Why would she come here? She does not even know that I exist."

"I'm afraid that is no longer true." Helen's hands tightened into a knot on her elegant lap. "She learned recently that you are her half-sister."

Virginia went quite still. "I see. How did that come about?"

"Perhaps it was inevitable. I told myself that no one would remember the old gossip. But there are always some who never forget ancient scandals."

"Yes," Virginia said.

"When Elizabeth came to me a few days ago, demanding answers, my first thought was that you had sought her out to tell her the truth. But I later learned that she got the story from a friend who had overheard her mother and another woman gossiping about the old tale. It seems the other woman was a client of yours." Helen looked down at her hands and then raised her eyes. "She remarked on the family resemblance."

"I am sorry," Virginia said gently. "I realize how upsetting this is. But I give you my word Elizabeth is not staying here with me. You may search the house, if you like."

Helen closed her eyes in anguish. When she opened them again, she looked more frightened than ever. "That will not be necessary. I can see that you are telling me the truth. I admit that I had pinned all of my hopes on finding her here. But if she is not in this house, where can she be?"

"I'm sorry," Virginia said again. "Perhaps Elizabeth is staying with a friend?"

"No, I'm certain that is not the case. I made a few discreet inquiries before I came here."

"I still do not understand why you believe she would have come to me."

"She is extremely curious about you. She has questions, you see. Questions I cannot answer."

"What sort of questions?"

Helen's mouth tightened. "My husband claimed to have some psychical powers. He said he could see shimmering currents of energy around people. He said the colors and hues of the wavelengths told him a great deal about the person. Indeed, he was always very good at predicting how others would act, and he had a knack for knowing when someone was lying. But I never believed he actually possessed paranormal abilities. However, when Elizabeth turned thirteen this year, she told me that she could perceive strange lights around other people."

"She inherited her father's aura-reading talent."

"For months I have tried to tell her that it was her imagination. I took her to our country house for a month. I thought the fresh air and daily walks would distract her."

"But she continued to see auras," Virginia said.

"Yes. When we returned to London last month I told her that she must not discuss the visions she has with anyone because people would think she was mentally unbalanced. That sort of chatter can ruin a young lady in society."

"Yes, of course," Virginia said evenly.

"After that lecture, she stopped talking about auras; at least she did not speak of them to me. But she has begun to take a great interest in all things paranormal. When I let her know that I was concerned, she informed me that the paranormal was all the rage and that her friends were very much intrigued by it. She made it sound as if attending séances and demonstrations of psychical talent were simply fashionable activities for young ladies."

"For many young ladies, that is true," Virginia said. "But Elizabeth is attempting to comprehend and accept her own talent. Surely you can understand that she does not want to believe that there is something wrong with her. She is seeking answers that will assure her she is not mentally unbalanced."

"I realize that." Helen tightened her gloved hands. "Learning that she has a half-sister who claims to possess paranormal talents, indeed a sister who makes her living with her abilities, was the final straw. I am convinced that she has set out to find you."

"I would have said that she could not possibly know my address. But since you are obviously aware of it, I suppose she might have discovered it, too."

"I have been aware of your address for some time," Helen said. "But I did not tell Elizabeth."

"If she knows anything at all about me, which I think we can assume is the case, she will likely know to make inquiries at the Leybrook Institute. That is how my clients contact me. Mr. Welch accepts the commission. His assistant, Mrs. Fordham, forwards all requests for consultations to me. I have received no notes regarding your daughter."

My sister.

Although she had been aware of Elizabeth since her birth, it had always been difficult to think of the girl as her sister. Mansfield's legitimate daughter existed in a different dimension. The world she moved in had nothing in common with the one in which Virginia lived.

Tears glinted in Helen's eyes. "Forgive me." She pulled out a delicate lace handkerchief and blotted up the moisture. "I have been living in a nightmare since I discovered she was gone. The thought of Elizabeth out there alone on the streets terrifies me. She has no notion of how to survive in the world. What if she has been kidnapped?"

"I will send word to Mr. Welch at the Institute," Virginia said. "I will ask him to be on the alert for a young lady making inquiries about my services. My housekeeper will have one of the street boys dispatch the note at once. If Elizabeth shows up, Mr. Welch will have his assistant keep an eye on her until I can get to the Institute to take charge of her. If I hear any news I will contact you at once."

"Thank you," Helen said, her voice leaden with anxiety. "I am so afraid that she will come to grief before I can find her."

"You said your daughter is an aura-reader."

"That is how she refers to herself."

"Is she a sensible young lady?"

Helen sighed. "I had always believed that to be the case until this morning."

"If she has a degree of common sense and if she can read auras, she is not as unprotected as you might think," Virginia said.

"How can you say that? She has no experience of the world."

"Her talent provides her with a strong intuitive ability that will surely help her avoid people who might be a danger to her. Aura-readers are very good at that sort of thing. That sensitivity will help keep her out of harm's way."

"She does seem to have recently developed very sound instincts when it comes to judging others," Helen admitted. "I can only pray that you are right."

Virginia rose. "I shall write the note to Mr. Welch immediately."

Helen got to her feet. "I am very grateful, Miss Dean. I realize that you have no reason to feel any vestige of obligation to Elizabeth."

"All I am going to do is send a note," Virginia said. "It is nothing."

Helen looked at her with an unreadable expression. "The gossip was right, you know."

"What do you mean?"

"There is a strong family resemblance. You and Elizabeth both have your father's eyes."

Helen went out into the hall. Mrs. Crofton opened the door for her with a respectful air. Helen went down the steps and got into the waiting carriage.

Virginia went into her study to write the note to Welch. After she gave it to Mrs. Crofton to send around to the Institute, she opened the bottom drawer of her desk and removed the photograph inside.

For a long time she sat, looking at the picture of her handsome, dashing father, her attractive mother and herself. She had just turned thirteen when the photograph was taken. She looked innocent and happy and loved. For all her budding psychical talent, that day she'd had no premonition that in a few short months her world would come crashing down around her.

TWENTY

The note from Mrs. Fordham, Welch's assistant, came within the hour.

> A young lady is here requesting a consultation with you. Won't give her name. I assume she is the one you asked Mr. Welch to watch out for. I informed her you would see her shortly.

Virginia dashed off a note to Helen and went upstairs to change into a walking dress. By the time she returned to the front hall to collect her cloak and gloves, Mrs. Crofton was waiting at the door. She had been uncharacteristically quiet since Helen had left. Evidently she had not yet recovered from the shock of discovering that her employer was the by-blow of a shady psychical practitioner and a gentleman descended from one of the most distinguished families in society.

"Please have one of the street boys take that note around to Lady Mansfield in Hamilton Square immediately, Mrs. Crofton," Virginia said. "She is very worried about her daughter."

"Yes, ma'am," Mrs. Crofton said. The words were stilted and tight. She opened the door.

Virginia went out onto the front step.

"Miss Dean?" Mrs. Crofton said quietly behind her.

Virginia paused. "Yes?"

"Under the circumstances, I think you were very generous to Lady Mansfield."

"It was not her fault that her husband chose to keep a second family on the side."

"He wasn't the first to do so, and he won't be the last. But it does not follow that you owe Lady Mansfield anything."

"My concern is for Elizabeth. She is the innocent one."

Mrs. Crofton looked knowingly. "She is growing up in luxury and will inherit a fortune. She will take her place in society and make a grand marriage. You will spend most of your life working for your living. You'll be fortunate, indeed, if you are able to put enough aside for your later years."

"You're right, Mrs. Crofton. Given the rosy future that you portray, I really do need to see about attracting higher-quality clients."

"Time you raised your fees, as well. People don't value services unless they pay dearly for them."

Virginia smiled. "Thank you for the advice, Mrs. Crofton. I shall consider it closely."

She pulled up the hood of her cloak and set off briskly into the fogbound afternoon. It was a fifteen-minute walk to the Leybrook Institute. There were usually a number of carriages and cabs parked in the street in front of the large building that housed the Institute's offices and meeting rooms. This afternoon was no exception. Lectures on the paranormal and demonstrations of psychical powers were given frequently during the week. They attracted enthusiastic audiences, which, in turn, generated clients for practitioners affiliated with the Institute.

Those who chose to associate with the Institute paid a portion of their fees to Gilmore Leybrook for the privilege, but Virginia considered the cost to be more than worthwhile. Her business had increased dramatically in recent months. She was now making twice what she had earned as a practitioner on her own.

She went up the broad front steps and into the marble-tiled hall. Fulton, the porter who sold tickets to the lectures and demonstrations, signaled to her.

"Miss Dean," he said. "Mr. Welch said you were expected shortly. Asked me to send you straight to his assistant's office. There is a young lady waiting to see you."

"Thank you, Mr. Fulton."

She went down a corridor lined with offices and demonstration rooms. A familiar voice drifted out from behind a closed door. Dr. Gatwood was giving a lecture to a group of fellow researchers.

"It is clear from my investigations that psychical energy is similar to electrical energy, but rather than passing through wires, it flows in the form of currents through the ether."

She went past the door and on down the hall. When she reached Mrs. Fordham's office she raised her hand to knock. For a few seconds she hesitated. What would she say to the sister she had never met?

Before she could come up with an answer, Jasper Welch opened the door of the neighboring office.

"There you are, Miss Dean," Welch said. He was

a serious, scholarly looking man in his early thirties with nondescript light brown hair that was starting to thin. He peered at her through his spectacles. "I see you got the message. Mrs. Fordham tells me the young lady is most eager to speak to you."

"I must thank Mrs. Fordham for being so prompt," Virginia said.

Welch lowered his voice and cast a meaningful glance at the closed door of his assistant's office. "Mrs. Fordham informs me that the young lady is obviously very well-bred. The girl wouldn't give her name, but Mrs. Fordham suspects she is the daughter of a very fine family. Just the sort of people Mr. Leybrook likes to encourage as clients, if you know what I mean."

"Yes, Mr. Welch, I know what you mean. If you'll excuse me?"

"Of course, of course. See you at the reception tomorrow evening."

"Certainly."

Welch popped back into his office and closed the door.

Virginia took a deep breath and knocked.

"Come in," Mrs. Fordham called, her crisp, no-nonsense voice tinged with impatience.

Virginia opened the door. Mrs. Fordham was at her desk. She was a woman of a certain age, prim, gray-haired and a model of painfully erect posture. She regarded Virginia with sharp, birdlike eyes.

"Miss Dean," she said crisply. "This is the young lady who is asking for you."

She inclined her head toward the girl, who sat, stiff and uncertain, in a wooden chair.

"Miss Dean?" Elizabeth asked with an air of barely suppressed hope. "I am Elizabeth."

My sister, Virginia thought.

"Hello, Elizabeth," she said quietly. "Your mother has been very worried about you."

Elizabeth blinked, startled. "She spoke with you?"

"Yes."

"I did not want to alarm her. But I had to meet you, and I knew that she would never approve."

"I am aware of that, but I must tell you that I sent word to her when I learned that you were here. She is no doubt on her way to collect you."

Tears glittered in Elizabeth's eyes. "But I must talk to you, Miss Dean. I do not know where else to turn."

"Why don't we go downstairs and have some tea while we wait for your mother?"

The tearoom was located on the ground floor of the Institute. The high Palladian windows looked out onto a large garden planted with a wide variety of herbs and plants reputed to have psychical properties.

Virginia and Elizabeth sat at a small table, cups and saucers, a pot of oolong and a plate of small, dainty cakes between them. The room was lightly crowded with a mix of outsiders who had come to attend the lectures and demonstrations, as well as a scattering of practitioners and researchers.

"When I first began seeing lights around people, I thought it was rather entertaining," Elizabeth said. She munched a bite of cake. "But Mama got upset when I told her about it. She said I must not tell anyone what

I could see. Her reaction frightened me. I tried to stop seeing the lights."

"But you could not stop perceiving the auras," Virginia said.

"Well, I could stifle the urge for a time, but it was like closing my eyes or holding my breath. After a while I just had to look."

"That is because using your talent is as natural and intuitive as using any of your other senses, like vision or hearing or touch. It must have been very difficult for you, coming into your new senses with no one to guide you."

"Mama said it was just my imagination. She said that if I told other people, everyone would think that I was mentally unbalanced."

Virginia picked up her cup. "You wondered if that might be true."

"Yes. For Mama's sake I tried to pretend that I was no longer using my other sight, but on a couple of occasions I felt I absolutely had to tell her what I had seen."

Virginia sipped some tea and lowered the cup. "Your talent is a form of intuition that allows you to tell a great deal about another person's character."

"Yes, exactly," Elizabeth said eagerly. "For example, a couple of months ago I was visiting a friend, Sophy Wheeler, when her elder sister's fiancé arrived at the house. He was shown into the library to discuss the marriage settlements with Mr. Wheeler. Before they closed the door I saw the two men talking. I opened my other senses, and I knew at once that the fiancé was lying about the state of his finances."

"What did you do?"

"I did not say anything to Sophy, but when I went home, I told Mama. At first she said it was none of our affair. But I knew she was concerned. The next day she went to see Mrs. Wheeler. She told her that she'd heard rumors about the fiancé's finances and that it might be wise to make a few inquiries. The next thing we knew, Mr. Wheeler announced that the fiancé was nothing but a fortune hunter. The marriage was called off. After that, Mama has paid more attention to my warnings. But she still insists that I not talk about my abilities with others."

"I must tell you that I think your mother's advice is sound," Virginia said. "Generally speaking, unless one is in the business, as I am, it is not a good idea to talk about one's paranormal senses with those who do not possess them. People are likely to think that you are odd, to say the least."

"But the public is fascinated with the paranormal," Elizabeth insisted. "They come to hear lectures here at the Institute and to watch practitioners give demonstrations. They hire consultants like you."

"Just because people are fascinated with the paranormal, it does not follow that they accept it as normal, if you see what I mean. People in your world will look at you askance if you claim to have psychical abilities. At best you will be considered eccentric, and that is not a good thing for a young lady of your rank and station."

Elizabeth flushed a deep red. "Forgive me. I never meant to bring up such a delicate subject."

"I was merely stating a fact. That does not mean that there are not a number of psychically talented people who move in your world, just as your father did. But they tend to keep quiet about their abilities. Some of them belong to a very respectable but secretive organization known as the Arcane Society, however."

"I have never heard of it."

"It maintains museums and conducts serious research into the paranormal."

"How does it differ from this Institute?" Elizabeth asked.

"Arcane is considerably more exclusive in the sense that all of their members actually possess genuine talents. I'm afraid the same cannot be said for many of my colleagues here at the Institute."

Elizabeth looked troubled. "But your talent is real. Why don't you join Arcane?"

"The Society frowns on those of us who must use our abilities to make a living. They believe we give the public a poor impression of the paranormal because there are so many frauds in our ranks."

"For my part, I am very happy to discover that I have a sister who also possesses a psychical talent," Elizabeth said. "I have felt so very alone."

"I remember how hard it was for me after Mama and Papa were killed. I was sent away to boarding school. It was a very good school, and everyone was quite pleasant, but none of the teachers took the paranormal seriously. I felt that I had to keep my own abilities secret."

"You must have been very lonely," Elizabeth said.

"That was the year that I came into my own talent. I had no one I could talk to about the things I was seeing in mirrors, but at least I knew something of what to expect because Mama and Papa had prepared me. I am sorry that you had no one you could talk to this past year."

Elizabeth glanced toward the door. "Oh, dear, Mama has arrived. I can see that she is quite upset. I shall have to go home with her. But I would very much like to meet you again for tea. Would that be possible?"

"I'm not sure your mother would approve," Virginia said gently.

Helen arrived at the table. She looked at Virginia.

"Thank you for sending me word that Elizabeth was safe," Helen said in a very low voice.

"Certainly," Virginia said, keeping her own voice just as soft.

Helen looked at Elizabeth. "You gave me a terrible fright."

"I am so sorry, Mama." Elizabeth blinked back tears and hastily jumped to her feet.

"Come," Helen said. "We must go home now."

"Yes, Mama."

Helen inclined her head at Virginia. "I am in your debt, Miss Dean."

"No," Virginia said. "You're not. I would have done the same for anyone in your situation."

"Yes, I believe you would have. Good day, Miss Dean."

"Lady Mansfield," Virginia said.

Elizabeth smiled at her. "Good-bye, Miss Dean. I am sorry that I frightened Mama, but I am so happy we got to meet."

"Good-bye," Virginia said.

She drank her tea and watched Helen and Elizabeth walk out of the tearoom. Neither of them looked back.

After a while she got up from the table and went upstairs to her small office. She unlocked the door, went inside and sat down behind the desk. She looked around, taking in the client chairs, the filing cabinet and the most recent issues of the Institute's *Journal of Paranormal Investigations*.

This was her world, she thought. This was where she belonged. She had a career that was important to her, and she had friends. She did not need her father's other family.

But it would have been nice to have had a family of her own.

TWENTY-ONE

"This was the first time you met your sister?" Owen asked.

"Yes," Virginia said. "I knew of her, of course. My father told me about Elizabeth when she was born. But I had never even seen her. To be honest, I was shocked today when Lady Mansfield showed up on my doorstep, asking if Elizabeth was with me."

They were in a carriage headed toward the scene of the second glass-reader murder. It was late enough to allow Virginia to read glasslight accurately.

Owen was not certain what to make of Virginia's mood. She was composed, but he had the impression that her thoughts were focused on something other than the case.

"Lady Mansfield obviously realized that it was only logical that her daughter would turn to you for answers about her talent," he said.

"Helen will have to confront the fact that Elizabeth cannot simply pretend she does not see auras. Elizabeth may be able to conceal her talent from her friends and acquaintances, but she can't deny her ability to herself."

"No, it is as much a part of her as her other senses. She needs guidance."

"I suggested to Elizabeth that she consider joining the Arcane Society."

"Good advice," he said.

"She wanted to start attending lectures at the Institute. I explained that Arcane did not approve of the organization, due to the high percentage of charlatans associated with it."

He watched her face in the shadows. "What was it like for you when you came into your talents?"

"I was thirteen. My parents had been killed a few months earlier. I was living at Mrs. Peabody's School for Young Ladies. I had been seeing shadows off and on in mirrors for some time, but nothing distinct. I will never forget the first time I saw a true afterimage burned into a mirror. My mother had explained to me how her talent worked so I understood what I was perceiving, but it was still a great shock. The images really do look like ghosts and spirits."

"Where was the mirror?"

"In the school library. The school was housed in a mansion that had been the property of a wealthy family for several generations. Some of the mirrors were very old."

"You saw something terrible in one of them?"

"Yes. The mirror was at the far end of the library. I had not been comfortable in that room, but until that day I hadn't understood why. That afternoon I walked past the mirror and felt that sensation of awareness that one sometimes gets in the vicinity of strong, violent energy."

"I know what you mean," Owen said.

"Instinctively I heightened my talent and looked

deep into the mirror. That was when I saw my first murder victim, a woman of perhaps nineteen or twenty."

"Surely the murder had occurred long before you went to live at the boarding school?"

"Yes, but I hadn't yet learned to sort out the sense of time that comes with the images. And murder always rattles the nerves, even if it is an old crime. I had to know what had happened, so I talked to some of the people who had worked in the school for a long time."

"Did you learn anything?" Owen asked.

"The old gardener had been employed by the former owners of the house. He told me the story. The young woman was a governess who was seduced by the eldest son, who was, in turn, engaged to an heiress. The governess got pregnant. The lady of the house let her go without a penny. The desperate governess tried to extort money from the lady by threatening to tell the son's fiancée about the pregnancy."

"So the lady of the house murdered the governess to make certain she did not jeopardize the marriage plans."

"There was a fortune at stake," Virginia said without inflection. "The family could not afford to have the fine marriage put at risk. So the lady of the house struck the governess on the head with a poker. The servants, including the gardener, were told that the governess had fallen and hit her head on a table, but they all knew the truth. One of the maids found the bloodstained poker."

Virginia fell silent. She went back to watching the scene outside the carriage window.

"How did you end up at the boarding school?" Owen asked after a moment.

"*Hmm?*" Virginia did not take her attention off the street.

"I have heard of Miss Peabody's school. It is not a charity orphanage. The fees are quite high. It takes in the illegitimate offspring of wealthy families who feel an obligation to care for the results of their indiscretions. The girls are educated for careers as governesses, ladies' companions and teachers. They are taught manners and etiquette. They do not go out into the world to work as maids or shopgirls."

Virginia turned back to him, eyes widening a little, as she refocused on the question. "My father provided for me in his will. The school fees were paid until I left at seventeen, and I even received a small bequest when I was ready to go out on my own. It was enough money to allow me to start my career as a glass-reader."

"That explains it," Owen said.

The carriage clattered to a halt. He opened the door, got out and turned to assist Virginia down to the pavement. They walked through the park and along a quiet street of modest houses.

"Mrs. Hackett lived in Number Twelve," Owen said.

Virginia studied the dark windows. "I wonder if there will be another clockwork device on guard."

"At least this time we will be prepared."

He used the lock pick to open the kitchen door of Number Twelve.

"I really must look into purchasing one of those tools," Virginia said.

He looked at her as he rose and twisted the knob. "Why?"

"I fancy the idea of being able to go through locked doors, I suppose. I'm not certain why. Perhaps I have a criminal mind."

"I don't think so. I believe you are attracted to mysteries because you have encountered so many that you have not been able to solve."

"I had not thought of it in quite that way. You may be right."

He opened the door into a darkened rear hall. Whispers of energy wafted through the atmosphere like an ominous scent.

"I think it is safe to say that Hackett did not die of natural causes any more than Ratford did," Virginia said.

"No. It was murder. But then, I have known that from the beginning."

They made short work of the ground floor and then climbed the stairs, listening for the thump and clank of a clockwork guard. This time there were no deadly surprises.

Virginia looked through the open doorway of one of the bedrooms. "I wonder why he did not leave a device behind at this house."

"He has concluded the experiment," Owen said.

"What an unpleasant thought."

He pushed open another door and heightened his talent. The mercury light indicating death by paranormal means shimmered in the atmosphere.

"This is where he killed her," he said.

Virginia walked into the bedroom. He felt energy

suffuse the atmosphere and knew that she had raised her senses.

"Mrs. Hackett was at her dressing table, just like Mrs. Ratford," Virginia said. "She is looking toward the bed, aware that whatever she sees is killing her and there is nothing she can do about it."

"In these two murders, at least, Hollister appears to have established a pattern."

"He requires a mirror, and he kills at night, because that is when glasslight is strongest."

"Do you perceive flames in that mirror?"

"Yes." Virginia contemplated the dressing-table glass again. "The fire is weak, but I can sense it. A small amount of raw energy somehow locked in stasis. It is very strange."

"At least we now have a sense of his motive for killing the glass-readers in their bedrooms in front of their mirrors." Owen surveyed the space. "But to accomplish his goal he had to gain access to the most private room in the house in order to set up the murder machines. I wonder if he took both women by surprise or if they invited him into their bedrooms."

Virginia turned away from the mirror. "I know what you are thinking. I am well aware that some women who claim to channel spirits have a certain reputation that attracts male clients. While that may have been the case with Mrs. Ratford, I am certain it was not true of Mrs. Hackett. She was a middle-aged woman who took her work quite seriously. I doubt very much that she would have invited a client upstairs."

Owen nodded, accepting her verdict. "You are certain that both women possessed some genuine talent?"

"Yes."

"Which means that out of all the charlatans and frauds in the psychical practitioner business, the killer managed to identify two true glass-readers."

"If he is a talent himself, as we suspect, it is not surprising that he could discern others with real talent," Virginia said.

"The other thing the victims had in common is that they were both affiliated with the Leybrook Institute."

"Yes, but what is the connection to Hollister?" Virginia asked. "Neither Lord nor Lady Hollister were clients of the Institute until Lady Hollister commissioned a reading from me."

"You were not chosen at random. Someone arranged to have you sent to the mansion. Who booked the appointment?"

"Mr. Welch or his assistant, Mrs. Fordham," Virginia said. "I'm not sure which one actually accepted the booking. The note came from Mrs. Fordham. She maintains the master appointment journal."

"Where does she keep the journal?"

"In her office."

"I believe I'll have a look at her files tonight."

"I'll come with you," Virginia said.

"No."

"You'll need me to show you exactly where to look," Virginia insisted.

"No. There is always a chance of getting caught when one engages in this sort of thing."

"Nonsense. I'm sure you won't let that happen."

* * *

There really was not that much risk involved, Owen assured himself an hour later. The Institute was deserted at night. Even if someone were to enter the premises, there was a number of exits that he could employ to remove Virginia in a timely manner.

"I don't understand," Virginia said. "There is no record of my appointment with Lady Hollister."

Owen struck another light and studied the appointment journal that was open on the assistant's desk. It showed no booking for Virginia on the night she had been sent to the mansion.

"How did you receive word that you had been requested for a reading?"

"The usual way. I got a message from Mrs. Fordham. It was a last-minute booking. Mrs. Fordham explained in her note that Gilmore Leybrook himself was eager for me to accept the commission. Leybrook is very keen on attracting high-quality clients to the Institute."

TWENTY-TWO

"What do you know of Gilmore Leybrook?" Owen asked.

"Very little, to be honest," Virginia said. "No one does. He is a talent of some kind, but I've never been certain of the exact nature of his ability. He arrived on the London scene about a year ago and established the Institute. He was successful right from the start."

"He must have money, in that case. The Institute is an expensive operation."

"One of Leybrook's many talents is his ability to attract funding for the Institute," Virginia said dryly. "He is charming and persuasive. There is something about him that draws people to him."

"A side effect of his talent, perhaps, whatever it is."

They were back on the street, walking toward the park, where Owen hoped that they would find a cab. That prospect was dimming rapidly. The streets around the Institute were empty. It was nearly midnight, and the fog had thickened to the point where the gas lamps appeared only as glary orbs in the mist, the light they cast all but useless.

Part of him was attuned to the currents of the night, listening for the sound of footsteps that might signal the approach of a footpad. But they had the street to themselves. No normal people, not even normal street thieves, went abroad at night in such an impenetrable atmosphere, he thought. But he and Virginia were not what most people would call normal.

It felt good to share the night and the hunt with this woman at his side. It felt right.

"If we are correct in our initial conclusions, you were the killer's intended victim the night you read the looking glass for Lady Hollister," Owen said. "But things went wrong. Hollister ended up dead, and you and one of Hollister's other intended victims, Becky, escaped. I am quite certain the second killer did not plan that ending to the affair."

"What was Becky doing there that night?" Virginia asked. "Why would she have been needed if I was the intended subject of the experiment?"

"Good question. I asked one of my aunts to stop by the Elm Street charity house today to inquire about Becky."

"You did?" Virginia turned her head quickly to look at him. "Was there any news of her?"

"My Aunt Ethel reports that Mrs. Mallory was able to persuade Becky to attend the charity school."

"I'm so glad," Virginia said. "If she learns typing or telegraphy she will have a chance to forge a respectable career for herself. She will be able to escape the streets. I still find it hard to believe that Arcane has taken over responsibility for the school."

"A sign of a change in the organization, perhaps," Owen said.

"I'm far from convinced that Arcane is truly changing, but I suppose I must allow for that possibility."

They walked in silence for a time, their footsteps echoing eerily in the fog.

"There is something else besides my talent and my association with the Institute that I have in common with Ratford and Hackett, now that I think about it," Virginia said after a while.

He glanced at her, but in the darkness she was all but invisible to the eye. But not to his other senses, he thought. He would always know when she was anywhere in the vicinity. Her energy would always thrill him.

"What is that?" he asked.

"Ratford and Hackett were both spinsters with no immediate family. So am I. The deaths of women like us, those who are alone in the world, are almost certain to go unnoticed by the authorities."

"The killer did not take Arcane and its new investigative agency into account," Owen said. A cold satisfaction flashed through him. "That will prove to be his great mistake."

"No," Virginia said quietly. "His mistake was that he did not take you into account, Owen Sweetwater."

At the end of the street, carriage lights glowed weakly in the fog.

"We're in luck," Owen said.

They quickened their pace. The driver was glad of the fare on what had evidently been a very slow night. Owen bundled Virginia into the cab and sat down across from her. The vehicle rumbled forward.

"I may have an idea," Virginia said with a meditative air. "I do not know if it will be of any use, but you might find it of interest."

"Tell me," he said.

"There is a social event planned at the Institute tomorrow night. Everyone connected to the organization will be there. Leybrook is giving a reception in honor of D. D. Pinkerton, the mentalist from America. Pinkerton arrived recently in London and is very popular. Leybrook hopes to persuade him to become affiliated with the Institute."

"You are thinking that perhaps the killer may be in the crowd?"

"If he is involved with the Institute, as you believe, then yes, it is very likely that he will attend," Virginia said. "Of course, there will probably be over a hundred people there. That makes for a very large pool of suspects."

"Yes, but we know a little more about him now. And I think there is every possibility that the killer will be drawn to you in the crowd."

"What makes you believe that?"

"You were the intended subject of his grand experiment, whatever it is, and you got away. You ruined his plans. He wanted you before, but now he will be obsessed with you."

"You sound very sure of your analysis of his thinking."

Owen looked out the window into the night. "It is what I do, Virginia. It is the way I hunt. I saw the killer's obsessive nature in the energy he left at the scenes of the murders. He is driven by a force that is as strong as physical passion. In fact, the compulsion is a form of sexual desire."

She frowned. "I don't understand."

Owen turned back to her. "When he returns to the scenes of the murders, he no doubt tells himself that he is merely studying the evidence of his successful experiments. But the truth is that the scenes of death arouse him in a sexual manner. He is thrilled by what he has accomplished."

"Thrilled by the act of murder?"

"The death scenes fill him with a ravishing sense of his own power. I suspect that in the past he has felt quite the opposite. Weak and powerless. Unimportant. But now he has found a way to make himself feel strong and powerful. He has become addicted to the sensation. He will continue to kill until he is stopped."

She shuddered. "And all the while he will tell himself that he is actually conducting some sort of scientific experiment."

"Yes. You say you plan to attend the reception at the Institute?"

"Certainly. The receptions are good for business. Leybrook gives them regularly. My colleagues and competitors will all be present."

"I will escort you."

She blinked. "Are you serious?"

"When it comes to the hunt, I am always serious."

She pursed her lips. "I really don't think that is a good idea."

"Why not?"

"I am planning to attend with a friend."

He felt his insides tighten. "A male friend?"

"No, a female friend. She owns a bookshop."

"She is single also?"

"Yes."

"That shouldn't be a problem."

"Owen, please, think about this for a moment. It is one thing to tell people that I am allowing you to conduct some tests and experiments on me. But if you appear with me at the reception, people may begin to suspect that our relationship is of an entirely different nature."

"An intimate nature, do you mean?" he asked without inflection.

Her mouth opened and closed, and then opened again. She waved her hands in a warding-off gesture.

"There was only the one incident," she said quickly. "I am fully aware that our interlude the other night was the result of the effects of the intense energy that we encountered at the scene of the murder. It affected our nerves."

He should have seen this coming, he thought, but once again he was blindsided by her failure to acknowledge the bond between them. Blindsided and more than a little annoyed.

"Is that all it was to you?" he asked. "Therapy for a mutual case of shattered nerves?"

"I realize that you never intended the evening to end the way it did," she said. She was very earnest. "It was my fault. I'm the one who invited you in for a glass of brandy."

Anger crackled through him.

"And now you do not want your friends and associates to see me with you in a social setting?"

"Damnation, sir, do not put words in my mouth. I am attempting to make it plain that I do not hold you responsible for what occurred between us. As a matter of fact, it is your reputation that concerns me."

He stared at her, nonplussed. "What the devil are you talking about?"

"It is common knowledge that you will soon be in the market for a wife."

He was stunned, shocked nearly witless. No one outside the family knew that he was hunting for a wife. No one outside the family understood why finding a mate was so important to a Sweetwater male. *No one.* It was the darkest of the Sweetwater family's many dark secrets.

"Where did you hear that?" he demanded, when he could collect his thoughts.

"I asked my friend Charlotte to look into your family background," Virginia admitted.

"She discovered that I am hunting for a wife?" He still could not comprehend how the wall of secrecy that surrounded the family had been so easily breached.

"She discovered that you are descended from an old, established family in which the men tend to marry, at the latest, in their early thirties." She cleared her throat. "It was obvious to both of us that you would soon be looking for a wife if, indeed, you hadn't started the process already. You obviously have a responsibility to your family."

Relief slammed through him. He settled back into the corner of the carriage. The Sweetwater secret was still safe.

"You're right," he said. "The men in my family are generally married by their late twenties or early thirties. You could say it's a tradition."

"Yes, of course," she said tightly. "In a proud family

such as yours you naturally want heirs to carry on the name."

"More like heirs to carry on the family talent," he said. "But when a Sweetwater sets out to find a bride, he does not concern himself with society's dictates and customs. He hunts for a wife the same way he hunts his prey. He follows his own rules."

"Owen—"

"I do not want to talk about marriage tonight." He drew her into his arms. "That is for the future. At the moment I would much rather kiss you."

Her lips parted on what he feared would be another question. He covered her mouth with his own before she could say anything else.

TWENTY-THREE

"Congratulations, you found our missing clock maker," Owen said. "But it appears that in addition to being a brilliant glasslight-talent, she is also highly intuitive."

"She must have sensed that someone was closing in on her and her business," Nick said.

They were standing in the shadows of the empty shop. Millicent Bridewell had disappeared, along with every trace of her clockwork curiosities.

Owen walked into the back room and studied the empty shelves and workbench. "Given her rather dangerous sideline, she no doubt made plans for just such an emergency departure."

"Want me to keep looking for her?"

"No, we cannot afford the time. She is Arcane's problem now. We must concentrate on our killer scientist. Are you free tonight?"

"I'm always free at night, you know that," Nick said.

"Good. I want you to accompany me to a reception."

"I detest social affairs," Nick said. "You know that,

as well. It is the primary reason why I spend most of my evenings with my books."

Owen walked out of the back room and headed toward the front door of the shop. "I don't enjoy such affairs any more than you do. But I need your help tonight."

Nick followed him. "Receptions are boring."

"I don't think this one will be."

"Why? Because it is being held at the Leybrook Institute? I don't see how that makes it any more appealing."

"We are not going to attend for the purpose of amusing ourselves. We will be hunting."

"Huh. I suppose that might make it a bit more interesting. How do you expect to find your killer in a crowd?"

Owen opened the door and went out onto the fog-bound street. "By now he will be obsessed with Miss Dean. I do not think that he can spend an entire evening in the same room with her without getting close to her at some point."

"Obsession is a strange and powerful force," Nick agreed. He closed the shop door. "It makes people do things that go against logic and reason."

"Exactly."

"Do you know, I have not seen you this intrigued by a case in a very long time."

"It is the most interesting hunt that has come along in a while."

"It came along thanks to J & J," Nick pointed out.

"Yes," Owen said. "I think the agency will become a regular, established client for us in the future."

"Because J & J and Arcane both hunt the same monsters?"

Owen smiled. "I predict a long and profitable partnership."

TWENTY-FOUR

Mr. Sweetwater is going to escort both of us to the reception tonight?" Charlotte emerged from an aisle of bookshelves, a stack of leather-bound volumes cradled in her arms. "Good heavens, Virginia, what do you think you are doing?"

"Trying to find a killer," Virginia said.

Charlotte set the stack of books on the table. "Does that sort frequent social affairs?"

"Mr. Sweetwater seems to think this one will definitely be at the reception."

"Why?"

"Because the monster is associated with the Institute."

Charlotte pondered that briefly. "Well, it is certainly true that everyone with any connection whatsoever to the Institute will attend the affair tonight. Those who don't show up will be notable by their very absence. But how will you explain him to people at the reception?"

"I had not planned to explain the killer's presence to anyone."

"That is not amusing. You know very well I meant how will you explain Mr. Sweetwater? It is one thing to allow people to think that you have agreed to let him study you, but the reception is not a venue for demonstrations of paranormal powers. It is a social occasion. You know what people will say."

"The awkwardness of the situation did occur to me, but oddly enough, after visiting the scenes of several murders in the past few days and concluding that I may be next on the killer's list, I find that I no longer care what people say about my association with Mr. Sweetwater."

Charlotte brightened. A knowing look illuminated her eyes.

"Well, that explains it," she said, satisfied. "And just when did you plan to confide in your closest friend? I refer to myself, of course."

"What are you talking about?"

"There is something different about you lately. At first I thought it was the excitement of pursuing a murder inquiry. That would certainly be more than enough to thrill the senses. But I had a feeling that there was more to it."

"Such as?" Virginia picked up the old book on top of the pile and opened it to the title page. *A Treatise on the Art of Summoning Spirits in Looking Glasses*. "Are these all of the books you have that touch on glasslight?"

"All of those that appeared to contain useful information."

Virginia considered the stack of books in front of her. "There aren't very many, are there?"

"Much of what has been written on the subject is superstitious nonsense. I didn't think you would want to waste time on works of magic and the occult."

"No, of course not." Virginia tapped the big book she

had opened. "But this appears to be a book on summoning spirits. What is that, if not superstitious nonsense?"

"Like many glass-readers, Llewellyn did not fully understand what he was viewing when he looked into mirrors. That doesn't mean he did not have some fascinating observations to make. And stop trying to avoid the subject of Mr. Sweetwater. Your relationship with him involves more than the investigation, does it not?"

Virginia sighed. "Is it that obvious?"

"It is to me." Charlotte smiled. "I have the distinct impression that you are no longer interested in booking an appointment with Dr. Spinner for one of his hysteria treatments."

Virginia felt herself turning red. "To be honest, the prospect of being treated with an electrical device was always somewhat worrisome."

"The dangers of electricity are well known." Charlotte's smile faded into an expression of concern. "But I think you may be facing another sort of danger."

"Trust me, I am well aware of the risk involved in hunting a murderer."

"I am speaking of your liaison with Mr. Sweetwater," Charlotte said gently. "Do not mistake me. I am thrilled that you are embarking on a glorious affair. Indeed, I envy you. But try to maintain some perspective."

Virginia raised her brows. "Perspective?"

"You must not lose your heart to Mr. Sweetwater. He will surely break it, even if he does not intend to do so. He comes from a different world."

"I understand. But really, Charlotte, why should I bother to protect my heart any longer? I will have the rest of my life to recover from a doomed love affair."

"Hmm." Charlotte considered the question for perhaps five seconds, and then she nodded once, emphatically. "You're quite right. After it is over, you will have the stirring memories. I, on the other hand, will have only the stirring recollections of my appointments with Dr. Spinner to warm my lonely old age."

"Assuming you do not get electrocuted."

Charlotte shuddered. "It is an alarming thought, isn't it?"

"So is the prospect of a broken heart. But at least one survives that sort of thing, or so I'm told. Looking on the bright side, I'm sure there will always be doctors offering treatments for female hysteria to whom I can turn after my liaison with Mr. Sweetwater comes to the inevitable conclusion."

"And given the amazing progress of modern science, we can no doubt look forward to many more advances in electrical devices of a medical nature."

"No doubt."

They looked at each other. For a moment neither of them spoke.Then, as happened so often between them, they both burst into laughter.

"Oh, Charlotte, what would I do without you?" Virginia said. She took out a handkerchief and wiped the tears away from her eyes.

"I would miss you even more than you would miss me," Charlotte said. She sobered. "Are you absolutely certain that your affair with Mr. Sweetwater will end badly?"

"I think it is the most likely outcome."

"But the two of you have so much in common."

Virginia frowned. "In what way?"

"It strikes me that your talents are quite similar."

"He hunts psychical killers. I see the dead in mirrors. How are those two talents alike?"

"Perhaps not alike but complementary, if you see what I mean. When you think about it, the two of you make a very good team."

"For goodness' sake, Charlotte, I would not want Mr. Sweetwater to marry me just because we make a good investigation team. Even assuming he was inclined to do so, it is not enough. You and I have both discussed this matter. We made our decision the night of my twenty-sixth birthday. We will marry for love or we will not marry at all."

Charlotte grimaced. "It certainly seemed like a very modern, very romantic notion at the time. But sometimes I wonder if perhaps we may have been a bit too hasty."

"Enough of this depressing conversation. Let's talk about something else."

"Such as?"

"I think there is someone who may be able to shed some light on this investigation."

"Who?"

"Lady Hollister's companion," Virginia said. "There has been so much going on in the past few days that we have all but forgotten about her."

"Why is she important?"

"She may well have been the last person to see her employer alive."

Charlotte glanced at the copy of the *Flying Intelligencer* on the table. "According to the report in the press, Lady Hollister's body was found by the housekeeper.

The rest of the staff was dismissed the morning after you were kidnapped."

"In which case the companion is no doubt searching for another post."

"Yes." Charlotte's eyes gleamed with anticipation. "I could make some inquiries among the agencies that provide hired companions, if you like. It might take some time, but it shouldn't be too difficult to find the woman who attended Lady Hollister."

"That's a brilliant idea," Virginia said. "How soon can you start?"

She was interrupted by the tinkling of the bell above the door of the shop. She turned to watch Owen walk into the room. It seemed to her that he entered on an invisible tide of power. The lower edges of his unbuttoned overcoat swept out around him. She thrilled to his presence as she always did, with a stirring sense of awareness.

He was followed by a tall, lanky gentleman in need of a visit to his barber. The long-haired man wore an expensively tailored but sadly rumpled suit. His tie was a shapeless knot at his throat.

"Good afternoon, ladies," Owen said. He came to a halt in the center of the room and inclined his head very formally in Charlotte's direction. "Miss Tate, I presume?"

Virginia remembered her manners. "This is Mr. Sweetwater, Charlotte."

Charlotte stared, fascinated, at Owen. "Yes, I know. Indeed, all the Leybrook practitioners are aware of your identity, sir."

Owen looked amused. "Miss Dean warned me that was the case."

Charlotte blushed. "You have a certain reputation in our world, Mr. Sweetwater."

"So I'm told." He moved one gloved hand toward the tall man in the rumpled suit. "Allow me to present my cousin, Nicholas Sweetwater. Nick, Miss Dean and Miss Tate."

Virginia and Charlotte both looked politely at Nick, but he seemed unaware of them. He had wandered over to the locked bookcase and was perusing the collection of ancient leather-bound volumes with great interest.

"I say, this collection looks a good deal more promising than I had anticipated, Owen," he announced. "When you informed me that we were going to visit a bookshop that specialized in the paranormal, I assumed the place would be rife with lurid books on magic and the occult. But I see what may actually be a genuine copy of Wakefield's *Notes on Alchemy*."

"It is most certainly a genuine copy of Wakefield's *Notes*, sir," Charlotte snapped. "I would not have taken the trouble to store it in that locked case if it was a copy or a forgery."

"What?" Startled, Nick turned around. For the first time he appeared to notice Charlotte and Virginia. He turned red. "Sorry. Good afternoon, ladies."

Virginia murmured a polite greeting. Now that she could see him more plainly, she realized that Nick Sweetwater was younger than Owen, twenty-eight or twenty-nine, perhaps. There was some family resemblance, most noticeably in the broad shoulders and lean physiques of the two men. But Nick's intelligent eyes lacked the dark knowledge that burned in the depths of Owen's disturbing gaze.

"That particular volume is extremely rare," Charlotte informed Nick in frosty tones.

"I am well aware of that," Nick said eagerly. "I would very much like to examine it to determine its authenticity for myself."

"I'm afraid that won't be possible," Charlotte said a little too sweetly.

"What do you mean? This is a bookshop. I am interested in examining a book that I might wish to purchase."

"I'm afraid I only allow *legitimate* practitioners of the paranormal and researchers who are known to me or vouchsafed by someone I trust to examine the books in the locked cases," Charlotte informed him in lofty accents. "Many of those volumes contain dangerous information. I cannot let just anyone read them."

Nick stared at her, shocked. Then he started to scowl. "I assure you I possess a fair amount of psychical ability. Just ask my cousin, here."

Owen caught Virginia's eye. She realized he was suppressing a grin.

"I am happy to verify that my cousin does indeed possess a high level of psychical ability," Owen said.

"What of it?" Charlotte shot back. "That is not as important as his standing as a researcher. What are his academic credentials?"

Nick's eyes narrowed. "I'll have you know, Miss Tate, that I can read a number of ancient languages, including three or four that are dead, and I have deciphered the codes of several old alchemists."

"*Hmm.*" Charlotte was not impressed.

"I have been a student of the paranormal since I was old enough to open a book. I have, in fact, written a few papers for the Arcane Society's *Journal of Paranormal and Psychical Research,* which is, I might add, a far more legitimate publication than the Leybrook Institute's ridiculous rag. It's true that I write under a pseudonym, due to the fact that my family does not like to see the Sweetwater name in print, but that does not alter the validity of my work."

"Oh, dear," Virginia murmured. "I'm afraid Arcane is not the most helpful recommendation, sir."

Nick switched his attention to her. "What do you mean?"

Charlotte cleared her throat. "For your information, Mr. Sweetwater, the Arcane Society carries very little weight in this shop."

"How can you say that?" Nick swept out a hand to indicate one of the shelves. "It looks like you've got several years' worth of the Society's *Journal* over there. Which means you've got some of my research papers sitting right here on the premises."

"I do subscribe to the *Journal,*" Charlotte agreed. "But that does not mean that I tolerate its members, which I have always found to be an arrogant and irritating lot."

"So do I," Nick shot back. "Which is why I am not a member of the Society."

Owen cleared his throat. "Well, that and the fact that Sweetwaters are not in the habit of joining organizations of any kind."

"That's not the point," Nick grumbled.

"No, it's not," Charlotte agreed.

Evidently concluding that the argument had gone on long enough, Owen took charge.

"Now that we have all survived the social pleasantries," he said, "I suggest we move on to the particulars of the situation that brings us together today."

"An excellent notion," Virginia said quickly.

"My cousin is assisting me in the investigation," Owen said. "This morning he tracked down the clock maker who made the clockwork weapons."

"That's wonderful news," Virginia said.

Nick grimaced. "No, it's not, I'm afraid. Owen and I paid a visit to the shop. It was empty. Mrs. Bridewell, the clock maker, has disappeared. There was no trace of any of her curiosities or her financial records left on the premises."

"Oh," Virginia said, deflated. "Now what do we do?"

"We will leave Mrs. Bridewell to J & J," Owen said. "I want Nick to help us with another aspect of the investigation. He has agreed to attend the reception at the Institute tonight. I want him to assess possible suspects in the crowd."

Charlotte narrowed her eyes at Nick. "Are you any good at that sort of thing, Mr. Sweetwater?"

"Yes," he said. "As a matter of fact, I am."

"How do you plan to get inside the Institute without a ticket?" Charlotte asked. "One must be invited to the reception or accompany an invited guest."

"I have already dealt with the problem," Owen said. "Nick will escort you, Miss Tate."

Charlotte's eyes widened. "What?"

"Nick has a talent for noticing small details. I want

his observations of the guests at the Institute to compare with my own."

"Excuse me—" Charlotte began in ominous tones.

"Everyone at the Leybrook knows who I am by now," Owen said, "or at least they think they know who I am. But no one will recognize Nick."

"I don't get out much," Nick explained.

"You will introduce Nick as a new practitioner who is eager to establish himself in your community," Owen explained.

Charlotte gave a small, ladylike sniff. "I cannot imagine that scheme working for even an instant." She glared at Nick. "What sort of talent will you claim to possess, sir?"

Nick flushed. "I will pretend to be one of those charlatans who summon spirits. It is the easiest talent to fake."

"Because there are no ghosts," Charlotte shot back. "By definition, everyone who claims to see spirits is either a fraud or delusional. But there are literally hundreds of mediums in London, sir, perhaps thousands. Your talent will not appear exceptional."

"Which is precisely the effect that we hope to achieve," Owen said smoothly. "No one will pay much attention to one more practitioner who claims to summon spirits. Nick will not be perceived as a serious competitor or threat to business by anyone present at the reception. That will allow him to make his observations without drawing scrutiny."

"I see," Virginia said quickly, before Charlotte could produce another argument. "A very ingenious plan.

I am also happy to say that Charlotte has offered to make inquiries at the agencies who provide paid companions. We suspect that Lady Hollister's companion will now be searching for a new position. Charlotte may be able to find her."

"Excellent," Owen said. He looked impressed and very pleased. "Thank you very much, Miss Tate. That will be extremely helpful."

"I'll see what I can do," Charlotte said, mollified by Owen's obvious gratitude.

"You will have to excuse us now." Owen strode toward the door. "Nick and I have a number of details to see to before tonight's affair."

Nick inclined his head toward Virginia. "A pleasure, Miss Dean." He looked at Charlotte. "It has been interesting, Miss Tate."

Both men were out the door and lost in the fog before either Virginia or Charlotte could even say good-bye.

"Well," Charlotte said, when she could speak. "Both Sweetwater gentlemen are quite expert when it comes to departing in a speedy fashion."

"Indeed," Virginia said. "One would almost think they had a psychical talent for disappearing."

TWENTY-FIVE

At eight forty-five that evening Virginia stood with Pamela Egan in a relatively quiet section of the Institute's reception hall. Together they surveyed the crowded room. Fifteen minutes earlier Virginia had seen Charlotte and Nick arrive. No one had appeared to take any notice of the couple.

When Virginia had walked into the room on Owen's arm, however, the reaction had been decidedly different. The short silence that had fallen on the crowd followed by the sudden burst of loud conversation had told the story. Everyone had noticed.

Pamela surveyed the scene. "There is no getting around the fact that Gilmore Leybrook is a pompous ass." She paused to down a healthy swallow of champagne. "Pity he controls the Institute."

"The good news is that I understand he is planning to tour the Continent soon," Virginia said.

"Bah. One can only hope that afterward he will feel compelled to tour America. When he is in London he lords it over the rest of us as if this were the Arcane Society and he was a genuine Jones."

"I suppose he is the nearest thing we have to a Jones here at the Institute. Let's be honest, Pamela, we are both making a good deal more money now that we can call ourselves Leybrook practitioners."

"Trust me, Leybrook is well aware of the fact that we are in his debt."

"It is the price of doing business, Pamela."

"*Hmmph.* A damn high price, if you ask me."

Pamela was a stately, full-figured woman in her early forties who conducted a successful business channeling the spirit of an ancient Egyptian princess. In tribute to the spirit that had done so much for her finances, she wore her artificially darkened hair in a style that her hairdresser had dubbed "the Cleopatra." An imitation-gold diadem set with glittering crystals circled her brow, enhancing the dramatic effect. Her eyes were heavily outlined in kohl, and her elegantly tiered gown was in a color known as Egyptian green.

Pamela had waited until Owen had left Virginia's side to collect two glasses of champagne before gliding through the crowd with the speed of a shark knifing through the sea.

She was a friend and former mentor who had offered kindness, support and excellent business advice when Virginia had embarked upon her own career as a practitioner. Virginia was very fond of her, but Pamela was a notorious gossip who prided herself on knowing the latest rumors and scandals.

"Speaking of Leybrook," Pamela said, "I have heard that the relationship with his latest assistant has already begun to fray."

"That didn't last long," Virginia said.

"His assistants never do." Pamela swallowed some

champagne and lowered the glass. "I suspect the charming Adriana has begun making demands."

"Leybrook changes assistants almost as often as he does his socks. Adriana must have known that when she accepted the position. It is no secret."

"True, but you know how it is. Each new assistant thinks that she will be the last." Pamela's mouth twisted in disdain. "If I didn't know better, I'd swear that Leybrook actually does have some talent: namely, a paranormal skill for seduction. What's more, he can work his charms on men as well as women. Just look at the way people are flocking to get closer to the Presence tonight. Our guest of honor has been all but forgotten. Poor D. D. Pinkerton is stuck in the corner with Edward Drummer, who is surely boring him to tears. I see Mr. Welch is making his way over there to rescue Pinkerton."

"It's not necessary to resort to a paranormal explanation for Leybrook's remarkable powers of attraction," Virginia said. "He is handsome, and he is exceedingly clever. One must give credit where credit is due. He's a brilliantly successful practitioner who draws sellout crowds wherever he goes."

From the moment of his fashionably late arrival that evening with his beautiful assistant on his arm, Gilmore Leybrook had been the star attraction. There was no question that he outshone the guest of honor.

Leybrook was holding court in the center of the room. He was tall, with chiseled features and a graceful, athletic build that was enhanced by his elegantly tailored evening clothes. His dark hair was cut in the latest fashion. No one knew where he had come from, but he had the manners and the accents of an educated gentleman.

Of course, Virginia thought, a good actor could mimic the attributes of the upper classes. Leybrook would not have been the first person of lowly birth to descend on the London scene and convince everyone that he had been born and raised in exclusive circles.

His assistant, Adriana Walters, looked as spectacular as ever tonight, but something in the atmosphere around her made it plain that she was not pleased. Her smile was tight, and her beautiful face looked as if it had been carved in stone. Evidently sensing she was being watched, she turned her head and looked straight at Virginia. There was so much rage in her eyes that for a few seconds Virginia could have sworn that she felt unwholesome energy shiver in the atmosphere.

"Oh, dear," Pamela murmured. "I know that expression on her face, and it doesn't bode well."

"You don't really think—"

"That the lovely Adriana is looking at you with murder in her eyes because she has reason to believe Leybrook is going to replace her with you? Yes, that is exactly what I think."

"Ridiculous. Why would Leybrook want me as an assistant? It's obvious that I lack all of the physical attributes he requires. My bosom is much too small, and my hair is too red."

Pamela assumed an air of ominous portent. Her voice dropped to a lower, huskier register. "The princess tells me that he has altered his requirements," she intoned.

Virginia ignored the theatrics. "Why would he do that?"

"I have no idea," Pamela said, her voice returning to normal. "At least you've been given some warning. And I'll add another word of caution."

"What?"

"I wouldn't accept any invitations to tea with Adriana. She's the type to dump a spoonful of cyanide into the cup."

Virginia smiled. "I'll bear that in mind, although I think it is highly unlikely that she will invite me to tea."

"In that case, let us turn to a far more interesting subject."

Virginia braced herself. "That would be?"

"Your association with Mr. Sweetwater, of course."

"I'm sure you've heard the news by now, Pamela."

"Oh, yes, it's all over the Institute." Pamela gave her a sidelong glance. "But is it true?"

"I have agreed to allow Mr. Sweetwater to study me while I employ my talents. He is convinced that he can measure my psychical energy patterns."

"You know what he did to Digby and Hobbes. After he exposed them as frauds, Leybrook was forced to release them from the Institute because of the bad publicity. Doesn't it concern you that you may be next? How can you prove that you have a true talent?"

"He claims to believe that I do have talent."

"I see." A glint appeared in Pamela's eyes. "That may explain the other talk that is going around."

"What do you mean?"

Pamela gave her a knowing smile. "Rumor has it

that your connection with Mr. Sweetwater extends beyond the boundaries of scientific research and experimentation."

You knew this was coming, Virginia thought. Nevertheless, she had not been expecting such a blunt approach. She ought to have known better, she thought. This was Pamela, after all, who had gone through almost as many lovers as Leybrook.

"Good heavens, wherever did you get that notion?" she managed lightly.

"Virginia, you are talking to me, not one of your clients. There is no point trying to finesse the situation. I know you too well."

"I would rather not discuss my relationship with Mr. Sweetwater," Virginia said quietly.

"You are a grown woman, no longer a young, green girl trying to establish her career. I respect that. But I am well aware that you have not had much experience with men."

"I have had any number of male clients."

"I meant experience of a personal nature, and well you know it," Pamela snapped. "Mind you, if you had chosen almost any other man for this sort of adventure, I would have been thrilled for you. Every woman deserves the opportunity to discover romantic passion. But why the devil did you decide to embark on an affair with Owen Sweetwater?"

"For heaven's sake, Pamela, will you please lower your voice?"

"No one could be more unsuitable for you. He might even decide to damage your career when your affair ends. You have worked hard to establish yourself. I do not want to see you throw away your future."

"I don't think Mr. Sweetwater will pronounce me a fraud," Virginia said.

She broke off when she sensed a presence behind her.

"Rest assured, that will not happen," Owen said, his voice very dry.

Pamela gasped and swung around so sharply that a few drops of champagne flew out of the glass in her hand. "Mr. Sweetwater. I didn't realize you were in the vicinity."

Virginia turned more slowly. Owen held two glasses of champagne in his hands. He was smiling his coldest smile. His excellently cut black-and-white evening clothes underscored the aura of raw power that always charged the air around him.

"Allow me to introduce a *friend*," Virginia said, laying subtle emphasis on the word "friend" so that Owen would understand that he was not allowed to be rude to Pamela. "Miss Egan is a highly regarded practitioner. She was very kind to me at the beginning of my career. Indeed, I owe much of my success to her advice and the introductions she was good enough to provide."

Amusement replaced the ice in Owen's eyes. His smile warmed several degrees. He inclined his head in a formal manner toward Pamela.

"In that case, it is a pleasure, Miss Egan," he said.

Pamela recovered her composure, but Virginia could have sworn that she blushed. "Mr. Sweetwater. I've heard a great deal about you."

"None of it good, I'm sure." He handed one of the

glasses to Virginia. "But believe me when I say that I have no reason to declare Miss Dean a charlatan." He took a swallow of champagne and gave Virginia an intimate smile. "In fact, I find her talents extraordinary."

"Will you be giving that information to the press at the conclusion of your study of her powers?" Pamela asked. "It might do wonders for her career."

Owen turned back to her, brows slightly elevated.

"I will be happy to inform the press that Miss Dean possesses genuine psychical abilities, but I doubt that she needs my acclaim. She seems to be doing very well on her own."

Pamela gave him a steel-bright smile. "There is no such thing as too much positive publicity in our business, Mr. Sweetwater. It seems to me that a few good words to the press is the least you can do for Miss Dean under the circumstances."

"Circumstances?" Owen repeated, somewhat ominously.

"I refer, of course, to the fact that you are taking advantage of Miss Dean's generous nature in order to pursue your research project," Pamela said coolly. "She is doing you an enormous favor, is she not, Mr. Sweetwater?"

Virginia winced. "It's all right, Pamela, I assure you."

Owen slanted a long look at Virginia. "Yes, Miss Egan, she is doing me a great favor."

"Then it is only right that you repay her when you end the project," Pamela said. "The most helpful way you could do that is by ensuring that she receives some attractive publicity that might send some new clients her way."

"I see," Owen said.

"After all, it is not as if you have anything else of lasting value to offer her, is it?" Pamela said very pointedly.

"Pamela, please," Virginia pleaded. "That's enough."

"Quite right." Pamela smiled at Virginia. "Enjoy the rest of the evening, my dear, and don't forget the warning from the princess."

"I won't."

Pamela whisked up her green skirts and swept off into the crowd.

Owen watched her leave. "What was that about a warning from the princess?"

"Nothing important. I wonder how Charlotte and Nick are making out. I have lost sight of them. Oh, damn."

"Now what?"

"Gilmore Leybrook and his assistant are coming this way. Well, I suppose it was inevitable."

Owen followed her gaze, suddenly very focused. The atmosphere around him became more highly charged.

"This should be interesting," he said.

TWENTY-SIX

T his isn't working," Nick said.

Charlotte had been about to take a sip of champagne. She paused and peered at him, squinting a little because she had stored her spectacles in the dainty beaded bag that dangled from the waist of her gown. For reasons she was not certain she wished to explore, she had concluded that afternoon that she wanted to look her best tonight. According to the fashion journals, spectacles were not the most attractive evening accessory.

The unfortunate result of her fashion choice was that the reception hall below the small balcony where she and Nick stood was a colorful blur. But this close up she could make out Nick quite plainly. He looked very fine in his evening clothes, she thought. True, she'd had to put her spectacles on in the carriage long enough to make some small adjustments to his appearance. But it had taken only a few minutes to redo the sad knot in his black tie. When she had mentioned, quite discreetly, that the buttons of his satin waistcoat had been fastened in the wrong order, he had immediately rectified the problem.

"What isn't working?" she asked.

"Owen's plan," Nick said. He sounded baffled. "I don't understand. When it comes to this sort of thing, my cousin's schemes invariably work quite well. But this one has certainly come a cropper."

He contemplated the scene below as though it was a perplexing puzzle. Although Charlotte could not make out details, she knew that the balcony, originally designed to conceal the musicians at a formal ball, gave Nick a panoramic view of the hall.

"I was under the impression that your task was to look for the subtle signs that might indicate that someone in the room had developed a pronounced or obsessive interest in Virginia," Charlotte said. "Really, sir, how difficult is that? You're supposed to have a talent for observing small particulars."

"Quite difficult, as it happens, because a number of people in the room appear to have a great interest in Miss Dean. The only people who have not been casting veiled glances at her and my cousin are the servants. There is a great deal of speculation going on down there."

"Speculation about her association with Mr. Sweetwater, yes, I warned Virginia about that. I knew everyone would assume the worst."

"Damnation. Surely they don't suspect that she is helping Owen investigate the murders?"

"No, of course not. It is much worse than that. They think she is involved in an illicit liaison with him."

"Is that all?" Nick looked considerably relieved. "No need to worry, then. I don't see why that sort of gossip should cause Owen any problems. For a moment there, you had me concerned that perhaps his plan was falling apart."

Charlotte gave him a long look.

"Did I say something wrong?" Nick asked.

"We are speaking of the reputation of my dearest friend. Do try not to sound so cavalier, sir."

"I fail to understand how conducting a liaison with Owen would damage Miss Dean's reputation. She is not an eighteen-year-old girl whose family is out to broker a social marriage."

Charlotte said nothing. She just looked at him again.

Sensing that he was on dangerous ground, Nick cleared his throat.

"Miss Dean is obviously a woman of the world," he said, somewhat weakly.

"As am I," Charlotte said. "Are you always this thick-headed, sir?"

He sighed. "When it comes to the nuances of matters such as this, I'm afraid so."

"It was quite rude of you to call attention to the fact that Virginia and I are women of a certain age."

"I never meant to imply that either of you is in your dotage," Nick said hastily. "Merely mature."

"Thank you," Charlotte said. "Allow me to explain the crux of the problem here, sir. While it is true that at her age Virginia is free to indulge in a discreet romantic affair, the difficulty in this instance is that the man everyone thinks she is having that affair with is your cousin."

Nick went blank. "What of it?"

"In case you have not noticed, no one in this hall tonight trusts Owen Sweetwater."

"I see." Nick looked as if he was beginning to comprehend the situation.

"Thanks to his recent hobby of exposing Leybrook practitioners in the press, those connected to the Institute now consider him a serious threat to everyone's career."

"I see," Nick said again.

"It was one thing for people to believe that Virginia was allowing him to study her powers. But now the rumors are going around that she is conducting an affair with him. They will no longer trust her not to betray their secrets to a lover. I fear that when Mr. Sweetwater concludes his investigation, she will no longer be welcome here at the Institute."

"Huh." Nick gave that some thought. "Perhaps she should consider joining Arcane. Come to think of it, both of you ought to join."

"Don't be ridiculous, sir. Arcane has never welcomed those of us who must make a living with our talents."

"They say that the Society is changing rapidly now that Gabriel Jones has assumed the responsibilities of the Master's Chair."

"It remains to be seen if Mr. Jones can reinvent Arcane," Charlotte said. "Even if that is possible, Virginia and I will still be obliged to work for a living. For all practical purposes, that means maintaining an affiliation with the Leybrook Institute. It is not her personal reputation that Virginia is putting in jeopardy by associating intimately with Mr. Sweetwater; it is her career, indeed, her entire future."

"I see," Nick said for the third time. He contemplated the scene below. "I'm afraid the damage in that regard, whatever it proves to be, may have already been done."

Alarmed, Charlotte plucked her spectacles out of her evening bag and pushed them onto her nose. She studied Virginia and Owen. It did not require any degree of paranormal intuition to sense the energy around the pair. Owen stood a little too close to Virginia, just inside the invisible sphere of personal space that a lady always kept in place around her person. There was something both proprietary and protective about his stance. It was as if he were sending a silent message to every other man in the hall, putting them all on notice of his claim on Virginia.

Virginia was in love, whether she knew it or not.

"Damn him," she whispered. She gripped the railing with her gloved fingers. "How dare he do this to my friend?"

Nick went still beside her. She knew that he was looking at her, not at the crowd down below.

"Miss Tate, do try to remember that my cousin established an association with your friend for the sole purpose of discovering the identity of a killer who may well intend to murder her," he said softly. "Owen is attempting to protect Virginia."

Charlotte pulled herself together with an effort of will. "Yes, of course. Forgive me. Sometimes my imagination runs away with my common sense. It may be that I have spent too much time studying the unique properties of the strong energy that is generated between two individuals of talent who are physically attracted to each other."

"What a coincidence." Nick was pleased. "I am very interested in the subject, myself."

"Mr. Sweetwater, really." She could feel the heat in her cheeks. "Are you always this blunt in your speech?"

"I have been told that I have a tendency to speak too directly at times," he admitted, abashed. "My apologies."

"Accepted," she said stiffly.

He cleared his throat. "Right, then, back to the business at hand, eh?"

"That is a very good idea."

"From up here it appears that the only other person in the room who is drawing more attention than Miss Dean and my cousin is that tall man in the center of the hall, the one accompanied by the large-breasted blonde."

"Gilmore Leybrook," Charlotte said. "He is the founder of the Institute. The blonde is his latest assistant, Adriana Walters. Leybrook has had a number of assistants."

Nick appeared deeply intrigued. "Interesting."

"Why do you say that? Because she is quite pretty?"

"*Hmm?* No." Nick gripped the edge of the railing with both hands. "I find it all very interesting because Leybrook is showing a rather intense interest in Miss Dean. He is moving toward her now. The fact that Owen is by her side does not seem to have put him off in the least."

Charlotte peered over the edge of the railing. "Oh, dear. You're right. Good heavens, surely you don't think that Leybrook has an unhealthy, obsessive interest in her?"

"Yes, I do," Nick said. "And so does Miss Walters."

"What does that mean?"

"It means, Miss Tate, that the danger to your friend is coming from a number of different quarters."

TWENTY-SEVEN

Gilmore Leybrook smiled at Virginia. "You and Mr. Sweetwater have caused quite a stir among the practitioners here at the Institute. I gather you have consented to allow him to study you while you work. How very daring of you, Miss Dean."

Owen drank some champagne while he listened to Leybrook talk with Virginia. Idly he toyed with the notion of ripping Leybrook's head off his shoulders. It would be a very pleasant, extremely satisfying project, but Virginia would probably not approve.

Good Lord, I'm jealous, he thought.

The realization jolted him. It had been so long since he had experienced the primitive emotion that he had almost failed to recognize it. There were, after all, other sensations that raised the hair on the nape of a man's neck and induced a fierce, battle-ready tension that tightened every muscle in his body. Hunting had a similar effect. But there was nothing else on the face of the earth that twisted the gut and threatened to override common sense the way jealousy did.

Approximately a minute after she had made the introductions, Owen had concluded that the founder and director of the Leybrook Institute was intelligent, cunning and ruthless. No great insight or intuition was required to produce that analysis. Those qualities were only to be expected in the man who had managed to create a successful financial enterprise based, for the most part, on fraud and deception.

The truly intriguing thing about Leybrook was that the atmosphere around him was ever so slightly charged with the telltale energy of some strong talent. Many of his practitioners were frauds, but Leybrook himself possessed a strong psychical nature. That made him far more dangerous than any charlatan.

"Mr. Sweetwater is a professional researcher," Virginia said. "I saw no reason not to allow him to observe me."

Adriana Walters smiled at Owen. "How fascinating, Mr. Sweetwater. Do tell us what you have discovered about Miss Dean."

Objectively speaking, Adriana was a stunningly beautiful woman, Owen thought. It was a pity about the eyes. They reminded him of the eyes of the clockwork dragon.

"I have no doubt at all about Miss Dean's talent," he said. "She is a very powerful practitioner."

Leybrook looked at him, one dark brow elegantly arched. Icy speculation glittered in his eyes. "Unfortunately you did not come to the same conclusion about two other practitioners associated with the Institute."

"I'm certain they will recover their careers," Owen said. "It takes more than a few negative comments in the press to destroy a clever practitioner. The public is only too willing to believe. But then, I'm sure you already know that, Leybrook. You have built a very successful business on that concept."

"Sadly, the two glass-readers who suffered mysterious and untimely ends in the past two months will not be able to recover, will they?" Leybrook asked softly.

Virginia froze. So did a number of other people in the vicinity. Heads turned. An acute and unnatural silence fell on the guests who happened to be standing nearby.

Adriana took a sharp breath. "Gilmore? What are you implying?"

Virginia's expression tightened. "We all know what Mr. Leybrook is suggesting. He is trying to plant the notion that Mr. Sweetwater had something to do with the deaths of Mrs. Ratford and Mrs. Hackett. That is quite untrue."

Leybrook turned back to her with an air of grave concern. "Can you be sure of that, Miss Dean? No one seems to know much about Sweetwater, aside from the fact that he evidently feels he has been appointed to pronounce judgment on practitioners such as yourself."

"I am positive, sir," Virginia said. She smiled coldly. "As it happens, I viewed the afterimages in the looking glasses at the scenes of the deaths. Both women were, indeed, murdered, but not by Mr. Sweetwater."

Leybrook and Adriana were transfixed. So was everyone else, Owen thought.

"Are you certain they were murdered?" Leybrook demanded.

"Yes," Virginia said. "Absolutely certain."

Owen sensed energy heighten in the atmosphere. Leybrook was unnerved. Adriana had gone pale.

"How, damn it?" Leybrook demanded. "I heard that there were no marks of violence on the bodies. No sign of poison."

"The spirits," Adriana whispered. "The rumors are true. The glass-readers summoned deadly entities from the Other Side."

Leybrook gave her a disgusted look. "Don't be ridiculous, Adriana."

"I assure you, no ghosts were involved," Virginia said. "Just a cold-blooded killer."

"Did you see his image?" Leybrook pressed. He was very intent, very focused.

"I have explained to you that I cannot see the faces of the killers in the mirrors. But Mr. Sweetwater was with me when I performed the readings. He was able to sense something of the psychical nature of the person who murdered Mrs. Ratford and Mrs. Hackett."

Leybrook gave Owen a hard look.

"What did you learn about the killer?" Adriana asked uneasily.

"It was clear that the person who murdered Ratford and Hackett took an unnatural and unwholesome thrill of a sexual nature from the acts," Owen said.

Adriana stared at him, appalled. "*Really*, Mr. Sweetwater."

"Really, Miss Walters," Owen said.

Leybrook's eyes narrowed. "I fail to see how that observation rules you out as the killer, Sweetwater."

Virginia smiled benignly. "I can assure you that Mr.

Sweetwater's passions, while strong, are not at all unnatural or unwholesome. Quite the contrary."

Leybrook shot Owen another scathing look and then glowered at Virginia. "I think you've had a little too much champagne, Miss Dean."

Virginia ignored that. "If Mr. Sweetwater were to commit a lethal act, I am certain that he would not derive a thrill from the business."

"Certainly not a sexual thrill," Owen said, gravely polite. "I prefer to get that sort of thing in the normal manner."

TWENTY-EIGHT

"Well, that certainly put the cat amongst the pigeons," Charlotte observed. "For heaven's sake, Virginia, why did you not simply wear a large sign on the back of your gown tonight announcing that you were involved in a romantic liaison with Mr. Sweetwater?"

"I didn't think the sign would complement my dress," Virginia said.

Charlotte glared at her. "I am serious."

"Sorry," Virginia said. "I could not seem to help myself. It is not as though the rumors about my relationship with Mr. Sweetwater were not already circulating."

"Rumors of an affair are one thing. An outright declaration is quite another. Until tonight we could always hope that there were at least a few doubts about the nature of your relationship with Mr. Sweetwater. Leybrook looked furious. This could well destroy your career, Virginia."

"I'll survive. I do have one thing going for me."

"What?"

"My talent is genuine."

They were standing on the crowded front steps of

the Institute, waiting for Nick and Owen to return with the carriages. It was nearly midnight. In the glary illumination from the gas lamps that bracketed the entrance, the busy scene looked as if it had been rendered in chiaroscuro, all light and shadow. The street was jammed with carriages and hansoms hoping for fares.

"Your talent may be real, but you know as well as I do that the average client cannot tell the difference between a fraud and the real thing," Charlotte said. "The reason your business is flourishing is because of your connection to the Institute, not because you can actually read mirrors."

"I did manage to make a living before I joined the Institute," Virginia said.

"Yes, but you are earning far more now, thanks to Leybrook making this Institute fashionable."

"Trust me, I am aware of the current state of my finances."

"In any event, as if the damage to your reputation was not enough, Nick tells me that the entire exercise tonight has been wasted. He claims that any number of people appear to be obsessed with you, including Leybrook and Adriana." Charlotte paused. "For somewhat different reasons, of course."

"Nick? You are already so well acquainted with Nicholas Sweetwater that you refer to him by his first name?"

"It seemed the most convenient way to distinguish him from your Mr. Sweetwater," Charlotte said. "It was getting confusing."

"He's not my Mr. Sweetwater."

"Hah. That is no longer in doubt, thanks to your remarks to Adriana and Leybrook. Honestly, Ginny, what were you thinking?"

"I'm not sure I was thinking. I just did not care for the way Adriana was looking at Owen."

"Gentlemen do have a difficult time looking her in the eye when they converse with her. Their attention tends to wander south. My point is that she is a nasty piece of work. If she thinks you are a threat to her position with Leybrook, there's no telling what she might do."

"I did get the warning about both of them from Pamela's ancient Egyptian princess," Virginia said. "But I very much doubt that Leybrook would be happy with me as his assistant, and I do not think that Adriana would murder me just because she lost her position."

"I wouldn't place any wagers on the lovely Adriana, if I were you," Charlotte said. "That woman is a viper. I am convinced she could be dangerous."

A voice rose out of the crowd on the steps: "Miss Dean, Miss Dean, one moment, if you please."

Virginia turned to see Jasper Welch bustling toward her through the throng. She smiled. "Good evening, sir. I saw you earlier from across the room, but you appeared to be feverishly busy attending to D. D. Pinkerton."

"He was being practically ignored. Everyone was trying to chat with Leybrook." Welch came to a halt in front of her. "It was quite awkward, given that the reception was in Pinkerton's honor. I felt obliged to do something to smooth over the insult."

"It was very gracious of you," Charlotte assured him.

"It has been a difficult evening." Welch took out a

handkerchief and wiped his brow. "I am very glad it is over. There are always so many details to attend to, and something always seems to go wrong. Poor Mrs. Fordham was overwhelmed. The caterer ran out of lobster canapés midway through the evening, and she was forced to send for more champagne."

"You did a brilliant job, as always, Mr. Welch," Virginia assured him.

Charlotte smiled. "Yes, it was a beautifully planned affair, sir. I do not know what Mr. Leybrook would do without you. I'm sure the Institute would collapse, were it not for your expert management."

"I could not handle any of it if it were not for Mrs. Fordham," Welch said. "She is a wonder."

"Speaking of Mrs. Fordham, I did not see her tonight," Virginia said.

"She was very busy behind the scenes," Welch said. "The crowd was larger than we had anticipated. Miss Dean, the reason I wanted to speak to you was to apologize for the unpleasant gossip that is making the rounds."

"Idle chatter," Charlotte said firmly.

"And certainly not your fault, sir," Virginia added.

Deep furrows of concern lined Welch's brow. "Nevertheless, I am very sorry for any embarrassment you may have experienced tonight."

"I shall recover," Virginia assured him.

"Of course, of course." Welch inclined his head in a small bow. "Dear me, I see Mrs. Harkins is having some difficulty managing the steps with her cane. If you will excuse me?"

"Of course," Virginia said.

"Good evening, Mr. Welch," Charlotte added.

They watched Welch scurry off to assist the aging Mrs. Harkins, a venerable practitioner who conducted séances twice weekly on Wednesday and Friday nights.

"The woman may be suffering from rheumatism," Charlotte observed softly, "but she is still doing more business than most of her competitors. I hear that she recently raised her séance fees yet again, and now counts Lady Bingham among her regular clients."

"Yes, well, Mrs. Harkins is an American," Virginia said. "You know how it is, the act from out of town always draws the largest crowd."

Like many who specialized in summoning spirits, Mrs. Harkins had originally hailed from America. The rage for the paranormal had begun in the States decades earlier, and American mediums still commanded considerable attention from the British public.

Charlotte raised her brows. "How fortunate for Mr. Sweetwater that he did not choose to make an example of Mrs. Harkins when he set out to expose a couple of fraudulent mediums last month. She'd have made mincemeat of him."

Virginia laughed. "I'm sure he has no idea just how lucky he was." She watched Owen emerge from the chaotic tangle of horses, carriages and people milling about on the street. "Mrs. Harkins has been looking after herself and her career for a long time. She has dealt with more than one investigator who sought to expose her as a fraud. She made them all look like silly fools for questioning her talent."

Owen reached the top of the steps in time to hear the remark. He grinned.

"I'm not a complete idiot," he said. "When I set out to expose a few frauds, I chose very carefully, I assure you. Sally Harkins was not on my list."

"Very wise of you, sir," Charlotte said. "Legend has it that Mrs. Harkins punished the last investigator who tried to expose her by revealing the name of his current mistress to a correspondent from the *Flying Intelligencer.* The gentleman's wife was not at all pleased when the item appeared in the paper."

"I did some research," Owen said. "I was aware of that story." He surveyed the busy street. "Where is Nick?"

"Here," Nick said, materializing out of the crowd. "I finally found a carriage. The driver is waiting in the lane, Miss Tate."

"Our carriage is across the street," Owen said to Virginia. "Are you ready to leave?"

"As the evening has apparently been a complete waste of time in terms of the investigation, I suppose so," Virginia said. "Not that it hasn't had its moments, mind you."

There was a short round of polite farewells, and then Owen was steering her through the crowd. He had his hand clamped around her upper arm. He was not hurting her, but the manacle-like grip spoke volumes about his determination to get her away from the Institute.

"Is something wrong?" she asked.

"Aside from the fact that tonight I discovered that Gilmore Leybrook wants you as his mistress, do you mean?"

She flushed. "Don't waste any time worrying about Leybrook. I am quite capable of handling him."

"He is determined to have you, Virginia."

"Pamela Egan did say something to the effect that he may be shopping around for a new assistant. But I assure you I have no interest in the position. I prefer to control my own career. I have no wish to work as another practitioner's assistant."

"I am not referring to the opening for a new assistant. Leybrook wants you in a much more intimate position."

"Nonsense. You're overstating the case."

"I saw it in his eyes."

"He does have a very unpleasant history of conducting affairs with his assistants," she conceded. "Indeed, he is known to select them for very specific physical attributes. I'm quite certain I do not meet his specifications."

"I think he may have adjusted some of the specifications on his list."

She glanced at him, startled. "How odd. Pamela Egan said much the same thing. Just what is this new attribute that might move me to the top of Leybrook's list?"

"Your talent," Owen said. "He has sensed that it is real."

"What of it? He possesses some talent himself. I'm sure of it."

"Precisely. I believe he has concluded that with you by his side he can take his financial empire to even greater heights. It's a logical move, when you consider it closely. The Institute is already a profitable enterprise. But just think what two people of strong talent could do with the business."

"If Leybrook offers me the position Adriana now

holds, I will decline. I have no interest in entering into a partnership with him."

"Even if it means making a great deal more money than you do now?"

"Make no mistake, I am as ambitious as any other practitioner. But I have my own long-range plans. They do not include Leybrook."

"You say that, yet you are affiliated with the Institute," Owen pointed out.

"Temporarily. I did not say that I could not do business with Leybrook. But I would never enter into a close partnership of any kind with him."

"You make such fine distinctions?" Owen sounded intrigued, not dismissive or critical.

"A close partnership is like a marriage, sir," she said. "To be successful, there must be a great deal of trust on both sides."

"And you do not trust Leybrook?"

"Oh, I trust him," Virginia said. "I trust him to always do what he perceives to be in his own best interests. As long as I keep that in mind, he and I can get along together at the Institute. At the moment our financial interests are aligned, as Mrs. Crofton would say. But that will not always be the case."

At the base of the steps the hair suddenly stirred on the nape of her neck. Her intuition sent a sharp jolt of warning through all of her senses.

"Owen?" she began.

But he was already reacting, pulling her aside so quickly that she stumbled and would have fallen if he had not steadied her.

A figure in a hooded cloak swept past so close that

the edge of the cloak whipped against Virginia. A gloved hand lashed out, missing Virginia's shoulder by inches. She knew that if Owen had not yanked her out of the way, the cloaked figure would have shoved her down the long flight of granite steps.

It was all over in an instant. The cloaked figure slipped away into the throng. The crowd closed up, oblivious to what had occurred.

"Wait here," Owen ordered. "Don't move."

He started past her. She knew that he was going after the cloaked figure. She put out a hand to stop him.

"Owen, no," she said urgently.

To her surprise he stopped. His eyes burned. "She tried to push you down the steps."

"It was an impulsive act. She is not our killer."

"Impulse or not, if you had gone down those steps you could have broken your neck."

"There are a lot of people in the way. I'm sure they would have broken the fall. It is more likely that I would have twisted an ankle."

"Owen, Miss Dean, wait."

The sound of Nick's sharp, urgent voice came from the street. Virginia turned and saw him plowing a path through the crowd. He had a firm grip on Charlotte's hand, hauling her with him.

Owen watched the pair come quickly toward them.

"What did you see?" he asked Nick.

"I glanced back in this direction just as I was assisting Miss Tate into a cab. Saw a figure in a cloak push through the crowd. Her movements were very deliberate. It appeared that she was determined to get to Miss Dean. Thought maybe she wanted to have a word with her, but there was something about the way she was moving that did not seem right. Then I saw Miss Dean stumble."

"Someone brushed up against me," Virginia said. "It was an accident." But even as she spoke, she remembered the frisson of intuition that had seared her senses.

"The woman in the cloak tried to push Virginia down the steps," Owen said.

"Who was it?" Charlotte demanded. "Did you see her face?"

"No, but I saw her glove and her shoes," Virginia said. "It was Adriana Walters."

TWENTY-NINE

I am very certain that Adriana acted on impulse," Virginia said. "Nothing more."

Owen looked at her from the opposite seat of the carriage. In the shadows of the darkened cab it was impossible to read her face. "She hates you."

"She is seething because she fears Leybrook is going to let her go, and she blames me. I understand. But she is not the one who murdered Ratford and Hackett. You said yourself, the killer is a man."

"It does not follow that she is not linked to the killer," Owen said. A fever was simmering in him, but it was generated by frustration. It had not been easy to let Adriana escape.

Virginia hesitated. "Well, I suppose anything is possible, but my intuition tells me that Adriana is not involved in murder."

"Intuition is not always reliable."

"Think about it, Owen. If Adriana was in league with the killer, she would have had no reason to try to push me down the steps. Hurting me or even killing me in that manner would not have achieved the murderer's ends. He is using his victims to lay down energy in mirrors. That requires planning and preparation."

"She is dangerous, Virginia."

"She is a woman scorned. I will be careful around her."

"You should have let me go after her."

"For pity's sake, Owen, what on earth would you have done with her if I had let you catch her? She would have declared the whole thing an accident and pointed out that nothing bad happened. What proof would you have had to offer that the shove was deliberate? And all of this would have taken place in front of an audience of people who do not trust you. It would have been a fiasco."

He said nothing.

"Well?" Virginia said. "What could you have done?"

"Frightened her out of her wits."

There was a short, startled silence.

"Yes, well, you can be quite intimidating. I have no doubt but that you could have thrown a good scare into her."

"I meant literally," he said very softly. "It is part of my talent. I could have gone further. I could have frightened her to death."

"Oh." Virginia cleared her throat. "I see. Have you ever actually—"

"Yes."

"But only monsters."

"Yes."

"Adriana Walters may be a problem, but she is not one of the monsters."

"They hide in plain sight, Virginia. That is what makes them so bloody dangerous."

"Which is why you need proof before you take such

permanent action. You have no proof to use against Adriana."

Owen tapped his fingers against the seat and switched his attention to the street scene outside the window. "You're right, of course."

There was a long silence.

"I do appreciate that you have committed yourself to protecting me while you hunt for the killer," Virginia said after a while.

He turned his head to look at her. "I would walk into hell to keep you safe."

There was a short, shocked silence.

"Owen," she whispered.

Tension, desire and a lot of hot but unfocused energy shimmered invisibly in the atmosphere. He dragged the carriage curtains shut and reached for Virginia. He drew her toward him, opening his legs to make room for the waterfall of skirts and petticoats between his thighs.

"You cannot begin to guess how much I want you," he said.

He pushed back the hood of her cloak, caught her face between his hands and kissed her, hard and deeply.

She returned the kiss with sweet, feminine excitement. His blood was already running hot in his veins, a volatile brew of sexual desire seasoned with the fierce, elemental need to protect Virginia. The knowledge that she wanted him brought the temperature to the scalding point.

He released her face and slipped his hands beneath the folds of her cloak. He found the hooks of the bodice and began to undo them one by one. She clutched his shoulder and made a soft, urgent little sound.

"Damned bustle," he muttered a short time later. "How the devil do women manage with the things?"

Her laugh was soft, husky and sensual. "Carefully, Mr. Sweetwater. Very, very carefully."

He would have taken her there in the dark, intimate confines of the cab, the bustle be damned, but for the unfortunate fact that the drive to her town house was far too short for what he had in mind. Nevertheless he could not restrain his passions entirely. By the time the carriage halted in front of Number Seven, the interior of the cab was as humid and scented as an overheated stillroom filled with exotic herbs and mysterious spices.

Virginia's hair had come free of her tightly pinned chignon, and he had one hand inside the partially undone gown. His own clothing was also in disarray. His tie hung loose around his neck, the front of his waistcoat was open, and so was the collar of his shirt. He was as hard, if not harder, than he had ever been in his life, with the possible exception of the last time that he had made love to Virginia.

"It seems we have arrived," he said against her mouth. He moved his thumb over one delicate nipple.

"Already?" Virginia sounded breathless and a bit dazed. She slipped her hands out from under his shirt with obvious reluctance.

"Perhaps we might continue this very enlightening conversation concerning the progress of our investigation over a glass of brandy?" he suggested.

"Excellent notion."

He smiled and raised the hood of her cloak back up over her head to conceal her tousled hair. She pulled the folds of the garment around her to hide the unhooked bodice. An edgy anticipation aroused his senses like a potent drug.

Somehow he managed a reasonably dignified exit from the carriage. Virginia's hand trembled when he assisted her down to the pavement, but she appeared outwardly composed, as always.

He paid the driver and waved the vehicle on its way. The need to get Virginia into the house and out of her clothes was almost overpowering, but he took a moment to survey the darkened street, looking for shadows within shadows.

One particular shadow shifted in the front area below the steps of Number Seven. A hand appeared out of the darkness, waving enthusiastically.

Virginia stifled a small yelp and peered into the inky depths. "What in the world? There's a man down there."

"Good evening, Uncle Owen," Matt said.

"Where's Tony?" Owen asked.

"He's in the garden, watching the kitchen entrance," Matt said.

"You're both supposed to be in the attic of the empty house across the street, damn it," Owen said.

"This is closer to the muffins and the coffee, sir," Matt said.

"What muffins and coffee?"

Virginia looked at him. "Owen, who is this?"

"My apologies, Virginia. Allow me to introduce my nephew, Matthew Sweetwater. He and his brother have been keeping an eye on this house for several days. Matt is the one who told me that you had not returned from the Hollister mansion the other night. Matt, this is Miss Dean."

"A pleasure to meet you, ma'am," Matt said respectfully.

"Mr. Sweetwater," Virginia responded automatically. She looked at Owen. "You said you had put watchers on my house, but I didn't realize they were your nephews."

"Didn't I mention that?" He took the key from her hand and opened the front door. "Must have slipped my mind. I've been somewhat preoccupied lately. Matt, what did you mean about getting closer to the muffins and coffee?"

"The housekeeper came out onto the front steps earlier this evening and signaled to us."

"Oh, dear," Virginia said. "She *saw* you?"

"Mrs. Crofton is a very observant woman," Matt said. "We realized she had spotted us, so we crossed the street to introduce ourselves. She invited us in for muffins and coffee."

"So much for instructing you in stealth and camouflage," Owen said. "Keeping watch on this house was supposed to be part of your training."

"Did you tell Mrs. Crofton that you were guarding the house?" Virginia asked, very anxious now.

"Yes, ma'am," Matt said.

"She must have been horrified," Virginia said.

"She didn't seem horrified, ma'am," Matt said. "She left extra muffins and coffee in the kitchen for us after she went upstairs to bed. Gave us a key. Told us to make ourselves at home."

"She'll probably give notice in the morning," Virginia said. "I'm certain her previous employer did not have the sort of personal life that required men to watch her house."

"What's done is done," Owen said. He opened the door and urged Virginia into the hall. "Forget my nephews and your housekeeper."

"Easy for you to say. I'm sure, given the Sweetwater status and fortune, that you and your family don't have any problem obtaining good housekeepers."

Owen got the door closed. "No, we don't. Most of our staff have been with us for years. Their parents worked in our parents' households. The positions have descended down through the family."

"How convenient," she grumbled.

He peeled off his outer coat and hung it on a hook. "If you need a new housekeeper, I'll see that you get one. Now, if you don't mind, I have something else I'd rather discuss."

"What?"

"This."

He trapped her against the nearest wall, pushed back the hood of the cloak and kissed her until her eyes heated and she was once again breathless. Only then did he raise his head.

"Right," she said, her voice low and sultry. "We'll discuss my staffing problems some other time."

"Definitely some other time."

He scooped her up, the skirts of her gown and the frothy petticoats spilling over his arms. Angling her so that she would not bang her head or her knees against the wall, he carried her down the dimly lit hall and into the study.

The curtains were drawn across the window, casting the room in deep shadow. The only light was the narrow wedge of illumination that came from the sconce in the hall.

He set Virginia on her feet and turned up one of the lamps so that it burned very low. He closed and locked the door, intensely aware of the flaring heat in his veins. When he looked back at Virginia she smiled. Her eyes were fathomless pools of promise. She did not say a word, but the energy of her desire flashed invisibly in the atmosphere.

She stepped out of her dainty evening shoes, raised her hands and undid the strings that bound her cloak at her throat. The thick woolen folds fell away, revealing her disordered clothing. He caught his breath.

"Virginia," he whispered. For a moment he could only look at her. Everything inside him tightened with longing.

He shrugged out of his evening coat, removed his waistcoat and dropped both over the arm of the nearest chair. He went to stand behind Virginia. Setting his hands on her shoulders, he bent his head and kissed the side of her throat. He felt a tiny shiver sweep through her.

Gently he eased the cloak off her shoulders and tossed it aside. He took down her hair. She was so soft and delicate. His own body was hard and tight, making him feel clumsy and awkward. The soft *pings* that sounded when he put the hairpins on the mantel seemed very loud in the shadows.

He turned her around to face him. Slowly, deliberately, he finished the task of unfastening the stiffly boned top of her gown. The bodice separated and fell away, revealing the gentle feminine curves underneath. He stripped the tight sleeves to her wrists and eased the rest of her clothing away until she stood before him, wearing only her chemise and stockings.

He fitted his hands to her waist, lifted her free of the heap of skirts and petticoats and set her back on her feet. She unfastened the remaining buttons of his shirt and flattened her palms against his bare chest. The touch of her hands made his temperature climb even higher.

"I love the feel of you," she whispered.

She kissed his jaw and then his shoulder. Her mouth was wet and warm, thrilling all of his senses.

"I can't take much more of that," he warned her.

She raised her head and smiled a devastatingly mysterious smile. Her eyes were brilliant with feminine power.

"I don't believe that," she said. "Not for a minute. You are always in control, Owen Sweetwater."

"That was mostly true, I think, until I met you."

He kissed her, a short, hard kiss that was fueled by the edgy urgency crackling through him. Then he turned away and picked up her cloak. He unfurled it with a sharp, snapping movement of his hand and let it fall on the carpet in front of the fireplace. The thick woolen folds spread out and fluttered to the floor, forming a makeshift bed.

He got rid of his boots, his trousers and drawers. When he turned back to Virginia he saw that she was staring at him in consternation. At first he thought she was transfixed by his erection. He did not know whether to be flattered, amused or worried.

"Is that a knife you have strapped to your ankle?" she said, and gasped.

He looked down at the leather sheath, chagrined. She had not noticed it the first time because he had made love to her without removing his trousers.

"Sorry," he said. "I tend to forget about it."

"How could you possibly forget a knife strapped to your ankle?"

"I have worn it since I was a boy. All Sweetwater men do. It's the family motto."

She raised her brows. "Just what sort of motto would that be?"

"Talent is useful, but always keep your dagger sharp."

"Not the usual family motto. But, then, I'm getting the impression that the Sweetwaters are not an ordinary family."

"That's not true," he said. "The Sweetwaters are really a very normal sort of family."

He unfastened the knife sheath and left it conveniently at hand. This time, when he looked at her he saw that she was, indeed, gazing at his erection.

"Is it always like that?" she asked.

His laugh came out as a groan.

"Only when I am near you," he said.

He knelt on the cloak and drew her down onto her knees in front of him. She reached out and took him in her hands, exploring him intimately. He closed his eyes briefly, his jaw clenching against the surging need that pulsed through him.

"I'm desperate for you," he said, aware that his voice was raw with need.

"You stir the most astonishing desire in me," she whispered. "I have never known anything like it."

"Then we are well matched."

He tightened his arms around her and kissed her, letting her feel the full force of his need. When she sighed and sank against him, her breasts pillowed against his chest, he moved his hand between her thighs. She was damp and slick, and wonderfully full to the touch. He stroked her carefully, seeking out the sensitive hidden places.

When he inserted a finger deep inside her she cried out and dropped her forehead against his shoulder. He felt her body draw tighter. Deliberately he inserted a second finger.

She gasped. Her small, delicate muscles closed even more securely around him. She released his heavy erection and clutched his forearms.

"Now relax," he whispered.

"I don't want to," she said into his shoulder. "I like it this way."

"You'll like it even better if you do as I say. I give you my word. Relax."

Her narrow passage loosened almost imperceptibly. He withdrew his fingers partway.

"Now hold me as if you'll never let me go." He pushed back into her.

She tightened snugly around him again. Another tremor went through her. She was very wet now. He breathed in the scent of her body.

"Yes," he said. "Like that."

He removed his fingers partway and eased his thumb up under the taut little bud of her clitoris until she strained against him. Then he penetrated her again with his fingers.

"You are as tight as a handmade glove," he said.

He hooked his fingers a little so that he could press them more firmly against the sensitive area just inside her hot channel. Then he slowly started to withdraw.

"No," she gasped, and tightened abruptly, trying to keep him inside. "Don't stop."

"I have no intention of stopping. Relax."

She did but just barely. She had the pattern of the dance now, and she was taking control, alternately clenching and releasing as he eased his fingers in and out of her. With each stroke he dragged his half-curled fingers against the roof of her passage, pressing harder and harder.

"Yes," she said. Her voice rose to a faint squeak. "*Yes.*"

He knew she was hovering on the precipice. He felt the sudden release of the tension deep inside her and sensed the onset of the small convulsions even before she did.

Her lips parted. He covered her mouth quickly with his own to swallow the sound of her climax. Her fingers dug into his arms.

He let her ride the currents, glorying in the knowledge that he was the one who had sent her soaring. When the small tremors started to ease, he pushed her onto her back, fitted himself to her and plunged deep.

"Owen," she managed. "*Owen.*"

He was beyond any coherent response, beyond the boundaries of his own control. He no longer cared.

He thrust in and out of her, his senses dazzled by the energy of their hot auras.

And then he, too, was poised on the high cliffs above the deep, mysterious waters. His release slammed through him, taking him over the edge. Virginia cried out softly again. Another rush of energy rippled through her.

It seemed to him that they fell together, their auras fused in a moment of searing intimacy. When the last of the shuddering waves faded he opened his eyes and looked down at Virginia's flushed face. She was watching him with a strangely intent expression.

Do you feel it? he wanted to ask. *Do you sense this bond between us?*

He rolled onto his back, taking her with him. She sprawled across his damp chest. He wrapped her close, indulging his exhausted senses in her warmth and the soft, vital weight of her body.

He let himself drift into the hazy place that marked the indefinable border between the dream state and the waking state. It was a good place, a fine place. He could not remember ever having been in a better place. He wanted to stay there until morning.

THIRTY

They called him Wolf because he was as fast and as savage as any beast of prey. He had bestowed the nickname on himself while still in his teens, when he had realized that he possessed senses that the other street boys did not have. No one had dared object.

His talent had served him well. Over the years he had acquired a brutal reputation that was the envy of his colleagues. He was known and feared on the dark streets of London's underworld.

Until recently he'd made a comfortable living taking care of problems for one of the city's most powerful crime lords. Luttrell had appreciated his talents and paid well for his services.

But all good things must come to an end, Wolf reflected. Luttrell had been killed recently by another crime lord, Griffin Winters. Luttrell's demise had thrown the always delicate balance of power in the underworld into disarray. To further complicate matters, Winters himself had sold off his operations and vanished. Some said he was no longer even in London. No one knew where he had gone, but one thing was certain. Until the surviving crime lords got things sorted out among themselves, hardworking men like Wolf were on their own, obliged to make their livings by hiring out their services to whatever clients came their way.

Business had not been what anyone would call brisk lately. When the small man who called himself Mr. Newton had approached him outside of a tavern last night and offered a job, Wolf had accepted without asking too many questions.

He waited now in the deep shadows of the graveyard one street over from Garnet Lane. If he had calculated correctly, Sweetwater would pass this way when he left the Dean woman's town house.

The anticipation of the kill sparked an intoxicating excitement. All of his senses were heightened, but he was not yet making any attempt to focus. For the moment, he simply savored the darkness and the prospect of what was to come. It had been a while since anyone had hired him to kill a man, but he knew he hadn't lost his lightning-fast reflexes.

As if in response to his own flaring energy, the handle of the strange mirror that the odd little client had given him seemed to grow warmer in his hand. He doubted that he needed the device, but Mr. Newton had been very insistent.

"He's a talent of some kind," Newton said. "I don't know what sort, but I'm certain he's strong. There must be no mistakes. You will not take any chances."

"I can handle myself."

"I'm not worried about you," Newton said. "I just want to ensure that you are successful. Use the mirror in exactly the way I described. It's dangerous."

Although the graveyard was shrouded in darkness Wolf was careful not to look down at the mirror. He had made that mistake the first time he had removed it from the black velvet bag, although he had been warned.

"Have a care when you handle the artifact," Newton said. "It responds readily to psychical energy. It is best not to look directly into the glass, but if you must, be certain to keep your senses lowered. It requires a great deal of talent to control the Quicksilver Mirror."

But Wolf's curiosity had got the better of him. He had removed the mirror from the sack and looked into it with his talent slightly elevated. He shuddered, remembering the dazzling energy that had temporarily blinded his senses. He did not want to speculate on what might have happened if the client had not come to his rescue.

"Fool," Newton said, yanking the mirror out of Wolf's hand. "I warned you. Too much of that energy and you will destroy your own senses permanently. The object of the exercise is to blind Sweetwater to ensure that he cannot use his talent against you. When you have dealt with Sweetwater you will return the mirror to me."

Wolf had been more careful after that. If the Quicksilver Mirror worked as advertised he had no intention of returning it to Newton. The relic might come in handy in the future. It would give him an edge against his rivals. In London's underworld there was always plenty of competition.

THIRTY-ONE

Owen felt Virginia stir in his arms. She gently pried herself free from his grasp. He let her go. The room immediately grew colder. Reluctantly he opened his eyes and looked up at her.

"It's getting late," she whispered.

"I know."

He levered himself up on one elbow and watched her get to her feet. Her hair was wildly tousled. Her stockings had come free of the garters and were draped around her ankles. The top of the chemise was crumpled at her waist. Her face and breasts were still flushed. He felt his senses stir.

"You look delicious," he said. "Good enough to eat. I believe I'm working up an appetite."

"There will probably be some muffins left in the kitchen," she said very seriously. She pulled the chemise up over her breasts. "Unless your nephews ate all of them."

He smiled and got to his feet. "I had another dish in mind. But it's getting late. You need your sleep."

She glanced at the tall clock in the corner. "Good heavens, it's nearly two o'clock in the morning. Your nephews will be wondering what is going on."

He fastened the front of his shirt, taking his time. "If either of them asks any questions, which I very much doubt, I will tell them that we were discussing the case."

"I dread facing Mrs. Crofton in the morning." Virginia leaned down to strip off her stockings. "I shall be lucky to get breakfast before she gives notice. She has been remarkably tolerant of the eccentricities of this household, but the business of bodyguards watching the house will be too much for her."

He reached for his trousers. "You know, Virginia, it is probably not a sound idea to go about in fear of your housekeeper."

"I'm not afraid of her." Virginia straightened and stepped into the center of the pool of fabric formed by her discarded gown. "Well, perhaps I am, in a manner of speaking."

"Why?"

"Don't you understand? No, you probably don't." Virginia inserted her arms into the sleeves of the dress and concentrated intently on doing up the hooks of the bodice. "If Mrs. Crofton goes back to the Billings Agency to seek another position, she will naturally inform Mrs. Billings of the rather odd goings-on around here. Mrs. Billings takes great pride in making certain her people are sent only to *respectable* employers. I suspect that after all that has happened here lately I will no longer qualify."

He thought about that while he secured the knife sheath to his ankle and got his trousers closed. He fastened his waistcoat with quick, practiced motions and pulled on his low boots. When he was dressed he crossed the room to stand in front of her.

"Is respectability that important to you?" he asked.

She raised her chin. "My father was a gentleman who kept his glass-reader mistress in the shadows. I have lived my entire life with the stain of illegitimacy. I am burdened with a talent for perceiving the most unwholesome afterimages in mirrors. That is not exactly a fashionable or ladylike skill. I make my living in a way that Arcane, the one organization that should accept and understand my psychical nature, finds disreputable." She fastened the last hook of her gown and dropped her hands. "Yes, Owen, respectability is important to me."

He caught her chin on the edge of his hand. "I grew up in a family that does not concern itself overmuch with the outward appearance of respectability. But the Sweetwaters do care a great deal about honor and courage and strength of will. It is how we have survived. Those qualities are what bind us together as a family."

She smiled. "I do not doubt that."

"You are endowed with all of those attributes that Sweetwaters hold dear. I would trust you with my life and my secrets."

She went still. "Truly?"

"Truly." He brushed his mouth across her parted lips and straightened. "Speaking of family secrets, I have revealed a number of them to you. Which leaves me with only one safe alternative."

"What is that?"

"You must marry me, of course."

Her mouth fell open. "What?"

"Otherwise I shall have to spend the rest of my life worrying that you will reveal all of the dark Sweetwater secrets to some other man."

"What?"

"I'm teasing you, of course. This is not the time to discuss our marriage plans. It is late, and you must go to bed."

He released her, picked up his black evening coat and headed for the door.

"Owen, wait."

"We will finish this conversation some other time," he promised. He unlocked the door and moved out into the shadowed hall, smiling a little when he heard the quick patter of her bare feet behind him.

"You cannot just run off like this," she hissed urgently. "Explain yourself, sir."

He opened the front door and paused long enough to steal one last kiss.

"There is nothing more to explain, when you get right down to it," he said. "I am asking you to marry me. I can only hope that you will say yes."

"Damn it, Owen—"

He went out into the night. She started to pursue him and then evidently thought better of it when her bare feet touched the cold stone of the step. She moved back into the hall.

The shadows shifted down in the front area.

"I'm leaving now, Matt," Owen said. "I expect you and Tony to take excellent care of Miss Dean."

"Yes, sir," Matt said cheerfully.

"Mr. Sweetwater," Virginia snapped, her tone excruciatingly formal. "You can't just leave like this. I have questions for you."

"Another time, Miss Dean," he said. "Don't forget to lock the door."

Virginia said something indistinct in a very low voice and closed the door with considerably more force than was necessary.

He listened for the rasp of iron on iron that told him Virginia had turned the key in the lock. When he heard it he went down the steps to the pavement.

"Uncle Owen?" Matt called softly.

He stopped. "Yes?"

"She's the one, isn't she? The woman everyone in the family says you've been waiting for."

"Yes," Owen said. "But I would take it as a favor if you don't mention that to Miss Dean."

"Why not?"

"Because she doesn't understand that, not entirely. Not yet. I'm trying to break it to her gently. She needs time to become accustomed to the notion of marriage to me."

"No offense, sir, but judging by the tone of her voice just now, I don't think you're doing a very good job of explaining the situation."

"What do you expect? It's the first time I've tried to do so."

"You mustn't hit her over the head with it. Women like to be romanced like the heroines in the sensation novels."

"What the devil do you know about sensation novels?"

"A man can learn a great deal about women from novels," Matt said. "You should try it sometime."

THIRTY-TWO

Owen went to the end of the street and rounded the corner into the narrow lane that bordered the graveyard. The gas lamps were few and far between now, but he scarcely noticed the deeper darkness. His senses were slightly elevated, as they always were when he walked the night. He registered the small sounds and the shifts in the shadows around him without consciously thinking about it.

The hunter in him was on the prowl, searching for the spoor of the monsters, but he was aware that something was different tonight. He did not feel driven by the relentless compulsion that had been riding him so hard in the past year. The obsessive need to hunt had faded to a normal level or, rather, a level that felt normal for a Sweetwater. The men of his line would never be wholly civilized, he thought. But it was good to regain a sense of balance and perspective, good to be able to ignore, for now, at any rate, the terrible allure of the abyss of night that had been calling to him for months.

And, yes, it was good to feel this pleasantly euphoric, if unfamiliar, sense of well-being. Virginia had given him back his future, although she did not realize it yet.

Virginia. She was his talisman. The bond between them gave him the power not only to resist the dark forces that had been drawing him toward the edge but to control them once more.

He had to admit that Matt had a point, though. *I'm botching the job of explaining the Sweetwater bond to her.*

He would have to come up with a better way of making sure that she understood their relationship. Although when he thought about the situation closely he could not comprehend the exact nature of the problem. Virginia was obviously attracted to him. There could be no doubt about the depths of their mutual passion. She was as warm and sweet as melted honey in his arms. Women were supposed to be especially sensitive to powerful emotions. Where the devil was he going wrong?

He sensed the faint shift in the atmosphere between one step and the next, a subtle whisper of heightened energy. The hunter in him pricked up his senses. There was another strong talent abroad tonight, close at hand.

He did not change his pace. He was too experienced to give any outward indication that he had picked up the telltale signals of the other's presence. Nevertheless, his senses flashed into full strength. He knew he was giving off a lot of hot energy. If the other sensitive was paying attention, he or she would surely realize that there was another talent in the vicinity.

It was not uncommon to encounter a stranger on the street who possessed a measurable degree of talent. But passing someone who was unusually powerful was a relatively rare experience. There were not that many high-level talents around. He could not afford to assume that this encounter was a coincidence, not when it was taking place so close to Virginia's address.

He studied the lane without appearing to do so. There was no one else visible. That meant that the other talent was probably concealed behind one of the ancient stone monuments or in the crypt up ahead.

The crypt, he decided. *That's the place I would choose for an ambush.*

He kept walking, waiting for his quarry to leap out of the shadows. He heard the faint rush of movement from the yawning darkness of the crypt a few heartbeats before the figure swept toward him. The preternatural speed and the certainty with which the attacker moved in the darkness told him everything he needed to know. He was dealing with a strong hunter-talent.

Although he was not a true hunter when it came to his physical abilities, he understood their nature and their talent, having grown up in a family littered with the breed. When they were in their full senses, their night vision was excellent and they moved with the speed and agility of wolves. He could not hope to match his attacker in those attributes, but he was not without resources. The critical thing was to make certain the other man did not get close enough to use his greater speed and strength against him.

He was prepared for the swiftness of the other man's movements. It was like confronting a charging wolf. What he did not expect was the blinding flash of paranormal fire.

It was as if a paranormal sun had struck a mirror. The night burned around him, searing his senses. He was engulfed in a blinding radiance.

His heart pounded. A terrible chill spread through his veins, icing his blood. He fell, landing hard on his hands and knees. It was all he could do not to collapse on the cold pavement.

He knew then that he was dying.

"Virginia," he whispered. The thought of never seeing her again was intolerable, but far worse was the knowledge that he was leaving her in grave danger. He had failed her.

"Virginia," he said again, louder this time.

It seemed to him that the cold brilliance faded ever so slightly around him, as if the simple act of saying Virginia's name had temporarily driven back the forces that had blinded him psychically and were now killing him.

The unnatural radiance moved closer to him. Although his paranormal abilities were gone, he realized he could still make out the crypt and the gravestones to his left. He could feel the pavement beneath his hands. He could hear the echo of the killer's boots on the pavement. He was rapidly losing his strength, but he still had his normal senses.

"My client wants you dead, Sweetwater." The voice came from the darkness beyond the senses-dazzling light. "But there is no great rush. I haven't had a job like this in a while. I'm going to take my time."

"Who hired you?" Owen managed.

"He called himself Newton, but I doubt that's his real name. Seemed to know a lot about you, though. He said you're a talent. Told me where I could find you. He knew all about your whore in Garnet Lane, you see."

"He gave you that device you used to blind me?"

"He called it the Quicksilver Mirror. Told me it was valuable and that he'd want it back as soon as I finished with you. But between you and me, I plan to keep it. Right handy, it is."

"Did he tell you why he wants me dead?"

"Doesn't seem to like you very much. I got the impression that you're standing in the way of something he wants."

Owen felt himself growing colder. His vision and hearing started to dim. The energy of the mirror was affecting his normal senses now.

"He gave you the mirror because he knew you couldn't take me with just your talent alone," he said.

"That's a bloody damn lie." Outraged by the insult, the hunter moved closer. "I could kill you before you take another breath. I don't need this mirror to finish you off."

Owen gathered what was left of his strength. It took almost everything he had, but he managed to move his hand back to his ankle. His fingers touched the sheath strapped to his leg.

"You're burning a lot of energy keeping that mirror hot," he rasped. "You're exhausting your talent."

"Unlike you, I've got plenty to spare," the hunter snarled.

The paranormal brilliance was definitely fainter now. The hunter did not realize how much energy he was using to wield the mirror. He was too excited, too focused on the thrill of the kill. Emotions were always the enemy when it came to this sort of thing, Owen thought.

"You're definitely weakening," Owen said. "You won't be able to finish this."

"Let's find out," the hunter growled.

The blinding paranormal radiance flashed once more, sending another searing wave of energy across Owen's senses. In the next instant the terrible light winked out like a gas lamp that had been turned down.

"Damn thing is broken," the hunter said. "But I told you, I don't need it."

"Not broken. You don't have enough strength left to focus it."

"*Bastard.* I'll show you who is weak."

The hunter hurled the mirror aside. It clanged on the paving stones. Owen was vaguely aware that he did not hear the sound of glass breaking, but there was no time to analyze the implications.

The hunter rushed toward him, moonlight glinting on the knife in his hand. He was not nearly as fast as he had been at the start of the confrontation. He had used too much energy controlling the paranormal weapon. But he was still quick and savage, still enraged.

Freed of the pressure of the mirror, Owen could breathe freely again. But when he tried to heighten his talent he got no response.

He yanked the knife out of the ankle sheath. The hunter reached for him, intending to lock him in a choke hold and secure him for the killing slash across the throat.

Owen twisted onto his side, managing just barely to

avoid the hunter's hand. He brought the knife up in the same instant, felt it sink deep into flesh.

The hunter grunted, recovering his balance with startling speed, and leaped back. The quick action caused him to pull free of the knife. Blood gushed forth from his chest.

For a split second, the hunter did not seem to comprehend what had happened. He looked down at the blood spraying out of his body, and then he raised his head to stare at Owen.

"No," he said. "No, it's not possible. You're not a hunter."

"You should not have called her a whore," Owen said softly. "In my family we do not allow anyone to insult our women."

The hunter stared, horrified and bewildered, for another second. He crumpled to the pavement.

Dragging in a lungful of air, Owen called on what was left of his resources to haul himself to his feet. It took just about everything he had left to stagger the short distance to the body. He knew before he checked for a pulse that the hunter was dead, but he crouched down and put his fingers on the man's throat. When it came to their work, Sweetwaters were always thorough.

He heard the others in the lane, but his head was spinning now. He tried to focus. One man, he decided, moving very fast, *hunter-fast.*

"Uncle Owen, are you all right?" Matt stopped at the sight of the body. "What happened?"

Alarm slashed through Owen. "You left Virginia alone?"

"What? No, sir, of course not. Tony is with her. She couldn't keep up with us, so they sent me on ahead. They'll be along any moment now."

"What the devil? You allowed her out of the house?"

"Couldn't stop her, sir. She said you were in terrible danger. Said we had to find you. Insisted on coming with us. He looked at the body. "Who is this?"

"Hunter-talent. Someone named Newton gave him a commission to kill me."

"Bloody hell." Matt surveyed him with concern. "Looks like he came close. Are you all right?"

Owen ignored the question. He was on the verge of passing out. He had to stay focused awhile longer.

"Make sure you get the weapon," he said.

"What weapon?"

"I don't know what it is. Never got a good look at it. He called it the Quicksilver Mirror. I heard him drop it on the pavement."

Owen turned to search the darkened street. The small movement cost him his balance. A great gray fog was enveloping his mind. He would have gone down to his knees if Matt hadn't caught his arm.

With Matt's help he made his way the short distance to the weapon. It resembled a lady's hand mirror of the sort one might see on a dressing table. It was lying facedown on the paving stones. He started to lean over to pick it up and spotted the black velvet bag nearby.

"Hand me that sack," he said.

Matt scooped up the bag and gave it to him. Owen crouched and gingerly picked up the mirror. He thought he felt a faint shiver of energy when his fingers closed around the handle, but his mind was so muddled now and his senses so unresponsive that he could not be certain. Careful to keep the glass aimed downward, he inserted the artifact into the velvet sack and tightened the strip of leather that bound it shut.

He reeled again when he tried to get to his feet. More footsteps sounded in the lane. He turned his head very cautiously, afraid he might humiliate himself by fainting dead away. His vision blurred, but he saw two people running toward him. Well, Virginia was running, he thought. Tony was loping casually alongside.

"Owen." Virginia rushed forward. "Are you all right?"

"Yes," he said automatically. Then he realized that was not true. "No."

"What?"

"Never mind." He thrust the velvet bag into her hand. "Take this. It's a weapon of some kind, a looking glass. The nature of your talent means that you are probably more qualified to handle it than any of the rest of us. But be very, very careful. It has blinded my senses, perhaps permanently."

"*No,*" she said. "They will revive."

He smiled a little at her fierceness and opened his arms to fold her close. But the black night closed in and began to seep through him.

Somewhere in the darkness he heard Virginia calling his name, speaking to him in that same bracing tone.

"I will not let you go, Owen Sweetwater. Do you hear

THIRTY-THREE

D o you think Uncle Owen's psychic blindness will be permanent, Miss Tate?" Tony asked.

"I have no way of knowing," Charlotte said. She closed the heavy volume she had been reading and glanced uneasily at the black velvet bag on top of the chest of drawers. "According to my research, the Quicksilver Mirror is capable of blinding the senses permanently and even causing death. The power of the device, however, is directly related to the psychical strength of the person who wields it. The stronger the talent, the more radiation the mirror emits. Conversely, the amount of permanent damage that is done to the victim's senses depends on how strong the victim is, psychically speaking."

"Owen will recover," Virginia said. She tightened her grip on his hand. "He is strong. I can feel his energy. He just needs time to heal, that's all."

They were crowded into her small bedroom. Owen was tucked into the bed. Matt and Tony had placed him there after carrying him back from the lane. He was in a profound but restless sleep. Mrs. Crofton had decreed that he be covered with only a sheet because he was feverishly hot. Virginia knew that the fever was psychical in origin, a result of the severe injury that had been done to his senses.

She had not let go of him since he had collapsed, unconscious. She dared not let go. She sensed that the link between them was his best hope. Her intuition told her that he was drawing on her strength to mend his shattered senses.

She had dispatched Matt to fetch Charlotte with instructions to bring all of the books on mirrors that were housed in the bookshop. They needed to know more about the strange hand mirror. Nick Sweetwater had arrived with Charlotte and the books. Virginia had been startled to see the two of them together at that hour of the night, but there had been no time to ask questions.

Mrs. Crofton loomed in the doorway, a steaming mug in her hand. "I have made a pot of coffee, as I doubt that any of you will get much sleep tonight." She looked at Virginia with her usual forbidding expression. "I brought some upstairs for you, ma'am, because I knew you would not be leaving this room for a time."

Virginia smiled. "Thank you, Mrs. Crofton. I appreciate that."

Mrs. Crofton dipped her chin in minimal acknowledgment of the gratitude and set the mug on the nightstand. She looked at Owen.

"He is still feverish," she said. "I'll bring some more cold washcloths."

"Thank you," Virginia said again.

Mrs. Crofton turned and stalked out of the room.

Nick watched her leave. He was clearly awed. When she was on the stairs, he turned back to Virginia. "Your housekeeper is extraordinary. You have two men guarding your house. You rush off into the night with no explanation. You bring an unconscious man into your bedroom and invite several people to join you. And yet she shows no signs of being alarmed."

"As I have told Owen, Mrs. Crofton is a gem of a housekeeper," Virginia said. "But I fully expect her to give notice at any moment."

"She doesn't appear to be about to do any such thing," Nick said. He turned back to Charlotte. "Is there anything more about the effects of the Quicksilver Mirror in that book?"

"Only that the device was crafted in the seventeenth century by an alchemist."

Nick frowned. "That means it dates from the time of Sylvester Jones. I wonder if he made it."

"I don't think he had anything to do with it," Charlotte said. "According to this book, the alchemist was a woman who called herself Alice Hooke." Charlotte took off her glasses and polished the lenses with a handkerchief. "The only reason I was able to find out as much as I did concerning the history of the mirror in such a short time this evening is because I had already done a considerable amount of research on the subject of looking glasses."

Virginia glanced at the black velvet bag. "Another mirror has popped up in this case. That cannot be a coincidence."

Nick looked thoughtful. "I agree with you. It is too much to believe that yet another powerful weapon based on glasslight would show up in this investigation unless there was some connection. But the Quicksilver Mirror is quite different from the curiosities. It is much older, for one thing."

"And is not a clockwork toy," Virginia said.

Charlotte tapped the large leather-bound tome she had been reading. "The mirror is much older, so we know it was not made by Mrs. Bridewell. But I agree, there must be some link to the case."

Nick frowned. "The mirror is a dangerous and no doubt valuable artifact, yet someone entrusted it to a common street ruffian to use against Owen this evening. Someone was very desperate to get him out of the way."

"Well," Charlotte said, "I'm afraid all we can do at the moment is wait and see if Mr. Sweetwater is strong enough to recover from the effects of the mirror."

"He will recover," Virginia vowed.

"We might have a better notion of his chances if we had some idea of just how strong the attacker was," Charlotte said.

"We have no way of knowing that now that he is dead," Tony said.

"He was certainly powerful enough to do serious damage with the damn mirror," Nick said grimly.

Virginia gave him a sharp, reproving glare. "The one thing we know for certain is that Owen defeated him. That means Owen is the stronger of the two."

Nick, Tony and Matt exchanged glances. None of them spoke.

"What is it?" Virginia demanded. "What's wrong? Why are you looking at each other that way?"

Nick cleared his throat. "We don't really know that Uncle Owen was the stronger in terms of talent, Miss Dean, not for certain."

"What do you mean?" she said. "He is the one who survived the encounter."

"But he used a knife," Tony said, as if explaining a very elementary principle to a not-very-bright child. "Not his talent. The mirror rendered his psychical senses useless."

Virginia frowned. "What are you saying?"

"Just that Uncle Owen did not survive because of his talent," Matt said.

"I see," Virginia whispered. She tightened her grip on Owen's hand.

Nick looked at the unconscious man. "He is a hunter of a sort, but he is not a true hunter-talent like Tony or Matt. His reflexes, eyesight and coordination are excellent but not preternaturally so."

"Is that why he carries a knife concealed in his boot?" Charlotte asked.

"No," Tony said. "He carries a knife in his boot because all Sweetwaters carry knives in their boots."

"Used to be a dagger," Matt offered. "But we have moved with the times."

"Family tradition," Nick explained. "In keeping with the family motto."

"Talent is useful, but keep your dagger sharp," Virginia quoted softly.

"It sounds better in the original Latin," Tony said.

Virginia gave him a weary smile. "No doubt."

"Owen's great talent is his ability to predict the behavior of the monsters," Nick explained. "Not his speed or his night vision."

Charlotte looked at him. "I can't see how the ability to predict the killer's behavior would have been enough tonight. I mean, he already knew that the footpad was trying to kill him."

"You'd be surprised," Nick said. "Owen has a knack for provoking people. He says that if a man can be prodded into losing his self-control, he can be manipulated quite easily, regardless of the level of his talent. I suspect that is exactly what happened tonight."

Tony looked at Owen. "It does appear that Uncle Owen sliced things a bit close, so to speak, on this occasion, however."

Virginia shivered. "Yes."

"Usually he leaves no trace of violence," Matt said. "But there was a lot of blood in the lane tonight. At first I feared that at least some of it was his."

Virginia shuddered at the memory of the blood on Owen's hands and clothes. "So did I."

"Do you believe that Mr. Sweetwater deliberately provoked his attacker into some reckless move?" Charlotte asked.

"Uncle Owen has a gift for shattering nerves," Tony said proudly.

Virginia looked at Owen. His profound state of sleep did little to soften the hard planes and angles of his face. Even unconscious, he managed to appear dangerous. His psychical senses had been blinded, but dark energy nevertheless whispered in the atmosphere around him.

"His aura no doubt unnerves some people," Virginia said.

"Perhaps that is the reason he has never married," Charlotte said.

Virginia realized that the three Sweetwater men were exchanging yet another mysterious look.

"What now?" she demanded.

Nick cleared his throat. "The reason Owen has never married is because he has yet to find the right woman."

Charlotte blinked and then smiled. "What a charmingly romantic notion."

"I'm not certain Sweetwaters can be called charmingly romantic," Nick said. "But we take marriage very seriously. You could say it's in the blood. A Sweetwater always knows when he finds the right woman."

Charlotte stopped smiling and narrowed her eyes. "How very convenient."

"Actually it can be very inconvenient," Nick said. "It isn't always easy to find the right woman. To tell you the truth, the family was starting to become concerned about Owen."

"Why?" Virginia asked.

Tony shifted uneasily. "We think he has started nightwalking. It's not a good sign."

"I don't understand," Virginia said. "What do you mean by nightwalking?"

Once again Nick, Tony and Matt exchanged looks. This time she knew she would not get any answers.

"It's hard to explain," Nick mumbled.

Charlotte fixed him with a glare. "What does a Sweetwater man do if he doesn't find the right woman? Does he content himself with a string of mistresses?"

Nick was looking ever more uncomfortable. Matt and Tony had evidently concluded they were out of their depth. They lurched toward the door.

"I think I need a cup of Mrs. Crofton's excellent coffee," Tony said.

"And perhaps another muffin," Matt added.

They went through the door and disappeared out into the hall.

An acute silence settled on the bedroom.

Charlotte peered at Nick. "Exactly how does a Sweetwater know when the right woman comes along?"

Nick blew out a deep sigh. "My father says it is a side effect of our talent. Something to do with our hunter's intuition."

Virginia looked at him. "But not necessarily something to do with love?"

The hunter in Nick must have sensed a trap. He glanced toward the door, as if longing to escape the room as Matt and Tony had done. But manfully he turned back.

"'Love' is a rather mushy word," he said weakly. "Hard to define, don't you think?"

Charlotte glared at him. "Not at all. One knows love when one experiences it. Isn't that right, Ginny?"

"Quite right," Virginia agreed. "We may never encounter true love, but that does not mean that women such as Charlotte and myself won't know it if we do run into it. Right, Charlotte?"

"Absolutely," Charlotte said.

Nick scowled. "But what will you do if you never discover what you believe to be true love?"

"Until then, there is always Dr. Spinner's treatment for female hysteria," Virginia said.

THIRTY-FOUR

Sometime later Virginia found herself alone with Owen in the bedroom. His temperature and the overheated energy of his aura were rapidly returning to normal.

She released his hand. Rising to her feet, she crossed the room to the chest of drawers. The velvet sack containing the mirror was on top of the dresser. When she picked it up a ghostly frisson of glasslight shivered across her senses.

She opened the sack and took out the mirror. The silver-and-gold handle was unnaturally warm in her hand. She carried the mirror to the window and examined the back of it. Strange crystals glittered ominously in the moonlight. An intricate Baroque design had been worked into the metal. It was too dark to make out the alchemical markings, but she could feel them with her fingertips. Small lightning flashes of power crackled through her.

Glasslight, a lot of it, was held in stasis in the mirror. All that was required to release the energy, she thought, was will and talent. It was a true paranormal weapon, one that was activated by the human mind, not by a clockwork mechanism.

Slowly, drawn by a compulsion that went far deeper than mere curiosity, she turned the mirror over to look at the glass. In the deep shadows of the bedroom she could not see her own reflection, but with her senses heightened she could perceive the energy that shifted in the surface of the artifact. It was as if she gazed into a pool of mercury. The Quicksilver Mirror seethed with the forces locked deep inside.

Dread and fascination consumed her. She looked deeper. Terrible afterimages appeared and disappeared like moving photographs trapped in the strange glass. She caught fleeting glimpses of the dead and the dying.

She saw fire as well, hot flames of silver and gold. The scorching, dazzling flames crashed and cascaded in the depths of the mirror. Her senses sang in response to the wild energy, urging her to unleash the forces in the glass.

She knew then with her glass-reader's intuition that any strong talent could use the mirror to blind or even kill. For a person with psychical abilities, the artifact was the equivalent of a gun. But someone endowed with a very special kind of talent could do much more with the device. She could set free the full power locked in the looking glass.

Someone with her kind of talent.

But what would one do with the strange energy that burned in the Quicksilver Mirror, she wondered. Then she thought about the weak energy that the killer had infused into the mirrors on Ratford's and Hackett's dressing tables and in the looking glasses on the walls of the terrible chamber beneath the Hollister mansion.

Again the question arose in her mind. Why would anyone try to lock power into a looking glass?

From out of nowhere she recalled something her mother had said a long time ago: *Power is power, whether it is normal or paranormal. It is always potentially dangerous, and there will always be those who seek to manipulate it for their own ends.*

"Virginia."

Owen spoke in his sleep, uttering her name in a raw, rasping voice that shattered the spell of the mirror.

She closed down her senses. The mirror darkened to an opaque gray. She inserted the artifact into the sack with shaking fingers and tied the cord.

Setting the sack on top of the chest of drawers, she went back to the bed and gripped Owen's hand. His fingers tightened around hers, but he did not awaken.

She contemplated the moonlit night on the other side of the window and thought about what she had seen in the Quicksilver Mirror.

THIRTY-FIVE

At ten minutes to five in the morning, Virginia sensed the subtle but distinct change in Owen's energy that told her he had surfaced completely from the depths. His breathing was relaxed, and his pulse was calm and steady. He was still asleep, but now his sleep felt entirely normal.

She released his hand.

"Virginia," he muttered. He did not open his eyes.

"I'm here," she said gently. "All is well. Go back to sleep."

He stirred, turned on his side and did as she instructed.

After a while she let herself out of the room and walked down the hall. She knew that Charlotte was asleep in the bedroom at the far end. She thought she heard Mrs. Crofton in the kitchen.

When she reached the foot of the stairs Matt spoke softly out of the shadows.

"Is Uncle Owen all right, Miss Dean?"

"He's quite well but still asleep. Where are Tony and Nick?"

"Tony's watching the back of the house. Uncle Nick is asleep in the parlor. Mrs. Crofton is in the kitchen.

She came down a few minutes ago. Said she wanted to get an early start on breakfast because there were so many of us to feed."

Virginia winced. "It is very decent of her to make breakfast for all of us before she gives notice."

"She didn't say anything about handing in her notice. Are you still certain that Uncle Owen will awaken with all of his senses?"

"Quite certain."

"That is very good news, indeed," Matt said. "We weren't looking forward to dealing with him if that turned out not to be the case."

Matt's obvious relief made her pause. "I understand your concern about the possible loss of his talent. It would be deeply disturbing for any strong sensitive to wake up and discover that his para-senses were blind. But what do you mean when you say that you weren't looking forward to dealing with him?"

Nick spoke from the shadowed door of the parlor. "You've said enough, Matt."

"Yes, sir," Matt said quickly. "Sorry. I keep forgetting that Miss Dean isn't family yet."

And that was all she was going to get out of him for now, Virginia realized. She turned toward Nick. "Good morning, sir."

"Good morning," Nick said. He rubbed his jaw, testing his morning beard. "All is well upstairs, I take it?"

"Yes," she said.

"Thank you," Nick said. He lowered his hand and looked at her with an intent expression. "The Sweetwaters owe you. We always pay our debts."

"This is ridiculous," she said, losing patience. "No one owes me a thing. For the last time, Mr. Sweetwater would have recovered on his own."

"Perhaps," Nick said. "Perhaps not."

"I give up," she said. "I'll see you both at breakfast."

"Yes, ma'am," Matt said meekly.

"Right, then," Nick said. "Breakfast. Sounds like an excellent notion."

Virginia went down the hall to the kitchen, mentally bracing herself for the next challenge of what was shaping up to be a difficult morning. The smell of hot coffee greeted her. She swept into the room, electing to go for a straightforward approach. There was no longer any point in pretending that hers would ever be a respectable household.

"Good morning, Mrs. Crofton," she said.

"Good morning, ma'am." Mrs. Crofton took a large frying pan down off a wall hook and set it on the stove. "Young Matt and Tony have been awake all night and are no doubt famished. I have a hunch the rest of your guests will wake up soon. What with one thing and another, I decided it would be best to plan an early breakfast. Would you like a cup of coffee?"

"I think I've had enough for a while," Virginia said. "I drank so much during the night that I doubt that I will sleep for a week."

"Some peppermint tea, then?"

"That sounds very good, thank you."

Mrs. Crofton disappeared into the pantry. "Mr. Sweetwater has recovered, I take it?"

"Yes, but he's still asleep. I expect he'll be down for breakfast."

"Very good." Mrs. Crofton reappeared with a small canister in one hand. She opened the container and ladled the herbal tea into a pot.

Virginia sat down on one of the long benches at the large wooden table. "Mrs. Crofton, I realize that the goings-on in this household, especially of late, are not at all what you are accustomed to."

"No, ma'am." Mrs. Crofton picked up the steaming kettle and filled the teapot. "This household is most unusual in a number of ways. Certainly not like any I've worked in previously."

"I know that you have been obliged to tolerate certain activities that you find unseemly and no doubt offensive to your high standards."

"I admit that I was somewhat unsettled by the notion of working for a psychical practitioner at first." Mrs. Crofton set the kettle aside and carried the pot to the table. "I was very sure that you were a fraud. But I soon changed my mind."

"You did?"

"Yes, ma'am." Mrs. Crofton put the teapot on the table and plucked a mug from a rack. She put the mug in front of Virginia. "I know now that you do, indeed, have a true talent. I also know that while some might call it a gift, it is also a burden. I've seen how the bad readings affect your nerves. I know that you suffer from poor sleep and nightmares after you've read the mirrors and seen things that no decent person should see."

"Yes, well, as I said, this is not a normal sort of house-hold. I do understand that in the past few days it has become even more bizarre. Last night was no doubt too much for you. Under the circumstances, I cannot blame you if you wish to give notice. Never fear, I will provide you with a good character reference."

Mrs. Crofton drew herself up proudly. "Are you dismissing me, ma'am?"

"What? Good Lord, no. I just assumed that in view of the odd activities around here of late, you would want to seek a position in a more respectable household."

"I went into service in a respectable household as a maid of all work at the age of twelve, Miss Dean. In that first post I was obliged to fight off the drunken attentions of the eldest son of the household. The lady of the house discovered us just as the young man was about to rape me. She blamed me and turned me off without a character."

Virginia frowned. "That was so unfair."

"It happens all the time. But I was fortunate. I landed on my feet in another respectable household. The husband took no interest in me. He seduced the poor governess instead. Got her pregnant. Needless to say she was let go. We heard later that she drowned herself in the river."

Virginia sighed. "She was certainly not the first young woman to take that path when she found herself in desperate circumstances."

"No, she was not. Since that post, I have worked in a number of other *respectable* households. In all but two of them, the husbands kept mistresses on the side. The sons frequented brothels and gaming halls. The women of the house were obsessed with jewelry, fine clothes, parties and their lovers."

"I see."

"The last post I held before I came here was with an elderly widow. I thought it was the perfect position. But toward the end she neglected to pay her staff. She was somewhat senile. Her family ignored her. I was the one who sat by her bedside when she died. She did not make provision for any of the servants in her will, and the family turned off all of us without a penny or a character. As a result, by the time I arrived on your doorstep, I was desperate."

"I understand," Virginia said. "You did not have a choice when it came to employers. But you do now, don't you? I'm assuming that the letter that you received from the Billings Agency the other day is an offer of employment in a more refined household."

"In her note, Mrs. Billings advised me that there was a position available in the household of Lord and Lady Ainsley. Mrs. Billings thought it might suit me."

"Lord and Lady Ainsley move in the very best circles. It sounds like an excellent position."

"I sent a note back to Mrs. Billings informing her that I was not interested."

Virginia put her mug down with enough force to create a sharp clink. "You did what?"

"This household is an extraordinary one in many ways, Miss Dean, but it is considerably more decent and, yes, more respectable than the majority of the other households in which I have worked. Furthermore, I find it interesting."

Virginia stared at her, dumbfounded. "Interesting?"

Mrs. Crofton wiped her hands on her apron. "I know very well what is going on around here, ma'am."

Virginia smiled ruefully. "One cannot conceal secrets from a good housekeeper."

"That's true. I know that you and Mr. Sweetwater are hunting a vicious killer, one who preys on women in your line of work. I also know that Mr. Sweetwater was very nearly murdered last night."

"That's true."

"It seems to me, Miss Dean, that you could use some professional assistance."

"From the police, do you mean? The thing is, we are investigating murders that were committed by paranormal means. There is no hard evidence to give to the police."

"I was not talking about assistance from the police. I was referring to myself."

"I beg your pardon?"

"There is something in this case that goes back to the Hollister household, does it not?"

"Yes."

"That was a large, wealthy household. There would have been staff."

"Yes," Virginia said, "but from what I observed, Lord and Lady Hollister employed remarkably few people for a house that size. What employees they did have all seem to have disappeared."

"Even if the Hollister staff was small, there would have been a housekeeper."

"Yes, there was. She let me in the day I went to the mansion."

"The world of those engaged in service in high-ranking households is a small one, ma'am. I spent my entire career in it until I came here. I might be able to find the Hollister housekeeper for you."

THIRTY-SIX

He awakened from the dark dream to the pale light of a drizzly dawn and a deep awareness of Virginia's strong, invigorating energy. He opened his eyes and looked up at the unfamiliar ceiling. He was lying on a bed, but he was quite certain it was not his own.

"It's about time you woke up," Virginia said. "Your relations downstairs have been very anxious."

He turned his head on the pillow and saw her in the doorway of the bedroom. She was dressed in a plain housedress. Her hair was neatly pinned into a simple knot at the back of her head. She had a mug of coffee in her hand.

"Virginia," he said. He sat up and started to push back the covers. He stopped when he realized he was nude to the waist. He glanced down and saw that he was wearing only his drawers. He yanked the covers back up over his hips and surveyed the decidedly feminine curtains, wallpaper and dressing table. "This is your bedroom."

"Yes, it is. It was much closer than your own, so we brought you here. It seemed more convenient." She carried the mug into the room, set it down on the bedside table and gave him a bright smile. "How are you feeling?"

He pondered that briefly. "I think I feel all right." Cautiously he heightened his talent. Relief flooded through him when he realized that his psychical senses were as strong as ever. "Yes. I'm fine."

"Good," she said. "Mrs. Crofton is preparing breakfast for all of us. I suggest you wash up, dress and join us."

He looked around. "Where are the rest of my clothes?"

"Tony discarded them. He went to your house early this morning to fetch some clean clothes for you. There was just too much blood."

He grimaced. Seeing him covered in the blood of a man he had just killed had probably not left a good impression on her.

"I understand," he said.

"You'll find everything you need hanging in the wardrobe. The bathroom is next door."

She turned to leave.

"Virginia," he said very quietly.

She stopped and looked at him. "Yes?"

"You saved me last night."

"No," she said. "You are a strong man. You just needed time to recover from the effects of the mirror."

"I can't believe that damned looking glass was so powerful."

"It was an alchemical weapon, not an ordinary looking glass. Charlotte and Nick have done some research into its origins. They will tell you all about it when you come downstairs."

He twisted the sheet around himself, stood and walked across the room to stand in front of her. "Whatever the hell it was, you are the reason I recovered with my senses intact."

"No, I could sense the power in you, even when you were unconscious. I knew that you would recover."

"Because I had you to hold on to." He tipped up her chin and brushed his mouth across hers. "There is a connection between us, Virginia. Admit it."

"Perhaps there is some sort of psychical awareness."

"Yes, there certainly is." He kissed her forehead.

"But that is not so odd, when you think about it," she said. She frowned in intense concentration, as though puzzling out a math problem. "We are both strong talents, and we have been intimate. Passion is a powerful force. It creates a great deal of energy."

"Indeed." He kissed her nose.

"While it lasts," she whispered.

She whirled and fled the room.

For some reason he was ridiculously pleased with her confusion. It was so unlike Virginia to get flustered. He told himself he would take it as a good omen.

He walked into the dining room a short time later and stopped at the sight of the large crowd gathered there. Virginia and Charlotte sat at the table, plates of eggs, toast and kippered salmon in front of them. Each was reading a morning paper.

"Ladies," he said. "You look lovely today."

Virginia glanced up from the *Flying Intelligencer*. She

surveyed him critically and appeared satisfied. "Good morning."

Charlotte smiled warmly. "It is good to see you looking so fit after your ordeal, sir."

"I expect to look even better after I've had breakfast," he said.

Nick, Matt and Tony were at the sideboard, helping themselves to generous quantities of food from the serving dishes.

"About time you woke up," Nick said. He ladled a mound of scrambled eggs onto his plate. "It was a long night, and none of us got much sleep, thanks to you, so we decided to start breakfast without you."

"I'm touched," Owen said. He realized he was hungry. He picked up a plate and examined the contents of the serving dishes. "What the devil are you all doing here at this hour of the morning?"

"We spent the night here," Nick said.

The swinging door between the kitchen and the dining room opened. Mrs. Crofton bustled into the room with a pot of coffee. Her eyes widened at the sight of Owen. She appeared pleased.

Pleased and decidedly more cheerful than usual, Owen thought. The housekeeper seemed almost energized.

"You're awake, then, sir," she said. "And looking quite fit, just as Miss Dean predicted." She set the coffeepot down on the table. "I'll bring out some more potatoes."

She whisked back into the kitchen. He knew at once that she was aware of everything that had happened during the night. He looked at Virginia.

"It is impossible to keep secrets from a housekeeper," she said. She went back to reading her paper.

Owen glanced at Charlotte, who made a show of turning a page of the morning paper that she was perusing.

He turned his attention to Nick.

"You all spent the night here?" he said without inflection.

"Yes," Nick said.

"Must have been somewhat crowded."

"We made do," Nick said easily. "Wanted to make sure you didn't do something melodramatic if you woke up and concluded that the mirror had permanently fried your para-senses. Try some of the salmon. It's excellent."

Owen picked up one of the large silver serving spoons. "When have you ever known me to be melodramatic?"

"First time for everything," Nick said. He took a bite of toast.

It dawned on Owen that Virginia and Charlotte were listening intently without appearing to do so. He concluded it would be best to move on to another topic, one more suited to casual breakfast-table conversation.

"What did you do with the body?" he asked.

Virginia choked on her tea and started to cough. Charlotte glowered at Owen.

He carried his plate back to the table, sat down and looked at both women. "Something I said?"

Virginia recovered and gave him a severe look. "We are eating breakfast, Mr. Sweetwater. Kindly save all talk of dead bodies until later."

He noticed that Nick, Matt and Tony were doing their best to conceal their twitching lips.

"Breakfast-table conversation in non-Sweetwater households generally takes a slightly different tone than it does at home," Tony said.

"Is that so?" Owen sat down at the table. "In that case, pass me the toast tray."

They gathered in the parlor after breakfast. Mrs. Crofton joined them. Owen did not ask her to leave. She knew too much already, he thought. She might as well hear the rest of it. After all, she was part of Virginia's household.

"We dumped the footpad's body in one of the old crypts," Nick said. "It will probably be ages, perhaps years, before it is discovered, if, indeed, it is ever found. But even if by some fluke someone stumbled over it today, there is nothing on it that will connect him to any of us. Everything about him, from his clothes to his rings and the kind of knife he carried, indicates he was a professional criminal."

"One of many who are now on the streets, looking for work, since Luttrell's criminal empire fell apart," Matt said.

"Don't worry, Uncle Owen, we took care of every detail," Tony added.

"I do not doubt that," Owen said. "What I find troubling about this situation is the Quicksilver Mirror."

They all looked at the black velvet sack on the coffee table.

"The artifact is an alchemical object, but it is, nonetheless, a mirror," Virginia said. "We have all agreed that it is too much to believe it turned up in the footpad's hands by pure coincidence."

"He told me that it had been given to him by his client, a Mr. Newton," Owen said.

"Who evidently has concluded that you are standing in the way of his plans," Charlotte observed.

"Which include Virginia," Owen said.

"It also means that Mr. Newton, whoever he is, knows or suspects that you are a good deal more than simply a researcher of the paranormal who specializes in exposing fraudulent mediums," Virginia said. "Otherwise he would not have given a hired killer from the streets such a valuable artifact to use against you."

Owen looked at Nick. "After breakfast you will see what you can find out about the hunter who attacked me last night. With his talent he will no doubt have had a reputation on the streets."

"Right."

Owen turned to Charlotte. "Any luck finding the missing paid companion?"

Charlotte frowned. "No, and it is rather odd. There are not that many agencies that supply paid companions to wealthy households. I made inquiries yesterday at all of the more exclusive agencies. None of them had any record of providing a companion for Lady Hollister."

"Another dead end," Owen said. "I think we must assume that the companion, whoever she is, may be involved in this affair. Either that or she is dead."

"Perhaps she saw too much and concluded that she needed to go into hiding," Virginia suggested.

"That is a third possibility," Owen said. "But regardless of where she is now, some agency must have sent her into that household."

"I'll make inquiries at some of the less exclusive agencies today," Charlotte said.

"Thank you, Miss Tate." Owen started to pace the room, trying to think of other possible angles that needed to be explored. The unpleasant energy stirring the hair on the nape of his neck told him that time was running out. The killer was becoming dangerously impatient. "We need to move more quickly in this affair. We know that the bastard is linked to the Institute and to Hollister. We have to find the connection."

Virginia cleared her throat. "Mrs. Crofton has offered to assist us with the investigation."

Owen glanced at Mrs. Crofton, who regarded him with an expectant, oddly hopeful air. It dawned on him that she not only seemed more cheerful and energized this morning, she appeared younger in some way.

"How do you propose to help, Mrs. Crofton?"

"I might be able to locate the housekeeper, sir."

"What housekeeper?" Owen said. Then comprehension struck. "The one in the Hollister mansion. Of course. Excellent notion. But if we cannot find the companion, how do you propose to locate the housekeeper?"

Mrs. Crofton beamed. "I have connections in that world, sir. If she is out there, I can find her."

Owen hesitated. "It is very kind of you to offer to assist us in this investigation, but are you certain you want to do this? There may be some risk involved."

"As I explained to Miss Dean, I am not unfamiliar

with risk, sir," she said. "Now, if there's nothing more, I'll be on my way."

"Where are you going?" Virginia asked.

"I believe I will start by speaking with a friend of mine who has a sister who is currently employed in the Overton household," Mrs. Crofton said. "The Overtons know everyone in the more exclusive circles, and therefore know all the gossip."

Virginia's eyes lit with understanding. "Therefore it follows that their staff will be equally well connected to those who are in service to exclusive employers. Brilliant, Mrs. Crofton."

"Thank you, ma'am." She hurried toward the door. "I shall get my bonnet and coat and be off."

Owen put up a hand to stop her briefly. "You will be careful, Mrs. Crofton."

"Yes, sir."

The sparkle of excitement in her eyes worried him, but he waved her on out the door and turned to Tony. "Matt will be Miss Dean's bodyguard today. I want you to go into the Hollister mansion and tear the place apart. Miss Dean and I did not have time to do a thorough search on our last visit to that house. Look for anything that might tell us how Hollister might have been linked to the Institute."

"I'm off," Tony said. He headed for the door.

"Whatever you do, don't get yourself arrested for breaking and entering," Owen called after him. "We have enough trouble on our hands at the moment."

"I'll be careful," Tony said. He went through the door.

"And make sure you keep an eye out for automatons," Owen called after him.

Nick pushed himself away from the wall he had been propping up and smiled at Charlotte. "You and I might as well get started on our projects. We both have a busy day ahead."

"Indeed." Charlotte got to her feet.

They both went out the door. For a time there was a great deal of noise and bustle in the front hall. The door opened and closed. The house was quiet again.

Owen looked at Virginia. "You and your female acquaintances appear to have a taste for adventure," he observed.

"Yes, well, none of us is getting any younger," she said. "I suppose it comes down to a choice between a dash of danger and adventure or an appointment with Dr. Spinner."

"About this Dr. Spinner."

"Never mind. What is our plan of action for the day?"

He reminded himself that the mystery of Dr. Spinner and his therapy for female hysteria was not the most pressing issue at the moment.

"I think it would be useful if you were seen going about your customary routine at the Institute this afternoon," he said. "We need more information from that quarter."

"You want me to try to discover some gossip concerning this affair?" she asked.

"Yes. Someone at the Institute must know something. You are the only one in a position to make inquiries."

"No offense, sir, but if you are seen hovering in my vicinity, I doubt very much that anyone will risk engaging in any sort of useful conversation with me."

"I'm aware of that," he said. "Which is why Matt will accompany you today."

Virginia glanced at Matt. "How do I explain his presence?"

"I'm sure you'll think of something," Owen said.

She turned back to him. "What will you do while Matt and I are at the Institute?"

"I am going to pursue some very boring research into Hollister's financial affairs. Now that both Lord and Lady Hollister are conveniently dead, someone has just inherited a fortune. I would like to know the name of the happy heir."

"You think that money might have been a motive in Hollister's death?"

"Money is always a strong motive."

"But I thought we concluded that there is some mad scientist running around in this affair," Matt said.

"In my experience, scientists, mad or otherwise, are always in need of money."

Virginia raised her brows. "That is a very good observation."

"Thank you. I try to do that every once in a while in the course of an investigation. There is another angle I want to explore as well. Now, then, before I leave, I have a small gift for you."

Virginia's eyes lit up with pleasure. "Really, sir, you shouldn't have."

He reached into his pocket, took out the lock pick and presented it to her. "My uncle designed it. Very simple to use. Works on most standard locks."

Matt got a pained expression. "Uncle Owen, that is not the sort of gift one gives to a lady."

Virginia blinked in surprise, but she recovered immediately and took the pick from Owen. She examined it with evident delight. "How thoughtful. I've been wanting one of my very own."

She was pleased, Owen decided. Satisfied that his first gift to her had been a success, he gave Matt a triumphant smile.

Matt rolled his eyes.

Owen headed for the door. "Matt, here, can teach you how to use it this morning before you go off to the Institute this afternoon."

THIRTY-SEVEN

The Institute was humming with activity when Virginia and Matt arrived. Practitioners, researchers and clients mingled in the halls and lounged in the tearoom.

Matt looked around with interest while Virginia handed her umbrella and rain-spattered cloak to the porter.

"So this is the Leybrook Institute," Matt said. "It's not quite what I expected."

"What, exactly, were you expecting?" Virginia asked coolly.

"I'm not sure," he admitted. "Everyone in my family assumes that most people who call themselves practitioners are charlatans and frauds. I didn't think this establishment would have such an academic atmosphere."

"Leybrook and everyone else connected to the Institute work very hard to create that atmosphere," she said stiffly.

Matt flushed a dull red. "My apologies, ma'am. I didn't mean to imply that you are a charlatan. Of course I understand that some practitioners are genuine talents.

And it certainly seems reasonable that they would congregate in professional surroundings like this."

Virginia waved his protests aside with an impatient gesture. "My office is upstairs."

"Yes, ma'am," Matt said. He followed her meekly across the grand front hall.

Welch's voice stopped her just as she was about to lead the way up the staircase.

"Good morning, Miss Dean," he called. He hurried toward her. "I've been waiting for you. I was about to ask Mrs. Fordham to send a note around to your address."

"Good morning, Mr. Welch," she said. "I'd like you to meet my new assistant, Mr. Kern."

"New assistant, eh?" Welch gave Matt a swift, critical appraisal and then nodded approvingly. "You look quite presentable, young man. That's important here at the Institute. We have an image to maintain, you know. Mr. Leybrook is very insistent on that point."

"Yes, sir," Matt said politely. "I look forward to assisting Miss Dean."

Welch turned eagerly to Virginia. "I have excellent news, Miss Dean. I am delighted to inform you that I have just received a request for a private consultation with you from a new client. A most exclusive new client, I might add. Mr. Leybrook will be very pleased."

"Who is the new client?"

"Lady Mansfield."

Virginia's stomach fluttered. She knew that the attack of nerves was fueled by the rush of mixed emotions. Uncertainty, curiosity and a deep longing to see her half-sister again swept through her. But common sense told her that any attempt to forge a bond with Elizabeth would be a mistake. It was not in the girl's best interests to maintain a personal relationship with an illegitimate half-sister, a sister who occupied a very different rung on the social ladder. Such an association could damage Elizabeth's reputation and even affect her marriage prospects when she got older.

Those who moved in elevated circles were far from naive. They were aware of the facts of life. It was not uncommon for gentlemen to produce bastard offspring. But society and the members of the gentleman's legitimate family never acknowledged such offspring socially.

"I'm a little busy at the moment," Virginia said weakly.

"Yes, yes, I know, but this is Lady Mansfield," Welch said. "Mr. Leybrook likes to encourage that sort of highflier."

"There are other glass-readers here at the Institute."

"Lady Mansfield was quite insistent. In her note she said that she wanted an appointment with you."

"I generally meet new clients here at the Institute for the initial meeting."

Welch gave her a reproving look. "You cannot expect a person of Lady Mansfield's consequence to come to you for a meeting. You must go to her. Naturally I told Mrs. Fordham to schedule the consultation."

Virginia sighed. "Naturally."

"It is for this Thursday afternoon at three." Welch smiled benignly. "In her note Lady Mansfield very graciously said that she would send her carriage to your address to convey you to the appointment. Just think, Miss Dean, you will not be obliged to hire a public cab. Isn't that splendidly generous of the client?"

"Splendidly generous, Mr. Welch. Thank you."

"Indeed, you're quite welcome. I can't wait to inform Mr. Leybrook."

Welch scurried away.

Virginia continued up the stairs, Matt at her heels.

What was Helen thinking? Virginia wondered. She was surely aware of the risks involved in promoting a connection between her daughter and her dead husband's illegitimate offspring. On the other hand, it was obvious that Helen genuinely cared for Elizabeth. Perhaps she had concluded that it would be best if Elizabeth were given some practical advice in regard to managing her talent.

At the top of the stairs Virginia led Matt along the hall to the door of her small office. She opened the small chatelaine purse that dangled from her belt and took out her key. Her fingers brushed against the lock pick. She smiled. Most gentlemen gave their lovers jewelry. The Sweetwater men were more original when it came to tokens of affection. After two hours of intense instruction and practice on every lock in the house, Matt had pronounced her quite adept at lock-picking. *You would have made a very good burglar, Miss Dean,* he'd said.

She opened the door of the office. Matt followed her into the small space.

"Leave the door open," she said in a low voice. "Our goal is to try to gain some information from my colleagues. The easiest way to do that is with casual conversation, and the quickest route to that end is an open door."

"Yes, ma'am," he said.

"There is no reason for you to stand around. Take one of the client chairs. I have a copy of the most recent edition of the Institute's *Journal* that you might like to examine."

"Thanks."

She sat behind the tidy little desk and plucked the copy of the Leybrook *Journal* off a nearby bookshelf. Matt took it from her and studied the cover with great interest.

"It looks very much like a copy of Arcane's *Journal of Paranormal and Psychical Research*," he said.

Virginia smiled wryly. "I believe Mr. Leybrook deliberately patterned it after the Society's publication. I told you, he is intent on establishing the credibility of the Institute."

Matt opened the journal and glanced at the table of contents. He grinned and read aloud, "An Investigation of Automatic Writing as a Method for Relaying Messages from the Other Side." He looked up. "The Leybrook *Journal* may look like an Arcane publication, but I can assure you that no self-respecting member of the Society believes that spirits communicate through mediums who transmit their messages with automatic writing."

"I'm aware of that," she said. "Leybrook doesn't believe in visitations from the Other Side, either, but he says that is the sort of paranormal investigation that intrigues the public."

"And sells a great many copies of his *Journal*."

"Yes." She reached for her appointment book.

She heard Gilmore Leybrook's confident footsteps in the hall outside her door just as she opened the book. He paused in the doorway. Matt got to his feet.

"Good morning, Virginia," Gilmore said. "Welch told me that you had arrived." He gave Matt a speculative survey. "He also mentioned that you have acquired a new assistant."

"I decided to follow your example, Mr. Leybrook," she said smoothly. "You have told me on more than one occasion that clients are always impressed by a practitioner who employs an assistant. Mr. Kern has accepted a position with me."

"I see." Gilmore did not look pleased. He ignored Matt and glanced at the open appointment book. "Busy day?" he said to Virginia.

"Not especially," she said. She was careful, as she always was with Leybrook, to use her most exquisitely professional tones. "I have an appointment for a consultation later this afternoon but no readings tonight."

"Welch tells me that you have attracted a very important new client, Lady Mansfield." Gilmore sauntered, uninvited, into the office. "Congratulations."

The small room was suddenly quite crowded, Virginia thought. The two men seemed to take up a great deal of the available space.

"Lady Mansfield has requested only a consultation," she said. "I doubt that she will become a regular client."

Gilmore lowered himself into one of the two wooden chairs arranged in front of the desk and hitched up his expensive trousers. "Let us hope that you can convince her otherwise."

Virginia smiled and prepared to lie through her teeth. "I will certainly do my best. Was there anything else, Mr. Leybrook? If not, I would like to prepare for my appointment."

"Yes, Virginia, there is something else." Leybrook cocked a dark brow at Matt. "Be so good as to step out into the hall, Mr. Kern. I wish to speak to Miss Dean privately."

Matt made no move to leave. He looked at Virginia for direction. She had known this confrontation was coming, she reminded herself. Best to get it over with as quickly and as privately as possible.

"It's all right, Matt," she said quietly. "Please wait in the hall. Mr. Leybrook won't be long. Take the *Journal* with you to read."

Matt did not look happy, but he did not argue. "I'll be just outside if you need me, ma'am."

"Thank you," Virginia said.

Matt walked out of the office. He did not close the door behind him. Leybrook got up and closed it quite firmly.

"Your new employee appears to be quite devoted to you," he remarked, returning to the chair.

Virginia readied herself for the skirmish. If she did not handle things very carefully, today could prove to be her last at the Institute.

"I believe Mr. Kern has a flair for the business," she said. "What was it you wanted to speak to me about?"

"Unfortunately it has become clear that Miss Walters is not suited to the position for which I employed her."

"I'm surprised to hear that. She appears to meet all your requirements in an assistant."

"I have changed some of my requirements."

"I see."

"As it happens, Miss Dean, I have concluded that you will suit the position very nicely. I have decided to offer you the post."

Virginia smiled with what she hoped was just the right degree of regret.

"I am certainly flattered, Mr. Leybrook, but I am afraid that I will not be able to take the position," she said. "As you can see, I have, in fact, just hired my own assistant."

Displeasure flashed across Leybrook's handsome face. It vanished in the next instant.

"It is hardly the same sort of position that I am offering to you," he said. "May I ask why you are not interested?"

"Do not mistake me, I am very aware of the singular honor you are offering. But I am determined to pursue my career as a glass-reader."

"I never meant to imply that I would expect you to give up your readings if you became my assistant," Gilmore said quickly. "The opposite, in fact. I have given the matter a great deal of thought, and I am convinced that working together as a team we could establish ourselves as the most fashionable glass-reading consultants in London."

She picked up her pen. "But you do not read mirrors."

"No," he agreed. He smiled. "My talents lie in other directions. But that does not mean we cannot conduct consultations as a team. You would perform the actual reading of the mirrors, of course."

"I see."

"But we would inform clients that while you can summon the spirits in the glass, I am the one who can actually communicate with them."

She tightened her grip on the pen. "You know that I don't summon spirits."

"Yes, but the majority of the clients believe that is exactly what you do. They think that you are a kind of medium, that you contact the Other Side through mirrors. It's a very good act, Virginia, but it lacks a crucial element."

"What is that?"

"The problem is that you do not give voice to the ghosts in the mirror. People want to communicate with the departed. In short, your act lacks the element of high drama. That is what clients seek when they pay a fee to a medium or a glass-reader."

She put the pen aside very deliberately and clasped her hands on top of the appointment book. "I told you when I applied to become affiliated with the Institute that what I do is not an act. The reason that the after-images don't speak through me is because they are not spirits. I have explained that what I perceive are psychical photographs, not ghosts."

"I understand. But that is precisely why you have not become the most successful psychical consultant at the Institute. It is why Pamela Egan channeling her ancient Egyptian princess and that old biddy Mrs. Harkins still pull in more clients than you do. People expect action at a séance or a reading. They want theatrics. They want to feel that there is active communication with the departed. I can provide that missing element in your readings."

"Indeed?" she said evenly. "How would you do that?"

He sat forward. "By working with you at each consultation. You would do what you always do, summon the spirits in their final moments."

"You mean summon the afterimages, which, I might remind you, only someone with my kind of talent can perceive."

"Ah, but that is where I come in." Leybrook smiled. "I can provide a visual element to the readings."

"I knew it," Virginia said. "You are an illusion-talent, aren't you?"

He hesitated, frowning, and then shrugged. "Yes."

"I suspected as much."

"For obvious reasons I prefer to keep the exact nature of my ability a secret. People want to believe that they are seeing real ghosts, not stage magic. In our performances I will create the illusion of visual disturbances on the surfaces of the mirrors while you read the afterimages. The clients will be enthralled."

"You intend to deceive them."

"Not at all. I will merely enhance the experience for them by providing some drama. You will relay to me what you see in the mirrors. At the same time I will provide the audience with the illusion of fog and images swirling in the glass. But we will add the finishing touch. After you tell me what you have seen, I will channel the voices of the departed for our clients."

"You will pretend to speak for spirits? But what will you say?"

"Come, now, Virginia, how hard can it be to speak for the dead and the dying? Mediums and séance-givers do it all the time. I will convey last messages to loved ones, perhaps a plea for justice in the event we stumble across a genuine murder victim, that sort of thing."

"Has it occurred to you that if you claim to speak for someone who is in the process of being murdered the client and very likely the police will expect the victim to name the murderer?"

"There are ways to finesse that angle," Leybrook said.

"How can you do that?"

"Mysterious clues from the dead will work nicely," Gilmore said.

"What sort of clues?"

"*Search for the blue door,*" Gilmore intoned in a deep, melodramatic voice. "*Listen for the hound at midnight. Read what is written on the stone at the bottom of the pond.*" He waved one hand in a dismissing gesture, and his voice returned to normal. "There are endless possibilities when it comes to clues from beyond the grave."

"I see."

"We will split the consulting fees sixty-forty," Gilmore added smoothly.

"I assume I'm the one who will receive the forty percent?"

"Correct."

"Under the terms of our current agreement I retain seventy-five percent of the fees that I charge," Virginia said.

"Any loss in profit to you under the new arrangement will be more than compensated for by an increase in business and in our fees."

"How very generous of you."

"Together we will not only make a great deal of money, we will take the reputation and the influence of this Institute to new heights." Gilmore's eyes hardened. He was suddenly very intense. "We will attract a greater number of *true* talents to work here, and not just those who would never be welcome in Arcane. I believe we have the potential to draw members from the Society itself."

"Do you really believe that?" Virginia asked.

"Yes. There are rumblings within Arcane. Not all of the members are happy with the new direction the organization is taking. Some are chafing under the limits that the Joneses have begun to set on the kind of research that will be condoned by the Society in the future. Furthermore, the establishment of Jones & Jones has created a great deal of resentment both within and outside of Arcane. Many feel that the Society has no right to police the rest of us."

She had always understood that Gilmore viewed Arcane as competition, but now she realized that his hostility toward the Society involved something more than business, something very personal.

"Mr. Leybrook, rest assured that I wish you well in your efforts to create an alternative to Arcane, but I cannot accept your offer to enhance my readings. I am not interested in going into a consulting partnership of the sort that you are describing."

"You wish to bargain for a higher percentage of the fees?"

"I am not trying to negotiate with you, sir. I am telling you that I intend to build my business my way. I do not want to deceive my clients, even if it means larger fees."

"It's Sweetwater, isn't it?" Gilmore surged up out of the chair and stalked to the window. He looked down at the street. "He is the reason you are turning down my offer. He has seduced you."

"The nature of my association with Mr. Sweetwater is none of your business."

"Do not bother to deny it." Gilmore shot her a scathing look. "I sensed the energy around the two of you last night. I suspect everyone at the reception did." His mouth twisted. "Hell, even nontalents can pick up on those sorts of currents."

Virginia could feel the heat rising in her face. She was very glad that Gilmore was watching the scene outside the window.

"What an extraordinarily ill-mannered and inappropriate thing to say," she said in her coldest accents. She was careful to keep her voice low, because she knew that Matt, with his hunter-talent hearing, was probably listening. "I have no intention of discussing my personal affairs with you, Mr. Leybrook. I will thank you to leave my office immediately."

Gilmore turned away from the window to face her. "You surprise me, Virginia. I never thought that you would become a gentleman's mistress. I was convinced that you had more pride than that."

"That's enough." She leaped to her feet. "Leave this office at once."

"You seem to forget, this office is the property of the

Institute, and I own the Institute. As long as you accept the benefits of affiliation with my organization, you will do as I say."

The door opened. Matt looked straight at Virginia.

"Is there a problem, Miss Dean?" he said.

"Get out of here," Gilmore ordered.

Matt ignored him. He waited for Virginia to respond.

She moved around the corner of the desk. "There is no problem, Mr. Kern. We are leaving now."

"Where do you think you're going?" Gilmore demanded.

"I am hereby severing my affiliation with the Institute. Good-bye, Mr. Leybrook. It will be interesting to see if you can create an organization that rivals Arcane. You have your work cut out for you."

"You can't just walk out of here."

She paused in the doorway.

"Watch me," she said.

Matt smiled at Gilmore. Virginia had seen Owen smile a very similar smile. *The Sweetwater smile*, she thought. It promised that bad things would happen.

"That's enough, Matt," she said quietly. "We're leaving now."

Matt looked disappointed, but he followed her obediently down the hall to the staircase.

Virginia looked down and saw Adriana Walters coming up the stairs.

"Walk out of this Institute and you can say farewell to your career, Virginia Dean," Gilmore roared from the doorway of the office. "I'll destroy your reputation in London. You'll be lucky to get clients from the gutters before I've finished with you."

She glanced back at him over her shoulder. "Why don't you go search for the blue door, Mr. Gilmore? Or perhaps listen for the hound at midnight? Better yet, try reading what is written on the stone at the bottom of the pond."

Gilmore's face suffused with rage.

Virginia continued down the stairs.

"You know, it would be very easy for Gilmore to break his neck on these stairs," Matt offered with a hopeful air. "Accidents do happen."

"That won't be necessary, thank you," Virginia said.

"Just a leg, perhaps?" Matt wheedled.

"No, Matt. I do not need the aggravation."

Adriana swept past, glaring.

"He's all yours," Virginia said.

"Bitch," Adriana hissed.

At the foot of the stairs the porter lurched out of his office to open the door. He handed Virginia her still-dripping umbrella and cloak, and shot a grim look at the top of the staircase.

"Is there a problem, Miss Dean?" he asked.

"No, Mr. Fulton, there is no problem. Not anymore."

"It's still raining outside, ma'am," he said anxiously. "I'll summon a cab for you."

"Thank you," Virginia said.

Outside on the front steps, Matt held the large umbrella for her while Fulton took out a whistle. In response to the piercing sound, a cab materialized out of the driving rain.

"Number Seven Garnet Lane," Matt said to the driver. He handed Virginia up into the cab and got in behind her. The vehicle rolled forward.

Virginia contemplated the rain through the window and pondered the disastrous turn of events. Her career and the secure, prosperous future that she had been attempting to create for herself now lay in smoking ruins. She was surprised to realize that she felt strangely numb. It would no doubt take a while for the shock to set in, she concluded.

Matt watched her from the opposite seat.

"Uncle Owen won't like it when he finds out that Leybrook threatened your career, Miss Dean."

Virginia frowned. "Let me make something very clear. I appreciate your sentiments on my behalf, but what just happened between Mr. Leybrook and me is my problem. I will deal with it. Is that understood?"

"Yes, ma'am, I understand. But I'm not sure Uncle Owen will see things that way."

"To clarify further, if I hear that Gilmore Leybrook has suffered an unfortunate or fatal accident of any kind in the near future, I will be very annoyed."

"Yes, ma'am. I was merely pointing out that Uncle Owen won't be happy."

"I am not particularly thrilled, myself. But I will not allow your uncle to use me as an excuse to do something dreadful to Leybrook. I was told that Sweetwaters only hunt the monsters."

"That's true."

"Heaven knows Gilmore has his faults, but he is not one of the monsters."

Matt regarded her with a considering expression. "Are you certain of that, Miss Dean? The monsters are usually well disguised. That is what makes them difficult to hunt. It is why J & J asked for our assistance in this matter of the glass-reader murders."

She could not think of a response to that. He was right. The monsters of antiquity were easy to identify. They had three heads or snakelike tails and a terrifying, demonic aspect. But human monsters all too often were chameleons who blended into society.

Fifteen minutes later the cab halted at her address on Garnet Lane. Matt took the umbrella and escorted Virginia up the front steps. The Sweetwater men might be assassins for hire, she thought, but they were very well mannered. Gentlemen to their lethal fingertips.

"Something amusing, Miss Dean?" Matt asked.

Virginia realized she was smiling. "No, not really."

She took out her key and gave it to him. He opened the door and ushered her inside. The house felt dark and empty. There were no footsteps coming down the hall from the kitchen.

"It looks like Mrs. Crofton is not yet home," Matt said. He planted the umbrella into the wrought-iron stand. "Perhaps she has had some luck locating the Hollister housekeeper."

"That would certainly be helpful." Virginia undid her cloak. "The hem of my skirts and my walking boots are soaked from the wet streets. I'm going to dash upstairs and change into some dry clothes. Why don't you go into the kitchen and put the kettle on the stove? There are some biscuits in the pantry. I'll join you shortly."

"An excellent plan," Matt said.

He assisted her with her cloak and then ambled happily down the hall, a young man in search of food.

Well, it was not his future that had just burned to the ground, Virginia told herself. The Sweetwaters enjoyed a very secure profession. There would always be monsters around to hunt, as well as people and organizations such as J & J who would no doubt be willing to pay well for the service.

She went up the stairs, the weight of her rain-soaked petticoats and skirts as heavy as the anchor of a ship. Or perhaps it was her mood that was weighing her down, she thought. She wanted very badly to talk to Charlotte, who was no doubt happily engaged in the exciting task of locating the mysterious paid companion.

At the top of the stairs, she went down the hall to her bedroom. Inside, she closed the door, unlaced her wet boots and stepped out of her damp clothing. She changed into a fresh petticoat and a simple day gown and secured the little chatelaine purse at her waist.

She crossed the room, went out into the hall and down the stairs. There were no sounds coming from the kitchen. That was curious. By now Matt should have gotten the kettle going and started rummaging around in the pantry for the biscuits.

"Matt? Did you find the tea things?"

She went through the doorway into the kitchen. There was no sign of Matt. The swinging door of the pantry was closed. She pushed it open.

She stopped at the sight of Matt sprawled unconscious on the floor.

"*Matt.*"

He did not move. But something else did. She heard the ominous clank and thump before the clockwork doll toddled out of the shadows. The automaton was nearly three feet tall, a chillingly lifelike replica of Queen Victoria. Every detail was exquisitely rendered, from the miniature crown set with crystals to the high-button boots and the dark mourning attire that Her Majesty had worn since the death of her beloved Albert.

The Queen's icy glass eyes rolled in their sockets and fixed on Virginia. Cold energy shivered in the small space. Virginia experienced the now-familiar chill with all of her senses. She fought back, heightening her talent.

The Queen clanked forward in her miniature boots. Desperate, Virginia pushed her talent higher. The clockwork doll stopped as though confused.

Virginia grabbed the nearest heavy object, a large iron skillet, and hurled it at the doll. The pan struck the curiosity full on, knocking the device off its feet. It toppled onto its back. The booted heels drummed relentlessly on the floor. The eyes rattled in the porcelain skull, seeking a target.

Virginia seized Matt's ankles and tried to haul him across the floor out of range of the doll. The Sweetwater men were not small, and they were evidently constructed of pure muscle and bone. The smooth wooden floor was in her favor, though. She managed to slide Matt's heavy frame halfway out the pantry door before she had to stop and gather her strength for another tug.

The clanking, thumping and rattling of the clockwork mechanism muffled the sound of the footsteps behind her until it was too late. She caught a whiff of a sweet, flowery scent just before the chloroform-soaked cloth covered her nose and mouth.

A man's arm wrapped around her throat and wrenched her back against a hard chest. She reached upward, trying to claw at her captor's eyes. Her fingers closed around a pair of spectacles. She ripped them off and dropped them to the floor. There was a sharp crack when the lenses shattered.

"You stupid woman," Jasper Welch snarled. "Why do you have to make things so bloody difficult? You have come close to ruining my great work."

She held her breath, but she had already inhaled some of the vapor. Her head was spinning, and the world was disappearing into a fathomless fog. She tried to struggle—at least, she thought she struggled—but she could not be certain.

She fell into an endless night.

THIRTY-EIGHT

Flames smoldered deep in the mirrors.

Virginia sensed the paranormal heat before she was fully awake. She knew glasslight the way she knew sunlight or rain. She did not have to look into the mirrors to know that they surrounded her and that they were infused with energy unlike anything she had ever experienced.

The power in the looking glasses called to her, triggering frissons of awareness, summoning her out of the darkness.

Warily she opened her eyes and beheld a dazzling, glittering wonderland of ice lit by massive glass chandeliers. For a few seconds she wondered why she did not feel the cold. It took her some time to realize that there was no ice. She was lying on a low bench in a long, high-ceilinged chamber that was entirely paneled in mirrors.

The room reminded her of the terrible chamber in the basement of the Hollister mansion, but this hall was fashioned on a far larger and grander scale, a palace room of mirrors. There were no windows, no obvious door.

The brilliantly reflective surfaces were everywhere.

They covered the walls and clad the stately columns. An elaborate mosaic of tiny mirrored tiles patterned the coved ceiling and accented the decorative molding.

And all of the mirrors simmered and seethed with the paranormal fires trapped inside the glass.

She struggled to a sitting position and discovered that the bench on which she had awakened was padded in white velvet. She was still wearing the day gown she had changed into before she was kidnapped. The small chatelaine purse dangled at her waist.

For a moment she sat there, entranced and intoxicated by the energy that flooded the gallery. After a while, she gathered her nerve, heightened her senses and looked deeper into the mirrors.

She was braced for dreadful visions of death, but there were no afterimages, no visions that indicated that people had been murdered in the glittering chamber. All she perceived was power, an enormous quantity of it, locked inside the looking glasses.

She had been reading mirrors since the age of thirteen, but she had never seen or experienced anything like what she was viewing now. She could not imagine how so much raw energy had been trapped in the mirrors.

Slowly, cautiously, she got to her feet and discovered that she was in a museum gallery. All of the artifacts and antiquities were fashioned of mirrors and glass. Each relic was displayed on a mirrored pedestal or inside a glass case. Combined with the mirrored walls, floor and ceiling, the effect was visually disorienting. She had to elevate her talent slightly in order to maintain her balance.

Her bedazzled senses whispered that not all of the energy in the room came from the mirrors. The antiquities around her were infused with power.

It occurred to her that the relics were very likely the source of the fire in the mirrors. Over time the looking glasses had absorbed the paranormal radiation that emanated from the antiquities.

One of the display cases sat on the floor. It was roughly the size and shape of a coffin. The case was draped in a white-velvet cloth. Virginia's intuition told her that she probably did not want to see what lay beneath the velvet covering.

She looked around, but there was no obvious way to tell which mirror concealed the door. There was always a slight draft across a threshold, she reminded herself. Perhaps if she walked the length of the gallery she would be able to detect a shift in the flow of air.

She made her way slowly through the room, the low heels of her walking boots ringing on the mirrored floor tiles. Each artifact she passed called to her senses. It took willpower to ignore the silent summons of an ancient urn fashioned of cobalt-blue glass. She had to force herself to look away from a gleaming obsidian dagger that reeked of dark glasslight.

Farther along the gallery she glanced into a case and saw a small statue of Pan formed of opaque green glass. She could have sworn that she heard the faint, lilting notes of the god's flute. The paranormal music was as unnerving as it was erotic.

But it was the long coffin-shaped case covered in white velvet that tugged most powerfully at her awareness.

She tried to ignore the pull of the covered case and moved on quickly, seeking the slight draft that would indicate a door. She passed another display case and saw that it contained a glass-plate photographic negative.

She told herself that she should not look at the image on the plate, but she could not resist. She glanced down and saw a picture of a woman. At first there did not appear to be anything extraordinary about the negative. Then she realized that the eyes of the woman in the picture glowed as though lit from within. The heat in the subject's eyes grew brighter and hotter the longer Virginia studied the image.

When she realized that she was reaching out to open the glass case, she gasped and stepped back quickly. The compulsion to touch the negative faded.

She turned away quickly and found herself staring, yet again, at the case draped in white velvet. She knew then that she could not escape the chamber until she had discovered what was concealed inside.

She crossed to the case, grasped a handful of the velvet, took a grip on her nerves and pulled the cloth aside.

She was prepared for the sight of the glass coffin. But it was the body inside that horrified her.

"Mrs. Crofton."

The housekeeper was dressed in the serviceable gown that she had been wearing when she left the house that morning. Her eyes were closed, as though she were asleep.

The knowledge that Mrs. Crofton had been murdered because she had become involved in the investigation sent waves of crushing guilt and rage crashing through Virginia.

Anguished, she raised the glass coffin lid.

Mrs. Crofton snored gently.

Light-headed with relief, Virginia reached inside and shook the housekeeper, gently at first.

"Wake up, Mrs. Crofton. Can you hear me? Please wake up. We must escape this place."

Mrs. Crofton grimaced in her sleep. Virginia shook her again, more forcefully this time.

"Mrs. Crofton, wake up."

This time Mrs. Crofton stirred, raised her lashes and peered up at her with glazed eyes.

"What?" she mumbled in a thick, drugged voice.

"We have to get out of here," Virginia said.

"So sleepy," Mrs. Crofton murmured. She closed her eyes again.

"For pity's sake, you are lying in a coffin, Mrs. Crofton. Unless you wish to be buried, I strongly suggest that you resurrect yourself immediately."

Mrs. Crofton's eyes popped open again. "Coffin? Made of glass?"

"Yes."

"I remember bits and pieces now. I think."

"You can explain later. We need to get out of here."

"I'll not quarrel with that plan."

Mrs. Crofton sat up, still noticeably groggy. With Virginia's help, she managed to scramble awkwardly out of the glass coffin. But it became clear at once that she could not stand. Virginia tried to steady her. Together they staggered a few feet.

"Can't," Mrs. Crofton whispered. "You must go on without me. Hurry. Before they come for you."

"I'm not leaving you in this place." Virginia got her to the bench and lowered her down onto it. "But I will be able to locate the door more quickly if you wait here."

Mrs. Crofton groaned, folded her arms on her knees and lowered her head.

Virginia rushed through the room, ignoring the pull of the artifacts.

A draft whispered beneath one of the mirrored panels.

"I found it," Virginia said.

Mrs. Crofton looked up, brightening a little.

"There must be a concealed lever, but I don't have time to search for it," Virginia said. "I will have to shatter the mirror to reveal the doorknob."

She went back across the room and picked up a heavy glass statue of a cat. Frissons of energy crackled through her. She paid no attention.

The mirrored panel swung open just as Virginia started toward it with the statue.

For a heartbeat she dared to hope that Owen would enter the room, coming to the rescue as he had the night he found her in the Hollister mansion.

But of course it was not Owen who walked into the mirrored chamber. One did not get that sort of good luck twice, Virginia thought.

A woman stood in the opening. She was tall, with a face that would have been quite pretty, had her eyes not been so ice-cold. Her dark hair was swept up into an artful chignon. Her elegant silver-gray-and-black gown was trimmed with glittering black glass beads. Strands of black glass gems sparkled at her throat and wrists. Obsidian earrings dangled from her ears. She gripped a pistol in one hand.

Virginia recognized her in spite of the fine clothes and expensive jewelry.

"Mrs. Hollister's paid companion," Virginia said. "I congratulate you on your wardrobe. It is certainly of a much finer quality than it was the last time we met."

"Good evening, Miss Dean. Allow me to introduce myself properly this time. I am Alcina Norgate. You are, of course, acquainted with my brother, Jasper."

Jasper Welch bustled into the room. He had a pocket watch in one hand. "It is nearly midnight. Time to ignite my Great Engine."

Alcina smiled at Virginia. "I'm afraid Jasper requires a contribution from you in order to complete his project. His grand experiment ought to have been concluded by now, but things did not go as planned that evening at the Hollister mansion. We have taken pains to ensure that this time matters will turn out quite differently."

"Quite differently, indeed," Welch said. He snapped the pocket watch closed. Reaching into another pocket, he produced a set of iron wrist manacles. "Only one set, I'm afraid. We didn't plan on two of you being present for the final phase of the experiment. But there's no reason you and your housekeeper can't share these."

THIRTY-NINE

Gilmore Leybrook was in his library, going over the latest financial reports for the Institute, when he sensed the ominous currents of energy. They rolled through the room like the waves of a dark, cold sea. Alarmed, he surged to his feet. He was suddenly sweating profusely. His heart beat too fast. Instinctively he looked around, searching for the source of the deadly danger that had invaded the room.

At first he saw nothing, but before he could assure himself that his imagination had overreacted, Owen Sweetwater came through the doorway, the wings of his long black coat flaring around him.

Gilmore stared at him, unable to breathe. He had never been so frightened in his life.

"I need an address, Leybrook," Sweetwater said. "You will provide it to me."

Anger surged through Gilmore, momentarily offsetting the raw terror that was roiling his guts. "Now, see here, I don't know who you think you are, but you have no right—"

He broke off, choking on another wave of panic.

"You will give me the address," Sweetwater said.

Gilmore crumpled back down on his chair. "Yes." He sucked in a breath. "Who are you looking for?"

Sweetwater told him. Gilmore gave him the address.

Sweetwater turned and went toward the door of the library. He paused briefly to look back at Gilmore.

"There will be no more threats to Miss Dean's career," Sweetwater said. "If I hear so much as a whisper of gossip I will assume it came from you, and I will come for you."

He did not wait for a response, which was just as well because Gilmore doubted that he was capable of speech.

He sat at the desk for a long time, collecting his nerve. After a while he got up, crossed the room to the brandy decanter and poured a large measure of the strong spirits into a glass. He downed the brandy in three swallows. Then he poured another glass.

After a while his nerves recovered somewhat.

One thing was clear, he would have to pursue his vendetta against Arcane without the assistance of Virginia Dean. Well, it was not as if she was the only powerful talent in London, he thought. He would find another who could help him destroy the Society.

FORTY

Y
ou do realize that Mr. Sweetwater and his associates will be here soon," Virginia said.

She sat next to Mrs. Crofton on the velvet bench, her left wrist bound to Mrs. Crofton's right wrist with the heavy manacle. The chain of the manacle had been looped around the center leg of the padded bench. The iron bench leg was, in turn, bolted to the floor.

Welch was busily arranging three clockwork curiosities, a large praying mantis, a monstrous scorpion and a giant spider. He positioned the terrible toys in a semicircle in front of Virginia and Mrs. Crofton, careful to make certain that the curiosities were out of range of their feet.

"Rest assured there is no way that Sweetwater can possibly learn the location of this house," Alcina Norgate said. "Just as he will never discover the identity of the glass-reader killer. I assume that is why he took up with you, is it not? It is the only explanation for his presence in this affair. I never did believe that he was merely an investigator who was out to expose a few pathetic fraudulent practitioners."

"You seem to have it all reasoned out," Virginia said.

"But why in heaven's name did you get involved with Hollister and his wife? They were both mad."

"Their eccentricities are what made the entire plan possible," Alcina said. "It was a somewhat risky venture, to be sure, but the results made the effort worthwhile."

Owen had been right, Virginia thought. Money had been the motivation for much of what had occurred. But she did not want to let Alcina and Welch know that Owen was closing in on the answers. She needed to buy time for Mrs. Crofton and herself.

"You were after the Hollister fortune?" she asked aloud.

Rage flashed in Alcina's eyes with the startling speed of a wildfire. "The Hollister money belongs to Jasper and me. It will soon be ours. Lady Hollister inherited her husband's fortune, you see. But I persuaded her to leave it all to me in her own will. I had planned to get rid of her in due course, but she very graciously took care of the problem herself. Now that she is dead, I am the sole beneficiary."

Suddenly it all fell into place, the disconcerting burst of fury, the talent, the obsession with the Hollister inheritance.

"You and your brother are Hollister's illegitimate offspring, aren't you?" Virginia said quietly.

Mrs. Crofton nodded with a knowing air. "Ah, so that's the way it is."

Alcina frowned. "Very good, Miss Dean. Did you guess the truth because you and I share the stain of illegitimacy?"

"Well, that, and because you and your brother are obviously as mad as your father," Virginia said.

The taunt proved to be a mistake. Fury flashed again in Alcina's eyes. She opened the nearest glass case, reached inside and took out a crystal pendant.

The pendant sparked. A senses-searing fire crackled in the room. Virginia had lowered her talent, but that did not save her from the shock of the pendant's energy. It was as if she had been struck by lightning. Instinctively she put up her free hand in a useless attempt to shield herself.

"No, Alcina," Welch shouted. Alarmed, he rushed toward her. "You must not destroy her senses. I need her and her talent."

"Miss Dean," Mrs. Crofton said urgently. "Are you all right?"

The white-hot energy ceased abruptly.

"Don't talk to me like that," Alcina shrieked. "Don't ever say such a thing again or I will blind you permanently. Do you understand?"

Virginia blinked several times. "I understand."

Cautiously she heightened her senses. When she perceived the heat in the mirrored walls and the dazzling energy of the artifacts around her, she breathed a small sigh of relief. Her talent still functioned.

"You are right about one thing," Alcina said, once again unnaturally calm. "My father was quite mad, and so was his ridiculous wife."

"How did you discover that Hollister was your father?" Virginia asked.

"The orphanage where Jasper and I were sent after our mother died burned down years ago. All of the records were destroyed in the fire. It wasn't until last year that I was finally able to locate a woman who had been close to our mother when they both worked as maids for Hollister's parents. Hollister got her pregnant when he was a young man. She was, of course, let go. She could not afford to feed her infant twins. She wound up in the workhouse, where she died of a fever."

Mrs. Crofton stirred on the bench. "An old and very sad story."

"True," Alcina said. "But Jasper and I decided to give our tale a slightly different ending. First, however, we had to find a way to survive in the world. When we left the orphanage, we were sent out to work in a wealthy household. Jasper was a footman. I was a maid. But I was fortunate in my looks. At the age of sixteen I succeeded in catching the eye of an elderly, extremely wealthy gentleman who had become senile. He had no close family to protect him from me. It was no trick at all to persuade him to marry me."

"Something tells me he did not last long after the wedding," Virginia said.

"He expired a month later. A great tragedy but one that passed unnoticed in the social world because he had not gone into society for decades. I inherited his fortune and this house. Jasper came here to live with me. We copied the manners and accents of our betters, and now we pass easily among them when we wish, as you do, Miss Dean. Really, we have so much in common."

Virginia waved a hand to indicate the contents of the mirrored gallery. "This collection is yours, I assume?"

"Yes." Alcina looked around with satisfaction. "I

have spent a great deal of time and money acquiring glass antiquities with a paranormal provenance. Jasper designed this chamber for me. We both inherited our father's talent, you see."

Welch looked around the room with a sense of satisfaction. "It was some years before I realized what was happening in this room."

"Over time the accumulated energy of so many relics imbued with psychical power has saturated the mirrors," Virginia said. "That explains the fire in the glass."

Curiosity leaped in Welch's eyes. "You can sense the power trapped in the mirrors? Yes, I suppose that is only natural, given the strength of your talent. Very good, Miss Dean. You might be interested to know that the process works both ways. As the energy has built up in the mirrors, the currents have been reflected back into the artifacts, enhancing the forces infused into them. Those forces, in turn, are reflected back into the mirrors. The process has gone on for over a decade. The result is that this chamber has stored an astonishing amount of powerful energy."

Virginia looked at Alcina. "When you discovered the identity of your father you began to plot your vengeance. You found a way into the Hollister household as Lady Hollister's companion."

Alcina gave her an approving look. "It was not terribly difficult. None of Lady Hollister's companions lasted long. I bought an inexpensive, tailor-made dress, pretended to be a respectable woman who had fallen on hard times and knocked on the front door. I told the housekeeper that I had been sent by an agency. No one asked any questions. I was accepted as Lady Hollister's companion almost immediately."

"Once inside the household, you began to take charge," Mrs. Crofton said. "You manipulated Lady Hollister, who was too mentally unbalanced to understand what was happening."

Virginia looked at Mrs. Crofton in surprise.

"I found the Hollisters' housekeeper," Mrs. Crofton explained. "She answered my questions, but she must have slipped a drug into the tea she served me."

"It was the same drug that we used on you, Miss Dean," Alcina said. "After Mrs. Crofton was unconscious, the housekeeper sent a note to me, informing me of what had happened. We had made a bargain, you see. I paid her a great deal of money to ensure that she would notify me if anyone came around asking questions. I sent Jasper to collect Mrs. Crofton."

"Gaining control of Lady Hollister must have been a simple matter," Virginia said. "It did not require any talent to manage her, and through her, the entire household. But Hollister would have been another problem altogether."

"My father was a rather dangerous man." Alcina smiled. "But when you discover a man's passion, you know what is required to control him."

"How long did it take you to realize that he was raping and murdering young prostitutes in that mirrored chamber below the mansion?" Virginia asked.

"Not long at all. I realized almost at once that something very odd was going on, of course, but Hollister kept his secrets surprisingly well. It was not as if he went about practicing his hobby every Saturday night. He often went weeks, sometimes months, between kills. But eventually the fever would come upon him and he would go off into the night to find a suitable victim."

"How did you learn the truth?" Virginia said.

"Jasper followed him one night," Alcina said.

"When I realized what he was doing with the street girls, I began to conceive my grand experiment," Welch said. "I had already discovered Mrs. Bridewell and her clockwork curiosities, and I had developed my theory. I was anxious to perform some experiments with the devices."

"You convinced your father to let you run those experiments on his victims," Virginia whispered.

"He was very enthusiastic about the plan when he realized that I was his son. He certainly got into the spirit of the experiments, I must say."

Virginia did not think she could be any more horrified than she already was. But a new chill slithered down her spine. She stared at Welch.

"You helped your father murder three street girls in the basement of the Hollister house, and then you murdered Mrs. Ratford and Mrs. Hackett," she said.

Welch scowled. "You speak as if I were a common criminal. I am a scientist. I have been carrying out experiments with glasslight for years, but it wasn't until I accidentally discovered Mrs. Bridewell's inventions that I was able to conceive of a way to realize the full potential of my work. My father and I worked together to perfect the process of infusing the death energy into the mirrors."

"Why did you stop using streetwalkers as your victims?" Virginia asked. "Why take the risk of killing Ratford and Hackett?"

"It occurred to me that if the subject that was to be extinguished—"

"You mean the murder victim," Virginia said.

Welch ignored the interruption. "If the subject was possessed of a talent that was sensitive to glasslight, the energy given off at death would have a natural affinity for mirrors and be far more readily absorbed by the glass."

Mrs. Crofton glowered at him. "What is the purpose of all this murdering? Why are you trying to infuse paranormal energy into mirrors?"

"Of course you do not understand," Welch said impatiently. "You are a housekeeper, not a scientist." He turned to Virginia. "But surely you, with your great talent, can perceive the potential of my work, Miss Dean."

"As far as I can tell, your only goal is death by glasslight," she said. "Where is the use in that? A gun would certainly be more efficient."

"Bah. You are as ignorant as your housekeeper. This is where you come in. Over time this chamber has absorbed a vast quantity of energy. It only remains to find a way to ignite the power in the mirrors."

"You think you can do that by murdering me and infusing my energy into the glasses?"

"Indeed. What's more, if my theory is correct, I will be able to construct other engines like this one."

"Good grief," Virginia said.

"Once I learn how to harness and control the energy

in the mirrors, there is no limit to what I can achieve. I stand on the brink of creating amazing weapons that will bring down armies yet leave buildings, roads and factories untouched."

"In other words, you are crafting a very large psychical cannon," Virginia said.

"Advanced weaponry is only one potential aspect of my work," Welch said. "Power is power. It can be used for an infinite number of purposes. A psychical scientist with a talent for engineering might find a way to use my glasslight generators to power ships and trains. One day someone might use one of my generators to unlock the secrets of the paranormal spectrum. Who knows what might be accomplished if mankind succeeds in comprehending the workings of the paranormal."

"And all of it powered by death," Virginia said. "Something tells me that is not going to generate a lot of enthusiasm in the general public."

Welch's face tightened with anger. "The public need never know that my Great Engines require the death energy of an occasional glasslight-talent or two to ignite them."

"A few glass-readers will disappear here and there, and no one will even notice. Is that the plan?"

"The reflective properties of the mirrors will magnify the results of each subject's contribution," Welch assured her.

"How do you plan to control your looking-glass engines? You said yourself that you do not know Mrs. Bridewell's secret for releasing the energy stored in glass by mechanical means."

"I am still working on that aspect of the problem," Welch admitted. "But it is only a matter of time before I reason it out. Meanwhile, igniting the energy in this chamber will have one very immediate and useful effect. It will vastly enhance the power of each of the objects in this room."

Mrs. Crofton looked disgusted. "You're turning these artifacts into weapons?"

"Weapons that are far more powerful than Mrs. Bridewell's toys," Welch assured her. "One can only imagine what devices I will be able to create in this chamber once I have ignited the mirrors with the energy given off by a high-level glasslight-talent like Miss Dean. And that is just a starting point. Future applications are unlimited."

"Mirrors break rather easily," Virginia said.

"If that was intended as an attempt at humor," Alcina said, "perhaps you don't understand why you are here today."

"I'm well aware of why you brought me here," Virginia said. "Your brother wants to murder me in this room because I'm the strongest glass-reader he has ever come across. There is a lot of energy trapped in these walls. He thinks he can use me to ignite it."

Alcina looked amused. "You are impressively calm about the situation in which you find yourself, Miss Dean."

"So are you," Virginia said. "Why are you allowing Welch to use this fantastic collection and these mirrors for his grand experiment?"

"The more powerful the mirrors in this room become,

FORTY-ONE

O ne last question," Virginia said. She looked at Alcina. "What went wrong that night at the Hollister mansion?"

"Everything went wrong that night," Alcina said, her face twisting with fury and remembered frustration. "Jasper and I always intended to kill Hollister, but we did not plan for him to die that night. We wanted him to suffer."

"And, of course, make a contribution to my Great Engine," Welch added. "Father was a fairly high-level glasslight-talent. Not nearly as powerful as you, Miss Dean, but certainly strong enough to enhance the store of energy in this chamber."

"The plan was to kidnap you and hold you in Hollister's basement until we could arrange to transport you here," Welch said. "We reasoned that if anyone noticed that you had disappeared, the investigation would get no farther than the door of the mansion. Hollister would see to it that it was stopped at that point."

"Hollister cooperated because you promised him that he could participate in the experiment, didn't he?"

"Yes." Welch smiled. "He was very excited. He even offered to toss in the little whore that he had picked up for his own amusement. Extra fuel, he said. Of course, he did not entirely understand what I meant by the word 'participate.'"

"But Lady Hollister finally snapped that night," Virginia said.

"It was something you said at the reading, you stupid woman," Alcina hissed. "You told her that you saw the ghost of her dead daughter in the mirror and that the girl had been murdered by someone in the household, someone the child feared greatly."

"Her own father," Virginia said.

"I'm sure Lady Hollister had long ago guessed the truth, but she refused to acknowledge it to herself all those years. Perhaps the denial is what drove her mad. But that night you ripped through her illusions by forcing her to confront the ghost of her daughter."

"Well, actually, I don't see ghosts," Virginia began.

"She thought you did," Alcina shot back, accusation ringing in the words. "You were not awake to watch her lose whatever frail grasp she had left on sanity, because at that point you were overcome by the drug I put in your tea. Lady Hollister thought you had fainted. I told her I would arrange to have you sent home in a cab. She went to her bedroom and locked the door. I assumed she was taking her laudanum. Hollister and I got you downstairs. We were about to lock you in one of the cells."

"That's when Lady Hollister arrived with the kitchen knife," Virginia said. "She stabbed him in the tunnel outside those cells."

"Hollister was taken completely by surprise," Alcina said. "So was I. By the time Hollister realized that his mad wife intended to murder him the knife was already in his chest. I won't ever forget the look on the bastard's face. Lady Hollister fled back up into the house. As he lay dying, I told my father who I was and that Jasper and I were going to inherit his entire fortune."

"But then you panicked and ran."

"I had no choice. I was afraid that in her madness Lady Hollister would summon the police. I did not want to be questioned by the authorities. They might have learned my real identity. I might even have been considered a suspect. There were no witnesses, aside from myself."

"How did I end up on the bed in the mirrored room with Hollister's body?" Virginia asked.

"I have no idea," Alcina said.

"I think that's enough chatter for now," Welch said. "Let us be off, Alcina." He leaned down to remove the keys in the three clockwork weapons. "We now have one minute to reach safety."

Alcina was already at the door. She opened it quickly and rushed out of the room. Welch followed, yanking the door shut. There was an ominous, muffled click when he secured the lock on the other side.

"I am so sorry, Mrs. Crofton," Virginia said quietly. She used her free hand to open her chatelaine purse. "I should never have allowed you to involve yourself in the investigation."

"Nonsense. I'm the one who made that decision. What's more, I'd make the same decision again." Mrs. Crofton sighed. "But in hindsight, it would have been nice to have been able to take along a pistol when I went to see the Hollister housekeeper."

"The Sweetwaters favor knives," Virginia said. "They are also fond of lock picks."

She took out the pick that Owen had given her and went to work.

Mrs. Crofton watched her intently. "Are you skilled with that particular device?"

"I've only had a few lessons," Virginia admitted. "But it appears that manacle locks are very simple in design."

She heard three ominous clicks. The tail of the scorpion twitched. The eyes of the praying mantis glittered. The spider's jointed legs creaked.

Cold energy shivered in the atmosphere.

There was a fourth click. The manacles parted and fell to the floor.

The energy from the three clockwork weapons was heightened rapidly.

"Dear heaven," Mrs. Crofton whispered. "What is that terrible sensation?"

"Glasslight," Virginia said.

She jumped to her feet and kicked over the praying mantis. The device toppled onto its side. The terrible chill from the remaining two curiosities was so strong now that she could scarcely breathe. She managed to topple the spider and then the scorpion.

But all three machines continued to respond to the presence of the human auras. The mechanical legs thrashed rhythmically. The glass eyes rattled in their sockets, pouring energy into the atmosphere as they attempted to fix on their targets.

Flames leaped in the mirrors, so powerful that even Mrs. Crofton could perceive them. She stared into the looking glasses, horrified.

"Oh, damn," Virginia said.

"The room is on fire," Mrs. Crofton said, and gasped.

"It's paranormal fire, Mrs. Crofton. I think the energy from the curiosities is fueling it. For now the flames are still trapped in the mirrors, but I do not know how much longer that will be the case. Come, we must get out of here. Hold on to my hand. Whatever you do, don't let go."

Mrs. Crofton needed no urging. She took a tight grip on Virginia's fingers.

Perhaps "death grip" was the most appropriate description, Virginia thought. They started toward the door.

The cobalt urn began to glow an eerie shade of blue.

"What's happening?" Mrs. Crofton demanded.

"The energy in this room is so strong now, it is activating some of the artifacts."

Virginia picked up a glass vase and hurled it at the mirror that concealed the door. The looking-glass panel cracked, splintered and fell to the floor, revealing the doorknob. Virginia seized it with her free hand.

"Locked," she said. "I'll need both hands. Keep a grip on my shoulder, Mrs. Crofton. Do not lose contact."

She went to work with the pick. The mirrors burned around her.

FORTY-TWO

S omething has gone wrong," Alcina said. "I can sense it."

"Nonsense." Welch examined his pocket watch. "I have calculated very carefully. Miss Dean is dying at this very moment. Her energy is being infused into the mirrors. You can sense the power because there is so much of it, but that is a good sign. It means that my Great Engine has begun to ignite. I have achieved what the ancients failed to accomplish, an astonishingly powerful alchemical furnace that will deliver up the secrets of the paranormal."

They were standing together in the library of the mansion, awaiting the conclusion of the experiment that was taking place on the floor above. Welch was beside himself with excitement. He had waited so long for this moment, he thought, overcome so many obstacles. Now, at last, success was within his grasp. By dawn he would be the master of alchemical power beyond description. The arrogant Joneses of Arcane would be forced to bow to his superior talents. Royalty would be dazzled.

But the true prize was beyond measure. He was certain that the energy trapped in the mirrors could do more than bring him great wealth and power. It would do what Sylvester Jones's formula had failed to achieve. It would enhance his paranormal senses, and if the ancients were correct, that enhancement would add decades to his normal life span.

A small, muffled explosion rumbled through the ceiling of the library. Alcina looked up, horrified.

"My artifacts," she shrieked. "Your engine is destroying them."

"Perhaps one or two of the relics will not survive the storm of energy in that room, but that is no great matter," Welch said.

"No, I cannot allow that to happen. They are too precious. They enhance my talent."

Alcina grabbed fistfuls of her skirts and ran out of the library. He heard her footsteps on the staircase.

"Alcina, wait," he called. "Come back."

He started after her, but the window behind him exploded inward with violent force. Glass rained down. Stunned, he whirled around.

A dark figure swept in out of the night. Welch felt a terrible force strike at him, nearly stopping his heart. Terror unlike anything he had ever known paralyzed him.

"Where is she?" Owen Sweetwater asked.

Welch's brain seemed to be fragmenting.

"Too late," Welch wheezed. "Experiment has started."

"Where is she?"

"You can't stop it."

Another wave of terror struck Welch.

"Upstairs," Welch managed. "She will still be alive. It will take some time to infuse her energy into the walls."

FORTY-THREE

C an you open the door?" Mrs. Crofton asked.

"I don't know," Virginia said. She tried to concentrate, but it was difficult because she was using so much energy to keep an invisible shield around herself and Mrs. Crofton. "This lock is much more complicated."

Across the room the interior of the glass coffin started to glow with an eerie green radiance.

Virginia sighed and straightened away from the door. "We're trapped in here, Mrs. Crofton. I do not have the necessary skill required to open this lock."

"We are dead, then."

"Maybe not. This is glasslight. Powerful glasslight, to be sure, but I know how to work it."

She took Mrs. Crofton's hand again and focused on the fire in a nearby mirrored wall panel. She opened her senses to the fullest extent. The flames inside the looking glass leaped higher. Without warning, they flashed free of the glass and lanced through the chamber. More artifacts exploded.

Mrs. Crofton gasped. "What is happening?"

"There is an incredible amount of energy trapped in these mirrors," Virginia said. "I am setting some of it free. If I can channel it, I might be able to use it to destroy the door."

"Won't it destroy us as well?"

"I think I can protect you as long as you hold on to me, Mrs. Crofton."

"Trust me, I won't be letting go anytime soon."

Another wall panel ignited, sending out flames of hot energy in response to Virginia's summons. She seized control of the currents and channeled them toward the door.

More artifacts were heating now, as the objects inside them responded to the wild energy in the atmosphere.

The door of the chamber began to shudder. When there was a great quantity of paranormal energy in the atmosphere, it affected the normal energy in the space.

The door started to char. In another moment it would surely burst into flames, Virginia thought. She would have to maintain very careful control of the energy she had unleashed.

The door slammed open. Alcina stood on the threshold, the rage on her face as hot as the storm in the chamber.

"What are you doing?" she shrieked. "You are destroying my artifacts, my chamber." She brought the gun up. "I will not allow you to do this to me."

Virginia released Mrs. Crofton's wrist and moved away from her. Alcina swiveled to follow Virginia. She no longer seemed to be aware of Mrs. Crofton.

"Run, Mrs. Crofton," Virginia whispered. "I will deal with this."

Mrs. Crofton hesitated and then hiked up her skirts

and fled through the doorway. She disappeared into a dark hall.

Virginia channeled some of the energy at the gun in Alcina's hand. The weapon glowed red. Alcina screamed and flung it aside. She ran to the nearest glass case, opened it and took out the obsidian dagger. She aimed the tip of the blade at Virginia.

Black flares flashed from the dagger. Virginia felt the blood in her veins turn cold. She could not move.

"You cannot do this to me," Alcina shrieked at Virginia. "I will not let you destroy me."

More energy arced from the tip of the dagger. But this time Virginia was ready for it. Her psychical resources were fading rapidly now. She was close to exhaustion. But she managed a dampening current of power.

The dagger heated with paranormal fire. Alcina screamed. Her body jerked violently. She tried to drop the dagger, but her hands seemed frozen around the hilt.

The chamber erupted into flames, the normal kind as well as the paranormal variety. Mirrors cracked, splintered, fractured and exploded. Virginia realized vaguely that the wood walls behind the looking glasses were burning. Smoke boiled into the atmosphere.

She tried to stagger toward the door, but it was a million miles away in another dimension. She knew she would not make it.

She fell to her knees, sliding into the darkest night she had ever known. Her vision wavered. When she saw Owen coming toward her through the storm of energy, she knew she was hallucinating.

"Virginia," he said.

She looked up at him, dazed.

"I meant to tell you that I love you," she said. "Too late now, though. You're not really here, are you?"

"I'm here, Virginia."

"Oh, that's right," she said, remembering. "You told me that you would walk through hell to save me."

"Yes."

He reached down, scooped her up into his arms and ran for the door.

The mirrored chamber exploded around them.

A short time later Owen stood with Nick, Tony, Matt and Mrs. Crofton in the shadows of a small park. With the exception of Virginia, who was sound asleep in Owen's arms, they all watched the big house burn. Flames roared from every window. Black smoke billowed into the night.

"Both bodies are inside the house?" Owen asked, mentally tying up loose ends.

"Yes," Nick said. "It will look like they died in the blaze."

"I didn't know paranormal fire could start a normal fire," Tony said. He sounded awed.

"There is no hard-and-fast line on the spectrum between the normal and the paranormal," Nick said. "How many times have I explained to you that it's a continuum? Get enough energy going in one section and it will affect the currents in the neighboring regions."

Matt grinned. "Thanks, as always, for the lecture, Uncle Nick."

"Huh," Nick muttered. "All I can say is Miss Dean must have set free a lot of very hot glasslight tonight."

"I don't know anything about this spectrum you're all talking about," Mrs. Crofton declared, "but I must admit that Miss Dean is a most unusual employer. My life has become a good deal more exciting since I entered her service."

"She'll fit in nicely with the Sweetwater family," Owen said.

"I see." Mrs. Crofton nodded in a knowing manner. "I had a feeling that might be the way of things."

Owen looked at her. "Plenty of room for you, as well, Mrs. Crofton."

"Is there, now?" Mrs. Crofton said softly.

"Recent evidence to the contrary, we're actually a very normal family," Nick said.

"Is that so?" Mrs. Crofton said.

"Assuming you can overlook our talents and the sort of work that we do," Tony added.

"Miss Dean says you hunt monsters," Mrs. Crofton said.

"You might call it the family business," Owen said.

"Would I get to do more of the sort of inquiries that I did this afternoon?" Mrs. Crofton asked.

"If you like," Owen said. "Sweetwaters are happy to take all the help we can get, so long as it comes from within the family."

"My inquiry today left me sleeping in a glass coffin."

"Perhaps you won't want to continue with a career as an inquiry agent," Owen said. "Understandable. There are other positions available."

"Might have been a different outcome if I'd been properly armed," Mrs. Crofton said. "A pistol in my handbag, for example, would have been useful."

"That won't be a problem in the future," Owen said.

FORTY-FOUR

Virginia opened her eyes and saw Owen standing at the window, looking out into the moonlit night. The sleeves of his shirt were rolled up on his forearms. His collar was open. He had one hand braced against the sill. The silver light limned his face in shadows and mysteries.

"Owen," she said softly.

He turned and walked to the bed. His eyes heated.

"How are you feeling?" he asked.

Tentatively she heightened her senses. There was no need to focus. One knew when one's talent was functioning properly, just as one knew if one's hearing or eyesight or sense of touch was working. She felt the familiar tingle of awareness.

"I feel fine," she said. "What of Mrs. Crofton?"

"She has concluded that she has a talent for the private inquiry business, but she insists on being properly armed the next time she goes off to track down persons of interest in a case."

"I told you at the start of this affair that she is an excellent housekeeper and that I was very lucky to have her."

"So you did. She seems to think that she is fortunate in her employer, as well."

"Hardly. I very nearly got her killed today."

Owen leaned over the bed, palms flattened on either side of her shoulders. "I'm the one responsible for what happened today. I put you both at risk."

"I was already at risk, if you will recall. That is why you came to me in the first place. You wanted to keep me safe."

"I failed."

"Here is what I know, Owen Sweetwater. If you had not come looking for me that night that I went to the Hollister mansion, I would likely never have made it out of that terrible place alive. The girl we found there would have died as well."

"Virginia—"

"If you had not convinced me that I was in grave danger, and if you had not allowed me to participate in the investigation, I would not have been prepared for what happened tonight. The lock pick you gave me helped save Mrs. Crofton and me. By the time I had finished dealing with Alcina Norgate, I was so exhausted I would not have been able to escape the flames. But you carried me out of that storm of energy and fire. All in all, I would say that you took very good care of me."

"However that may be, I swear I will do an infinitely better job of taking care of you in the future."

She touched his hard jaw. "Will you?"

"I have no choice," he said. "Last night when I carried you out of that chamber you said you loved me."

"Yes."

"I realized I had never told you that I love you. I have loved you since I watched you give the reading in Lady Pomeroy's drawing room. I will always love you."

A sensation of radiant joy rushed through her. Mercilessly, she crushed it with an act of will.

"You don't have to romance me," she said. "I understand that what you believe we have is some sort of psychical bond. But it is enough. For now."

He leaned down and kissed her forehead. When he raised his head, his eyes burned. "For a man like me, there is no difference between the psychical bond and the bond of love. It is all one and the same."

She searched his face in the shadows. "How can you know that?"

"Sweetwaters take this kind of thing very seriously. It is part of our talent. Trust me, I am certain."

"You must realize that I will not be the mistress of a married man. I will not live in the shadows as my mother did."

"Has some married man asked you to be his mistress?" Owen's eyes glittered with dark laughter. "If so, give me his name and I will see to it that he disappears."

"I am serious."

"You insult me gravely if you think that I am the kind of man who would keep a lover on the side while I married another woman and fathered children by her. I realize that may be common in society, but we do not do that sort of thing in the Sweetwater family." He smiled a quick, wicked smile. "Our ladies do not condone the practice."

She stared at him. "But you must marry a woman of your own station. It is your duty to your family."

He stopped smiling. "My family hunts monsters, Virginia, not foxes or deer or squirrels. What is more, we do it for money whenever possible. It is, as I made clear to Mrs. Crofton, the family business. I'm afraid that there is no getting around the fact that we are in trade. Where does that put us on the social ladder?"

"I hadn't thought about it in those terms," she admitted.

"Sweetwaters are not bound by society's conventions when it comes to marriage. We cannot afford to abide by them. For us, too much depends on finding the right woman. I have found you. You are what I need to help me survive the night."

"I don't understand."

"Sweetwater men must marry women who can accept the talent and the compulsion that drives us to hunt, strong women who can be our partners as well as our lovers. We must choose women who can keep and protect the family secrets."

"Well, yes, I can understand how trust would be of paramount importance in a Sweetwater marriage, given your family's eccentricities, but that's not my point here."

"It goes far beyond trust," Owen said evenly. "It is a matter of survival."

"What are you talking about?"

"I am going to tell you the greatest Sweetwater secret of all. The men of my family can survive the hunt over time only if we succeed in finding the right women. Each of us must find the one with whom we can truly bond. If we fail to establish such a connection, we are doomed."

"To die?" She gasped, horrified. "I can't believe that."

"Death is not what we fear. In the end we all die.

What the men in my family risk is far worse, the slow, cold, empty doom we call nightwalking. When a Sweet-water becomes a true nightwalker he is consumed utterly by the passion for the hunt. Nothing else matters. The bloodlust is the only emotion he can feel, an absolute obsession that can never be satisfied. There is no peace, no rest, no other passion. The darkness takes over. He seeks the only escape available to him."

"Suicide?"

"You could call it a form of suicide, perhaps." Owen straightened away from the bed. "The Sweetwater who becomes a true nightwalker starts to take great risks. He shuts himself off from the family. He begins to hunt alone. He goes out again and again, seeking prey. Eventually he miscalculates. Some say deliberately."

She shuddered. "That night, after you were attacked, one of your nephews said something to the effect that your family was worried because you were starting to walk the streets at night. Now I understand the concern. Are you sliding into this dangerous obsession you speak of?"

He smiled. "Not any longer. I have found you." Methodically he began to unfasten his shirt. "Now all I have to do is convince you to marry me."

This was the one man she could trust, she thought, the one she had been waiting for. If he said he loved her, she could believe him.

She smiled slowly. "Well, when you put it that way, I can hardly refuse."

His hands dropped away from the unbuttoned shirt. His eyes burned with a stark hunger.

"Virginia—"

"I love you, Owen Sweetwater. You are the only man who has ever understood me, the only one who can handle my talent. I need you as much as you need me. I will love you to the end of my days and beyond, if such a thing is possible."

He smiled his dangerous smile. "That's how it's supposed to work."

He sat down on the edge of the bed. One boot hit the floor, and then the other. Virginia watched as he unbuckled the leather sheath containing the knife and placed it on the nightstand.

He stood long enough to remove his trousers, and then he came to her in a fever of passion. She shivered when he touched her, thrilling to his touch, as she always would. A great longing built deep inside her.

She felt his strong fingers move on her, stroking all the secret places. When she touched him intimately he shuddered in response. She could feel the perspiration on his sleek back.

He lowered himself on top of her and slowly, reverently joined their bodies together, generating the intimate currents of the most powerful force on the spectrum—the energy of love.

FORTY-FIVE

"How did you find us last night?" Mrs. Crofton asked.

They were gathered once again in the tiny parlor. The space was crowded. Virginia and Charlotte occupied the sofa. Mrs. Crofton sat on one of the dainty chairs. The four Sweetwater men ignored the spindly furniture. They lounged around the room like great cats or propped themselves gracefully against the walls and mantel.

"I discovered that a woman named Alcina Norgate was the sole beneficiary of Lady Hollister's will," Owen said. "But it appeared to be a dead end. So I went back to the start of the case and considered events from another angle."

"What angle?" Nick asked.

Owen gripped the marble edge of the mantel. "It occurred to me that the killer was too sure of himself, too certain that his experiments with Ratford and Hackett were not likely to be disturbed. Later, after I did disturb them, he felt confident enough to place the curiosities on guard."

"I understand," Virginia said. "You wondered why he felt comfortable returning again and again to the scenes of the crimes."

"It is not uncommon for a villain to do that," Owen said. "But this particular killer seemed especially casual about it. There was one obvious reason why that might be true. If he owned the houses, he could make sure they remained empty as long as he wished."

"Of course." Enthusiasm leaped in Nick's eyes. "He did not need to fear that a new occupant would move in."

Owen looked at Virginia. "I paid a call on the agent who rented this house to you. It took some time, but I eventually discovered that Welch was your landlord. I also learned that he owned the two houses that had been rented by the glass-readers who were murdered."

Tony grinned. "As my father would say, that is an example of the importance of basic detective work. No paranormal talent involved."

"It wasn't proof that Welch was a murderer," Owen said. "But it did raise some interesting questions and suggested some answers."

Virginia winced. "No wonder Mr. Welch was so helpful when I signed the contract with the Institute. He was delighted to find another glass-reader. He directed me to the agent who rented this house to me. I expect that is how the other two glass-readers came by their leased houses as well."

"Yes."

Charlotte looked at him, intrigued. "How did you discover Mr. Welch's address?"

"That was not so easy," Owen said. "The agent did not have it. He simply deposited the funds into a bank account. But I was fairly certain someone else did know where Welch lived."

Mrs. Crofton's brow wrinkled. "Who was that?"

Owen looked at her. "Gilmore Leybrook."

Virginia raised her brows. "You called on Leybrook?"

Owen smiled his Sweetwater smile. "He was very helpful."

Virginia groaned. "I doubt that. Please tell me that he is alive and in reasonably good condition."

"Leybrook is recovering from a shock to the senses, but he is fine," Owen said.

Virginia decided not to pursue that subject. She turned to Mrs. Crofton. "What did you learn from the Hollister housekeeper?"

"Mrs. Tapton was deep into her gin when I found her. She talked quite freely. Told me that Lady Hollister was mad but that Hollister himself was the one who terrified the staff. The only reason Mrs. Tapton stayed was out of loyalty to Lady Hollister. She had been with her since Lady Hollister was a girl in her teens. When Lady Hollister entered the mansion as a young bride, the housekeeper went with her."

"Did the housekeeper and the rest of the staff know what was going on in the basement of the Hollister mansion?" Charlotte asked.

"No, I don't think so," Mrs. Crofton said. "I'm sure they sensed that something dreadful was happening inside that house, but they took the sensible approach."

"In other words, they did not go looking for trouble," Virginia said.

"They were paid well to look the other way," Mrs. Crofton said. "And it is not as if the Hollister household was the only one in London that held secrets that the staff preferred not to know."

"No," Owen said. He caught Virginia's eye. "Every house holds a few secrets."

"Some secrets are decidedly more dreadful than others," Virginia said briskly. She frowned in thought. "There is still one question that we have not answered. Who helped Lady Hollister stage the scene in the mirrored room under the mansion so that it would appear that I had murdered Hollister?"

Mrs. Crofton looked at her, surprised. "Isn't it obvious? Who else could the lady of the house count on at such a time?"

"Of course," Virginia said. "The housekeeper."

FORTY-SIX

"Well?" Virginia said. "Have you decided whether or not to make an appointment with Dr. Spinner?"

"I have decided that I won't require Dr. Spinner's therapy after all." Charlotte poured tea into the pot with a serenely confident air. "As it happens, I have recently discovered another very effective cure for female hysteria."

"Have you, indeed?"

"It is, I suspect, the same therapeutic remedy that you have begun to employ."

Virginia smiled knowingly. "I had a feeling that might be the case when I saw you with Nick this morning. There was a certain energy in the air around you."

"I love him, Virginia." Charlotte carried the pot to the table and sat down. "I don't understand it, and I certainly cannot explain it, but I realized the day I met him that deep inside I *recognized* him. It was as if I had been waiting for him to walk through the door of my shop my entire life."

Virginia thought about the night that she had met Owen's eyes in the mirror at the Pomeroy reading. "I know what you mean."

"It was all very odd and confusing, I must admit. Nick says it was the same way for him, but he claims that it always happens like that for the men of the Sweetwater family when they find the right woman. He thinks it is a side effect of their talent, something to do with their ability to survive their peculiar psychical natures."

They were seated in Charlotte's small kitchen. Outside, the morning was sunny and warm. It felt to Virginia as if all of the shadows and darkness that had haunted her world for the past few weeks had been burned away by the fires that had been unleashed in Alcina Norgate's mansion.

There would be more shadows and more darkness in the years ahead for both Owen and herself. It was the nature of their talents and the work that their abilities compelled them to do. It was also the nature of life. In that sense the Sweetwaters were no different from any other family, she thought. But she knew now that the bond of love that she shared with Owen would see them through the years ahead, regardless of what the future held.

She picked up the teacup that Charlotte had filled. "Perhaps it's true what they say about love between two strong talents," she said. "It does forge a metaphysical connection."

"Just like in a sensation novel," Charlotte said.

Virginia laughed. "Something tells me that no sensation novelist would approve of the heroine marrying into the Sweetwater family. That particular family does possess some unusual secrets."

"*Bah*. Every family has secrets."

"You're right." Virginia raised her cup in a small salute. "And you and I will keep those secrets."

"Absolutely," Charlotte said.

The bell over the door tinkled. Owen walked into the shop. Nick was with him.

"We're in here," Virginia called through the doorway of the back room.

Owen came to stand in the opening. He looked at the pot on the table and smiled.

"Excellent," he said. "There's tea."

Nick ambled into the room, rubbing his hands in anticipation. "I am sorely in need of a cup. Are there any biscuits to go with the tea?"

"In the cupboard," Charlotte said. "Help yourself."

"Thank you, I'll do that."

Owen sat down next to Virginia. He took her hand underneath the table, gripping her fingers tightly. She felt the energy of his love enveloping her and knew that she would sense that energy for the rest of her life.

"My Aunt Ethel has given strict instructions for Nick and me to bring both of you to dinner this evening," Owen said.

"We are to meet the rest of your family?" Charlotte asked, startled.

"Some of them." Owen made a face. "They won't all be there this evening, but there will be more than enough, believe me."

Nick opened a cupboard and took out a package of tea biscuits. "It will be relatively painless, I assure you," he said. "Everyone is very excited to meet both of you. They had almost given up on Owen, and they were starting to fret about me. They will all be overjoyed to make your acquaintance."

"No need to be concerned," Owen said. "Talent aside, Sweetwaters are actually a very ordinary family."

"Right," Nick said. "Ordinary to the point of being rather dull." He came back to the table with the biscuits and sat down. "Is there any tea left?"

Virginia and Charlotte exchanged glances, and then they looked at Owen and Nick. Both men munched on biscuits, oblivious.

"Ordinary," Charlotte repeated.

"Dull," Virginia said.

Owen smiled, his eyes heating.

"Don't worry," he said. "You'll both fit right in."

FORTY-SEVEN

W hat was Papa like?" Elizabeth asked.

Virginia put her teacup gently down on the delicate china saucer. She thought for a moment. "While you do not remember Papa at all, my own memories of him amount to little more than fragments of a photograph. The only reason I can recall what he actually looked like is because I do have a photograph that was taken the year that he and my mother died."

Virginia had arrived at the Mansfield house a short time earlier. She had sent around a note declining Helen's offer of the Mansfield carriage. Instead, Owen had escorted her in a Sweetwater carriage. He was now waiting for her in the park across the street.

When she had been ushered into the elegant drawing room, Helen and Elizabeth greeted her. Virginia had not been surprised to discover that Helen did not really want to consult about a mirror reading.

"Elizabeth wants to talk to you," she had said. "I hope you will be kind enough to answer her questions."

Virginia had expected Elizabeth to ask questions about her talent. Instead, the girl wanted to know about their father.

"I have a photograph, too," Elizabeth said. "It was taken on my parents' wedding day. Papa looks quite handsome."

Virginia thought about her own precious photo. "Yes, he was a fine-looking man. But what I remember is the energy around him. When he walked into a room, people were immediately aware of him. They greeted him warmly. Everyone wanted to be his friend. For his part he was gracious to one and all, high and low."

Helen paused her teacup in midair. A wistful smile fluttered around her lips. "That's true. Robert always treated those who served him with respect. They, in turn, would have done anything for him."

Elizabeth sat forward eagerly. "What else do you remember about him, Miss Dean?"

Virginia smiled. "Please call me Virginia."

Elizabeth brightened. "Thank you. And you must call me Elizabeth. Everyone else does, and you are, after all, my sister."

Virginia waited for Helen to dispute the relationship, but she said nothing. She took another sip of tea instead, and waited for Virginia to continue.

"Very well, then, Elizabeth," Virginia said. She thought for a moment. "Your father—"

"*Our* father," Elizabeth insisted.

"Yes," Virginia said. "Papa was always cheerful. I do not recall him ever losing his temper. When he came to see us he brought me presents."

There was no need to explain that the small gifts were intended as silent apologies for all the broken promises and all the times that he had failed to visit.

"Did he take you to fairs and museums?" Elizabeth asked.

A forgotten memory flitted through Virginia's head. "I remember a trip to a museum when I was your age. Papa wanted to show me some artifacts that he believed were infused with paranormal energy."

"That must have been exciting," Elizabeth said.

"It was. That was the day he told me that I had a baby sister. He said that he looked forward to showing you the artifacts when you were old enough to sense the energy in them. He said the paranormal was part of our heritage and that we should understand it."

"He talked about me?" Elizabeth asked.

"Oh, yes," Virginia said. "He was very fond of you." She looked at Helen. "And of your mother, too. He was proud of you both."

Helen raised her brows at that.

Virginia smiled at her. "It's true. As my mother once told me, in his own way, Papa loved both of his families."

Virginia took her leave a half hour later. Helen saw her to the door.

"I hope you will come back to visit Elizabeth again soon, Miss Dean," she said. "Please know that you are welcome in this house at any time."

"That is very kind of you, madam."

"Call me Helen," she said.

"You must call me Virginia, as Elizabeth does."

The butler opened the front door. Virginia was surprised when Helen followed her onto the front step and out of earshot of the servant.

"He was not a bad or evil man, was he?" Helen said quietly.

"No," Virginia said. "Papa enjoyed life."

"Perhaps to excess," Helen said dryly. "But in his boundless enthusiasm for it, he was careless of the happiness of others."

"Yes."

"He never wanted to consider the consequence of his actions, and he never was called upon to do so. He got away with that attitude because he could charm the birds out of the trees as well as every woman in range of his smile." Helen shook her head ruefully. "I swear, that was his true psychical talent."

"You may be right," Virginia said.

Helen fixed her with an intent look. "But I will say this much for him, he fathered two fine daughters, of whom he would have been proud. Thank you, again, for your kindness to Elizabeth."

"She is my sister."

"And we are forever linked as family," Helen said. "Do not forget that."

Virginia looked across the street and saw Owen lounging, arms crossed, against the side of the gleaming black Sweetwater carriage.

"As it happens, I am to be married soon," Virginia said.

Surprise flashed across Helen's face, but she recovered quickly and smiled. "Congratulations." She glanced across the street at Owen and the sleek carriage. "Dare I ask if that is your fiancé?"

"Yes. Mr. Sweetwater." Virginia raised a hand to signal Owen. "I will introduce you."

Helen watched Owen straighten away from the carriage and start toward them across the street. "Sweetwater. I think I have heard of the family. It's an old one, I believe. But I know nothing about them."

"The Sweetwaters rarely go into society," Virginia said.

Owen smiled at her. He was halfway across the street.

"Can I ask you a personal question, Helen?" Virginia said.

"My daughter asked you a great many personal questions today. The least I can do is answer one for you."

"Knowing what we both know about my father, it has occurred to me from time to time that while I'm sure he always intended to provide for me, it is unlikely that Papa actually got around to doing so in his will."

Helen did not look away from Owen. "I don't know what you mean, Virginia."

"Even if he did remember me in his will, I cannot imagine that he went to the trouble of ensuring that I would attend Miss Peabody's School for Young Ladies in the event of his death. He would have assumed that my mother would be around to take care of me. I'm sure it never occurred to him that there was a possibility that I would be orphaned."

Helen sighed. "It was not in Robert's nature to plan for the future, nor did he like to contemplate the prospect of his own death. He lived too much in the moment."

"You were the one who saw to it that I went to the

Peabody School, weren't you? You were the one who
paid the fees all those years and made certain that when
I graduated I received a bequest to see me started in
life."

"It was only a small amount," Helen said. "I should
have done more for you. But it took me a long time to
overcome my own pain and anger. You see, I loved Robert with all of my heart. I believed he loved me. I never
realized that he had a second family until the day I was
informed of his death. It came as a great shock."

"But you nevertheless made certain that I was not
sent to the workhouse or a charity orphanage. You
ensured that I was given a fine education and taught
proper manners. You gave me what I needed to survive
as a woman alone in this world. I will always be
grateful."

Helen smiled. "Nonsense. I may not possess any psychical ability, but my intuition tells me that you would
have survived quite nicely on your own resources, Virginia Dean. You are a woman of many talents."

And then Owen was there and Virginia was introducing him to Helen and a very excited and curious
Elizabeth, who came rushing out the door to meet him.
There were congratulations on the forthcoming marriage and promises to attend the wedding.

Eventually Owen took Virginia's arm and escorted
her to the waiting carriage. He handed her up into the
cab, got in and closed the door.

"I take it your visit with your sister and her mother
went well?" he asked.

"Yes," Virginia said. "Very well."

Owen smiled and pulled her into his arms. His eyes, those dark, haunted eyes that she had sensed from the beginning could promise heaven or hell now promised a lifetime of love.

The small vehicle was traveling too fast on the narrow, twisted road that snaked along the top of the cliffs. Charlotte Enright heard the insectlike whine of the tiny flash-rock engine behind her and hastily stepped off the pavement onto the relative safety of the shoulder. A moment later, one of the familiar low-powered Vibes that visitors rented to get around on the island careened out of the turn.

The driver hit the brakes, bringing the open-sided buggy to a halt beside her.

"Hey, look what we have here," the man behind the wheel said to his two passengers. "It's that weird girl with the glasses who works for that crazy old lady in the antiques store. What are you doing out here all by yourself, Weird Girl?"

There was enough light left in the late summer sky to illuminate the three young men in the car. Charlotte recognized them immediately. They had wandered into Looking Glass Antiques earlier in the day, drawn into the shop not because of an interest in antiques but by the rumors that swirled around her aunt.

"Didn't anyone ever tell you it's dangerous to hang

out on empty roads like this late at night?" the man in the passenger seat asked.

His voice echoed along the lonely stretch of road that led to the Preserve. The laughter of his two companions sent icy chills through Charlotte. She started walking. She did not look back. Maybe if she ignored the three, they would leave her alone. She quickened her pace, walking faster into the rapidly deepening twilight.

The weird girl with the glasses who works for the crazy old lady in the antiques store. The words might just as well have been emblazoned on her T-shirt, she thought. She was pretty sure that just about everyone on the island, with the exception of her friend Rose, thought of her in exactly those words.

The driver took his foot off the brake and let the Vibe coast slowly alongside Charlotte.

"Don't run off, Weird Girl," the one in the passenger seat called out. "We've heard that it gets a little strange out here after dark. Guy back at the bar guaranteed us that if we could get into the Preserve on a moonlit night like this we would see ghosts. You're from around here. Why don't you show us the sights?"

"Yeah, come on now, be friendly, Weird Girl," the driver wheedled. "You're supposed to be nice to tourists."

Charlotte clutched the flashlight very tightly and kept her gaze fixed on the dark woods at the end of Merton Road.

"We'll give you a ride," the driver said, mockingly lecherous. "Come on, get in the car."

"All we want you to do is show us this place they call the Preserve," the one in the backseat urged. "From what we've seen today, there sure as hell isn't anything else of interest on this rock."

Charlotte wondered how the three in the car had found their way all the way out to Merton Road. Only the locals and the summer regulars were aware that the old strip of pavement dead-ended at the border of the private nature conservancy known as the Rainshadow Preserve.

The trio in the Vibe were a familiar species on Rainshadow during the summer months. The type typically arrived on the private yachts and sailboats that crowded the marina on the weekends. They partied heavily all night long in the dockside taverns and restaurants, and when the bars closed down they moved the parties to their boats.

"Come back here, damn it," the driver ordered. He wore a pastel polo shirt that probably had a designer label stitched inside. His light brown hair had obviously been cut in an expensive salon. "We won't hurt you. We just want you to give us a tour of the spooky places the guy in the bar told us about."

"Forget the ugly little bitch, Derek," the man in the backseat said. "No boobs on her, anyway. Trying to get into this Preserve is a waste of time. Let's go back to town. I need a drink and some weed."

"We came all the way out here to see the Preserve," Derek insisted, his tone turning surly. "I'm not going back until this bitch shows us where it is." He raised his voice. "You hear me, Weird Bitch?"

"Yeah," the man in the passenger seat said. "I want to see the place, too. Let's make the bitch show us."

Charlotte's pulse pounded. She was walking as

swiftly as she could. Any faster and she would be running. She was very frightened, but her feminine intuition warned her that if she ran the three men would be out of the Vibe in an instant, pursuing her like a pack of wild animals.

"Is she ignoring us?" the man in the passenger seat asked. "Yeah, I think she's ignoring us. That's just flat-out rude. Someone needs to teach her some manners."

"Damn right, Garrett," Derek said. "Let's get her."

"This is stupid," the man in the backseat said. But the other two paid no attention to him.

Derek brought the Vibe to a stop and jumped out. Garrett followed—so did the man in the rear seat, albeit with obvious reluctance. Charlotte knew that she had no choice now but to run. She fled toward the woods at the end of Merton Road.

Derek and Garrett laughed and gave chase. Charlotte's only hope was to reach the dark trees up ahead. If she could get even a short distance into the Preserve she might be able to lose the three behind her. It was common knowledge on the island that things got very strange inside the Preserve.

There were risks to the strategy. She might get lost herself. It could be days before she was found or managed to stumble out on her own, if ever. According to the local residents it was not unheard of for people to disappear for good inside the Preserve.

The pounding footsteps got louder. Derek and Garrett were gaining on her. She could hear their harsh, angry breathing. She knew then that she probably would not be able to outrun them.

She was almost at the end of the pavement, thinking

she just might make it after all, when a hand closed around her arm and dragged her to a halt.

She whirled, all of her still developing para-senses hitting the upper limits of her talent in response to the adrenaline and fear flooding through her. The driver, Derek, was the one who had grabbed her. Garrett hovered nearby. The third man hung back, clearly uneasy about the way the violence was escalating.

With her senses in full sail, she could see the dark paranormal rainbows cast by the auras of the three men. For all the good that did her, she thought bitterly. She did not need to see the flaring bands of ultralight to know that, of the three, Derek was the most unstable and, therefore, the most dangerous. Why couldn't she have been born with something flashier and more useful in the way of a talent? The ability to deliver a psychic hypnotic command or a freezing blast of energy that would stop Derek cold would have been nice.

She had no choice now but to fight. She flailed wildly with the flashlight. A brief flicker of satisfaction swept through her when the metal barrel struck Derek on his upper arm. She hauled back for another blow.

"Who do you think you are?" Derek snarled. "I'll teach you to hit me."

His face twisted into a vicious mask. He shook her furiously. The flashlight fell from her hand. Her glasses went flying.

Garrett laughed nervously. "That's enough, Derek. She's just a kid."

"Garrett's right," the man from the backseat said. "Come on, Derek, let's get out of here. We've got a lot of drinking left to do tonight. I need my weed, man."

"We're not leaving yet," Derek said. "We're just starting to have some fun."

He drew back a clenched fist, preparing to deliver a punch. Charlotte raised both arms in a desperate attempt to ward off the blow. At the same time, she kicked Derek in the knee.

Derek howled.

"Are you crazy?" Garrett said.

"Bitch," Derek screamed. He shook her again.

A shadowy figure materialized out of the woods. Charlotte did not need her glasses to see the obsidian-dark hues of a familiar ultralight rainbow. Slade Attridge.

Slade moved toward the driver with the speed and lethal intent of an attacking Specter-cat.

"What the hell?" Garrett yelped, startled.

"Shit," the man from the backseat cried out. "I told you this was a bad idea."

Derek was oblivious to the danger. In his rage, he was obsessed only with punishing Charlotte. He did not realize what was happening until a powerful hand locked around his shoulder.

"Let her go," Slade said. He wrenched Derek away from Charlotte.

Derek screamed. He released Charlotte and frantically tried to scramble out of reach. Slade used one booted foot to swipe Derek's legs out from under him. Derek landed hard on the pavement, shrieking with rage and pain.

"You can't do this to me," he screeched. "You don't know who you're messing with. My dad will have you arrested. He'll sue your ass."

"That should be interesting," Slade said. He looked at the other two. "Get him in the Vibe and get out of here. Come anywhere near her again and you will all wake up in an ICU or maybe just plain dead, depending on my mood at the time. Is that understood?"

"Shit, this guy's crazy," the man from the backseat whispered. He ran for the vehicle. "You guys do what you want. I'm out of here."

He hopped into the driver's side, rezzed the little engine and put the Vibe in gear.

"Wait up, damn it." Garrett raced toward the Vibe and jumped into the front seat.

Derek staggered to his feet. "Don't leave me, you bastards. He'll kill me."

"It's a thought," Slade said, as if the idea held great appeal. "Better run."

Derek fled toward the Vibe, which was now halfway through a U-turn.

He lunged forward and managed to dive into the back of the buggy.

The Vibe whined away into the night and vanished around a turn.

A hushed silence fell. The eerie quiet was broken only by the sound of labored breathing. Charlotte realized that she was the one trying to catch her breath. She was shivering but not because she was cold. It was all she could do to stand upright. Great. She was having another stupid panic attack. And in front of Slade Attridge of all people. Just her rotten luck.

"You okay?" Slade asked. He picked up the flashlight and put it in her hand.

"Y-yes. Thanks." She struggled with the deep, square

breathing exercise the para-psychologist had taught her and tried to compose herself. "My glasses." She looked around but everything except Slade's darkly luminous rainbow was indistinct. "They fell off."

"I see them," Slade said. He started across the pavement.

"You m-must have really g-good eyes," she said. Geez. Now she was stuttering because of the panic attack. It was all so humiliating.

"Good night vision," Slade said. "Side effect of my talent."

"You're a h-hunter, aren't you? Not a g-ghost-hunter but a true hunter-talent. I thought so. I've got a c-cousin who is a hunter. You move the same way he does. Like a b-big specter-cat. Arcane?"

"My mother was Arcane but she never registered me with the Society," Slade said. "She died when I was twelve."

"What about your father?"

"He was a ghost-hunter. Died in the tunnels when I was two."

"Geez." She wrapped her arms around herself and forced herself to breathe in the slow, controlled rhythm she had been taught. "W-who raised you?"

"The system."

She went blank for a moment. "What system?"

"Foster care."

"Geez."

She could not think of anything else to say. She had never actually met anyone who had been raised in the foster care system. The stern legal measures set down by the First Generation colonists had been designed to secure the institutions of marriage and the family in stone and they had been very successful. During the two hundred years since the closing of the Curtain, the laws had eased somewhat but not much. The result was that it was rare for a child to be completely orphaned. There was almost always *someone* who had to take you in.

Slade seemed amused. "It wasn't that bad. I wasn't in the system long. I bailed four years ago when I turned fifteen. Figured I'd do better on the streets."

"Geez." *No wonder he seemed so much older*, she thought. She was fifteen and she could not imagine what it would be like trying to survive on her own.

At least her pulse was starting to slow down a little. The breathing exercises were finally kicking in.

"You're Arcane, aren't you?" Slade asked.

"Yeah, the whole family has been Arcane for generations." She made a face. "Mostly high-end talents. I'm the underachiever in the clan. I'm just a rainbow-reader."

"What's that?"

"I see aura rainbows. Totally useless, trust me." She tried to focus on Slade as he reached down to pick up her glasses. "They're probably smashed, huh?"

"The frames are a little bent and the lenses are scratched up."

"Figures." She took the glasses from him and put them on.

The twisted frames sat askew on her nose. The fractured lenses made it difficult to see Slade's face clearly. She knew exactly what he looked like, though, because she had seen him often in town and down at the marina

where he worked. He was nineteen but there was something about his sharply etched features and unreadable
gray-blue eyes that made him seem so much older and
infinitely more experienced. Other boys his age were
still boys. Slade was a man.

She and Rose had speculated endlessly about where
he had come from and, more important, whether or not
he had a girlfriend. If he was dating anyone they were
very sure that she was not a local girl. In a town as small
as Shadow Bay everyone would know if the stranger
who worked at the marina was seeing an island girl.

He had shown up in the Bay at the start of the tourist
season that summer, looking for work. Ben Murphy at
the marina had given him a job. Slade rented a room
above a dockside shop by the week. He was polite and
hardworking but he kept to himself. Occasionally he
caught the Friday afternoon ferry and disappeared for
the weekend. It was assumed that he went to a larger
town on one of the other nearby islands—Thursday
Harbor, maybe—or maybe he went all the way to Frequency City. No one knew for sure. But he was always
back at work at the marina on Monday morning.

"Lucky I've got a backup pair of glasses at my aunt's
house," Charlotte said.

She was immediately mortified. She felt like an idiot
talking about her glasses to the man who currently fea-
tured so vividly in her fantasies. Not that Slade knew
about his role in her dreams. She was pretty sure that
to him she was just the weird girl who worked for her
crazy old aunt in the antiques shop.

"What are you doing out here at this time of night?"
Slade asked.

"What do you think I'm doing out here? I wanted to see the Preserve. My aunt talks about it sometimes but she won't take me inside."

"For good reason. It's beautiful in places but it's dangerous in some parts. Easy to get lost inside. The Foundation that controls the Preserve put up those NO TRESPASSING signs and the fence for a reason."

"You were inside just a few minutes ago. I saw you come out through the trees."

"I'm a hunter, remember? I can see where I'm going."

"Oh, yeah, the night-vision thing."

"Are you sure you're okay? Your breathing sounds funny."

"Actually, I'm getting over a panic attack. I'm doing a breathing exercise. This is so embarrassing."

"Panic attack, huh? Well, you had good reason to have one tonight. Getting assaulted by three jerks on a lonely road would be enough to scare the daylights out of anyone."

"The attacks are linked to my stupid talent. I started getting the attacks when I came into my para-senses two years ago. At first everyone assumed that I was just reacting to the stress of high school. But finally my mom sent me to a para-shrink who said it appeared to be a side effect of my new senses."

Great. Now she was babbling about her personal problems.

"That's gotta be tough," Slade said.

"Tell me about it. If I run hot for any length of time, I start shaking and it gets hard to breathe. I was really jacked a few minutes ago so I'm paying for it now. I'll be okay in a couple of minutes, honest."

"You should go home now," Slade said. "I'll walk with you and make sure those guys don't come back."

"They won't return," she said, very certain. She finally managed to take a deep breath. Her jangled senses and her nerves were finally calming. "I don't want to go home yet. I came all the way out here to see the Preserve."

"Does your aunt know where you are?"

"No. Aunt Beatrix took the ferry to Frequency City today to check out some antiques at an estate sale. She won't return until tomorrow."

Slade looked toward the dark woods. He seemed to hesitate and then he shrugged. "I'll take you inside but just for a few minutes."

Delight snapped through her.

"Will you? That would be wonderful. Thanks."

He started walking back along the road toward the woods. She switched on the flashlight and hurried to catch up with him.

"I heard someone at the grocery store say that you're going to leave Rainshadow for good tomorrow," she said tentatively. "Is it true?"

"That's the plan. I've been accepted at the academy of the FBPI."

"You're joining the Federal Bureau of Psi Investigation? Wow. That is so high-rez. Congratulations."

"Thanks. I'm packed. I'll catch the morning ferry."

She tried to think of what to say next. Nothing brilliant came to mind.

"Do you think those three guys will try to have you arrested?" she asked.

"No."

"How can you be sure? They might remember you from the marina."

"Even if they do, those three aren't going to go to the local cops. If they did they'd have to explain why they stopped you on the road."

"Oh, right." Her spirits lightened at that realization. "And I'd tell everyone how they attacked me. Chief Halstead knows me and he's known Aunt Beatrix forever. He would believe me long before he took the word of a bunch of off-islanders."

"Yes," Slade said. "He would."

She was surprised to hear the respect in Slade's voice. She glanced at his profile.

"I saw the two of you talking together a lot this summer," she ventured.

"Halstead is the one who suggested I apply to the academy. He even wrote a recommendation."

That evening Slade gave her a brief glimpse of the paranormal wonderland that was the Preserve by night. And then he walked her home, saw her inside the cottage on the bluff and waited until she locked the door. She listened to his footsteps going down the front porch steps; listened until he was gone and the only sound was that of the wind sighing in the trees.

The following morning she went down to the ferry dock. Slade didn't see her at first. He lounged against the railing, a duffel bag slung over his shoulder. He was alone. There was a handful of other passengers waiting for the ferry, but no one was there to see him off to his new life in the Federal Bureau of Psi Investigation.

She approached him cautiously, not certain how he would react. She knew that as far as he was concerned she was just a kid he had helped out of a jam and then humored with a short trip into the forbidden territory of the Preserve.

"Slade?" She stopped a short distance away.

He had been watching the ferry pull into the dock. At the sound of her voice he turned his head and saw her. He smiled.

"I see you found your backup glasses," he said.

"Yes." She felt the heat rise in her cheeks. Her second pair of frames was even nerdier than the new pair that had gotten busted last night. "I came to say good-bye."

"Yeah?"

"And to tell you to be careful, okay?" she added very earnestly. "The FBPI goes after some very dangerous people. Serial killers and drug traffickers."

"I've heard that." His eyes glittered with amusement. "I'll be careful."

She was feeling more awkward by the second. At this rate she would have a panic attack without even raising her dumb talent.

She held out the small box she had brought with her. "I also wanted to give you this. Sort of a thank-you gift for what you did for me last night."

He eyed the box as if not sure what to make of it. It dawned on her that a man who didn't have a family of his own probably didn't get many gifts. He reached out and took the box.

"Thanks," he said. "What is it?"

"Nothing important," she assured him. "Just an old pocketknife."

He got the lid off the oblong box and took out the narrow black crystal object inside. He studied it with interest. "How does it work? I don't see the blade."

She smiled. "Well, that's the unusual thing about that knife. It was made by a master craftsman named Vegas Takashima. He died about forty years ago. He was Arcane and he made each knife by hand so his pieces are infused with a lot of his creative psi. Whatever he did made the blades almost indestructible. You'll eventually figure out how it works and when you do, you'll see it's still good. It will last for decades, maybe another century or two."

"Thank you."

She hesitated. "I tuned it for you."

Slade raised his brows. "You can tune objects that are hot?"

She shrugged. "Provided there's enough energy in them. It's a rainbow-reader thing."

"What does tuning a para-antique do?"

"Nothing very useful," she admitted. "But people seem to like it when I find the right object and manipulate the frequencies to resonate harmoniously with their auras. Just a trick."

He hefted the Takashima knife on his palm and smiled slowly. "It does feel good." He closed his fingers around the black crystal knife. "Like it belongs to me."

"That's how the tuning thing works," she said earnestly. "It's not a real spectacular talent but my family feels I may have a career selling art and antiques."

"Is that what you want to do?"

"No." She brightened. "I want to get a degree in para-archaeology and work for one of the Arcane museums. Or maybe go underground with some of the academic and research people who explore the Alien ruins."

"Sounds exciting."

"Not as exciting as the FBPI but I'd really like to do it."

"Good luck."

"Thanks."

He slipped the knife into the pocket of his jacket. The ferry was docked now. The three other people who had been waiting for it started down the ramp. Slade hitched the duffel bag higher on his shoulder.

"Time to go," he said.

"Good-bye. Thanks for last night. And remember to be careful, okay?"

"Sure."

He leaned forward slightly and kissed her lightly on the forehead. Before she could decide how to handle the situation, he was walking away from her, boarding the ferry.

She stood on the dock until the ferry sailed out of the harbor and out of sight. Just before it disappeared, she waved. She thought she saw Slade lift a hand in farewell but she couldn't be sure. Her backup glasses were fitted with an old prescription and her distance vision was blurry. Or maybe the problem was the tears in her eyes.

She made a promise to herself that morning. When she went home to Frequency City at the end of the month she was going to get a trendy new haircut and a pair of contact lenses. Common sense told her that she was highly unlikely to ever meet Slade Attridge again. But just in case she did get lucky, she was going to do her best to make certain that, whatever else happened, he didn't kiss her as if she were his kid sister.

*Chilling paranormal suspense in a small California town,
by the* New York Times *bestselling author of
the Arcane Society novels*

JAYNE ANN KRENTZ

THE SCARGILL COVE CASE FILES

As the director at Jones & Jones, a psychical investigation agency, Fallon Jones solves crimes
of a different nature. Jones's latest case involves
a body found in the basement vault of a local
bookstore—and scratchings on the inside of
the door that seem to be a coded message . . .

Available online only!

penguin.com/especials

M939T0811

*There are as many mysteries above ground
on the world of Harmony as there are underground . . .*

From *New York Times* Bestselling Author

JAYNE ANN KRENTZ

writing as

JAYNE CASTLE

An Arcane Society Novel

CANYONS OF NIGHT

Book Three of the Looking Glass Trilogy

The island of Rainshadow is home to the mysterious, privately owned woods known only as the Preserve. Now, after fifteen years away, both Charlotte Enright and her teen crush, Slade Attridge, have returned to the island. But will their psi talents and Slade's dust bunny companion be enough to keep them from getting drawn in to the darkness at the heart of the Preserve?

jayneannkrentz.com
penguin.com

M996T1011

"Simply irresistible."
—*Booklist*

From *New York Times* Bestselling Author

JAYNE ANN KRENTZ

An Arcane Society Novel

IN TOO DEEP

Book One of the Looking Glass Trilogy

Scargill Cove is the perfect place for Fallon Jones, confirmed recluse and investigator of the paranormal. It's a hot spot, a convergence point for unusually strong currents of energy, which might explain why the town attracts misfits and drifters like moths to a flame. Now someone else has been drawn to the Cove—Isabella Valdez, a woman on the run from some very dangerous men. Soon Isabella begins working as Fallon's assistant, but after a routine case unearths an antique clock infused with dark energy, Fallon and Isabella are dragged into the secret history of Scargill Cove and forced to fight for their lives.

jayneannkrentz.com
penguin.com

M997T1011

From *New York Times* bestselling author
JAYNE ANN KRENTZ
also writing as
AMANDA QUICK
and
JAYNE CASTLE

Psychic power and passion collide
as a legendary curse ignites a dangerous desire . . .

THE DREAMLIGHT TRILOGY

Fired Up
Burning Lamp
Midnight Crystal

Praise for the trilogy:

"[A] captivating novel of
psychic-spiced romantic suspense."
—*Booklist* (starred review)

"A top-notch performance."
—*Publishers Weekly* (starred review)

"Sharp wit; clever, complex plotting;
intelligent humor; and electric sensuality."
—*Library Journal*